He stood next to the w  glistened from his dark locks.

Brigid watched as they trailed down his chiseled torso, traveling down to where his tartan was wrapped low on his waist. The wind whipped at the folds of his plaid, the power coiling within and around him, as mystical as the land he stood on.

"*Ancient warrior*," she uttered softly.

When she looked up into his eyes, they smoldered with desire, and it startled her. A sensual shiver ran through her, wanting to be crushed within his embrace. The raw desire to be in this man's arms, touching and tasting him, was so potent, she could feel her heart hammering inside her chest.

He tilted his head to the side, as if studying his prey.

Brigid didn't know if she should run or step into his massive arms.

He took a step toward her, and her pulse quickened. The very air around her seemed electrified. He then took another...*and* another, until he stood merely inches in front of her.

Her breathing became labored, as he bent his head leaning close to her ear. She was engulfed in a sensual haze wanting his lips to touch her anywhere and put an end to her torture. His mouth was so close, she could feel a dark lock of his hair against her cheek, and she shuddered.

"Bring me back *my* sword," he growled into her ear.

Brigid's eyes flew open, clutching the sheets as the last fragments of her dream faded.

*For Christine
Believe in the magic
of Scotland!*
Mary Morgan
8/31/19

Dragon Knight's Sword

by

Mary Morgan

*Order of the Dragon Knights Series,
Book One*

Dragon Knight's Sword

Cover Art by *Debbie Taylor*

The Wild Rose Press, Inc.
PO Box 708
Adams Basin, NY 14410-0708
Visit us at www.thewildrosepress.com

Publishing History
First Faery Rose Edition, 2014
Print ISBN 978-1-62830-397-1
Digital ISBN 978-1-62830-398-8

Order of the Dragon Knights Series, Book One
Published in the United States of America

Dedication

For John, my knight in shining armor.
You swept me off my feet when you slipped and fell
that very first day.

Prologue

They were an ancient order descended from the great Tuatha De Danann, a tribe from the Goddess Danu. Half human and half fae, each blessed with mystical powers. They were also given holy relics and guardianship over the dragons.

They were called *Dragon Knights*.

With the dawn of Christianity, the dragons were systematically hunted down and slain leaving only one. The Dragon Knights took her from Ireland to a land across the sea, settling in the great glen near Urquhart. The clan was known as the Mackay Clan, descendants from the MacAoidh.

Yet, there were those who deemed the Order had too much power, and they tried to possess it for themselves. They were evil and twisted, and their plan succeeded one fateful night.

The Clan Mackay is no longer.

The Dragon Knights scattered across the land.

Yet out of the darkness, one will fight for redemption.

He will pave the way for the others.

And before his journey ends, Duncan Mackay will witness that the power of love can heal and destroy in one swift stroke.

Chapter 1

Scotland 1204
Standing Stones near Urquhart Castle

The air hung still with the mists swirling about them, each one gasping for breath. Their swords covered in blood, not one of them had the courage to look at the other, for their crime was too heinous. Even the nocturnal creatures that hovered nearby were shocked into silence from what they had witnessed.

Four men, brothers of the Clan Mackay, stood over two bodies lying dead beneath them, one their sister, the other an enemy. At that moment, their deed would not go unpunished. It resonated through their bones, *nae*, through their souls. They stood on holy ground drenched with blood, tainting the place, and fouling the air.

"*Nae*." An anguished shout tore from the throat of the oldest brother, Angus. "What have we done?" Angus's sword dropped to the ground and with it, himself, cradling his baby sister, Margaret. The sob that wrenched from him made his other brothers snap out of their warrior trance, each dropping their weapons.

Duncan stood still, horror filling him with what had happened. His face a mask of stone mixed with the blood and grime of the battle.

The other two brothers, Stephen and Alastair, had

collapsed against the stones, neither fully comprehending what had just happened. They only knew their sister was now dead.

"I told ye all to let me go after them," Angus choked out. "Ye knew better, Duncan! By all the saints, why could ye not listen?" Angus shook with rage and despair. "Why, Duncan?"

"Ye know why, brother," Duncan, tersely replied. "She would not listen to us, Angus. And after the last row ye had with her, I thought it best to handle it without ye." Waving the air with his fist, he spat, "Christ, Angus. Did ye want her to marry the bastard? Would ye have seen the marriage of two feuding families tear apart the sanctity of the Order?"

"Would ye have seen the death of our sister in this?" Angus snapped.

Duncan reeled from his words.

Angus gently laid Margaret back down, wiping a bloodstained lock from Margaret's face. He stood to face him. "Do ye ken where ye stand, Duncan?" His hands pointing in all directions. "It is sacred ground we have violated. Do ye not see the stones? There will be consequences, brother. All of us will pay the price. Not only is our *Meggie* dead, but ye have cursed our brothers as well."

Duncan could hear no more, realizing Angus was indeed correct. He staggered to the ground, resting against one of the standing stones. What had occurred here on this night, this place, should never have happened. They were all men of honor, belonging to an ancient order with codes, which they adhered to—not only in their lives, but in battle as well. They had crossed that boundary.

Now, all was lost.

"Wait, Angus. Ye cannot blame Duncan alone." Stephen crept from the shadow of the stones, still stunned from what had occurred. "We also understood what had to be done, brother. It is the only way this could have ended. We are brothers, one and all. We fight as one. Did ye expect us to remain locked behind closed doors like frightened women? None of us has ever charged into battle without the other. Why was this different?"

Angus slowly raised, his fists clenched. No longer looking at his sister, he faced them all. "By all that is holy, Stephen, I expected ye to understand better than any of us. Ye ken the code, ye ken what *will* happen," he spat.

Grasping Stephen's shoulders he hissed, "We will *all* pay for this. Most of all, we have lost Meg..." Angus pushed back from Stephen, his grief too overwhelming.

At that moment, Duncan noticed one was eerily quiet. He looked to his youngest brother, Alastair, still slumped against the stone. His head tilted upwards, as if waiting for what he knew would be coming. If only they could have stopped their sister. But no, Meggie had a mind of her own, as did all of the Mackays.

Duncan blamed himself. He alone could have prevented this bloodshed. He glanced down at his hands covered with the blood of so many. Clenching them tightly, he forced himself to look away.

Alastair stood, and walked toward his brothers. "Angus, what happens now?"

"We wait." Angus knelt one more time and kissed Meggie upon her brow. Retrieving his sword, he stood to await their judgment.

Slowly snaking around each of the stones, the mist grew heavier, and the winds howled like a banshee. Lightning split across the night sky, charging the air with a power not of this realm. It was as if the world split open. The brothers stood still awaiting their fate.

There from the mists she came, ever so slowly. The wind whipping her long ebony hair as she walked toward them, fury etched on her face. Her dress was of midnight blue. Along the bottom, edged with silver, were Celtic spirals. A silver torque gleaned around her neck. She seemed to be from the stars above. In one hand she carried a staff and in the other, a crystal sphere. Fear and her power had frozen them where they stood.

She stopped in front of the tallest stone and looked down at Meggie, tears streaming down her face.

Duncan tried to speak, but found he could not do so, watching in horror when the woman knelt and whispered something in Meggie's ear.

Then with great care, the woman placed the crystal upon Meggie's chest. It began to shimmer with an iridescent glow. The woman continued to speak and Duncan realized he heard the word *draconis*. He wanted to move, but found like his brothers, it was impossible.

The woman slowly rose up. Holding the crystal sphere upwards, and with a crash of her staff upon the ground, the sphere vanished. Instantly, all became quiet. The lightning ceased, and the wind became no more than a whisper.

The brothers found they could move again.

Stephen and Alastair dropped to the ground. Angus started forward, but the woman raised her staff to halt his approach. It was then that Duncan noticed her eyes, for they glowed like gemstones. Duncan thought her to be the most beautiful woman he had ever seen, but he also realized what she was.

She was the Guardian, and she was here to deliver their fates.

Angus stepped forward and knelt down before her. "Lady, I am the eldest of the Clan Mackay, and I beg mercy for my brothers. Spare their lives. I offer mine in payment for what has transpired here on hallowed ground."

"Nae!" roared Alastair, pushing up from the ground. "Ye cannot take the blame entirely, Angus. I am at fault, also." He stood between the Guardian and Angus.

Stephen moved forward and knelt beside Angus, as Duncan staggered forward, too.

"Stop little brother," Duncan replied wearily. "We are all in this together, yet it is I who has killed our sister." Then he placed his hand on Angus's shoulder, kneeling before the Guardian.

Alastair, still in shock, sank to the ground, fists balled against his head in agony.

"What is done is *done*!" yelled the Guardian. Her words were like ice across their faces. "Blood has been shed here this night. You are the Dragon Knights, the Keepers. You have failed, and the world you know has been altered. You think I'm here to take your lives?" Anger infused her words, her rage felt by each brother. "No, you shall live, but each of the sacred relics which have been entrusted to your clan for more than a thousand years will be taken. Your names will be removed from the hallowed halls of the Order."

She leveled her gaze at each of them. "No, Angus Mackay from the Clan Mackay, you and your brothers *will* live!"

Duncan gasped, comprehending this was far worse than they could have imagined. It was one thing to take their lives, but to destroy their family's name and honor went without measure. To live with this shame would be their punishment. He would have preferred living in Hell than to live with this disgrace. He looked across at each of his brothers, knowing they felt the same as he.

Their names tainted for all eternity. Men of honor—no more.

The Guardian continued speaking in a language not spoken in a thousand years. Raising her staff above, she chanted the curse as the words resonated within their very souls.

"Across the sea their destiny awaits. A love will meet through time and space.

"To right a wrong within this place. Beneath the gate to test your fate."

And with her final words, she slammed her staff into the ground, and their world went black.

Chapter 2

Present Day—Seattle, Washington

"If one observes a rainbow, they may see the road through time."

Wicked beast!

It mocked her from the depths of its cold dark place, and she was powerless to continue any further. To think it had won under its square dark shell made her teeth clench. There must be a way to coax it out of its blinking doom.

"Hellfire and damnation!" shouted Brigid Moira O'Neill, slamming her palm onto the antique oak writing desk, causing the mouse to flip and sail across the room. "Some days, I think we would be better off without them."

Brigid sat, hands on either side of her temples, staring at her computer screen, which had frozen for the tenth time that morning. "Bloody technology," she muttered.

The thought had occurred more than once if it was worth perusing estate sales for specific artifacts, *or* if she should just show up at the auction houses and take her chances. She grudgingly had to admit, since she started scanning the internet she was able to snag some unique items before they went public.

"Why can't it be simple?" She swiped at a dark red curl which had come loose from her ponytail and continued to glare at the screen.

A dream come true. Or so she thought, until this morning when her computer fizzled out, *again*.

"What in the blazes have you done to the computer now, Brigid?" sighed Lisa. She bent to retrieve the mouse that landed near the door, and set it back near the computer.

"Should we just try rebooting, and give it a rest, say about thirty seconds?" The smirk in Lisa's smile said it all. "Here, let me take a look."

Brigid was just not capable of working out the kinks of high-tech gadgets. Hell, she still had problems with her cell phone. At least Lisa was here to sort out the techno beast. She was done doing battle with it.

Exasperated, she huffed off the chair, deciding what she needed was a cup of tea to calm her nerves. "It's all yours," she snorted.

Lisa shook her head shooing Brigid out of the room. "Go make us some tea, and make a call to Berkeley Auction House to find out what time the sale starts."

"Heading there now," she replied with a wave of her hand.

Debating whether to toss in a few shortbread cookies, she heard the bell go off in the shop. "Drats. No rest for the weary."

Heading downstairs, she noticed it was Mike, the Fed Ex guy. "Gosh, must be my lucky day," she snickered with a roll of her eyes.

Mike was always trying to get a date out of her. However, he was forty, twice married, and Brigid only twenty-five. Mike was nice, but she was not ready for *any* relationship. Her last one was a total disaster. When it ended, Brigid concluded there were no men in this century that would be of any interest to her—*ever*.

Mike was peering closely at a *sgian dubh* in the glass case, and Brigid approached quietly.

"Hi Mike, what do you have for us today?"

He jumped back so fast at her greeting he almost knocked over the full regalia of armor to the left of the case. "Christ, Brigid!"

Brigid stood there, hands on her hips. She was trying hard to keep from laughing, but Mike was so easily spooked sometimes.

"Humph!" He flipped out his scanner making notes, when Brigid noticed the long box lying on the ground near the door entrance.

Frowning, she wondered what the box held. She was curious, knowing they had not placed any orders. "Hey, I'll clear these items off the table."

"Let me help you," said Mike

"I wonder what it could be. We don't have anything outstanding," she muttered as she continued moving items to the counter.

Mike placed his scanner on the counter. "Whatever it is, it's traveled far, *and* it's addressed to you, Ms. Brigid O'Neill, care of MacDonald and O'Neill Antiques. Sign here."

Brigid looked at the box. It was over six feet long, and when she peered at the label, she only noticed one word—*Scotland.*

She whipped around, grabbed the scanner to hastily sign, and then literally shoved him out the front door— "Thanks, Mike"—closing it on his stunned face.

"Hmmm...let's see what's inside you." She glanced at the handwriting on the box. There wasn't a return address listed anywhere.

"Lisa, box from Scotland," she yelled.

Lisa stumbled down the stairs, slamming the door behind her. "Sheesh, Brigid! What did you purchase now? Wait—did you say Scotland?"

"It's been some time since we've had anything from the bonny shores of Scotland," she said in a far off tone.

Her fascination with anything Scottish came from a desire deeply embedded within her Celtic blood. Perhaps it all started when she was a child, sitting on her grandfather's knee listening to his bardic tales. Not only did he tell her stories of myths and legends, but of the great battles as well. Brigid would sit for hours enraptured by the stories, seeing the great men and women. Knights in shining armor, swords held high, rescuing damsels in distress. She wished every night she could be transported back in time within her dreams.

Already starting to open the box, Brigid was careful not to damage its contents. When she peeled back all the openings, there was another box enclosed, which was made of wood.

"It's oak," whispered Lisa, running her hands over the wood. They both were now carefully removing the cardboard that surrounded the wooden box. After what seemed an eternity of removing each of the sections, they stood back to determine their next move.

"What beautiful craftsmanship," gushed Brigid.

On the sides were carvings of Celtic spirals, but that was not what drew her attention. It was the dragon on the front panel. It not only was intricately carved, but also looked as if it was burned into the wood. Celtic symbols and writing, which Brigid could only assume were Gaelic, covered the rest of the box.

She reached out hesitantly placing her hand along the dragon's head, when a wave of dizziness blurred her vision. Her breathing became shallow as if all the air forced out of her lungs. The room blurred and colors swam before her eyes.

"*It is your beginning and your end...*"

"Whoa, Brigid, are you all right?" Lisa asked, placing an arm around her friend.

"Did you hear that?"

"Hear...what?"

Brigid looked up at Lisa, noticing her skeptical frown, "Nothing, just nothing."

"Do you need to sit down? You look a bit queasy."

"Yeah, I'm feeling light-headed. Must be the excitement, right?" Brigid rubbed her temples and the faintness passed. She stood there, eyes transfixed on the box. Great, now she was hearing voices.

"Hey, Bree, what's lying near your feet?"

Brigid glanced down and bent to retrieve the envelope. It was yellowed and worn. On the back was a red wax seal. "I don't recognize this crest. What do you make of it?"

"You're asking me? I studied business, and *you're* the history major." She scooted past Brigid. "Do you think it's a clan emblem?"

"Honestly, Lisa, I've never seen anything like it. It's just a dragon on the seal, similar to the one on this box. See, look at them both." Brigid glanced back at the dragon carving on the box, being careful not to touch it this time.

She was still a bit light-headed, and went over to grab one of the oak chairs. She kept looking at the envelope and back at the box. Normally she would have been giddy, jumping for joy and tearing apart the envelope, *and* the box to view what was inside. However, somewhere deep within her, her instincts were screaming as if her life would never be the same.

"Oh for Pete's sake, Bree, open the damn envelope." Lisa's voice interrupted her thoughts.

Fingers trembling, Brigid broke the seal with one swift flip. Pulling out the sheet of paper, yellowed with age, she opened it and began reading.

"Across the sea your destiny awaits...To right a wrong within this place...Beneath the gate to test their fate...Return this sword to its rightful place."—Clan Mor Mac Aoidh/Mackay

"Sword?" they both said in unison.

"What the hell does it mean?" Lisa was peering over Brigid's shoulder reading the note, too. "Return the sword to...*where*?"

She shrugged, "Not a clue. I'm unsure of this clan's crest. I know of the Clan Mackay, but the other? It might possibly be the first clan's name."

Brigid placed the note down and rose slowly. Her curiosity was piqued, and she wanted to know what was inside the box. The letter had said something about a sword, but she had to see it for herself. The possibility of a Highland sword in their possession made her senses spin. She held one hand against her heart, trying to stop the pounding from within and reached out with the other, ever so gently.

Lisa was watching her with just as much awe.

13

Her hand touched the wood, and a sense of familiarity tugged at her. She gradually traced the spiral symbols on the front, as she moved her hand along the side looking for a latch. A small smile curved her mouth when she touched the bronze latch and flipped it open. Carefully, Brigid lifted the lid, opening the box.

"Oooooh, my stars," Brigid gasped. "You are a *beauty*."

"I'll second that," sighed Lisa.

Using both hands, Brigid lifted it up only to stumble back a few feet from the weight of the sword, grateful for the support of the counter. Lisa rounded about to the other side to view it, though careful not to stand directly behind Brigid. For at that moment they both were speechless.

Not only was Brigid impressed by the hilt and the stone in the center, but the carving on the blade itself. Engraved on the blade, right below the hilt, a dragon gleamed brightly.

"This is a magnificent sword. Look at the engravings on the blade."

Lisa stepped around the counter, holding out a cloth to help lay it down on the oak table.

"See the carvings on the hilt, Lisa? They are definitely of Celtic origins, and this stone is beautiful. It almost looks like an emerald, but it has striations running through it." She kept running her hand over the hilt, exploring it with a reverent touch.

"Hey, Bree, it looks similar to Connemara marble," said Lisa, grabbing a magnifying glass from the desk to get a closer look.

"Connemara marble is from Ireland, so what would a Scottish sword be doing with a piece of Irish marble in its hilt?" Brigid asked mystified.

Lisa just shrugged her shoulders, while continuing her exploration of the sword.

Brigid moved over to the box and noticed a leather bag inside. The bag was meant to contain the sword and had a leather handle to wrap around the shoulder. As she lifted the bag out, musty smells assaulted her senses—ones of leather, dirt, grass, and some other metallic smell. The bag itself, though worn, was richly designed. Whoever had sent this, realized how much it would mean to Brigid, and that was the only information she could fathom from all of this.

The note made positively no sense at all.

"I know of only one person who can help us, Lisa." Brigid placed the leather pouch back in the box.

"Who?"

"I'll have to pay a visit to an old friend at the university. Perhaps Professor McKibben can shed some light on our Scottish sword." She paused in thought before adding, "I'll go tomorrow morning. He doesn't have any classes until the afternoon." Brigid had kept in contact with her history professor, and considered him more like a grandfather and mentor.

"You're not taking the sword to him, Bree, are you?" Lisa looked up from the sword with a look of a protective mother.

"Give me some credit, Lisa," she scoffed. Flashing her a smile, she pulled out the digital camera from behind the counter. "I'll take some pictures, but I think I will take the note with me."

Brigid rubbed her hand along the hilt of the sword, and gripped it firmly, feeling a bit braver than earlier. "Who was the warrior that wielded you, mighty one?"

****

He stood next to the waterfall. Beads of water glistened from his dark locks.

Brigid watched as they trailed down his chiseled torso, traveling down to where his tartan was wrapped low on his waist. The wind whipped at the folds of his plaid, the power coiling within and around him, as mystical as the land he stood on.

"*Ancient warrior*," she uttered softly.

When she looked up into his eyes, they smoldered with desire, and it startled her. A sensual shiver ran through her, wanting to be crushed within his embrace. The raw desire to be in this man's arms, touching and tasting him, was so potent, she could feel her heart hammering inside her chest.

He tilted his head to the side, as if studying his prey.

Brigid didn't know if she should run or step into his massive arms.

He took a step toward her, and her pulse quickened. The very air around her seemed electrified. He then took another...*and* another, until he stood merely inches in front of her.

Her breathing became labored, as he bent his head leaning close to her ear. She was engulfed in a sensual haze wanting his lips to touch her anywhere and put an end to her torture. His mouth was so close, she could feel a dark lock of his hair against her cheek, and she shuddered.

"Bring me back *my* sword," he growled into her ear.

Brigid's eyes flew open, clutching the sheets as the last fragments of her dream faded.

Chapter 3

"Do we bend history to our beliefs, or does history lead us there?"

The traffic was horrendous this morning on Hwy 5, and Brigid was relieved to be at the university. She parked in the visitor's space and grabbed her backpack. Throwing the hood up over her head, she stepped out, noting the rain had turned from a light mist to a steady downpour.

The University of Washington was a large campus, but Brigid knew it well, knowing which paths and shortcuts to take. Glancing at her watch, she noticed it was eleven. Professor McKibben took his tea around this time, yet tea was not what she needed to steady her nerves.

Actually, Brigid thought she could use a wee dram after last night. The dream she had was so powerful in its intensity, it had taken her several moments to realize she was in her bed, and not in a forest with a sinfully gorgeous-looking Highlander. She could still feel his breath on her skin, and she shivered.

"I receive a Scottish claymore, and I'm instantly having dreams of sexy Highlanders. What would the psych department make of that?"

Shrugging off the remnants of the dream, she quickly climbed the steps leading to the second floor of the building, smiling to herself at the numerous times she ran up these stone steps in anticipation of her visits with the professor. She had lost her parents to a car accident when she was an infant, and was raised by her grandparents. When she was nineteen, her grandfather died suddenly and then her grandmother soon thereafter; the grief was so overwhelming, she would walk through her days in numbing pain. Soon thereafter, she met Professor McKibben. He had filled the void, becoming not only her mentor, but her family, too.

So deep in her thoughts, she didn't see the couple emerging through the doors, almost colliding with them. "Oops, sorry."

His girlfriend giggled and pulled him back into her arms walking slowly down the steps, resting her head against his shoulder.

With a sigh, Brigid looked at them, so happy and in love. They only had eyes for each other. Another depressing thought to add to the growing list she was compiling.

"That's right, Bree, no guy in your life, only in your dreams," she muttered.

Walking through the doors, she was amazed at how nothing really changed on campus, as those same feelings crept over her in anticipation of learning something new.

As Brigid entered, she saw the professor's secretary, Ms. Peterson, sitting at her desk. Her glasses were perched on the bridge of her nose, book in hand, looking as regal as she always did.

"Good morning, Ms. Peterson." Brigid dropped her backpack and went to her.

"Oh, Brigid, what a delight to see you on this dreary morning," Ms. Peterson exclaimed, as she put her book down and removed her glasses, finally embracing Brigid in a motherly hug.

"I've missed you too, Ms. Peterson," sighed Brigid.

"Well, Brigid, what brings you to us today?" Ms. Peterson stood back and looked up at Brigid. "Are you here to visit, or do you have something for us?"

Brigid turned and reached for her pack. "A little of both; however, I do have something I need the professor to look at. It arrived at the shop yesterday morning, and I don't have a clue as to the sender."

She pulled out the envelope and held it against her chest. "I know I should have called first, but there's just something different, almost unique about this latest artifact. I don't understand any of it." Brigid continued to ramble.

Ms. Peterson held her hand up and with a nod to Brigid, turned toward the door to the professor's office. "Well, my dear, you should consult him right away. It seems this can't wait any longer, and since when do you need to call for an appointment? Your visits are always welcome.

"Professor, look what the wind blew in," as Ms. Peterson opened the door to his office, giving Brigid a reassuring squeeze on her arm as she guided her inside.

Archibald McKibbon was standing over his desk, papers laid haphazardly across it, books opened not only on the chairs, but on the floor as well. He was mumbling to himself, and his hair looked as if he had continually run his fingers through it, indicating to Brigid, he was deep in concentration.

"Hello, Archie," she said, smiling.

"Brigid! What a sight for sore eyes this morning." He dropped the book he was holding to reach out and gather her into his arms.

"Missed you, too," as she snuggled into his embrace.

Archie drew back frowning. "I've been back for some time, and was wondering when you would show up on my doorstep. Don't tell me you've got a man in your life and you're too busy to visit an old friend?"

He released her and went to the door, where Ms. Peterson greeted him with a fresh pot of tea and an extra cup.

"Och, thank you, my dear," he murmured.

"You've just returned a few weeks ago from Scotland, *and* I considered how involved you are right before classes start," Brigid replied rather dryly. "You could have called *me* when you returned, too," she stated, as she removed a text on ancient clans from a nearby chair and sat down.

He gave her a smile and pulled another chair out to sit beside her. "I know. I should have called earlier, but with the start of the new session—well, you understand how that can be, Brigid." He took her hand and gently squeezed it. "Now, how have you been?"

Brigid was still holding the note and Archie glanced where she had it pressed against her heart. He frowned nodding toward it. "I suppose what you're holding is of great importance for you to have a death grip on it?"

Nodding her head, she handed the note to him.

Archie stood to retrieve his glasses from his desk, and wandered over to the window to read the letter. "So my dear, where did you say this letter came from?"

"That's the problem. Lisa and I don't have a clue, no return address, or any information regarding the sender. *Nothing*," sighed Brigid.

He moved back to his desk to study the letter with a magnifying glass. With a sigh, he sat down, removing his glasses. "Well, this I do know, they, the MacAoidh, are an ancient family. Supposedly, their origins can either be from the Picts or Irish."

"There's more than just this letter," she said slowly.

He glanced back at the letter, then snapped his head back up. "The sword, too?"

"Oh yes, and it is magnificent." A cool breeze drifted past, and she hugged her arms around herself.

Archie got up and walked over to his mahogany cabinet. Grabbing two glasses and a bottle of Glenmorangie, he promptly poured them both a drink.

"I believe this calls for a wee dram." Raising his glass toward Brigid, he toasted her. "Slainte," then tossed back the drink in one gulp.

She did the same, letting the afterglow of its effects wash over her taut nerves. Drawing her attention back to the professor she asked, "So, what more can you tell me about this clan?"

"They were part of an ancient one," he replied.

Archie strolled over to a glass-enclosed bookcase, taking with him a set of keys he snatched from his desk. "These are books dealing with ancient Scotland, beginning of the clans and their history. Ahhh, here we are." The book he withdrew from the case was massive and leather bound, looking no worse for wear.

"Well, my dear, let us see if your clan mentioned in the letter is in this book. MacAoidh clan...hmmmm," then continued to read in silence.

The only sounds in the room were the methodical ticking of the clock, and the patter of rain on the window. Brigid's mind started to drift to thoughts of her dark Highlander.

Archie spoke in a hushed tone. "Brigid, does this sword have a dragon emblem etched on it?"

She blanched. "Yes! Does it say something in the book?" Leaning over the desk, her heart slammed into her chest.

There in the ancient text was a picture of the sword—*her sword*!

"Sit down, Brigid, and I'll tell you a story.

"There is an old legend claiming the MacAoidh, which now in present day are known as the Mackay clan, were the Keepers or Guardians of some ancient relics. Let me see where it states this." Folding back the pages carefully until his hand stilled. "Here it is, the MacAoidh clan were part of an order called Knights of the Dragon Order. They were entrusted with relics from the Order in the year 149 AD."

"149 AD?" Brigid whispered.

Archie only nodded. "For over a millennium, the Clan MacAoidh protected these relics until a battle was fought on Samhain, in the year 1204 AD; between the MacAoidh, better known as the Mackay, and clan MacFhearguis. Margaret Mackay was killed by her brother, Duncan, on sacred ground. The relics were taken from them that night, never to be held by the MacAoidh clan again." Archie removed his glasses, walking back to the bookcase to retrieve another old book from the shelf.

"So horrific. What could have happened?" Shock

filled Brigid with the revelation of finding out that her sword could have belonged to such a violent family.

However, were not all the clans feuding and violent during those times?

She shot a look at Archie. "There's more." Standing, Brigid started to pace, since she was never any good at sitting still.

Archie waited patiently, hands clasped behind him.

"When I opened the box and placed my hand over it, I had this feeling of déjà vu. As if, I knew this sword. I became light-headed and the world tilted. I don't know how else to explain it."

He just nodded.

"I also thought..." She threw her hands up exasperated. "I *thought* I heard a voice." Shrugging she added, "I didn't want you to think I was crazy."

"Och, Brigid, I would never think that of you." Archie came over and placed a firm arm around her. "There could be a number of reasons as to what happened to you. Yet an artifact carries with it the story or the history of itself within. And yourself being a sensitive soul, you might have intuitively sensed its— vibrations? Or, you had not eaten breakfast and were dizzy from the excitement?" Archie chuckled at the last comment.

"I know, it all *does* sound silly, but I can't help but feel like I've just opened Pandora's box." She laughed nervously.

"Yes, it wouldn't be the first time someone opened Pandora's box, and it usually took a hero to seal it once again. Come sit down, Brigid. Let me look in another book to see if we can glean anymore from this story of the Mackays, and the relics they speak of."

"I think I'm losing my mind!" Brigid exclaimed, as she jumped up to retrieve her camera from her backpack. "I completely forgot about these!"

Archie took his time going through the digital photos until he slowly brought his gaze up to hers. "Stunning, positively stunning, Brigid. Very old craftsmanship, too. It's a shame you could not bring it here. I would like to see this sword." Handing the camera back to Brigid, he went back to the bookcase, pulling not one, but several more rather large old books. He was mumbling to himself, as he started looking through the first book. "No, this won't tell us anything, just more on the early clans. Yes, this is what I was looking for."

She rolled her eyes. "What? Ancient Scottish legends? It's going to give us some insight on the family and sword?"

"Tsk, tsk, Brigid. Many of your legends are based on facts. Bards would weave a tale, based on the event. Now mind you...sometimes they did exaggerate the tale, but in the end, there were some basis of truth to their story. Yes, just as I thought," tapping his finger on the page which caught his attention. Archie turned the book around, as Brigid got up and walked over to the desk.

"The Legend of the Knights of the Dragon Order, by Eoghan the Bard. Okay, so now you want me to read a *faery tale*?"

"Brigid O'Neill! I'm ashamed of you. You of all people should believe in the legends. So now you're telling me, what, no?" Archie frowned at her as he leaned across the table to pull out another book.

Brigid cringed. "I do, but I don't see how a bardic

tale can help us." With a sigh, she slumped down into the chair and started reading aloud.

"Legend of the Knights of the Dragon Order...They were shrouded in mists and myth, for they came from the stars. The Tuatha De Danann, or as they were sometimes referred to, the Shining Ones, descended upon Eire bringing with them their beasts, the dragons. Great power and magic these dragons possessed. Governed by none, they lived in peaceful harmony with the people of Eire. Magically bonded with the Shining Ones and with the land...they dwelled."

Brigid peered up at Archie with a skeptical frown.

"Keep reading," he said, pointing at the book.

"With the dawn of Christianity, dragons were hunted and killed, since it was believed they were evil. Fearing the dragons would be no more, the Tuatha De Danann chose one of their kind, a male, to marry one of the females of Eire. Out of this union, five sons were born, each one entrusted with one of the relics, and the Order of the Dragon Knights was formed. The Shining Ones believed in time they would come back to dwell with the people of Eire. However, the persecution of their beliefs and the fear of these dragons led to a fury of destruction of these peaceful creatures, leaving only one remaining dragon.

"At that time, the Clan MacAiodh, five brothers, left Eire with the relics and the last remaining dragon. Legend states, Manannan Mac Lir gave them safe passage over the sea to Scotland. There, they traveled deep into the Highlands, settling within Glen Urquhart."

"Brigid, I think you need to take a look at this," bringing over another book.

She struggled for breath at what she saw. "Those are the relics?" She could not take her eyes off the drawings in the book.

Archie began reading. "The Order consisted of five relics, the sword, stone, axe, shield, and book; each one possessing some sort of magical power, linking them not only to the dragons, but to the Tuatha De Danann, or the realm of faery. The relic was bonded with each person."

He paused in thought before adding, "If your sword is indeed one of these relics, Brigid, you have in your possession the sword of Duncan Mackay."

Frowning, she looked up at him. "But why send it to *me*? Who would want me to have it? If the legend states the relics were taken from this clan, then where have they been *hiding?* And why now?" Brigid paused, attempting to fathom all of this. How could it be? Yet, there before her eyes in the picture was her sword, in every detail—including the dragon.

"What am I supposed to do with it, Archie?"

"I believe I may have your answer. Let me look at the note again."

Brigid reached for the note, handing it to him.

"Yes…" he muttered, reading its contents once again.

"Yes, *what?*"

"I can only explain its partial meaning. This letter is meant for you, and its meaning is very simple. You must return the sword to its home...its *rightful* place."

"And where would that be?"

"Scotland. Where else?"

The look Brigid gave him was incredulous. "What? Are you *serious*, Archie? What makes you suspect, or believe it's meant for me?" Brigid shook her head and went to stand by the window.

The rain was now coming down in torrents, and again an eerie tingling sensation started at the base of her neck. The memory of her dream came back to haunt her. Didn't he tell her to bring back his sword? Goosebumps trickled down her arms. Yes, she always did believe in faery tales and legends, but this one? A small part truly believed. However, another part screamed...*nonsense*.

She laid her head against the cool pane of the window. "What became of this Clan Mackay, Archie?"

"First Brigid, to answer your previous question, the note *is* addressed to you, and it states what you must do. I understand it may sound preposterous, but again, we both believe in the legends."

He went over and placed his hand on her shoulder, giving it a gentle squeeze, he guided her over to the chair. "You could always go to Scotland and present it to the clan Mackay?"

She nodded slowly, trying to absorb his words.

"Second"—he stretched out both arms to relieve the tension of reading for the past few hours—"they say the brothers vanished, each to his own hell. The locals claim their spirits roam the glen even to this day."

She watched as lightning flashed in the sky. "Knights, relics, fae, dragon—wait a minute...*dragon*? If the knights vanished, what happened to the dragon? Did it disappear, too?"

A gleam shone in his eyes, as Archie gave a chuckle. "Ah, Brigid, have you not heard of the Loch Ness monster? Well, some say she lives beneath Urquhart Castle and roams Loch Ness, waiting for the day of the knights' return."

Chills crept down her. "So-o-o, you're telling me the Loch Ness monster is really a *dragon*?"

"Indeed it is."

"Does all of Scotland believe it's a dragon?"

He shrugged.

She just shook her head, tossing her curls about, as a bout of hysterical laughter threatened to spill out. *Oh, Bree, what are you going to do?*

Closing the book, and placing his glasses down, Archie looked directly at her. "Well, lass, what *are* you going to do?"

"I don't know. It's *so* overwhelming, and I keep asking myself, *why me*?"

"Well, Brigid, sometimes the fae choose special ones to entrust great tasks."

"*Stop*," halting the rest of his words with her hand. "I may believe in legends, and perhaps a lone dragon, but I don't know about the fae singling out humans for heroic missions."

She stood, grabbing her coat and putting it on. When she picked up the note, Brigid almost believed anything could be possible. But now...she was just tired.

Archie stood watching as she gathered her items, wanting to say more.

"Let me sleep on it, Archie. There's too much to comprehend." She gave him a half smile and went to embrace him, feeling oddly sad.

"Then sleep well, bonny Brigid," and then Archie looked into her face one last time. "Call if you need anything."

Brigid smiled again. "I will."

Stepping outside, she walked briskly to her truck. The rain had stopped, and the sun had broken through the clouds with sunbeams streaming through. Brigid tilted her head up and soaked in the last rays of light before they slipped away.

Chapter 4

October 1205—Castle Creag

"The difference between justice and righteousness is often times blurred."

They were as one, rider and horse along the water's edge, racing faster with each thunderous crash of the ocean's waves. Spray covering both, the wind whipped a fury around them, as they continued to move with the elements. To look at them, one would not be able to distinguish between beast and man, for each melded into the other. Fear and madness drove them both, and neither cared if the gates of Hell opened and swallowed them within. The anguish they lived with was far greater than the fires and demons of Hades combined.

Oh, how the rider longed for release of his pain...faster and faster he urged his beast on. Sand and spittle flew into his face, but he did not care. Nothing mattered anymore to him. There was no light, no hope, and there certainly were no gods! His soul was damned for all eternity.

He would live in agony here until they dragged his wretched soul away.

Lightning splintered across the sky, and the rider shoved his fist in the air, daring it to touch down upon him. He continued to ride, pressing on toward oblivion.

He shook the water free from his face, noticing Cormac Murray standing along the turret wall, hands clasped behind his back and watching the fury of the storm unleash across the land.

It was always the same, Duncan contemplated. Cormac ever watchful for his return.

Yet in the year since he came stumbling across his threshold, haggard and with the blood of his sister still on his tunic, Cormac had been unable to do anything to help him.

He would not let him.

For almost a month, he could not speak. The death of Margaret by his hand left him scarred, bitter and hell bent on trying to destroy what little was left of his soul.

Oh, Cormac had tried, but after months of pleading with him, he made the decision to stand back, though only from a distance. Duncan remembered the day Cormac ordered his men to stay clear from him, and he threatened to cleave his friend in two. On several occasions when they were sparring, a rage would descend over him, forcing Cormac to pull back and stop.

The rage in him always ready to do battle.

Duncan slowed his pace as he neared Castle Creag, as both he and his horse were breathing heavily. For a few brief hours, he was alone in his grief and the world itself, separated from all. Now, as the stone fortress loomed in the distance, he almost turned away. He feared he was no longer human—devoid of all emotions. Those he encountered required civility on his part, one he was unable give.

There was only Cormac, and at times, it was near to impossible to be around his friend.

Duncan sighed, becoming aware they were moving closer, Brandubh's steps matching the mood of Duncan. There was a screech from above the trees, and Duncan saw a falcon circling above one of the oaks.

"Hold, Brandubh," commanded Duncan. He strained his head to the side watching the falcon riding the wind. Something or someone had caught its eye, and it descended with talons pulled forward, perching itself on the limb of a birch tree.

"Are ye friend or foe? If ye bring a message, show me now." Tired and exhausted from his ride, Duncan ran his fingers through his hair and clicked the reins of Brandubh on toward the castle.

Duncan's mood was still foul as he and Brandubh passed through the portcullis of Castle Creag. He dismounted and heaved a heavy sigh, for strolling toward him was Cormac.

"You've the look of the devil that's been to Hell and back again. I thought perhaps we would train in the lists this morn, my friend." Cormac motioned to the young lad watching Duncan. "Take Brandubh to the stables and have Tiernan tend to him." The young lad held back, yet Duncan nodded to him, handing over the reins.

"Inform Tiernan I will be there shortly," said Duncan giving a gentle pat to Brandubh.

"Aye, my lord, I will." As the lad took the reins, he walked proudly through the bailey as if he had just been presented with a gift.

"I am in no mood to listen to your lectures, Cormac." Duncan strode passed him and entered castle walking into the great hall. He went straightway to the pitcher of ale and poured himself a mighty portion, draining the ale in one swallow.

"Och, ye wound me, Duncan." Cormac pounded his fist against his chest. "No lectures from me, just sage wisdom." He proceeded to pour himself some ale, and went to stand by the fire in the hearth, rolling the goblet between his hands.

Duncan stood across from him, raising an eyebrow in his direction, "*If* I wanted sage wisdom, I would seek out the druid."

Cormac tossed back the ale and turned toward the table filling his goblet again. "I think it is time ye sought out the druid, Duncan. For ye dinnae ken what has become of yourself. It has been almost one year's passing since Meggie's death."

Duncan threw his goblet into the hearth and lunged at Cormac, his hands against his throat, shoving him back onto the wall. "Do not *ever* speak her name in my presence again!" Duncan's eyes burned not with fury, but with a pain of one tormented.

"It is time, Duncan," choked out Cormac.

Duncan slowly released his hold on Cormac and turned toward the hearth placing his massive arms against the stone. The fire was blazing, but Duncan could not feel its heat. An aching sadness surrounded his heart, freezing it from all warmth.

"Aye, Cormac, ye do not have to tell me again. I will seek out the druid. What is done cannot be undone. But I swear to ye, I will fight to retrieve the relics and restore our family's name." Duncan fisted his hands against the stone and pounded against them. "It is madness it went this far, Cormac! Bloody MacFhearguis and the whole lot of them!" he spat out.

He moved away from Cormac and went to pour

himself another drink, heaving himself down into one of the chairs.

Cormac sighed. Pouring himself another cupful of ale, he sat across from Duncan. "I ken this feud is ancient. Ye fight for the same cause—one on the side of righteousness, the other—*the MacFhearguis*, to use the relics and their power for evil. Same cause, different purposes."

"Do ye ken how long we have been protecting them?" Duncan said quietly. Until this moment, he had not spoken of that night or of the events which led to the violent tragedy.

"Aye, my friend...aye."

Duncan looked up at his friend, nodding his head slowly. Taking another gulp of ale, he looked within the cup, as if the solution to all his problems would be illuminated from within.

Cormac waited in silence for Duncan to continue.

"Where do ye suppose the Old One lives these days?" Duncan asked.

"Ye ken he cannae be far from the loch. Several of my men have recently seen him at the north end. I will send for the healer. She may know."

He got up and walked to the entrance of the hall, bellowing, "Someone fetch Finn and send him to me!" Cormac stood hands fisted at his hips and waited. "Blasted young'un, never around when I need him, but bloody sulking about when not needed." Cormac shook his head, but his face betrayed a smile.

"Have ye checked the lists lately?" Duncan smirked, since he had observed the lad many a morn when he was there.

"Sweet Brigid! What do ye mean at the lists?"

Cormac cupped his hands on either side of his mouth and roared, "Finn!"

They heard the pattering of feet across the stone floor, and a lad of nine winters ran into the hall colliding with Cormac, who all but yanked him up by his tunic and tucked him up against him.

"By all that's holy, Finn, do not tell me you have been in the lists?" Cormac asked sternly.

Finn cocked his head to the side, and the expression on his young face was one of surprise, but only for an instant.

"Oh sir, I cannae go into the lists. I just watch from the slats on the outside." Finn's chin tilted up in a defiant air, which made it difficult for Cormac to keep a stern face on the lad.

"Humph! Well, I've been hearing otherwise, Finn." Cormac released Finn and with arms crossed over his chest for emphasis, gave him a stern look. "I need ye to go fetch the healer. No stopping or dawdling. It is urgent, Finn."

"Oh yes, my lord." Finn's chest swelled with eager anticipation to serve.

"Remember, no side journeys, right, lad?"

Finn nodded in agreement and with a tousled shake of his hair from Cormac, the lad was off and running.

"Do not think this changes anything," said Duncan. Grabbing a ewer off the table, he strolled out of the hall.

"What the bloody hell does that mean?"

Duncan stopped and glared at Cormac over his shoulder. "I will not have ye or any druid tell me what to do."

Cormac waited until Duncan was out of sight

before he uttered, "Bloody bastard. If only it was so simple, my friend—*if only*."

****

It was coming upon nightfall and yet, no sign of Finn. Duncan was beginning to worry the lad had fallen into trouble or worse, mischief, when the great doors opened to reveal a small, old woman covered in a green woolen cloak. She walked into the hall and stood before Cormac, blue eyes blazing with fury.

"Ye send a wee one to fetch me, Cormac Murray? When there is no one who requires my tending? Tsk, tsk, lad."

Duncan saw Cormac flinch at her words, especially since she had done so within hearing of others in the hall. Seeing the fury simmering in his friend, he strode forth, placing a hand on his shoulder.

"Och, Matilda, do not stir the beast from Cormac. His wrath can be far worse than mine, healer," said Duncan, embracing her in a huge hug.

Matilda had been the healer for their clans for as long as Duncan could remember. She had helped in the birthing of his da, and with Duncan, his brothers and sister. No one person knew how old she was, but when she demanded respect, it was to be given.

"It has been many moons since I've set my eyes on ye, Duncan. Ye should have come to me sooner." Matilda took her gnarled hands and reached up to touch Duncan's face, tears streaming down hers. He took her hands and kissed them tenderly, closing his eyes to the pain that shone in hers.

Shaking his head, he whispered, "There is naught ye could have done. This is my pain and burden alone." Duncan released her hands and brought a chair for her.

Unpinning her cloak and tossing it on the bench beside the chair Duncan pulled out, Matilda looked to Cormac, saying, "Finn is tending my horse and I've sent him to the kitchens for his meal. I told him I would see to ye straightway. He already has a stubborn streak, one I could only assume he would get from his laird, whom he worships."

"Humph," grumbled Cormac, as he pulled a chair out and poured some ale into two mugs. "I sent Finn to fetch ye for the purpose of finding the old druid." Cormac held her steady gaze, and she slowly turned to face Duncan.

"Have ye not heard from your brothers, Duncan?" whispered Matilda.

Duncan shook his head no, and with bitterness in his words replied, "I cannae go back to my home, Matilda. I have destroyed all of their lives. It is best they never see me again." Pounding his fist against his chest, Duncan spat out, "It should have been me who died that night. For to see my brothers now would be a reminder of what I did. I killed our sister and destroyed our entire family in one blow." The blaze of his words etched across his face.

Trepidation crept through her voice. "Then why do ye seek the druid?"

Duncan stood and went to stand by the fire, a chill spreading through his being, though he knew it was time. He would do anything to reverse the curse, even sell his soul. His plan was simple and damn anyone who got in his way. He turned to her and in a steely voice uttered, "I seek the Old One to undo the curse."

Matilda gasped, "Och Duncan, do not mock the gods and goddesses. There was a reason ye were cursed. Ye and your brothers are all guilty. Ye sought blood vengeance and then took it to holy ground."

"This is the only way." His eyes daring her to challenge him.

Placing her hand on his heart, and looking up into his eyes, she spoke softly. "Ye cannae undo what is done. Margaret is gone. Ye and your brothers *are* cursed. However, there may be a way to find peace and to renew your name among your clan."

"*Peace*?" Duncan roared, pushing her hand aside. "I will not have peace in this life, or in the next!" Slamming his cup down, he stormed out of the hall.

Frowning, she looked at Cormac, who sat with arms crossed against his chest, staring at her. "He needs to seek the Old One, but not for the reasons he wants. 'Tis time he journeys on his quest. Only then, will he find peace. If he continues to battle with his demons, I fear he will become one."

"Aye, Matilda, I do understand. I will see him safely to the druid. Tell me though, how do his brothers fare?"

Sadness swept over Matilda's features.

"Och, Cormac, 'tis a sorry plight they are all in. Divided and tossed across the land, that is how they are. Angus has deserted Urquhart and is fighting in tournaments. Stephen has fled to a monastery, and Alastair has taken up with the Norse men, raiding the seas."

"It is worse than I feared." Cormac frowned. "Ye speak of this quest, Matilda. What of it?"

"Aye, Cormac. I will tell ye how to find the Old One, but tread carefully. Duncan must remember what the Guardian foretold. Therein lies his quest for redemption. Her words were a message for *all* of them."

"*If* what ye say is true, Matilda, what can be done? Can the Old One bring back Meg? Will the Order be restored to the Mackays? I honor the ancient ways, but even this is beyond my comprehension."

"Tsk, tsk, Cormac, ye should ken better. Besides, I feel in my bones time is running out." As she walked over to Cormac, she jabbed a finger at his chest, "Travel quickly and be on guard. There are enemies not only of men, but the magic they possess too!

"Now, Cormac Murray, I am weary. Would there be a place to put my head this night?"

Grabbing her cloak off the bench, Cormac went over and placed it across her shoulders. Confusion still battled within him. Knowing there might be a possibility to heal his friend and his brothers gave him...*hope*.

The question was would Duncan be ready and willing, or was his soul already damned forever?

Chapter 5

"A warrior often walks alone in battle, though he may have many around him."

"Well, it's about time, Brigid! Where have you been? Oh, let me guess, to Scotland and back?" Lisa was at the register taking out the day's receipts.

"I'm sorry, Lisa." Dropping her backpack, coat, and hat unceremoniously on the counter, Brigid went and gave Lisa a hug. She almost felt as if she had been to Scotland and back again, with all the researching she had done today.

Lisa kept on organizing the receipts, harrumphing at Brigid through the hug. "As if a hug is the cure-all. Well, you're just lucky this was a slow day. I was only peeved for a few minutes anyway, mostly I was worried." Lisa stopped what she was doing, giving Brigid a concerned look.

Brigid cringed. "I brought you a mushroom burger and sweet potato fries from O'Malley's." She held the bag in front as an offering of good will.

"Humph! Your apology comes at a cheap price." She took the bag, giving her a partial smirk. "You could have called."

"I have *so* much to tell you about the sword." Looking around she noticed the sword was not on the counter and visibly out of sight. "Where is it?" A look of panic took hold of Brigid.

"Settle down, Bree. I couldn't have an ancient claymore just lying on top of the counter. I placed it in the storeroom, and let me tell you, it's not a lightweight sword."

Rubbing her forehead and realizing Lisa would guard the sword at all costs, Brigid nodded. "Thanks, and again, I'm sorry. I do have so much to tell you, but I think we should sit down."

Lisa angled her head to the side, eyebrows raised in question.

They both went upstairs to the living room. Sitting down on the large sofa, Brigid began her story, starting at the university.

For the better part of an hour, Brigid unfolded the tale of the Order of the Dragon Knights, telling Lisa what she and the professor had found out in their research, ending with her visit to O'Malley's. Keeping her hands clasped firmly in her lap, Brigid waited for a response from Lisa.

"Do you hear yourself? That's crap!" Jumping up, Lisa threw up her hands and continued her rant. "Now mind you, Bree"—pointing a finger at her—"there might and I mean *might* have existed an order, but I don't believe they were part of some faery beings." Brigid winced and started to interject, but Lisa held up her hand halting whatever she was going to say. "Let me finish. They were probably an order, say on the same grounds as Uther the Pendragon. You know how stories were told in those days. They were highly embellished and overexaggerated."

Brigid shifted uncomfortably on the couch. "I believe some legends are true."

Lisa started to laugh. "Really, Bree? So what you're telling me is the Loch Ness monster, which by the way does *not* exist, is really a *dragon*?" Now Lisa was laughing uncontrollably, and Brigid started tapping her foot to prevent an angry assault of words at her friend.

"You've spent all day listening to faery tales. Sheesh, Bree, I want a day off like that, too." Lisa just shook her head with a look of nonbelief.

"Finished with your ranting, Lisa? Are you going to continue to lash out at what I consider some heavy information? I *do* believe in faery tales, legends, *and* the Loch Ness monster!"

"Since when? I thought they were just stories for you, considering your heritage. You know I love to listen and read them, too...but this?" Lisa started waving her hands again. "It's just nonsense. Hell, you don't even know who sent this. It could have been some crackpot idiot! Did Professor McKibbon agree with this theory of yours?"

"As a matter of fact, he did. And, he's the one who told me I needed to return it."

"What—*where*?"

"Scotland, where else?"

"*Right*." Shaking her head, Lisa looked at Brigid as if she had lost all marbles and any sense of logic just flew out the window.

Fury over her friend's outburst was evident in Brigid's green eyes, which were blazing. She expected Lisa to think her story incredible, but not on this level. Yet, the more Lisa ranted, the more Brigid was realizing it *was* the right thing to do.

If she was ever going to win Lisa over to her side ,

she needed to tame her temper. *Breathe, Bree; one, two, three, four, that's it. Damn! Unclench your hands—five, six, seven, eight, nine, ten.*

"Listen, Lisa, I honestly think I have to return it to Scotland. I can't really explain it. It's something I believe was entrusted to me to do."

Lisa gave her a skeptical look, but kept her mouth shut.

"Yes, it *does* sound crazy, and I have to admit at first, I thought it was a joke. But Lisa, I *saw* the sword in several very old books. It is an ancient sword belonging to the MacAoidh clan. Detail by detail down to the dragon emblem."

"Bree, where in Scotland are you taking the sword? And once there, what are you planning on doing with it?"

And therein was the problem. She had no idea where to take the sword, *or* to which branch of the Mackays. "I don't know," she sighed.

"Exactly my point. Insanity," clipped out Lisa, as she stormed out of the room.

****

"Are you prepared for your destiny, Brigid?" The mists swirled around them both, the dew of the grass glistening at their feet.

"Will you let your heart guide you to him?"

She heard the sweet music of harps and drums in the distance. The air was warm and smelled of flowers. She never felt as alive as she was at this moment.

"Will you stand beside him, though death may come to you both?"

She could hear the tinkling of water flowing in the distance, and she knew she was safe.

"Yes," Brigid answered softly. "I am ready."

"Take my hands, Brigid."

Brigid heard a bird's caw overhead, and then gazed at the woman beside her, placing her hands in hers. She was so beautiful it hurt to look at her. Her hair cascaded down her back in black waves, and her eyes were luminous. The light from their surroundings reflected in them.

"Do not fear me, little one," as she brushed her hand against Brigid's cheek.

The woman spoke in a strange language she had never heard, but could fully understand. It was full of melody and the air shimmered, making it impossible to see.

"You are ready, my child. Seek out the standing stones of Tulare, near Urquhart Castle. There your destiny waits."

She continued speaking in her beautiful language, and Brigid had the sensation of floating.

****

Brigid awoke immensely better than the night before. The sun was streaming in through her bedroom window and for once, she was glad it was not raining. Sitting up, she remembered the strange dream she had. She could still smell the scent of flowers, and the beauty of the place. Then she remembered the most important thing about the dream.

A huge smile came over her face. "I know exactly where to take you."

Any doubts she had yesterday were now gone. She didn't know what was at the end of her journey, only realizing she had to return the sword back home. It wouldn't make sense to anyone else. Even her logical side did not understand. However, her heart, no, her soul, cried out that it was her destiny.

"I may not be able to erase a curse from centuries past, but I can bring closure by returning the sword to its clan."

It was still early in the morning, but Brigid got up. Pulling out her suitcase, she started packing. Keeping it lightweight was the only option, since she would be bringing the sword.

Going to her computer, she checked flights to Scotland. Her only possible flight was one in the afternoon leaving Seattle, with a stop in Chicago, before departing to Glasgow. It would be a long flight, but she didn't care.

She pulled out her passport, grateful she still had a few years left on it. Then digging out one of the books she brought back from Professor McKibbon's library, she placed it in the suitcase. The book contained the legend of the Dragon Knights and further information regarding the clan. She wanted to know as much as possible about them before she stepped on Scottish soil.

There was only more item to take care of. She had to tell Lisa she was actually going. This was the hardest part of all of this, fearing her friend would freak, considering she was doing this alone. Then there was their store. Yes, Lisa could manage the store by herself, but they were partners. Therefore, Brigid sent an email to the professor asking if he knew anyone who could pitch in and help Lisa out, say, as a part-time assistant. She also informed him of her decision to take the sword to Scotland. Of anyone, she reasoned he would back her up and keep an eye out for Lisa.

Before Brigid realized it, a few hours had passed.

Stepping out of her bedroom, she saw Lisa's bedroom door was open, and hoped to find her in the kitchen.

Heading downstairs, she decided to look at the sword. A sword, which had only been in her possession a few days, yet she felt had been hers all along.

Walking into the room, she saw the sword lying on one of the back tables. As she stood in front of the table, Brigid brushed her hand along the leather pouch, absorbing the feel against her fingers. Lifting the flap, she pulled out the sword halfway. Taking the hilt, she turned it over to look at the back and noticed strange markings—*ogham* writing. "Damn! How did I miss these? If only I had seen these yesterday." She realized it was too late for Archie to help her translate the writings, making a mental note to tell him later.

Gliding her fingers over the writing she muttered, "Are you the sword of Duncan Mackay?" Goosebumps traveled up her arm, and slowly she placed it back inside.

Heading back toward the kitchen, she noted all the lights were off and Lisa nowhere in sight. Then she recalled that today was Tuesday, and she was probably at the gym teaching a yoga class.

"Of all days to make quick decisions," she remarked, or as Lisa would say, *rash and insane*.

"My decision...my fate."

Hiking back upstairs, sword across her shoulder, she went back to her room and wrote Lisa a long letter, explaining everything.

Brigid checked her computer again for any messages and was relieved to see one from Archie. He told her not to worry, since he would check in on Lisa. In addition, he was contacting a friend in Glasgow to help her with transportation and a place to stay. He wished her a safe journey, and if not for the fact he had classes, he would have accompanied her himself. In addition, he said that his friend could be trusted for anything she required.

"Bless you, Archie—you always know what I need."

She included this last bit of information in her letter to Lisa, stating she would be returning in a week's time. Folding the letter, she placed it on the office desk they shared.

"Love you, Lisa," she whispered.

Grabbing her coat and suitcase, Brigid took one last look at the store and walked out onto a path she was uncertain of, but fully prepared to face.

Chapter 6

"Who is stronger? The warrior with his sword, or the fair maiden who holds his heart?"

Duncan stood on the parapet, hands braced along the wall, watching the stars fading fast as the first rays of dawn touched down upon the land. He was always fascinated by the shifting of night into morning, where if one were ever observant you would be able to view both at the same time. Somewhere in that brief moment of suspended time, he allowed himself to believe hope was possible.

Perhaps Cormac was correct. He should try to reunite with his brothers and mend their broken family. Yet, as he clenched his fists, he knew in his heart they would never truly be whole again.

"Och, not in this life." Taking his hands and running them across stubble and worn face, knowing he had to do something.

He believed in the old ways, and taking a deep sigh, realizing how long he had not asked, Duncan said a reverent prayer to the gods to guide him to the Old One. Perhaps there, he would find the answers for not only himself, but for his brothers as well. The night stars had vanished, and the glow of the morning dawn now shimmered across the land.

Duncan turned from the wall and went to prepare

for the journey ahead.

****

"Can I not go with ye?" Finn asked, feeding an apple to Brandubh.

Cormac was tending to his horse and the supplies. "Nae Finn, and if I were ye, I would not have Duncan find ye feeding his horse again."

"But he likes them."

"Aye, he does." Cormac chuckled to himself, noticing Duncan striding toward them.

"Ahem...Finn," and with a nod to the lad, Cormac indicated that Duncan was approaching with his ever present scowl etched across his face.

Finn's raised his in time to see Duncan, and he attempted to scamper away. Duncan grabbed the back of his tunic, almost lifting him off his feet.

"I'll take those apples from ye, Finn, and if I find ye are giving any to Brandubh, I'll tan your hide."

"Och, Duncan, leave the young'un alone." Matilda came out to the bailey just in time to see Duncan towering over Finn. She walked toward them, placing her hand on Finn's shoulder. "Finn, go fetch my basket. I'm off to gather herbs for Moira. She's making curded beef soup, and I ken how much you favor it."

Finn scooted past Duncan, making sure not to make eye contact with him.

Duncan tossed his satchel across Brandubh and mounted his horse while adjusting his sword. Grabbing the reins, he ran a gloved hand over Brandubh's head. With a curt nod at Matilda, he took off toward the gate. Cormac soon followed closely behind them.

Matilda crossed her arms around herself, feeling a cold shiver pass through her. Tilting her head up toward the sky, she suspected the weather would not give them any burden today. However, on the horizon there was a tempest brewing, and she feared Duncan was standing on a precipice—one which could send his soul to oblivion.

"Oh Mother Danu," she whispered. "Hear my prayer for Duncan." As she gazed upon his leaving, she spoke a blessing of protection, tears glistening in her eyes.

"Power of the Raven be yours. Power of the Eagle be yours. Power of the Fianna to guard ye on your journey," and with a thought of the One God, she added, "and the Power of Michael and his shield to protect ye."

Wrapping her shawl more tightly across her shoulders, she turned to go find Finn, believing she had done all she could.

Duncan's journey was now beginning.

****

They had been traveling several hours, with only the sounds of the forest and their horses. Both men quiet in their own thoughts.

Though the morning was crisp, the sun was a welcoming light and a balm for Duncan. Most days, he preferred the wind and rain, but this morning he was grateful for the sun and its warmth. He tilted his head back, eyes closed, and breathed in heavily. The battle still raged inside him, yet somehow a spark of something he could not recognize flared within. Could Matilda be correct? She spoke of peace, but he realized it was impossible. The only hope he could bring himself to accept was to undo the curse for not himself, but for his brothers.

He had meant to ask Matilda if she had any news of his brothers, but feared it would only add more to his burden, which was already too heavy for any ordinary man to carry, and he was not ordinary.

No, Duncan understood that he and his brothers had the blood of the fae. They were not immortal. Nevertheless, each one was gifted with a certain power tied to the elements. When the Guardian had stripped them of their relics and the responsibility of guarding the last dragon, he thought their powers would be taken as well. Yet, being blood bound to the fae, could not strip out their heritage.

Not even the Guardian could.

Duncan found that his power was now a curse. He could control the winds and storms, but when his mood altered, he could not control what would happen to the skies. After the battle and death of Meggie, he had let his emotions dominate his powers. For many months afterward, storms raged. Why Cormac never asked him to leave was a question that still haunted him.

A falcon's cry drew him from his thoughts, as Cormac rode up alongside him.

Cormac narrowed his eyes. "This one has been following us for some time."

Duncan drew up the reins for Brandubh to halt, and looked up at the falcon. "*She* has been watching me these past few months. If my instincts are sound, she will lead us to the druid."

"Instincts? Meaning your *fae* instincts?"

"For the moment, aye."

"I think it is best we keep her in our sight." Cormac stated, shifting on his horse to get a better view.

Duncan was still gazing at the falcon when he

spoke, "Nae, she will keep *us* in her sight and guide us if we falter from the path. I believe she is guiding us to the druid and will warn us of danger. It is wise to keep moving." Duncan watched her for a few more moments, then gave a nudge to Brandubh to move on.

"Och, ye would have to mention danger, or are ye just itching for a fight, Duncan?" he muttered aloud more to himself, and urged his horse onward.

****

Deep in the forest—MacFhearguis land

The fire blazed hot and fierce—flames snapping like claws, reaching for him. Bones and blood scattered around the forest floor, the smell, and taste of the kill flowing through his body. This carnage was necessary; for he sensed the shift of power at dawn's first light, an uneasiness settling within.

If anyone ventured onto the site, it would sicken them and they would destroy him.

Yet, it had to be done. He had to *know*—had to see it for himself. Only then would he learn through his visions the truth.

The pain was like a knife, blinding him. He roared and fell to the ground holding his head. "Yes," he rasped out. "Let me see." Half images flooded him and the searing pain had him gasping for breath. He was near to passing out, when all the other images disappeared, and only one remained.

"Duncan Mackay," he snarled, licking the blood from his lips. The first Mackay had set forth on his quest.

"By all the gods and goddesses, ye shall fail, or die on your journey!" His hands dug into the dirt and leaves, waiting for the pain to ease. Slowly, he stood on shaky limbs, needing the support of his staff, his face a mask of rage.

The druid named Lachlan turned and grasped the severed head of the serving girl he had killed, tossing it into the fire.

Chapter 7

"When the worlds of fae and human are open, the reflection of love shimmers like a rainbow."

The sun's fading light and warmth were ebbing quickly on the horizon, and Duncan sought shelter among the trees for the night. Choosing a large oak tree with dense foliage, Duncan dismounted and led Brandubh to the other side of the tree. In the distance he could hear water flowing, which meant fresh water for the horses and themselves.

After they tended to their horses, Cormac pulled out some oatcakes, dried meat, and hard cheese. Both men not weary, apprehension filled their minds and bodies. Cormac was the first to speak.

"What will ye gain from the druid?" he asked while chewing on his dried meat.

Duncan sat silent, no emotion showing on his face. What could he say? Did he truly know what he would ask of the druid? He was so sure of his path yesterday morn. Yet the moment he had stepped outside of the castle, his purpose had become clouded. With a sigh, he stood, and fisted his hands on his hips, looking up at the night sky.

"Did ye ken the fae descended from the stars, Cormac? What a sight it must have been." Duncan shook his head as he walked over to the oak tree, leaning his shoulder against it, more for comfort than support.

"It was a night such as this, a brisk chill in the air, stars shining like glass, and Meggie was still alive." When he looked at Cormac, his eyes shone brightly. "She was so full of light and love. We wondered how one could live among brothers whose moods darkened as sure as the sun rose each morn. She said it was her mission to bring laughter to such morose men."

"What happened?" Cormac asked.

Duncan turned from his friend and stood with his back to him. He had not spoken of that night until now. He could not bring himself to look at Cormac whilst telling the tale.

"Angus and I were going over plans for the east tower, and Stephen was with his scrolls." Duncan could see every detail of that night. It lived within his thoughts constantly.

"Alastair was off with one of his latest wenches, deep in his cups, when Hamish came running in shouting that Meggie had left with her horse. We all thought him a bit daft at the time, since Meggie was always with the horses, until he said she was meeting Adam MacFhearguis, and they were going to be handfasted. He had heard her talking to her horse and singing.

"Angus stood so fast the pitcher of mead spilled everywhere. As he spoke, he kept a firm grip on my shoulder to let me know that I should not leave. He told Hamish not to tell the others, saying he would handle it. He did not want bloodshed if possible, and cast his eyes at me when he spoke this. Angus then told him to have Tiernan prepare his horse.

"When Angus left the hall, I went for my sword and stormed out, taking off on Brandubh. My rage was so great, the skies started to darken. I had no control." Duncan drew his hand through his hair, his nostrils flaring.

"There was only one place where Meggie would take him to handfast, and that would be to the sacred stones. By the time I reached them, the storm was fast closing in." He closed his eyes recalling the smell of that night—lightning flashing the night sky, and thunder so fierce, it shook the ground.

Duncan clasped his hands behind his back, slowly turning toward Cormac. "There they were in the middle, wee Meggie with our sworn enemy. All I could think of was blood and rage, and it was all for the MacFhearguis.

"Adam saw me first, and seeing my fury ran to put himself in front of Meggie. It was all my madness needed. I saw him as the enemy, and Meggie needed saving. By the time our swords clashed, the storm was upon us. I heard Meggie screaming and calling out to Angus to stop. I did not see that my brothers were there, swords drawn.

"The ground was muddy and I continued to battle the MacFhearguis and then my brothers." Duncan pounded his fist against the tree. "I did not see her coming."

"She stepped in front of Adam?" whispered Cormac.

"Aye," Duncan nodded.

"The fool lass had her arms outstretched calling my name, and I drove my sword into her."

Duncan dropped down against the tree, head in his

hands. When he spoke, there was bitterness in his words. "Ye asked me why I seek out the druid." His hands clenched. "It was with magic we were all cursed, and it will be magic that will unbind us. In truth, for my brothers, my soul is already damned, and I cannot undo what has happened."

Cormac then sighed, "So your plan is to sacrifice your life, using magic for redemption of your brothers."

When Duncan lifted his head, his eyes were cold shards of glass, gleaming in the night.

"Aye."

Chapter 8

"They say that Ireland and Scotland were once joined, until a dragon's tail smashed onto the land and separated them in two."

If anyone had told her a week ago she would be standing on Scottish soil, Brigid would have laughed in their face.

Yet, here she was.

The long flight and layover in Chicago did not dim her enthusiasm in the least. She felt like shouting for joy and tried to keep her eyes from tearing, lest others would think her some crazed American.

Thank goodness, Archie had contacted officials not only in the States, but also in Scotland alerting them that she was entrusted with an ancient artifact. He had faxed the appropriate paperwork and officials even had a copy of her passport. How he managed to know the proper contacts *and* to do it so quickly, was still a mystery to her.

Deeply breathing in the cool, crisp Scottish air, she closed her eyes and uttered a quick prayer of thanks for her safe journey here. Hugging the sword in its leather pouch more closely to her body, she opened her eyes and looked about.

Standing outside Glasgow's airport, she looked about as cars, buses, and people passed her by. She expected Archie to send her a text letting her know the name of his friend he was sending, but she hadn't heard a word since she left the States.

For a brief moment, the doubts started to creep into her thoughts as to her purpose here in Scotland. It was still unclear. However, this invisible pull, somewhere deep, urged her to continue.

Mind and soul playing a tug-of-war dance.

Then Brigid saw him. He stood heads over everyone else, walking toward her. It was as if the masses of crowds parted for him. He looked like a Viking straight from medieval times. His hair was golden and fell in waves just to his broad shoulders. And oh, those eyes. All she could think of was she had never seen that color of blue before. They seem to sparkle. The air had a chill, but this man wore nothing more than a form fitting black tee and jeans, which were excessively tight.

He oozed raw masculinity and more.

Brigid shook her head, fearing the jet lag was making her vision blur. But when she opened them, there he was standing in front of her.

One of his eyebrows arched, and he spoke. "Brigid O'Neill, do you always stand with your mouth open?"

The Viking god spoke. Brigid took a step back to gaze up at him, almost colliding with a passerby, a blush spreading from her neck to her cheeks.

"Wh...*who* are you?" gasped Brigid.

One side of his mouth tilted upwards in a half smile, "Conn MacRoich, at your service, fair lady. Archie sent me to assist you." His gaze traveled down to where she had been clutching the sword.

Brigid became aware of the shift in his eyes, as if

he went from being someone entirely different, then back to his former self. It was just for a brief moment. She told herself it was probably the jetlag causing her vision to blur.

She shook her head and smiled wearily, "I'm sorry, I'm just tired, and I was not expecting someone like you."

Conn, aka the Viking god, took the half smirk to a full-blown dazzling smile and crossed his arms across his chest.

"Come, lass, time to start your journey into Scotland. You'll feel better away from the city." Conn took her one bag and motioned for her to join him. Again, the crowds seem to part for him, and Brigid just stared in awe at her Viking.

"Oh, Archie, you truly did send a protector," she whispered.

Conn led her to his jeep around the corner. Loading her bag in the back, he turned to her. "Perhaps you'd like to place your sword in the back, Brigid?"

"Yes, thanks, Conn," but before she started to remove it from her shoulder, her head snapped up. "How did you know it was a sword?"

Conn did not answer her, and again his eyes shifted colors before he got into the driver's side.

Brigid placed the sword in the backseat and scooted in beside Conn. Confusion now took first place over the jetlag.

"Seatbelt, lass," Conn said, giving her a wink. He slapped a pair of shades on, looked over his shoulder, and took off.

"Conn, *how did you know*?"

"Archie told me you were bringing an ancient

artifact with you, and since I'm an expert in swords, you might say I recognize a sword when I see one. Also, I recognized the markings on the leather pouch. You've got a special friend in Archie. It's near to impossible for one to get into Scotland with an artifact without any questions."

"Did he tell you about the legend, too?"

"Nae lass, I already know about the legend. It's an ancient one, which the bards have been telling in my family for a thousand years."

"Then do *you* believe in the legend, and that this sword is one of the Knight's relics?" Brigid looked back at the sword, still so unfathomable to her that this could be one of their relics.

"Aye."

"How can this sword be connected?"

He glanced at her. "It has the mark of the Order on the pouch, and I can read the ogham on it."

She simply stared at him, again with her mouth open. Finally realizing it, she snapped it shut. "Not many can read the ancient language."

"I'm curious, Brigid, why didn't you take the sword to Archie?"

Sighing she looked away from him. "I really wanted to, but I was just so scared in the beginning. It all seemed so mysterious on its arrival, and I didn't want Archie thinking I had just acquired another random piece for the store. Everything happened so quickly, that there wasn't even a chance for him to see it. It all seems surreal." Shaking her head, she turned to look out the window.

They were no longer on a main highway, but somehow he maneuvered them onto a back two-lane road, and the land rolled around them in waves of green. They had just passed Rannoch Moor and the beauty of it took her breath away. Sheep dotted the hills and every once in a while she would see a stone circle, whose ancient stones beckoned to her, reminding Brigid of a past which was alive with pagan beliefs.

The scenery captivated her as she found it difficult to continue to keep her eyes open. Just before she drifted off, she thought Conn mentioned something about the Grampian Mountains.

****

The tall dark figure stepped forth from the shadow of the trees, and she froze.

Her *warrior* had returned.

Raw masculinity poured off him, and her legs went weak. His stance was fierce, and his gaze at her spoke of lust and possession.

He was unlike any man she had seen before.

Brigid licked her lips, and watched as his eyes followed the movement. She was locked into eyes that were flared with desire.

"Who are you?" she asked breathlessly.

His eyebrow rose a fraction, as if sending the question back out to her.

"Ye ken who I am," his husky burr low and seductive.

He moved slowly toward her, the heat from his body flooding her senses. She could hear lightning and thunder rumbling in the distance.

"Say it...say my *name*," he murmured across her cheek, right before his lips devoured hers, and her world dissolved in a dizzying vortex of pleasure.

With a gasp, Brigid woke up.

Chapter 9

"Fair lass come to me in my dreams, for I shall be well again."

Duncan awoke with a start, surveying his surroundings. It was still dark, but the air hummed with the approaching dawn.

The chill of the morning could not put out the fire which drummed through his veins and surged to his cock. The woman within his dream was like none he had ever seen. She was standing within the stones, a vision of light. The storm lashed about her, yet the elements did not touch her. She was tall, and wore clothing he had never seen, molding her body in luscious curves. Yet, it was the hair and those eyes—auburn hair that glittered like fire, and eyes the color of emeralds.

Her luminosity invaded his darkness, seeking to calm the demon beneath.

She had held out her hand to him, as if inviting him into her arms. He craved her with a primal need—to taste and devour. The desire was so intense the ground shook beneath him.

Just thinking of the dream made him place his hand over his cock and squeeze. Oh, how he lusted after her. It had been too long since he had a woman, and he needed his lust sated. If he concentrated on the vision from his dreams, he could come in a few strokes. His cock throbbed against the folds of his plaid.

"Nae," he whispered. "There shall be no release, no pleasure."

Throwing off his wrap, he stood and walked over to the clearing between the trees. Taking deep breaths, he squashed the feeling down deep. Running a hand through his ebony locks, he looked out at the night sky. It was only a dream, yet so powerful in its intensity.

Duncan could not remember the last time he even had a dream.

He needed to find the druid, and put an end to this madness. This was his quest. Emotions started to swirl again from the dream, and again, Duncan fought the lust that surged through him, taunting for the pleasure it would gain.

Turning aside, he went and grabbed his sword and made for a clearing he had seen earlier. Some training in the dark would harness his emotions and hone the other muscles.

There would be no more sleep, no more dreams tonight.

Chapter 10

"They say that a dragon's bite is worse than the fire they breathe."

Bolting upright, Brigid rubbed a hand across her face.

"You all right, lass?" Conn glanced at her sideways.

Hugging her arms tightly around her she replied, "Just a dream."

Brigid was too embarrassed to look at Conn, focusing her eyes out to the mists, which had started to swirl around the hills. Her breathing labored, as she recalled the intensity of her vision. This was the second time her Highlander invaded her dreams—this one more powerful than the first.

It was so erotic, she felt damp in her jeans, causing her to blush even more. When her Highlander had turned toward her, he reminded her of a Celtic god, arousing such a passion that she felt crestfallen that it was only a dream. Never in all her life had she felt such desire.

Angus Og, god of love came to her thoughts.

A nervous laugh escaped from her. "Land of myths and legends, right, Conn?"

"Aye, and they can be mighty powerful." He nodded toward a place to their right. "Ancient ruins of long ago, though still powerful to this day."

"Oh my...Conn," gushed, Brigid. "Can we stop for a moment?" The need for fresh air and the ruins of a castle were the perfect excuse.

Conn pulled to the side of the road, finding a small path that would lead them closer. "The magic of the land always calls to those who can hear her."

"I've only viewed Scotland in artifacts and books trying to capture this." She waved her hand about. "The beauty here is surreal. The books don't do it justice."

He laughed. "No, I suppose they wouldn't. One must *touch* the stones to get a sense of the past."

Her eyes lit up. "Yes, exactly."

Seeing a spot where he could park, he drove off the main part of the road.

She quickly stepped out and walked up the hill. The brisk, misty air invigorated Brigid as she climbed, each step taking her closer to the ruins.

They were magnificent, granted it was no longer habitable, but she could almost see what their former life had been like. The ruins spoke to her, beckoning her closer. She was in awe of their beauty with moss and wildflowers competing for space within the crevices and around the ground.

A rabbit skittered across and ran through a stone arch and she followed his path.

Upon entering, she gazed on what appeared to be a magical place. Sunlight glittered through the trees and onto the moss-covered stones, shimmering with a brilliance that astounded her. Carefully moving within the enclosure, she reached out to touch one of the walls. She was transported back to a time when survival upon the land and people were essential. Closing her eyes, she could almost hear the clang of swords and fragmented sounds of the people who lived among these walls. Laughter and song flittered across her senses, and she smiled.

Belonging filled Brigid's spirit.

Slowly, she opened her eyes, breathing deeply. Often contemplating why she would feel displaced in her own country, heck, even her own time, brought back those questions. "What do I have in common with the people of the past?" she whispered.

Her dream invaded her thoughts, again.

"If only he really did exist. I'm in Scotland and already dreaming of tall, dark, and gorgeous looking men." She snickered. "I was already dreaming of them back home."

Laughing softly to herself, she noticed a stone lying near some heather. It was quite unlike the other small stones lying around the ground. Crouching low and being careful not to touch the thorny parts of the heather, she picked it up. Holding it in her palm, it felt smooth and its color reminded Brigid of obsidian glass. Raising it above her head, she tried to peer inside. "My first treasure on my quest." Tucking the stone into her jacket, Brigid took another deep breath, and with reverence thanked the spirits for the gift, sending back thoughts of love.

"Is that a pebble you've found there?" asked Conn.

"Oh!" Brigid swung around so fast she tripped over a tree root. Trying to catch herself she landed in the arms of Conn, who had moved with incredible speed to break her fall. The contact with him made her skin tingle, as if he was charged with electricity. When she looked into his eyes, they did those strange shifting of colors she had seen earlier.

Conn released her gently backing away. "Come, lass." He turned and started toward the car.

"Who the hell are you?" she muttered, following in his steps. Her mind spinning questions about this man. "Viking god, Celtic god? Get a grip, Bree."

However, the only man who seemed to stir her was the one in her dreams.

****

It was midafternoon when they arrived at Rowan Cottage. Brigid said a mental thank you again to Archie for booking a room so quickly and near Urquhart Castle. The cottage was nestled among the evergreens. White washed on the outside, it looked so stark against the trees, with the front door painted a bold red. Smoke was coming from one of the chimneys, giving it a warm and inviting presence.

"Lovely," Brigid smiled, turning to Conn. His eyes were not on the cottage but seemed to be looking at something beyond the trees. Turning back toward her, he only nodded in agreement then got out of the car to get her luggage.

They didn't even get a chance to go through the door of the inn when a small, elderly woman came bustling out the front door. Her gray hair was woven in a braid, which fell down her back, and her white apron was covered in dust from flour, reminding her of a gnome. She grasped Brigid's arms and gave her a fierce hug.

"Welcome to Rowan Cottage, Brigid O'Neill. I'm Kate Tooley. Hamish, my husband, is tending to the horses. You'll get to meet him at supper." Kate engulfed Brigid with a feeling of motherly love, and she found she was speechless. Looking over to Conn, she could see laughter dancing within his eyes.

Mrs. Tooley then went to embrace Conn who literally picked her up in a bear hug, twirling her around. In just the short time she had spent with Conn, she had thought him reserved, and yet here he was acting the child. Laughter came forth from both of them, and Brigid stood transfixed by the scene.

"It's good to see you, Conn. It has been many moons since you visited. Shame the good folk for keeping you too long away," she chided.

Mischief gleaned in his eyes when he spoke, "Aye, it has, my wee Kate."

Conn released her, and she walked over to link her arm with Brigid. "Now, let us get you inside. You must be famished. I'll have the kettle on for a spot of tea and scones before supper."

"Thank you, Mrs. Tooley," responded Brigid, relieved to have found her voice.

"Whist, lass, call me Kate. We do not stand on high and mightiness here," giving Conn a wink as she said the last.

"I think I'll go find Hamish and let you two be." Conn disappeared through the front door, but not before Kate yelled out, "Conn, she has the first room on the right. You can place her bag there."

"Aye, wee Kate."

"If I may ask, Mrs Too...," Kate held up one finger as if to stop Brigid from saying the rest. "I mean Kate, how long have you known Conn?"

"Well, we've known Conn all his life. We ken his parents. He's a fine young man, though stubborn at times, which comes from his Da." Kate chuckled softly.

Seeing that Brigid's brow was furrowed, Kate replied, "Do not worry, Archie would have sent none but the best to look after you."

"Archie seems to have taken care of everything. I forget sometimes that Scotland is his home, too."

"It still is, Brigid."

They stepped inside the cottage and Brigid thought she stepped right into the play of Brigadoon. Never before had she seen so much display of tartan. The warmth of the dark wood blended with the furniture, making it feel so cozy. Turning toward a room to the right, she thought it to be the sitting room. Light spilled into the room from the window, casting a serene glow on the two tartan chairs placed in front of the glowing fireplace. Various portraits of men dressed in kilts, some of which looked rather old, adorned the walls. It was a room she could get lost in with a good book.

"Let me show you your room, lass." Kate's touch on her arm shook her out of her halo of peace.

"Yes, that would be nice."

Following Kate up a large staircase that led to the top landing, where one could either choose to go left or right, they turned right down a long hall. Kate stopped at the first door and opened it. Again light flooded this room, too. The colors were warm and muted, a fire blazing in the fireplace. Conn had placed her suitcase at the end of the bed.

Brigid's heart skipped a beat when she entered. "It's beautiful, Kate."

"Good. Now I'll let you be. I'll have tea waiting in the sitting room we were in, or would you rather I bring a tray up to your room? It's been a long journey for you today."

"No, Kate. I would love to come downstairs. Just let me freshen up a bit."

"The loo is beyond this door." Then Kate gave her hand a squeeze and left silently, closing the door behind her.

Removing the sword, Brigid laid it on the bed—her thoughts immediately returning to the present. She had absolutely no idea what she was going to do with it, though her heart told her this was the right path.

Someone had entrusted the sword into her care. She wondered who and why, a thought that was always nagging at the back of her mind, especially on the flight over. Since the moment she landed in Scotland, she felt a kindred spirit to the land and though it made no sense to an outsider such as Lisa, it did make sense to her.

The sword was now a part of her—hers to protect. The rest would fall into place, and the answers to her questions would unfold.

Chapter 11

Castle Leomhann—1206
Home of the MacFhearguis Clan

"Would that he could, the warrior could not remove the thorn from the beast."

Michael MacFhearguis sat in his chair at the end of the long table, twirling the wine in his cup with one hand, the other placed around the waist of the bonny lass that was sitting on his thigh. She kept nudging herself back and forth, and if she did not quit moving, he would plunge his cock into her right there.

Laughter rang out at the other end of the great hall where several of his men were engaged in a story of yet another raid gone very well. Each one's tale a bit more varied than the next. He had gained more cattle in this raid, which would see them through the long winter.

Without thinking, his hand went up to fondle the lass's breast and she gasped, parting her legs. Tipping his cup into his mouth, he swallowed the last of the wine then placing it down on the table. Grabbing the other breast, he rasped into her ear, "You've best be careful, Caitlin, or I'll lay ye across this table and take ye in front of everyone."

Her eyes went wide as she turned toward him. "Och, Michael not here."

Yet, the look in his eyes told her he was serious, and she scooted off his lap so fast, Michael burst out laughing. With a smack on her rump, she scampered out, a scowl upon her face. Turning around before she left the hall and fisting her hands on her hips, she stuck out her tongue at him and gave him a wink.

He arched a dark eyebrow at her envisioning all the things she could do with that tongue of hers, *and* he was fully prepared to have her start with his cock. Just the image made his balls tighten more. "Later, my bonny Caitlin," he said to himself. Michael knew she would be awaiting him in his chambers.

"One of these days she's gonna tie ye down permanently, Michael." Patrick smacked his brother on the shoulder as he rounded to sit in a chair next to him, proceeding to pour himself some wine.

Ignoring his brother's comment, Michael just grumbled low in his chest and watched Patrick pour some wine in his cup. There would be time to bed Caitlin. He needed to know if Patrick had any news regarding their brother Adam. He had been missing for nigh three months, and no one had seen or heard from him.

The past year was bad enough on them all, what with the death of Adam's beloved Meggie. To find they were lovers planning on handfasting had stunned the entire clan. Therefore, it came as a shock when Adam came home that night covered not only in his blood, but of Meggie's too.

The war cry had gone out to take vengeance on the Mackays, but Adam had pleaded with them not too. Michael thought he was daft and with fever, not realizing Adam was planning his own revenge. It was months before Adam could walk on his own, for his wound almost ended his life several times. They owed much to their own healer and of the druid Lachlan.

When Adam did regain his strength, he was still not himself. It was as if a changeling had come in the night and stole their younger brother away, replacing him with one who was restless, temperamental, and prone to pick fights with his men.

Then they received news the Mackays were missing, too. Michael thought it no great loss, for he thought they wielded too much power, and the two clans had fought for centuries over the glen. Their lands were now empty, and Michael took it as a sign from the gods that the evil had been banished. He had considered sending Adam to the north to stay with their uncle, but on the following day Adam had left, telling no one.

"Well?" Michael questioned. "Have ye found him?"

Patrick sighed, gazing into his cup, "Nae, Michael. It's as if he vanished when he stepped outside these walls."

"Damnation!" shouted Michael, as he slammed his cup onto the table, frightening the dog that lay nearby. "What news of Alex?" he asked.

"None, he is near Mackay land in the north."

"No fears, brother," said Michael. "Their land is barren of people, and the Mackays are scattered." He waved his hand in the air. "Do not worry about Alex. Our brother can hold his own."

Patrick held back his words, gripping his cup more tightly. It was awful Adam was missing, but Alex was on enemy land and regardless what Michael said, his gut told him the Mackays would one day come forth and the real battle begin.

Without warning, the hounds started to whine. Michael turned, noticing the druid Lachlan coming toward them. His men who were making merry with some of the lasses had fallen silent upon seeing the druid. Michael sensed his men feared the druid more than him, their laird.

Michael bowed his head in reference. "Greetings, Lachlan."

"Greetings and blessings of light," replied Lachlan, a smile curving his mouth.

Patrick stayed seated and had yet to acknowledge Lachlan, when Michael made a gesture toward Patrick in warning.

Patrick glared at Michael before turning toward Lachlan. Standing, he nodded his greeting in silence to the druid. Patrick honored the old ways, but for some unknown reason he could not fathom, he did not like the druid. He would never forget the day when Lachlan came to the castle telling them that not only was their father dead, but the great druid, Emer, had died with him.

Lachlan's claim was one where Liam Mackay had killed them in battle and plunged his sword into their father's heart. Then removed the sword and beheaded the druid, Emer. Lachlan was a young druid at the time and had witnessed it from the trees. Not knowing what to do, he waited in fear for Liam to leave, and then tried in vain to save their da, but had failed. He came to the MacFhearguis's and sworn a fealty to serve the clan. His vow was to regain the relics and the power of the glen to the new laird, Michael.

Patrick's warrior's instinct told him it was false,

and it stood as barrier between him and his brothers, with many a day spent in dissension. Adam and Alex both supported Michael in his decision to retain Lachlan as counsel, but Patrick would not. Alex only recently bent more to his side, but still kept silent, saying there needed to be proof of the druid's wrongdoings. In the end, Alex would obey his brother, their laird, until that day of reckoning.

Patrick only acknowledged the druid's presence for the sake of his laird—nothing more. Moving aside, he went over to the hearth and stood.

"Sit, Lachlan. Wine?" Michael asked.

"Certainly."

A servant came forth bringing a cup for Lachlan.

Lachlan nodded his thanks to Michael and took a seat next to him, without giving Patrick any acknowledgement. Taking a sip of the wine, he placed his cup down and spread his palms down upon the table.

"I bring ye grave news, my laird, one which will surely be of concern to ye. Duncan Mackay has left upon his quest to seek out the sword."

Michael's lips thinned and he slammed his fist onto the massive table. "Nae!" he roared.

Patrick had sense to stay by the hearth and not breathe a word. For if Lachlan's words were true then it would mean war again with the Mackays. His only concern was for Adam. *Where are ye, Adam?*

Michael stood and looked at Patrick, anticipating his thoughts. "We need to find Adam, now!"

"I know, brother," responded Patrick. He walked over and placed his hand on Michael's shoulder. "I'll ride out with some of the men before dawn's light."

Michael tensed, then placed his hand across Patrick and laid it on his shoulder. "I ride with ye." He then faced Lachlan. "Where did ye hear this news, and do ye ken where the Mackay is traveling?"

Patrick blanched. He had never heard Michael ever question Lachlan.

Lachlan slowly looked up from his cup of wine. "A vision came to me by the great goddess, one ye should heed, my laird."

Michael stilled himself shortly in thought, and then nodded to Lachlan in understanding. Making his way from the hall, he motioned for his men to follow.

Moving away from the hearth, Patrick went to follow Michael, but not before Lachlan stopped him with his words. "Travel quickly, lest your brother die at the hands of that beast Mackay."

Patrick slowly turned, steeling his emotions as he spoke. "We shall see if the Mackay is indeed a beast." He left, leaving Lachlan in his place.

"If ye are not careful, Patrick, ye may be the brother to perish. One can only pray to the gods for it to be so," as an evil smile spread across the druid's face.

Chapter 12

"If you lead the dragon to safety, will he choose the path filled with light or will he want to remain in the dark, therefore believing himself saved?"

They had traveled during the day, and night was approaching fast. Stopping only once to tend to their horses and their needs before journeying onward, they made sure their new traveling companion was never far from their sight.

Cormac slowed, watching the falcon.

As if sensing his thoughts, Duncan said, "Yes, she never ventures far, as if she is guiding us." He slowed Brandubh, the horse snorting as if in agreement with Duncan.

"It cannot fool ye either," Duncan muttered, as he laid a gloved hand on Brandubh's mane. "It's leading us to the druid, aye?" Brandubh gave another snort and Cormac laughed.

Duncan chuckled softly and then froze. Something or someone was in the trees ahead of them.

Cormac was the first to unsheathe his sword, as Duncan did as well, dismounting quickly from Brandubh. Giving a quick nod to Cormac and a wave of his hand to signal where he was going, Duncan moved as a warrior approaching his enemy. Sword arm raised, he was prepared to do battle with whatever was behind the trees.

A screech from the falcon sent both horses darting back and forth, hoofs stomping the ground in protest. The falcon dived and swooped at Duncan, talons outstretched as if to tear at him. If Duncan had not moved fast enough, he would have been doing battle with the falcon.

The falcon descended again. Cormac had Duncan's back as Duncan was ready to lunge at what or who was coming forth. He did not want to kill the bird, but he feared it was a distraction with the real enemy in front of them.

"Sorcha, stop...*nae*!"

The air hummed with energy as an old man emerged from the trees, staff held high at the falcon. The falcon swooped at an angle over them before taking flight high over the treetops.

Words spilled forth from the man which neither Cormac nor Duncan could understand, each still in their warrior stance.

The energy instantly flowed around Duncan, as if he was suspended in time itself. Colors danced, lightning flashed across the sky as thunder rumbled in the distance. His sword arm vibrated with the power. A power connected with the man in front of him.

Reality slammed into Duncan. This was no ordinary man. Slowly he lowered his sword arm, breathing heavily.

"Duncan?" Cormac hissed. "What are ye *doing*?" Cormac still held his sword raised, glancing not only at the skies but also at the man in front of them.

"I believe we have found him, Cormac." Duncan knelt before the druid. The one man who could take back what had happened twelve moons ago. Relief spread through him realizing there might be a chance to make amends. A spark of something lit within, as if he was coming to the end of his journey in this life.

"Rise, Duncan Alexander Mackay. Ye do not kneel to me, my son. Ye are still a Knight of the Order, and I should pay respect to ye and yours." The druid placed a firm hand upon Duncan's shoulder.

When Duncan spoke, he kept his gaze upon the ground. "Do ye ken why I am here?" he asked.

"With magic ye and your brothers were cursed, and with magic ye wish to undo the curse."

Duncan's look of surprise shattered the pain on his face as he looked up at the druid.

"Who are ye?"

"I am known as Cathal."

Cormac had been standing at a distance, but when he heard the druid mention his name, he stepped closer.

"The great druid, Cathal? Greatest warrior and counselor to King William?"

Cathal smiled at Cormac's words, "Aye, son...I am. And to the Mackays."

Duncan was now standing, for he could not believe that here before them was one of the greatest druids of all time—the same druid who had counseled his father in his early years.

"It is told ye were killed in battle," uttered a shocked Duncan.

Laughter roared from Cathal. "Do the bards still weave that tale and that I slew giants, as well? As ye can see my son, I am very much alive. Now, *Sir* Duncan, ye and your friend must be weary and hungry. Come, we have much to talk about." Still laughing and shaking his head, Cathal turned and went into the trees.

"Sweet Brigid," murmured Cormac. "What just happened?"

Duncan gazed transfixed on the spot where Cathal disappeared into the trees. Slowly he turned to Cormac, "It would seem I have indeed encountered the one and only person who can help. *In truth*, I do not think he will like my plan."

"What the bloody hell is *your* plan, Duncan?" Cormac moved in front of Duncan, piercing him with a glare.

"I cannot say for certain anymore." Duncan stepped past Cormac and went to follow Cathal.

The small stone cottage belonging to Cathal did not do him justice, thought Duncan. This was a great druid. However, to look at him now, anyone would think him to be a simple woods dweller. His clothing consisted of an old brown robe, knotted at the waist with leather, and on the belt hung a pouch. The only glimmer of status on him was the torc around his neck. Duncan wore a torc as well, yet his was of silver, whereas Cathal's glistened of gold.

They followed Cathal into the cottage, ducking low at its entrance. When they stepped inside, they noticed the roof extended much higher. Duncan and Cormac exchanged curious looks.

Seeing their puzzlement, Cathal chuckled, "Aye, it is deceiving from the outside for that purpose. An illusion ye could say." He winked. Moving over to the hearth, he lifted the lid on a pot simmering over the flames and tossed in some herbs. Without turning, he motioned to them. "Sit, ye must be famished."

Cormac, always in need of a meal, removed his

sword and sat down at the table where bread and berries were set out. Cathal brought over steaming bowls of what appeared to be a hearty soup. Duncan slowly put down his sword, sitting down across from Cormac. He bent inhaling the rich, steamy aroma and immediately, his stomach gave a tremendous rumble.

"Aye, good to hear your body is hungry for some food." Cathal placed his hand upon Duncan's shoulder, and then moved to take his place at the head of the table.

"Let us give a blessing to the Great Mother for providing us with the hare, which will nourish us." They each bowed their heads as Cathal finished the blessing.

Pouring some wine into a mug, Cathal passed it to Duncan and filled one for Cormac and himself.

Duncan frowned as he peered inside the mug.

"Ye may wonder where would I come upon wine? Let us just say, I still receive visitors who may need my help. I am not a druid without resources."

Duncan took a swig of the wine and proceeded to eat his meal in silence. He wanted this over with. The pretense that all was right with the world was a thorn in his side, yet each bite of the soup seemed to calm his restless spirit. He tried to listen to the conversation Cormac was having with Cathal, but his thoughts kept drifting to the conflict within himself.

Why had he let Cormac ride with him? The man was positively too cheerful *and* talkative. What jolted him out of his thoughts was Cormac's palm slamming down upon the table in laughter.

"Did ye hear that, Duncan? Cathal beat King Henry in a game of chess in order to proceed with the release of our King William." Cormac just shook his head in disbelief.

"Aye, the Treaty of Falaise," spat Duncan, his tone hardened. "We had to pay the cost of the English army's occupation of Scotland—a bloody tax!" He slammed his fist onto the table. "We should have taken them by force."

Cathal slowly put down his spoon and drank a swill of wine. Placing both hands down on the table, he rose slowly. The look he cut him was enough for Duncan to know he was angry. "Ye cannot always rage a battle with sword extended, Duncan, for death will surely follow every time, as ye well ken."

Duncan rose so fast the cups toppled over and his chair went crashing backwards. As a trained warrior, he reached for his sword at his waist, until he remembered he had removed it earlier. Fury etched across his face, since he knew the meaning of Cathal's words. He had killed in a rage of anger resulting in the death of Meggie.

He did not need reminding.

"Duncan?" Cormac had moved quietly next to him ready to block his move if needed. His constant mood shifting kept Cormac on the defensive ever since they left on this journey.

Breathing heavy, Duncan looked at Cormac, and holding up his hand to stop him from saying anymore, he bent to retrieve his sword, then walked out of the cottage. A roll of thunder clapped in the distance.

Cormac's brows drew together in an agonized expression. He reached for the pitcher of wine, poured a hefty amount into his cup, and drank deeply.

Cathal's eyes were still on the door where Duncan

had stormed through. Slowly shaking his head and running a hand down his beard, he went over to the fire standing with his back to Cormac. "Ye cannot go any further with him. His path is now one he must choose and make alone. He must remember the curse. From there his path will be set out before him."

Stunned by Cathal's words, he asked, "Can ye not help him?"

"Nae." Turning back from the fire Cathal came and put his hand on Cormac's shoulder. "This is his and his alone. I can only help him to remember the words of the Guardian, no more."

"I dinnae believe it is what he seeks. I fear it is something else."

"Aye, Cormac. If he chooses unwisely, then all is lost. Stay, rest by the fire. I shall seek him out. Your journey ends here."

Cathal started for the door, as Cormac asked, "Do ye think it wise to go out there with no weapon?"

"Cormac, do not forget I am a *druid* and not without my own protection. But I thank ye for your concern."

Yet, the moment the door closed, Cormac grabbed his sword. The least he could do was stand guard outside. Cathal might be a great druid; however, he still was a man, and Duncan had a powerful arm.

****

The sun was setting in the distance, its last rays of light glinting off the trees. Darkness came quickly this time of year, and Duncan felt himself shift into the vast darkness. He came close to thrusting his sword into Cathal, and it did not bode well with him. He did not need reminding of what he had done. His emotions were like a double-edged sword, and the battle was fierce at times—one he could not control.

Sorcha flew overhead, and he watched as she flew down, perching herself onto a branch not far from where he stood. Standing still, he kept his eyes transfixed on her.

Cathal approached Duncan with caution. "She is a beauty, my Sorcha."

Duncan kept his focus on Sorcha as he lamented, "My apologies, Cathal. I let my rage get the best of me."

Cathal nodded his head in acceptance of Duncan's apology.

Moving closer to Sorcha, Duncan decided to ask the question that had been burning within him, since the onset. Stopping just below the tree where she sat poised watching him he asked, "Do ye ken why I have come to ye?"

"I would rather ye tell me."

"I wish to forfeit my life in the rite of blood magic to restore my family's honor and that of the Order. I give my life freely and with my oath I want unbound what has been bound." Turning back from Sorcha, Duncan looked into the blazing eyes of Cathal and knew his answer.

"Follow me, Duncan," said Cathal. Sorcha decided she would follow, too. Flying ahead of him, she let out a screech.

Fists clenched, Duncan hesitated, since his instincts told him Cathal would probably not grant his request. Taking a deep breath, he followed in Cathal's wake.

Walking for almost an hour, they finally emerged into a clearing out from among the trees into a stone circle. In the middle was a singular stone slab. It was now dark, and the crescent moon shone her light just enough for Duncan to make out the shape of Cathal, who was near a pit opposite the slab. He was murmuring in a low voice, his back to Duncan and his hands outstretched over the pit. With a mighty roar and a clap of his hands, a fire had blazed forth from the pit. Bending down, Cathal picked up some dirt, tossing it into the fire. He then turned toward Duncan.

"Come and sit near the fire."

"Will ye not help me?" Duncan had not moved to sit, still standing where he had entered the grove, his stance agitated and battle ready.

"Aye, Duncan, but"—he held up his hand to silence Duncan—"on my terms. Do ye remember the night the Guardian cursed ye?"

Instantly, the wind whipped a fury around them and thunder rumbled closer. Duncan's eyes started to flash. "Ayyyee," ground out Duncan.

"Good," nodded Cathal as he moved closer to Duncan. "I ask ye once again, come, and sit."

"Nae!" he roared.

"Then ye will remember only fury, and it will not help. Ye need to recall the words of the Guardian!" Cathal spoke more harshly than he intended.

The wind was now a howling banshee and lightning split the night sky. Duncan unsheathed his sword so fast, Cathal feared for a mere moment he would strike him down. The night sky opened and huge raindrops descended on them both. The fires hissed with each spattering of rain, but it still kept burning. Aware of Duncan's power, Cathal had infused the fire with earth magic to keep it going.

"Arghhhhhh, take my blood, druid, but do not ask me to recall that night!" shouted Duncan, stepping closer to Cathal.

Lightning split across them and sliced into a tree near Cormac. He cursed under his breath, shifting slightly.

"*Control your emotions*! Ye are still a Knight of the Order! If ye want my assistance, ye will find the strength and balance." He slashed his hand through the air. "This is not helping!"

Something flashed in his eyes and with a roar, Duncan collapsed to the ground on his knees. He was breathing hard and trying to control the blinding fury, which begged for release. Cathal was correct. He still was a Knight, that and his powers were all he had left. Deep within his soul, he pulled out that which he had retained—his honor. He shook, taking in deep gulps of air, letting it calm the demon back into its cage.

Moments passed before the rain became a soft mist, and the wind a gentle breeze around them. Cathal slowly stepped to where Duncan had knelt. Placing his hands on his head he whispered, "*Remember*."

Through the tangled web of Duncan's mind, the words started spilling forth from his lips...

"*Across the sea their destiny awaits...A love will meet through time and space...To right a wrong within this place...Beneath the gate to test your fate.*"

A slow smiled spread across Cathal's face as he bent down to look into Duncan's eyes.

"All is *not* lost, my son. The Guardian is sending ye help."

With a look of utter confusion on his face, Duncan had only one thought. *Who*?

"Come—let us sit by the fire."

Looking up from Duncan, he waved to Cormac, standing within the trees. "Ye might as well join us, too."

Chapter 13

"For the dragon transformed her tears of sorrow into diamonds, and the brilliance reflected in them sparked joy into her heart."

Somewhere in the distance, Brigid heard the sound of bagpipes, and slowly started to smile. Hamish had told her last night she would awake with the sound of the pipes. She let the melodic tune of old soothe her taut nerves and snuggled deeper into her pillows.

"Thanks, Hamish," she whispered.

When he had finished, she tossed the covers off, and quickly dressed. The aroma of food could not keep her lying about.

Besides, Scotland beckoned.

****

Brigid only wanted a light breakfast, which was difficult to do considering the feast Kate prepared. Her eyes popped wide at the side table set up against the wall. She had never seen so much food at breakfast. If she ate like this every morning, she would soon be packing on more weight, and she already had trouble with the extra ten pounds she could never seem to get rid of.

The banquet was one fit for a king. There were bangers, rashers, eggs, several different kinds of breads, porridge, two cheeses, butter, jams, and a huge selection of fruit.

"Decisions, decisions," she mumbled.

Prior to entering the room, toast and coffee had been on her mind before taking a walk. However, her stomach had other plans, rumbling very loud in protest at the sight in front of her.

Brigid held her plate against her, inhaling the aromas. "Scrumptious. Perhaps, I'll just have one rasher, which puts American bacon to shame."

Before she knew it, she had loaded up her plate with a little of everything. Deciding to eat her feast in quiet company, she cast a glance around the room. She spied a cozy corner where sunlight was streaming through the beveled windows.

Kate bustled in bringing out plates of scones, fresh from the oven. She looked up to see Brigid, and was pleased to see her eating her meal with relish. Wiping her hands on her apron, she grabbed the pot of coffee, briskly moving toward her.

"It's a grand day indeed when I see a lass breaking her fast properly," she said, pouring some coffee into Brigid's cup.

Brigid drew back, placing her fork down. "I can't help myself, Kate. This is delicious. I really should not be eating this much."

"Pish, posh! You're a wee lass, and the Highland air makes everyone hungry," asserted Kate.

"You have got to be kidding me?" Brigid almost choked on the scone she was devouring. "I am not a *wee* lass by any means. Just look at my hips."

"Brigid, don't you let anyone tell you otherwise. If I think you're a wee lass, then so be it. That's the trouble with this century with all the lasses fretting about the look of their bodies. Tsk, tsk." Taking her pot of coffee, Kate kept muttering some more as she walked out of the room.

"Thank you, Kate." Smiling, she no longer cared that she had two scones, rashers, eggs, one sausage, and some blueberries with cream. Finishing the last of her coffee, she went to find Conn. She wanted to visit the ruins of Urquhart Castle.

Brigid found him in the stables with Hamish, tending a newborn colt. He never said a word when she asked if he could show her Urquhart Glen and the castle, only nodded.

The sun was warm, though the day was still brisk. October in the Highlands was showing its golden autumn splendor. Trees decked out in red and golden hues against the pines took her breath away. How could anyone ever leave this place? However, that's exactly what she was going to do after she returned the sword.

Brigid made a mental note to contact Lisa and Archie when she returned to Rowan Cottage. She had left both of them voice messages when she landed in Scotland, but had not personally spoken to either. Though it had only been a couple of days since she left the States, Brigid felt as if weeks had passed. Time moved different in the Highlands, and she made a second mental note to take this serenity with her when she returned home.

Conn had his window open, and the air whipped through making her curls more of a tangled mass. Tugging a band from the pocket of her jeans, she pulled her thick tresses over her shoulder and braided it.

"Would you like me to close the window, lass?"

She waved her hand at him. "Oh no, Conn, I don't

mind the cool air, it's just my hair is more trouble when it's open. Some days, I think I should just cut it all off."

Conn frowned and shook his head. "Your hair is like burnished copper, a rare beauty."

Brigid's jaw dropped. No one had ever called her hair a beauty. On the contrary, many had made fun of the mass of curls. Tucking a stray curl back behind her ear, she felt pretty for the first time in a long, long time. "Thanks Conn."

"So, is this part of Urquhart Glen? Where is the castle?" Glancing out the window, Brigid was looking at the most scenic part of their journey along the banks of Loch Ness.

"Aye, we are in Urquhart Glen, and soon you shall see the castle. It was once a mighty fortress with a proud clan that stood within her walls." His mouth was tight and a grim expression shown on his face. "Now it's only ghosts who haunt the stones."

"See the mound of wild looking grass over there?"

She angled her head. "Yes."

"It's *Both Ghlas-bheinn*—translated, it means, hut of the gray rock. And further up the road you will see *Tigh a' Chait*, house of the cat."

Laughing, Brigid saw new insight to this magical place. "I suppose that rock over there has a special meaning, too." She twisted around so she could catch a glimpse of the hut of the gray rock.

"Och, Brigid, do not laugh. For you mock the good folk, and I ken well their wrath when provoked."

When she glanced back at Conn, she noticed that he was not smiling. "You're serious?"

"Aye, as you should be, too."

Brigid believed, but she found it fascinating that

this man, who looked like a Viking god and dressed like a Harley biker, would truly believe in faeries. If he were in any other place than here, she would have laughed until her sides hurt.

As she was gazing out toward the loch, her senses became alive watching the water lapping along the edges of the bank. Waves gently weaved and flowed as if caught up in a mystical dance. What lay beneath these waters, she pondered. "They say that a monster lives beneath the loch. What do you believe, Conn?"

A smile curved ever so slightly, and he slowly looked at her before turning his gaze back toward the road. "What do *I believe*?" He paused to consider her question, for his answer could only confuse and possibly frighten her. Yet...she *was* the chosen one and did have a right to know some truth. He was always one to bend the rules just a wee bit to see what reaction he could glean.

As they were coming upon Urquhart Castle, Conn pulled onto a path away from the tour buses, but not too far for them to walk. "We'll walk from here."

Stepping out from the car, Conn headed toward the loch. Brigid followed tucking her hands into the pockets of her coat. A brisk wind had descended onto the loch, bringing the chill of the Highlands with it.

Conn stood legs apart with his hands on his hips gazing out toward the loch, sensing Brigid's approach. He removed his sunglasses and stuffed them in the pocket of his jacket.

"You asked me what I believed. Well, I shall tell you," as he gestured in a sweeping motion with one arm. "This here is a great magical place where within the depths of these waters, a dragon, the last of her kind, lives. She was brought with the fae and lived to see the last great battle only to flee in the end. She now resides here, protected. Yet, on rare occasions, she awakens from her slumber and ascends to the realm of humans."

Breathing deeply, Conn turned toward her, his eyes burning brightly. "It is not a myth nor legend, lass, but the truth I have told you. Just as you carry the sword which is an ancient relic, so she is what you call Nessie."

Brigid stepped back, "Who...*who are you?*"

"I think you know the answer, Brigid."

Arching her eyebrows, she replied, "Other than a nickname for you, I don't know what you're talking about."

Conn reached out with his fingers gently tipping her chin up toward him. "I'm not a Viking god, Celt yes, Viking, nae," and with that, he left her standing speechless along a bank as ancient as time itself.

Chapter 14

"In the veil between the worlds remember the faery folk who guard the ancient places and protect the last dragon."

"Egotistical man!" she shouted. Brigid watched as Conn walked back up toward the road, her anger boiling. How *dare* he make fun of her, and how in the hell did he know about his nickname she gave him?

Kicking up her heels, she took off after him. By the time she made it back up the road, he was almost at the entrance of Urquhart Castle.

"Wait just one bloody moment, Conn!" Now she was running after him. "Stop!"

Conn halted, slowly turning to face her. He had his hands on hips, with an arrogant look on his face.

Breathing hard she managed to spit out, "How did you know that's what I call you?"

Arching an eyebrow at her, he answered," I heard you tell Kate." He walked through a tunnel, which led to the ticket counter. Turning back toward a confused-looking Brigid, he grabbed her elbow and directed her down a dark tunnel leading out onto the castle grounds.

Yanking free from Conn, she snapped, "I don't recall saying *anything* about you to her!"

"Perhaps when you were mumbling in your sleep in the car?" He just shrugged. "Now would you like to see the remains of this grand castle, or are we going to stand here all day and argue?" A glint of humor sparked in his eyes.

"I would never..." and then a blush crept up her neck, spreading across her face. It dawned on her that he thought her dream was about him.

Biting her lip, she looked away and stepped past him, for if she had muttered something aloud, it was more to do with the man in her dreams and *nothing* to do with Conn. He might think he's some kind of Celtic god, but to her, he was just a man with an immense ego that rivaled his height.

Tucking the embarrassment within, she thought back to his earlier words. She had heard the tales that the Loch Ness monster was indeed a dragon from Archie, but the way Conn had described it, was as if he had witnessed some fantastical myth come to life. His face had transformed as he was telling the tale, speaking with reverence. Either he was very serious, *or* he was teasing her. Brigid made a mental note to call Archie and tell him what she thought about his choice of a guide.

"You may think you're a Celtic god, but don't all men think they're some kind of god?" she muttered with a smirk.

She followed along the path winding up to the castle ruins, aware that there was hardly anyone else around. As she came closer, she had that eerie sense of déjà vu. It was as if she had walked among the walls before, whispers of voices from long ago echoed around her. Shaking her head, she squeezed her eyes shut until the sensation stopped. When she finally opened them, her gaze drifted beyond the walls toward the Great Glen and the loch.

Placing a trembling hand against her heart she whispered, "It's beautiful *and* sad at the same time. The majesty of this place is incredible." Tears glinted in her eyes as a sense of sadness engulfed her.

Conn had quietly walked into a portion of the ruins. As he placed his hand on the stones, he gazed up into the sky.

Brigid stood watching him.

"When the English soldiers left in 1692, their last act of vengeance was to blow up part of the castle. That way it could not be used as a stronghold for the Jacobite rebels. It was a bloody battle, and it left many without a home. Now here it stands, still in ruins—a ghost of its former self."

Shoving himself away from the wall, he muttered a curse as he walked away from her.

****

They spent several more hours among the ruins, Conn answering many of her questions regarding the castle and the Mackays. The Mackays were the original owners and builders of Urquhart, but after the battle, they had dispersed to other parts of Scotland, never to be heard from again. Then the Durwards took over the castle and from there the MacDonalds. Finally, the Grants were the last owners. They were the ones who had built the most prominent feature of the entire castle—the tower house at the northern end of the promontory.

Conn then went on to describe in detail the outer and inner close, the great hall, and the chapel, which Brigid found fascinating. Apparently, the chapel was the site where St. Columba baptized a Pictish nobleman and his family in 580 AD.

Legend states even the faery folk thought him a great healer not only with words, but also of plants and animals, so they let him lay the first stone for his chapel here.

Conn was a walking encyclopedia of Scottish lore.

"If the Mackays of Urquhart are no longer in existence, where should I return the sword? Should I just hand it over to the Scottish Trust?"

"Nae, lass. The Mackays may not possess Urquhart, but the Order still lives. You wouldn't want to hand over a sacred relic to the Trust. They would just see it as an ancient sword to be displayed in glass and locked in a room. Nae, you must return it to a Mackay."

Shocked, Brigid asked, "Well then, who?"

"I've heard a Mackay lives a few kilometers north of here at Castle Aonach. I could take you there in the morn."

"Why not now? We could at least talk to this Mackay."

Irritation laced his words. "Lass, *first*, you don't have the sword and *second*, I would have to check with Hamish or Kate to see if this Mackay still resides at the castle."

"Mackay or not, I'm not about to turn over an ancient artifact to someone I don't know, unless they are part of a historical society. I just wanted to talk to them. I'll bring the sword, but that doesn't mean I'm handing it over to them." Walking away, she headed for the entrance of the tunnel, leaving a stunned Conn, shaking his head.

"Blessed Danu, give me strength to deal with this lass," he muttered.

Chapter 15

"Round and round they went singing, dancing, and laughing, till the darkness came, bringing with it evil, which spread like a cloak of thorns."

Brigid was famished by the time they came back to Rowan Cottage. When she entered, there was a note on the entry table addressed to her and Conn. It stated that on Fridays, there was live music and storytelling at the local pub called the Black Swan. Kate insisted that she come on down to get a true flavor of Scotland.

"Well, it looks like we'll be eating at the Black Swan for dinner," showing Conn the note.

Rubbing his hands together to ward off the chill, he remarked, "Aye, it's Friday, and you don't want to miss a great meal and singing at the Black Swan." Turning, he headed back out the front door.

"I'll be there in a few minutes, Conn. I just want to freshen up a bit," she called out.

"No worries, lass. I'll keep the car humming and warm," as he gave her a wave over his head.

Dashing up the stairs, all Brigid could think about was a warm meal and a pint. The day had drained her emotionally, and she couldn't think of anything better than being at a pub—*especially* in the Highlands of Scotland.

Walking into the bathroom, she splashed cold

water on her face, noticing she had sprouted more freckles from being out in the sun. A little makeup would help to cover them, but she didn't want to keep Conn waiting. The anticipation of food and a pint was causing her stomach to rumble. Braiding her hair quickly and securing it with a leather thong, she finished with a bit of lip-gloss and changed from her tee shirt to a pale green sweater.

Catching one more glimpse of herself in the mirror, she grabbed her leather jacket and purse, as she headed out the door.

****

As they approached the Black Swan, they could hear laughter spill out from the entrance and the smells of food assaulted Brigid before she set foot inside. "I'm really here in the Highlands," she whispered to herself and smiled.

Conn held the door open and as soon as they entered, cheers erupted from the crowd when they saw him. Hellos were exchanged with claps on the back, and even those daring gave hugs. It was as if he was being treated to a hero's welcome. They simply adored him. Smiling, Brigid just stood back to take it all in, since seeing Conn laugh and jest was something she had yet to witness.

"Well, there you are!" Kate came up behind Brigid, taking her arm and leading her to one of the tables near a small platform for the performers. "I thought it best you should have front row seating."

Hamish was heading slowly toward them with a tray full of pints, trying not to bump into anyone along the way. Brigid held her breath watching him make his way to their table. He was doing some fancy maneuvering to squeeze past a raucous pair of men.

"Here you go." Hamish set down the tray passing the pints to her and Kate.

"I see Conn is talking with the MacGregor's." He nodded to where Conn was standing with a group of men.

"Do they always acknowledge Conn that way?" Brigid asked, still watching as others greeted him as if they had not seen him in ages.

Kate looked back toward Brigid with a look that was more cautious as she spoke. "Aye, it's been some time since Conn's returned to these parts."

"Did he grow up here?" Brigid asked, as she took a sip of her pint. "Delicious," she muttered softly.

"He has family near and around these parts, but nae, he did not spend his young days here," responded Kate.

Laughter warm and rich came forth from Conn. Brigid continued to be in awe of this man until suddenly a sharp memory invaded her thoughts—the man in her dreams. Why would her heart dwell on a fantasy when here in front of her were real live men? So many too, she thought, *and* they made them big here in the Highlands. Yet, there he stood within her thoughts and heart—her dream Highlander. "Ridiculous!" she snapped.

"Brigid?" Kate had placed her hand on Brigid's with a questioning look on her face.

"Nothing, Kate," giving her a small sad smile. "I'm just thinking utter nonsense and how my life seems to be a bit...*lonely*. I've only been here a few days, but it seems as if my soul has found a home here in Scotland." With a sigh and another gulp of her pint, she continued, "I think things will have to change once I return back to the States." Brigid squeezed Kate's hand in reassurance, and returned to look out at the crowd.

"Perhaps, your man is closer than you think," said Kate squeezing Brigid's hand back.

She managed to shrug and say offhandedly, "Not enough time, unless he's here in the pub tonight."

"One never knows, lass," laughed Kate. "Tell me about your store in Seattle. Do you sell many old antiques?"

Brigid smiled just thinking about her shop—a shop that gave her joy and kept her grounded. A shop to let her explore Scotland until the day she received the sword, sending her on a journey she was still trying to figure out.

As she continued to talk to Kate, Conn strolled over, sitting down across from her. Then Hamish sauntered over bringing them their meal. And what a meal it was. There was shepherd's pie, cheesy potatoes, and fresh baked bread. More pints were ordered, and the conversation turned livelier. The atmosphere was warm and infused with friendship. Brigid loved every bit of it. It took her mind and heart off her nonexistent love life, and the trip back home, which had left her with a sinking feeling within.

"Oh, look," exclaimed Brigid. "They're setting up for the music."

Conn leaned lightly toward her, since the noise in the pub had risen considerably. "They're called the Wicked Brothers."

"Are they really related?" she asked, smiling.

"Nae, not by blood, only by clan." He leaned back sipping his pint.

The crowd had started to quiet down. A couple of men came over to the table, and Conn introduced them to Brigid as Rory and Liam MacGregor. They had the same build as Conn and similar striking eyes. Rory's hair was more golden than Conn's, and Liam's had reddish hues streaked throughout. She wondered if all of Conn's *cousins* were this tall and gorgeous. He explained they were distant cousins. However, Brigid thought they all looked like brothers.

She watched as they bantered back and forth, and at times, it seemed as if they had their own mental conversation going on. They joked with her and asked her if Conn had been taking care of her. Then they would wink at Conn and laugh, as he gave them a scowl.

"Listen, Brigid, if you tire of this old man, just give me call," spouted Liam with a wink.

Blushing, she just shook her head no. All these men were so ruggedly handsome, but again an ache for someone else skittered across her skin. When she looked into Liam's eyes, there was a glint of something else, but Rory slapped a hand on his shoulders, and the moment was lost. Brigid had never been the focus of so much attention. She thought herself too tall, too curvy, and hair that at times was just a wild mass of curls.

Sitting back, she told herself she was going to enjoy all of this attention, and the sexy scenery, too. Another round of pints was ordered, and the music started.

The Wicked Brothers played for the crowd for over an hour. Then they started taking requests. Some of the requests were ballads, and others were playful and more current. They became loud and boisterous until they sang the ballads. Brigid knew most of the older ones, and the crowd became silent during the mournful ones. She became tearful just listening to the words and haunting tunes.

Kate was silently weeping as well, and passed her some tissue. Looking up, Brigid saw another man had come forth. "Who's that?"

"It's, Tuck, the storyteller," sniffed Kate. "He is one of the best here in these parts."

He reminded Brigid of a gnome. His face was old and weathered with deep penetrating eyes that spoke as if they had seen much of this world, and gray hair that stood up in spikes at various places on his head. He placed a stool in the front, and the band became a quiet accompaniment.

The chatter in the room became silent, as he put up his hand to signal the start of his story. "Let me tell you a story of our dragon who dwells in the loch and silently awaits the return of her knights."

Brigid gasped, placing a hand over her heart.

He glanced her way, and as he tilted his head, he gave her a knowing smile, then continued in his telling of the tale. She sat enthralled, already knowing much of the story, but he recounted details as if he had witnessed them. She found it fascinating that at the end of the story—there was hope. A round of cheers and clapping ensued.

Brigid was stunned when Tuck jumped off the stool, and walked over to their table. Introductions were exchanged, and Tuck took a chair next to Brigid.

"Well, well, so this is the bonny lass who has kept Conn absent from the glen." Tuck chuckled as he gazed at Brigid.

Embarrassed by his words, she quickly said, "He's just showing me around the glen. However, I'm sure I can do fine by myself if he's needed elsewhere."

Conn just sat there with his arms folded across his chest, an arched eyebrow the only response to Tuck and her statements.

"I found your story fascinating, Tuck." Brigid was hesitant, but she realized Conn had probably told Kate and Hamish about the sword. Therefore, what could be the harm in telling Tuck?

He swiveled toward Brigid. "Ah yes, one of the saddest, too. You ken the tale?"

"Yes, and I believe I have one of the relics."

"Sweet Danu! Then 'tis true?" Tuck looked at Conn for confirmation.

Conn gave one nod meaning he was correct.

"Tell me, Brigid, how did you come upon the sword?"

She recounted from the beginning how she received the sword, leaving out the details of her dreams. She managed to convince Tuck that after doing some research with Archie, it was determined that she should return the sword to the Clan Mackay here in Urquhart Glen.

Conn added, "Kate believes the mistress of Castle Aonach is a Mackay, and possibly descended from the original Mackays of Urquhart."

Tuck nodded and took a swig of his ale. Then exhaling slowly, his gaze focused on Brigid. "Lass, what you have been entrusted to do is not for the weak. Your journey is about to begin."

She was startled by his words and took a quick breath of astonishment. "*What*?"

He jumped down from his chair, went over, and grasped both of her hands, placing a kiss on each. "May the light of the fae guide you on your path, for danger lurks within the shadows." Giving her a slight bow, he turned to Conn, quietly speaking. Apparently, it was not for her ears for he uttered it in Gaelic to him.

Then with a nod of his head, he left a stunned and speechless Brigid.

Chapter 16

"The dragon looked down upon the young knight, and asked, What is the difference between a myth and a legend?"

"*Who*?" Duncan rasped. With a look of puzzlement over his features, he waited for an answer.

Holding his palm up to still any more questions, Cathal glanced up toward the night sky as if listening for something. Gazing back toward Duncan, he just shrugged his shoulders and went over to the fire. Bending down, he grabbed some more dirt and tossed it onto the blaze, which seem to respond in kind with more heat.

Duncan ran a hand through his hair and across his face in frustration. He was bone tired, and the fire was not reaching the chill within. Cormac sat next to him in brooding silence, sword extended across his knees.

Cathal came forward and sat down. "I can only tell ye that the Guardian is sending someone of great importance. Ye must be mindful and alert, my son." Sighing, Cathal continued, "Life is sacred, Duncan. To forfeit a life will not end or break the curse."

"Ye dinnae ken that," Duncan said wearily.

"Ye are still blinded by fury and grief and cannot hear the words of the Guardian. Yes, there is danger in your path, but there is also hope." He hesitated briefly before stressing, "Margaret is *gone*. However, ye have a duty to unite your brothers and heal the scar, which has continued across your lands."

Duncan stood and went before the fire, hands outstretched in front of the flames. He remembered the words of the Guardian, but he still did not know their meaning. What *if* Cathal was correct? Had he really been blinded by his grief this past year so as not to see another? Perhaps there was another path. Sweet Meggie was gone, and he owed it to his brothers to bring them back to the Glen. They may not want him in their lives, but he would sell his soul to bring them back home.

He could only nod solemnly in agreement with Cathal.

"We shall spend the night here with ye, yet in the morn we shall part. Ye must find this person, Duncan. I sense the dark shadows following this one, too. Only *ye* can be their protector. I don't see from which direction they will come, but ye will ken when the time is near."

Cormac looked questioningly at Cathal. "I dinnae agree with ye, druid." A muscle clenched in his jaw, as he continued to shake his head in disagreement.

Duncan sighed. "He is correct, my friend. I go forth alone."

****

Duncan spent the rest of the night in fitful dreams. Visions of the night Margaret died tormented him and others of demons lashing out.

However, in those darker moments, a light of beauty streamed through his dreams. She whispered to him of hope and faith. Then when the demon was ready to rip out his soul, she reached for his face with both hands and took his mouth, breathing life back into him in a searing kiss. She tasted of honey, flowers, and *hope*. Breathing in a sweetness that rocked him to the core, he responded by cupping her face and delving his tongue into her mouth to savor her sweet nectar. He felt her moan deep within him, and he shuddered with passion so deep, it pounded the blood throughout his body.

He broke from the kiss, still cupping her face when he gazed into the most bejeweled eyes of green he had ever seen.

Duncan awoke to warm lips touching and caressing his face, until the lips snorted. "Out of my face, ye foul-smelling animal." Grimacing Duncan got up off the stone slab and patted Brandubh on his side. "Ye are a sore sight for these eyes, my friend, but your breath is one of a beast."

Brandubh snorted as he bobbed his head.

He rubbed at his face trying to erase the memory of yet another intensely erotic dream. If he closed his eyes, he could conjure up the lovely vision again. Scowling, he fought back the desire. Why he thought one would haunt his dreams he could not fathom, and there was no time to dwell on them, either.

Looking around, he saw Cathal was as good as his word. Both he and Cormac were gone. There was a sack, which upon opening contained some oatcakes, hard cheese, acorns, dried beef, and apples. He chuckled softly, knowing Cathal had included the apples for Brandubh. The druid had a soft spot for all animals, especially his warhorse.

"It appears Cathal intends to keep ye in good spirits on our journey."

Brandubh snorted, taking his front hoof and

stomping the ground. Duncan took out his dirk and sliced an apple, giving some to him before taking a slice into his own mouth.

Glancing skywards, he noticed the sky was cloudless and the sun a warm cloak around him.

He had two thoughts—to find this person, whoever they may be, and second, he would seek out his brother, Angus. His gut told him that he probably was at Urquhart Castle. However, where he would find the other person to aid him on his quest was a mystery.

"One task at a time," he muttered.

His soul was still heavy, yet for the first time since that awful night, a renewed sense of purpose filled him. There was hope for his brothers and their lives, and he would do whatever it took.

His fate, though, was still at a crossroad.

Standing, he loaded what little he had onto Brandubh. Breathing deeply the crisp morning air, he mounted his horse and moved silently onward.

Chapter 17

"It is said some souls are connected by an ancient calling, which echoes through time until they are one."

Brigid awoke with a start not fully realizing where she was. Clutching her sheets, she kept blinking her eyes adjusting to the sense of half dreaming and being awake. The smell of food brought her more into the reality of being fully conscious, and her shoulders sagged.

She had spent another restless night of dreams with her Highlander and her temples throbbed. Each time she would awake, she could still feel his arms around her, his scent lingering on her lips. She was on fire from his touch. How could a dream feel so real?

The moment her journey brought her to Scotland, she had not had one good night's sleep. Her eyes narrowed. This all started the moment she received the sword.

"Damn you!" she yelled, punching her pillow. Placing her head in her heads, she felt an ache she could not fully comprehend. Her Highlander had invaded her dreams every night, and exhaustion had frazzled her nerves. On some unconscious level, she felt as if she had known him all her life.

Moving slowly out of bed, she went and stood at the window, staring out among the sheep that dotted along the valley. She had made the decision last night to return the sword today. Tomorrow her plans would take her to Edinburgh for some sightseeing. Afterwards, she would head back home.

Swallowing the lump in her throat, her heart told her that this was her home.

Brigid loved the Highlands, but it was time go. Faery tales steeped in legend had made an impact on her. She was being foolish to expect anything more.

"If only..."—her breath fogging part of the window—"I may never find out who sent me the sword, but does it matter now?"

A smile spread across her face as she spotted a little lamb running and jumping to catch up with its mother. Yes, she would miss the Highlands, but who's to say she couldn't return one day.

Turning from the window, Brigid retrieved her suitcase and started packing.

****

Castle Aonach was located toward the northern part of the Great Glen. The road had sharp turns and at times narrowed to one lane. Brigid would hold her breath as Conn navigated the path a bit too fast. The view as always was spectacular, and though the morning was brisk, she rolled down the window to breathe in the scent of the air.

"You're a true Highland lass now, wanting to take in the mists."

She swiped at a loose curl. "I feel as if I can't get enough. I'm trying to absorb as much as I can before I leave."

A frown skittered across his features, and Brigid wondered what that was about.

"Conn, what's wrong?"

"Nothing, just what you would call...deep in thought?"

"Right." Yet she thought there was more, but kept silent.

"Here it is, Castle Aonach."

"Wow!" Brigid gasped, placing her hand to her chest.

It was beyond what she envisioned. Brigid expected a small dwelling, not this great expanse of stone structure. A turret stood in the middle as if welcoming all visitors. Then she understood its meaning—Castle Aonach meant *gathering place*. They went over the bridge and under an arched entrance into a large courtyard.

"When was this built, Conn?"

"I believe it was built in the year 1210 as a second home for the Mackays, a distant relative of the ones of Urquhart."

"You're kidding, right? 800 years ago? It looks so...*new*."

"It would depend on what your meaning of *new* means," he chuckled.

Brigid got out of the car and stood looking around, feeling a sense of warmth prickle her senses. Shaking it off, she took the sword out of the back seat and slung it carefully over her shoulder. It would have been nice if Conn had asked to help, but he never once mentioned to even look at the sword, much less help her carry it.

"So much for chivalry in Highland men," she snorted, following Conn up to the entrance. When she finally made it to the door, her mouth dropped open as it was promptly closed.

"What's wrong?"

Conn grasped her elbow to move her back down the path. "The butler said his mistress is not home. She is visiting friends on the Isle of Skye and will not be returning until the end of the month."

She glared at him. "This can't be happening!"

Continuing to move her along, he added, "He then suggested we call to make an appointment."

Jerking free of his grasp, she waved her hands up in frustration and stormed off into the direction of the pine trees across from the entrance.

Conn just stared at her fading back. He stifled a retort and watched until she was out of sight.

He was leaning against the car for some time thinking it best to give her some distance, until a bird's screech caught his attention. A falcon was hovering in the distance and understanding flooded him. She had gone in the direction of the stones.

"Bloody hell!" What a fool he was to let her go off in that direction, knowing she was not ready.

Conn cupped both hands over his mouth, speaking in Gaelic to the falcon. The bird swooped and flew off in Brigid's direction, as Conn took off running through the trees.

****

Brigid was angry, tired, and frustrated. She did not plan on waiting until the end of the month for Mistress Mackay to return. She wanted answers now, and she wanted to return the sword.

There were two options. One, she could take the sword back to Seattle, or two, she could turn it over to the Scottish Trust.

Shoving a fist into the air, she yelled, "And I'm

pissed off at whoever sent me this sword. Legends, my ass!" Picking up a stone, she tossed it hard across the path.

Walking faster and deeper into the trees, she tripped on a root branch and lost her footing, which did not help with the sword, its weight propelling her to the ground. One arm had managed to hold the strap, but her right hand and arm slammed onto the edge of a sharp boulder.

"Damn, damn, damn." Slowly rolling over, she saw her hand was bleeding. Using her good arm, she tried to remove the sword, which was proving to be difficult, since it required both hands.

Looking up, she noticed she was in a stone ring. In all, there were five standing stones and one long, horizontal stone in the middle, which Brigid assumed was probably an altar. On each of the stones, carved from top to bottom, were Celtic symbols.

Brigid tried to stand, but started feeling dizzy. Staring across the stones, she wondered if Conn had followed her.

"Probably not, he's probably in the car," she gritted out. She wasn't bleeding much, though still worried about getting any blood on the leather pouch.

"Blood or dirt? What shall it be?"

Wiping her palm on the grass, she thought she heard shouting in the distance. Her mind was spinning, and the pressure in her ears was getting worse. Lying down with the sword behind her, Brigid managed to position herself out from under the strap. Yet, in twisting to get it off, her bloody hand touched the sword handle, which had come out of the pouch. "Crap," she mumbled.

Instantly pain slammed into her with full force. Pressure started to build in her ears, and the pain seared her thoughts, taking control of her body.

It seemed as if time had stood still.

Slowly, she lifted her head to a sound of someone calling her name. Her vision blurred, and she thought she noticed Conn standing at the edge of the trees.

Why didn't he help her? And *why* was he yelling?

"Don't move, Brigid!" Conn was standing on the opposite side of the stones, a look of terror etched across his face. Conn had to steady the portal immediately. A portal she opened when her blood came in contact with the sword.

If he didn't, Brigid would die.

He quickly stripped off his jacket and shirt. Needing to feel the earth beneath him to call upon his powers, he removed his boots. Raising his arms out and upwards, Conn started chanting the ancient language of the fae, keeping his eyes on Brigid.

The pressure easing somewhat, Brigid managed to bring her head back up. However, the pain continued to rock her body, keeping her on the ground. Blinking her eyes to focus, she was shocked at the man before her.

Conn stood arms outstretched and emblazoned on his arms and torso were Celtic tattoos. They glowed, and Brigid could see the light and energy swirling around his body. She tried to understand what he was saying, but the words didn't make sense.

His eyes caught hers and she reached out for him. "Help me, Conn," she whispered, as a tear fell down her cheek. The pain was too much. What was *happening*? Looking back down at her hands, she started to tremble.

"Brigid!" Conn rasped out. Holding control of the portal took all of his strength, and he could only do so for a few moments more. Her life force started to fade from his sight, and he raised his arms higher. In his mind, he reached out for the goddess Danu, the mother of all, his prayer a silent plea for help. He felt her soft touch and then turned his direction back to Brigid.

"Damn it, Brigid, *look at me*!"

"Conn?" The pain eased somewhat, and glancing at Conn she saw that his face was one of pain, too.

"You only have mere minutes, lass. Can you hear me?"

Swallowing, she nodded.

"Take the sword to the Mackay."

Shaking her head she sobbed out, "She's gone."

He tried to keep his voice calm. "Nae lass, not *that* Mackay. Find Duncan."

"What?" she croaked out. "Duncan? Duncan Mackay?"

A quiet stillness settled within Brigid, and she knew she was dying. It was as if she was being absorbed into the ground. Her breathing became labored, and her thoughts muddled. Nothing mattered anymore. There was no point in fighting.

"Lass, look at me."

Her head was heavy, but Brigid looked up into brilliant eyes that blazed. In that instant, she realized Conn was not human. Struggling for breath, she choked out, "Wh...*who* are you?" Why won't you help *me*?" Brigid struggled to say the last.

Arms still extended, Conn feared the portal was closing too quickly. He had to prepare her for what was on the other side. "Brigid, I am a Fenian warrior of the fae, sworn to protect you, and if you want to live, you *must* take the sword to Duncan Mackay." His arms shook trying to contain the power. "I told you before, I'm not a Viking god, but a Celt, lass. I can only stabilize the portal for a few more moments. I am not allowed to cross into the realm. It is only for you. The sword belongs to the Mackay of the past. You must return it to him!"

The world exploded in one bright flash of light and pain, leaving Brigid no time to laugh at Conn's words.

Chapter 18

"Time is like a river, which with the ebb and flow of its currents, may venture off in many different directions."

Duncan swayed on Brandubh as if he had been struck. Both rider and horse had come to a halt. Sucking in his breath, he reached for his sword, more on instinct.

Recognition flared instantly in him.

The sword of the Dragon Knights—*his sword*, was nearby. He had not felt its magic since that fateful night. Yet in this moment, it resonated within his very soul.

It called to him.

Brandubh whinnied and shifted uneasily, sensing the magic, too. Reaching out toward him, Duncan patted his mane. "Aye, ye felt it, too."

Scrutinizing his surroundings, Duncan lifted his hand from the hilt of his sword. With a slow smile, he understood his destiny was about to change. For the first time in many a moon, Duncan raised his head and said a silent prayer to the goddess, placing his fate in her hands.

Calling forth his powers, he listened and waited until the breath of the wind touched his face, swirling around them both. "Let us follow the path of the wind,

Brandubh, and pray it will lead us to the sword."

Brandubh raked his hoof in leaves and mud several times, as if in agreement.

Then they rode off.

****

Castle Leomhann

"*Nae!*" Lachlan screamed, as he took hold of the stone wall, smashing his fist against it. Blood oozed from his knuckles and trickled down within the crevices. He did not feel the pain, just the power rush over him.

It could not be.

It was impossible.

All this time he did not think it could be done.

He tossed it aside many moons ago, but here in this dark corridor, he felt the shift of power and a crack of the worlds sliced open.

There wasn't a moment to be lost. He had to move quickly and find the source.

Shoving himself away from the wall, he placed his fist in his mouth and licked away the blood and flesh. "Ye will not fulfill your quest, Duncan Mackay," he hissed. "If I have to slay ye myself, then so be it."

Slinking back down the dank corridor, Lachlan already started forming a plan, one that didn't include the laird knowing the sword was closer than they thought. Lachlan had plans for the relics; such power to be harnessed with his own would put fear into any clan.

Nae, he would keep silent for now.

All he required was for the MacFhearguis to search out and find Duncan. Once he was killed, he would move on to the next Mackay. One by one they would all die. Then each of the relics would come into his possession. In the end, he would have the greatest treasure of all—the great dragon.

"Then I shall spit on the fae." Laughter, evil and low spilled forth from him as he walked faster, grazing his hand against the walls, spilling more blood.

****

Glen Urquhart Forest

Holding the sickle tightly, for fear it would slip into the stream, Cathal tried to steady himself.

The first wave of power had washed over him. Then a second one had followed, causing him to lose his balance and fall to his knees. His body trembled with its raw intensity and his vision blurred.

His thumb nicked the bottom of the sickle and blood seeped forth. Seeing this, he took it as a sign from the fae, and taking in a deep breath, he set the sickle aside. Placing his hand with the injured thumb into the ground, he uttered softly, "I give my blood freely to the Great Mother, for it is in her power to give life. Oh Great Mother of us all, blessed Danu of the fae, let me see who comes forth, so that I may assist."

The world stopped for Cathal, and a great wave of energy burst forth shoving him across the ground, landing some stones away. The motion caused him to lose his breath, and he fought to find air again. It shook him to his soul.

The message was clear.

He could not help.

Wiping his hands, which were shaking across his face, he noticed his thumb had healed and gave a blessing of thanks.

Cathal was still too weak to stand, so he crawled slowly over to a nearby oak, taking solace in its strength.

Trembling slightly, he glanced upwards. "If I cannot help them, then show me what I *can* do."

In that moment, the Guardian smiled.

Chapter 19

"A knight in shining armor may not want to rescue the damsel in distress, fearing she will steal his heart."

Brigid was cold. It was her only thought, that and her mouth tasted of copper.

Something or someone was close. She could sense the movement of it, yet it was a struggle to open her eyes. Finally, the warmth of the sun brushed gently on her face, soothing away the heaviness. When she opened her eyes, two dark brown ones stared back at her from the grass. A nut-brown hare sat munching on some grass, content to keep her company.

Breathing deeply, a trembling Brigid sat up sitting cross-legged and brushed the curls out of her face. She glanced around at her surroundings, noting she was still in the middle of the stone circle, though something was different—out of place. The trees were not as big and she didn't remember seeing foxgloves—yet, there she sat in a cluster of them.

Something was not right. She blinked several times trying to remember. Suddenly, memories flashed liked lightning within her mind, and the reality of what Conn told her sent her senses spinning.

The logical side of her brain clashed with the dreamer.

Conn was not human and whatever happened to

her was very real. Where was she? The area did look familiar. Her thoughts went back to what Conn told her. Only one thing he spoke of shook her to the core, and Brigid croaked out his name, "Duncan Mackay."

Conn could not have possibly meant *the* Duncan Mackay. "Impossible. He lived in the thirteenth century," her voice devoid of emotion.

"*No*, this can't be."

Hugging her arms tightly around herself, she rocked back and forth in a state of disbelief. Wiping another curl out of her face with the sleeve of her leather jacket, she watched as the hare stopped chewing and scampered off toward the trees.

"Great, even you little one are scared by his name too. You wouldn't happen to know where I could find *him*."

Overwhelmed by fear was enough cause for Brigid to harness it and become angry. "This is *insane*!" A battle of emotions waged a fight inside her until she spotted the sword lying a few feet to the right of one of the stones.

Testing her strength, she slowly crawled on all fours, and then stood, walking slowly over toward the sword. It was still partially exposed from the pouch. Remembering, Brigid drew up her injured hand, noticing it had healed. Bending down, she trembled as she placed her hand above the blade—the very blade that was absent of her blood, as if it had been cleaned. Shoving her fist into her mouth to stop the force of tears that threatened to spill, she gathered what little strength she had and placed the sword back into its pouch.

Standing back up, Brigid glanced upwards toward the sun and saying a silent prayer and ending it aloud,

"Because I sure don't know what the hell I'm doing."

Then, braiding her mass of curls that had bits of leaf and grass strewn in, she dug into her pocket for her leather tie. Gathering up the sword, she eased it over her sore shoulder and walked over to one of the stones, which stood at least ten feet.

Placing her hand on the cool, smooth surface, she traced her finger around and in its spirals. "Any help from this realm would be greatly appreciated." Remembering what her grandmother had taught her so many years ago about the fae, Brigid pulled a strand of hair loose from her braid. With a sharp tug and snap, she placed the strand at the bottom of the stone as a gift. "Give me strength, too."

Taking one last deep breath, she turned and walked out of the stone circle to the only place she thought might help. To Castle Aonach—the Mackay house.

She only prayed it was still there.

****

They had been riding only a few days, but the longer they went without any sign of the Mackay, the more it made it difficult for Patrick to squelch the uneasiness in the pit of his stomach. He rubbed his gloved hand over his chin, watching Michael talking sternly to one his men. He considered how much more any of them could take with his rage on edge these many moons, seeing the bloodthirsty look of revenge on his brother's face. Michael was a changed man, but they all had changed that night when Adam returned covered with the blood of him and Margaret.

Finding Adam would help to ease this disquiet, not the Mackay. They were wasting precious time, and were venturing onto Mackay land, as well. When did

Michael bend the law to his will? Nae...this was not the brother or laird he knew. It was time to seek out Alex. He needed his brother's aid. Or else, there would be more blood spilled, and he feared it would not be a Mackay's.

Instantly, Michael roared a curse, and jerked his steed toward Patrick. "Someone was here a few days past, made camp by the stones. It must have been the Mackay," Michael snarled.

Patrick raised a brow in question. "Why the Mackay? It could have been a traveler."

"It is Lachlan who brought us this news, and I must go with that." He flung his arm outwards. "No one else would travel in these damned parts."

"All he said, brother, was the Mackay had left on his quest, and he did not ken where. We should seek out Alex. He may have news of Adam."

"*Ye question me*?" Clenching his fists in front of his saddle, Michael kept his gaze fixed on Patrick, until a cry of a falcon brought his attention upwards. It was a beauty, raven black with white markings—a rare one indeed.

He watched it circle and make one last cry, before it flew off toward the north, toward the Great Glen, where he knew Alex was. He eyes remained fixed on the bird until he could no longer see it in his sight. Could it be an omen, he thought? Shaking his head, he whipped his attention back toward Patrick. His fury now ebbing some, he edged his horse closer to his brother.

Clamping his hand hard on Patrick's shoulder, Michael looked at him directly. "Let us go forth and seek out Alex." And in a hushed voice for only

Patrick's ears, he added, "Yet, if we encounter the Mackay, I will take my sword and run him through."

Patrick watched as Michael galloped off, giving commands to the rest of the men. He realized he had been holding his breath and exhaled slowly.

"Damn ye, Mackay! Why could ye not stay silent? Ye don't ken what you've started." His horse stomped one foot anxiously, ready to be with the rest. Patrick held him steady, not wanting to join his brother just yet. He wanted to place some distance until Michael's anger cooled.

****

Duncan could smell them, or smell someone. It was a faint sweet smell, and he had seen Sorcha overhead, giving him the warning there were riders in the distance. There had been no one in these parts for many a moon. In years past, travelers would travel through Mackay land and be welcomed.

A sense of sadness engulfed him, as he dwelled on happier times, when all was well with the clan, and laughter filled the great hall. They were a proud and fiercely loyal family, one filled with love. His parents were devoted not only to them, but to each other. The death of their da destroyed their mother and she went quietly to the *land of forever* a few moons after him. It was rough in the beginning. It was up to Angus to keep them together. Margaret was still young, but he was determined to keep them all at Urquhart.

To find a love like his parents shared was not possible in his future.

A twig snapped, and he stilled Brandubh. Dismounting quietly, he took out his sword. The movement had come directly ahead near the stream.

The closer he crept, the stronger the scent. It reminded him of flowers. He moved closer, edging between the trees, sword extended, battle instincts ever present.

Duncan came to a full stop, unable to fathom what he saw.

Sweet Danu! Crouched behind a rock looking out toward the stream was a lass. A lass who was dressed in the most peculiar clothing. He noticed she was perched as if she was hiding from someone or something, moving up and down trying not to be noticed, and at the same time watching.

What had captured his sight was not the long dark red braid that hung down her back waiting to be pulled, but the way her trews molded her bum. So round and luscious, intoxicating from where he stood, calling him to take and plunder her where she stood. Instantly, lust surged forth like a wild beast, and he wanted to take her over the rock and mount her from behind.

Then the glorious form stood, and turned around facing him, a look of shock etched across her face. Duncan lowered his sword arm, and stood motionless.

Nae, it could not be! It was the lass from his dreams.

Time stood still.

He heard her give a slight gasp, placing a fist against her heart, which caught his attention. When she took a step backwards, she landed against the boulder.

Duncan's eyes narrowed.

Dreams or not, he was not about to be swayed by the goddess who stood before him. He tried hard to squelch the lust that overtook him earlier. In truth, looking in those lush green eyes made his head swim. He could get lost in those, oh aye, and so much more.

"Who are ye?" Duncan croaked out.

"Brigid...Brigid O'Neill," she stammered. "*Who are you?*"

The lass had a strange form of language, which caught Duncan off guard again. She could possibly be a spy, and he hesitated in his answer.

He shifted his stance, then piercing her with his eyes and a cock of his dark brow, he replied, "I am Duncan Mackay of the Clan Mackay, and ye are trespassing on *my* land."

Chapter 20

"Let me look through the looking glass and see my true love, lest he comes forth and tarnishes my vision of him."

"*You* are Duncan Mackay?" Brigid swallowed the fear that had started to churn in the pit of her stomach when Duncan announced who he was.

Shaking, she leaned into the solid rock for support. Standing before her, she was looking at the man from her dreams. Yet, this was no dream, and this man was *very* real. He looked right at her as if he wanted to devour her. She saw the shock and yes, the lust that was evident when her gaze traveled down the length of him.

Snapping her gaze back up to his large eyes, eyes so blue, it reminded her of the sea on a stormy day. His hair was glossy black and lay against his shoulders in soft waves, tempting her to run her hands through them. A chin that was square and strong with a dimple in the middle, and a nose, which had probably been in several battles, but somehow added strength to his features.

She had thought Conn to be tall, but this man was a giant. He had to be at least six feet six inches, though she could be wrong.

He probably was taller.

His plaid was wrapped around his long tunic in such a way, one couldn't see where it started or ended.

However, what caught her eye was the glint of his silver torc, making him appear more primal than any man she knew.

Brigid wanted him, wanted him like no other. She didn't know who he was, just that he was here in the flesh—wanting to taste, and take him within her. Heat flooded her cheeks. She needed—no, *craved* his touch.

He was her knight, to take and plunder and she would surrender.

"Where are your clansmen? Why are ye here?"

Her knight had spoken again. However, *her knight* had a name.

Of all the faery tales she'd listened to, she would have never thought this one would be possible. No, it couldn't be—not *the* Duncan Mackay from the thirteenth century? The very one who killed his sister? How is it possible that a monster could look so good? Looks can be deceiving, her grandmother once told her.

Her knight was in truth a *murderer.*

"I feel like I fell down the rabbit hole." She slumped down on the grass, wiping a hand across her brow.

No sooner did she collapse than giant arms swept her back up, the contact sending shivers up her spine.

"Let me *go!*" Shoving with all her might, she twisted to get out of his arms. Duncan quickly released her. Obviously, he didn't want any contact with her, either.

"I will ask ye again, lass, why are ye here?"

"How do I know?" Her hands started to shake as he took a step forward.

"Bloody hell." Breathing hard, Brigid glanced around to where she spotted her sword, lying a few feet away. If she was quick, she could make a dive for it. Foolish thought. What good would it do? Her strength was no match against this Highlander.

"The truth?" Fear crept into her voice.

Pointing her finger in the direction of the sword, she exclaimed, "*That* is why I'm here! Someone sent me the sword, and apparently, I've just found out I'm to return it to you! At least that's what *he* said before I blacked out." Waving her hands about, Brigid kept rambling as if the words had a voice all their own. She could no longer contain them.

"So you see, I've brought back your sword, and now *my* question to you is how the bloody hell am I going to get back home?"

Gritting his teeth, he tried hard to follow what she was saying, but the lass had a language that was different from any he had known and she was talking so fast, he found it difficult to understand her ranting. His eyes darted away from her, catching the light off some object. Disbelief at what he saw nestled in the grass and he shook his head.

Could it be?

Duncan dropped his sword and walked past her to stand over the one thing that could help change the course for his brothers.

Raking a hand through his hair, he knelt down slowly and reached out with a trembling hand for the pouch.

Brigid thought she heard him moan and hesitated before she stepped closer. She could now see he was shaking, and it took all of her control not to give him comfort. She could swear Duncan was crying and speaking softly in what she knew to be Gaelic.

She continued to stand a few feet away when he spoke in a harsh, raw voice, "I thank ye for bringing me my sword." And with the swiftness of a warrior, he was in front of her, just mere inches from her face and a dirk at her throat.

"I will not ask again. *Where* are your clansmen?" his tone ominous.

She was stunned. Here she was feeling sorry for the crying Scotsman, the next, she wanted to take a rock and bash it over his head.

Infuriating man.

"I will tell you everything if you remove the piece of metal from my throat," hearing the bitterness spill over in her voice. She saw a flicker of something move within his eyes, and his breathing labored.

Slowly, Duncan removed his dirk from her skin, but chose not to release her, yet. He liked the feel of her and she smelled of wildflowers. The beast roared inside of him, beckoning him to move his hands down and cup her breasts. With control he thought he did not possess, he dropped his hold of her, stepping back. Placing his dirk back in its sheath, he crossed his arms over his chest and waited.

"First, don't you *ever* put a knife to my throat again. Second..."

"It is a dirk."

"Yes, I know...whatever." She threw up her hands. "Second, I don't have *any* clansmen with me!"

"Third...owww."

"Whist, lass," hissed Duncan in her ear, grabbing her firmly around the waist and yanking her toward the ground behind the boulder. He held her firm against his chest, and again it took all of his control to fight the temptation his body was craving. He could feel the roundness of her breasts against his arm and a shiver went through him. What was wrong with him? No lass had ever had this pull on him. What he needed was to bed her quick, and then he could focus. He would keep the lass with him until he found out the truth.

Aye, he would have his answers and perhaps a wee bit more.

Forcing the lustful beast back inside his cage, he looked outwards. "Bloody MacFhearguis!" he snarled.

Brigid swallowed. "Did you just say *MacFhearguis*?"

"Do not fear, lass, they are passing through, though why they are here is a question I would sorely like to ask."

"Sure, what's to fear?" *Except this gorgeous Highlander holding me.*

Scanning the area where the riders had been, they waited a few more moments before Duncan finally released his hold on her and slowly stood up. She watched as he walked over to the sword, hesitating briefly before picking it up. Turning, he walked back and extended his hand out to her. "Come, lass, I will keep ye safe."

Brigid had no other choice but to follow this man. She would not show her fear of him, *or* her burning desire to have sex with him. Her faery tale come to life with a knight in tarnished armor. Except this faery tale was a tad scary.

How in the hell was she going to get back to her own time? Did he not hear her earlier?

Until she could figure this out, she would continue to use her fear as a shield and weapon. At least she knew he would protect her. But for how long? For all she knew, he could be a thirteenth century bipolar maniac.

Shaking, Brigid got up from the ground without the aid of his hand. The less contact with this man the better, she thought. He just stood there, devilishly handsome.

"Where are you taking me?" she asked.

There were touches of humor around his mouth and near his eyes when he spoke. "To see a druid about a dragon."

Chapter 21

"Do we listen to the Song of Truth when it plays its tune upon our heart strings, or do we silence it within the tomb of ice we call fear?"

The crisp autumn air felt good as Brigid followed Duncan through the trees. For the moment, she welcomed the distance between them. The power of attraction hummed through her veins. However, she couldn't get the thought out of her head that this man killed his sister.

What the hell happened that night?

She started to laugh and cupped her hand across her mouth. "I think I'm going insane," she whispered. "Here I am worrying about something, which supposedly took place eight hundred years ago. *Wait!* I'm here in this time, so it just happened. Now he's talking about druids *and* dragons?" There was the question of the sword too, she realized. It had been passed down through the ages and landed on her doorstep, only to be brought back through time.

Just trying to formulate all the pieces caused Brigid to burst out in hysterical laughter. There was just no way she could stifle it.

Duncan paused, glancing back over his shoulder at her with that arched brow, which made him so sexy and dangerous looking. A gentle breeze caught his hair and a dark lock fell across his eye, creating a more alluring effect.

Shaking her head, she paused waving him on. "I'm fine."

A muscle clenched along his jaw and he turned, continuing through the dense foliage, muttering something about a daft lass and not right in the mind.

"I heard that! You should be the one to talk, Duncan Mackay."

Turning around a sharp bend, Brigid came to halt. Standing a few feet in front of her was the most beautiful horse she had ever seen. Most of the horses she had ridden were brown or sable, but this one was black as ebony with no traces of any other color. His proud stance spoke majesticly, an animal meant for kings and queens—of the faery realm.

"Hello, there." Brigid held out her hand, palm up toward the horse. "I'm sorry I don't have any treats, but may I touch you?"

"Nae! He does not take kindly to strangers." Duncan stepped in front of his horse, blocking her path.

Brandubh snickered, and Brigid had a feeling it was directed toward Duncan. She sidestepped past Duncan, proceeding to ignore him. Placing her hand gently on Brandubh's muzzle, she spoke softly to him. He moved his head up and down as she continued to speak in soft words.

Duncan stood glaring at them both.

How dare he—that traitorous beast! Brandubh was not an easy animal. Many feared the great beast. But nae, the lass had walked right up to him and started to stroke his mane, speaking words as if they were friends.

He watched how she leaned close to his head,

while keeping a hand down upon his mane. Just the vision was enough for him to want her hands on *him*! Her backside was so verra tempting, and he wondered why she would choose to wear this type of clothing. Did she not know the affect it would have on men? All her curves so lusciously displayed. He continued to enjoy watching her backside...again.

Swiping a hand through his hair, Duncan took a deep breath as he grasped her up and tossed her across Brandubh. Then swinging himself up and over, he positioned himself behind her.

"Owww! I *do* know how to mount a horse. You could have hurt me, or your horse!"

Duncan snorted. "I can assure ye *Brandubh* was not injured."

Brigid gave him such a look of scorn that Duncan had to look away, so as not to laugh. What a feisty, fiery lass.

"You're just angry Brandubh likes me!"

"Humph!" He knew of only way to stop her from this chatter and with his left arm, he wrapped it around her waist and pushed her back against him. Gathering the reins with his right hand, he gave them a quick snap and they were off.

The moment Brigid landed against his back, she went still and silent. Good, he thought, yet the nearness of her was awakening all his senses. Her braid was starting to come loose and strands of curls were tickling his face. He inhaled the sweetness and with every step Brandubh took, her breasts would bounce on his arm, sending tremors straight to his cock.

By the gods, it had been far too long since he had a woman.

Duncan was grateful the journey to the druid would not be a long one. If they moved quickly, they would be there by early morn.

He was still uneasy with the sighting of the MacFhearguis on his land. His uneasiness had more to do with his brothers, especially Angus. He needed to be warned. It had been twelve moons since he had seen his brother. There had been no news of them; however, he never once asked Cormac.

Duncan would rather face a demon than face his brother. Since this mess was his fault, he would do whatever it took, and damn the outcome to his soul.

Chapter 22

"If one trespasses through time and space, who will pay the gatekeeper?"

"Do you think we could stop for a moment?" Brigid asked.

The only response she got was a grunt. Her shoulders slumped, but she wouldn't be dissuaded. They had ridden endlessly, and the jostling on the horse was not helping her situation. She desperately needed to relieve herself.

What a brute! How could she have stirrings for this man? In addition, why in the blazes did he haunt her dreams? He should have stayed within those blasted imaginings. Now she was smack in the middle of God knows where, with him—in the flesh.

Brigid gave him a sharp elbow when he pulled her more closely against him.

He followed with another grunt.

Did he just laugh at her? The man was an ogre. "If you don't want me making a mess on you and your horse, I would advise you to stop and let me have some...personal time," she spat out.

"*Personal time?*" he growled out.

Blasted man. "I have to relieve myself. Now!"

"Aye. Ye could have said so to begin with."

Dismounting from Brandubh, Duncan leaned up to

help her down and was rewarded with a slap across his arm. Grumbling, she attempted to get off on her own and slipped almost falling off. Managing to finally succeed, she let out a curse, not caring if he could hear. When she glanced over her shoulder, he was smirking at her. "What, never heard a woman swear?" she muttered, stomping off into the trees.

Crossing his arms over his chest, he followed the movement of her bum as it disappeared through the thicket of pines, along with her fiery temper.

"She's a daft one, but a beauty," he muttered.

Brandubh gave a snicker in response.

"So ye fancy her? Humph! Might I remind ye, she may be the enemy."

Duncan surveyed their surroundings. He had not planned to tend to a woman's needs. There was little food and ale and only the brat on him for warmth, which he would have to share.

"Lugh's balls." He grimaced.

They would ride as long as they had sunlight, since the thought of him wrapped against her body surged forth the lustful beast. It was going to be a verra long night.

Watching her emerge from the trees, he saw she was still muttering to herself.

Placing her back on his horse, he swung up behind her. "We'll be riding not much longer and then we will stop for the night."

She only nodded this time.

Good, he thought. His mood was becoming foul, and he would rather she kept quiet.

****

The first stars were winking down at them as

Duncan pressed Brandubh further. He would use as much of the gloaming as possible before they stopped for the night.

The moment the lass had dozed off, she fell back onto his chest. Gathering her more tightly against him, Duncan felt guilty for taking advantage of her lush curves across his arms. Just this once, he let himself enjoy her scent and warmth.

Who was this strange woman who first appeared in his dreams? Did his powers now extend to one of visions? Nae, it could not be. Only his brother, Stephen had the gift. Now his dream was here—in his arms, flesh and blood.

She mumbled something incoherent as she slept. Duncan shook his head. The lass talked far too much when she was awake, and continued in her sleep.

"Daft, indeed," he drawled.

Duncan proceeded onward for another hour until he found shelter secluded from any worn path. When Brigid awoke, she didn't say a word as he drew her down off his horse. She followed him through the dense foliage.

Noticing a large oak near its end in life, Duncan dropped his provisions against it. Large and partially hollowed out at the base, it would provide protection from the brisk night air. The other trees would help in keeping the winds at bay, as well.

Taking out an apple for Brandubh, he settled him nearby. "Rest well, my friend."

Stepping back toward the oak, he undid his plaid, placing it on the ground. Then he retrieved the leather-skin. "We will rest here for the night." He took a sip of what little he had left of the ale.

"We...we're sleeping here?"

"Aye."

Hugging her arms around herself, she tried to keep the panic out of her voice. "And where might I ask, am I to sleep?"

Duncan smacked his hand down on the ground next to him. "Right here, lass."

"*With you?*" she squeaked. She didn't want to be so close to him. It was torture being in his arms on the horse, and feeling his every movement, but here—*on the ground?* Snug as a bug in a rug?

"No!"

Duncan let out a loud sigh, followed by a silent curse. "I ken ye are not happy with the prospect, but nor am I."

Rising slowly, he stepped forward. "I give ye my word I will not have my way with ye. It will get mighty cold, and I only have one brat. It would be best if we shared."

"Yeah, I've heard that line before."

Duncan just shrugged, keeping his focus elsewhere.

She snorted. "Can't you just build a fire?"

He cocked his head at her, giving her a queer look. "Take a look around ye. Does it look like we can have a fire? Even if we could, I would not take the risk of alerting any others.

Her shoulders slumped. "Do you at least have some food and drink?"

A small smile curved his features. "Just a wee bit, but enough."

Darkness enveloped them, except for the sliver of the crescent. The ale Brigid drank took some of the chill off, but the food was another issue altogether. Some dried piece of meat, too tough to chew on, and a chunk of stale bread was their meal. He wasn't lying when he said he only had a *wee bit*. In the end, she had given up on the meat.

He was as still as stone next to her, yet the heat radiating from him was better than a small fire. She caught a glance at his profile within the shadows; strength and power oozed off him. Each time she gazed into eyes of sea blue, she almost swooned.

It was ridiculous to feel this way. Hell! She didn't even know him. What was she thinking? Behaving like some love-starved girl. She wanted to pinch herself from this dream that was turning into a nightmare, and she started to fidget.

"Do ye need some personal time?" Duncan's voice was low and soft in the darkness.

"No," she blew out, exasperated. She was wound so tight, and nowhere to go or even think. "How far will we have to travel tomorrow?" she asked.

"We'll reach Cathal midmorning."

"Hmmm, is he a good friend of yours?" She played with the edge of his plaid.

He muttered something unintelligible under his breath.

"Okay, will he know how to help me?"

Now, he snorted his response.

It was like prying teeth from an elephant, Brigid thought. "Why do you want to ask him about a *dragon*?"

"To cleanse the sword."

Success! She finally got an answer. "Why do we need to cleanse the sword?"

Sweet mother Danu! Would the lass ever stop her infernal list of questions? He did not want words from her mouth. Nae, he wanted to bring forth sweet moans from those rosy lips.

"Well?"

"Bloody hell, woman!"

He had to end this now. He cupped her chin and rubbed his thumb over her bottom lip. *Big mistake, Duncan*. His mind now screaming at him.

"Hush," he rasped out. His lips barely grazing hers.

The physical contact with her mouth sent shockwaves throughout his body. He released her suddenly and stood. "I'll be back," he uttered hoarsely.

Brigid couldn't move, frozen by his touch. She drew forth her trembling hand to touch her mouth. His lips were like lightning on her body, and she quivered.

Who was this scarred warrior, and why did she have this connection? *And why did she let him kiss her*?

Hugging her part of the plaid more firmly around her, she settled back more into the tree, letting the music of the night soothe her spirits. Within moments, Brigid drifted off to oblivion.

****

Brigid was disoriented. Images flooded her mind like a jumble of mismatched puzzle pieces. Nothing fit. She kept trying to match each picture, but they wouldn't hold together. Fear and trepidation slithered inside until she felt the fire. The heat soothed and coaxed the icy fear from her veins, and she snuggled deeper into its embrace.

"Be careful, lass. I may want to explore ye further." Duncan's burr brushed along her neck.

Brigid's eyes flew open as the shock registered

within her mind and body. Trying to scramble away from huge arms that had her in an embrace was a futile attempt.

"Whoa, lass."

She swallowed. "Let me go."

Suddenly the heat evaporated, as Duncan released his hold on her. He stood quickly, making his way toward Brandubh.

"I will give ye a few moments for your...*personal time* before we leave."

"Thank you," she grumbled more to herself. Stepping through the pines, she cringed. It was going to be a *very* long morning.

Chapter 23

"A dragon's color changes as often as its emotions. The trick is seeing the shimmer before the change."

Cathal sensed the rider approach while he was walking back to his cottage. Strangely, earlier in the morn, he felt the need to forage for mushrooms for his soup. Looking in his basket, he noticed there was plenty for a large batch. The goddess was telling him that he would be providing for company. He smiled, but when the rider emerged from the trees, he was stunned.

Duncan had returned, and with him was a beauty dressed in odd clothing. No dress or headpiece, but by the gods, she was wearing trews! There was a glow around her body, and instantly he understood she was from neither this land—nor this realm. The fae had sent this lovely creature to assist Duncan.

"Sweet Danu," he whispered, laying down his basket of mushrooms and herbs. "Welcome back, Duncan."

Duncan dismounted and reached for Brigid. Placing her gently on the ground, Cathal noticed neither of them looked at each other, the tension visible for all to see.

They were both breathing hard as Duncan stepped aside, presenting her to Cathal.

"Cathal, this is Brigid O'Neill."

"From the great O'Neill's? Across the sea from Dalriada?"

Duncan just shrugged his shoulders, then turned and removed the sword strapped to Brandubh.

"She had this with her." Duncan held out the sword to Cathal, as if it were an offering.

"By the great Mother, can it be?" Cathal stepped closer and held his hand over it, closing his eyes.

"It hums with energy." He opened his eyes looking at Brigid. "Though, it is not with the energy of the knight, it is yours." He stepped toward her and held his hands out to her.

Brigid held up her hands, shaking her head. "No-o-o, I don't know what you mean." She started to back away from him, but slammed into Duncan.

Sensing her fear and wariness, he bowed his head. "Blessings of light, my child. I must apologize. Come, ye must be tired and hungry," extending his hand out to let her pass.

Brigid scampered past the druid toward the cottage. "Energy, my ass," she mumbled. "Wait till I see Conn, that is *if* I ever see the man again." Then she started laughing.

"That one is daft." Duncan nodded his head toward Brigid. "She laughs out loud to herself and talks in a strange tongue. Did ye not see her clothing?" He ran a hand through his dark locks in frustration. "Why would an *O'Neill* have the sword?"

Cathal smiled, "Och Duncan, she is a bonny lass, but she has been touched *and* sent by the fae. She is from a land not of this time, chosen by the Guardian, if I am not mistaken." Placing a hand on Duncan's shoulder, he added, "Remember, the O'Neills were the first to be blessed by the fae with gifts. Therefore, it makes sense that the relics have been placed with the descendants of the first family—the original owners. At least the sword has."

Giving Duncan a shake, Cathal leaned down and gathered his basket. "Come, let us eat. Then ye can figure out how to tell the lass *she* needs to take the sword to the great dragon to have it cleansed."

Walking away from Duncan, Cathal could almost hear his mouth drop open in shocked silence. He let out a burst of laughter that caused Sorcha to swoop out from her perch nestled in the trees. She circled above him as he made his way to the cottage. "I do not want to be around them when he tells her about the dragon, aye, Sorcha?"

Sorcha let out a caw and took off higher toward the upper branch of an oak.

****

Brigid approached the cottage, which was hidden in the dense cluster of the trees. When she opened the door, she paused in utter amazement. A mere small cottage was what she perceived from the outside, but when she looked beyond and stepped inside, it was transformed to a massive interior.

Cautiously entering, she surveyed her surroundings. The hearth was set toward the back of the wall, which was in reality part of the solid rock mountain. A long table and chairs were set in the middle and several large beautifully carved wooden chairs were placed on either side of the hearth. To the right set deeper within the rock, was another table with herbs laid out with some tucked inside the crevices. She realized this was a storeroom for the harvesting and drying of herbs.

Her eyes drew her to the opposite side of the room where she noticed an alcove, which appeared to be Cathal's sleeping quarters, heavily laden with furs. Brigid longed to lie down between them and close her eyes. The aroma of food and warmth was overwhelming. So much had happened, and placing her palms over her eyes, she sighed. Without realizing, she swayed, and the room spun.

Duncan was there in two strides, tucking her against him. Holding her for a moment more, he raised a shaking hand and brushed a stray curl that had come loose from her braid and tucked it ever so gently behind her ear. "Are ye feeling better, lass?"

His words sounding hoarse and his breath warm on her face sent a fire down her spine. Leaning more into him, she felt more than just his concern, his arousal.

Brigid stepped back with flushed cheeks, seeing the invitation in the smoldering depths of his eyes. If Cathal were not standing in the doorway, she would have given herself over to this mighty Highlander. Words seemed to escape her, and she shook her head to let him know she was fine. Turning back from him, she went over and sat down by the hearth.

Cathal coughed when he entered. "What ye need is some food and rest, Brigid. I will just be adding some of these mushrooms to the stew of roots and herbs."

Moving to the table of herbs, he poured some liquid into a cup. Coming back to her, he thrust the cup at her. "Drink this, lass. It will ease your spirits and the body, too."

"What is it?" Brigid took the cup from Cathal and

sniffed its contents.

"Wine mixed with herbs."

Sipping the wine, she let the liquid permeate its heat within, feeling a sense of calm. Leaning back in the chair, she watched the flames dance. However, part of her vision was also on the tall, dark, and dangerous-looking Duncan. He had placed the sword along the wall, and was saying something to Cathal before he started for the door.

"You're not leaving?" she asked, almost jumping out of the chair.

A slow smile tipped the corners of his mouth, as he shook his head no. "I'm tending to Brandubh, and then I'll return."

"Oh, okay." Settling back in the comfort of the chair, Brigid smiled.

Cathal continued stirring the stew, adding mushrooms and more herbs. Placing the ladle down, he went and sat down directly across from Brigid. Leaning back against the chair, he drew in a long breath and closed his eyes.

Was the man going to sleep? I need answers.

When he opened his eyes, he smiled.

"Ye have questions."

"Yes. How do you know?" Brigid replied mystified.

"I am a druid."

"I've never met a druid before, only a Fenian warrior."

Cathal's smile faded. "What is his name?"

"Conn, Conn MacRoich."

"Do ye understand what he is?"

"I didn't find out until moments before I blacked

out and awoke here in this time. What is the year, Cathal?" she asked, hesitantly.

"The year is 1205. Why was he with ye?"

"Oh my...1205," she whispered. Swallowing, Brigid continued, "Conn was sent by my friend, Archie McKibbon to be my guide in Scotland." Then Brigid's mouth dropped. *Maybe Archie is not what he appeared to be, either. No, it couldn't be, could it?*

Stunned by her news, Cathal now understood why the fae did not want him involved. This was larger than even he could have envisioned. By sending Conn, their elite warrior, meant the situation was extreme. This was beyond his realm of reasoning.

"What is your year, Brigid?"

"It is 2013. It seems strange saying that." She gave him a weak smile.

"Hmmmmm," said Cathal, frowning.

"Do you think my friend could have been a Fenian warrior, too? He was my professor in college, but from Scotland." *You're rambling, Bree.*

Glancing back toward her he answered, "I do not ken what professor or college is, but I have not heard of his name. Yet, Conn...yes, the name I am familiar with."

"*You are*?" she gulped, afraid to know the answer.

"Aye, it appears your guide is the leader of the Fenian warriors, which is a branch of the Fianna and the right hand to the fae."

Brigid's eyes went wide. She had heard of the Fianna, and Fenian warriors—names she associated with the Irish Republican Army in their earlier days, not some kind of faery beings.

"Why would the leader of the Fenian warriors be

interested in me? And what *are* the Fenian warriors?"

Cathal leaned forward piercing her with his eyes. "They are descended from the fae, the Shining Ones, and are the protectors between the realm of this world and theirs. They mingle and live among us, and some are known to travel between time itself. Ye ken of the fae, right?"

Brigid nodded. She had grown up listening to the tales of the great Shining Ones, the fae. They had arrived in Ireland as one of the great invasions and over time, those who were left created a world underground.

Her grandparents had always had great respect for the fae and spoke of the tales many times. It was not a myth or legend, but fact for them. It was a belief she held dearly. A stab of pain pierced her heart remembering her grandparents. They had always wanted to take her to Ireland and Scotland to show her the sacred places. They never made the journey.

Cathal had yet to answer her question, so again she asked, "Why Cathal, would a great Fenian warrior be interested in me?"

"I cannot say for sure, lass."

"Oh, Cathal," sighed Brigid. "Why *am* I here? Duncan has the sword now. Why can't I just return home?"

Cathal chuckled and stood, going over to the pot of stew. "Would it be so simple, lass. Duncan must go on his quest, and ye must accompany him. Ye are still the keeper of the sword, and Duncan knows this well."

Brigid gripped the cup she had been holding more tightly. She stood slowly and walked over to the table, placing the cup down for fear she would toss it against the wall.

Pounding her fist on her chest, she snapped back at Cathal, "I *still* don't understand why I'm involved with a man who has killed his sister! What the bloody hell happened that night, and how did I become involve in an ancient curse?" She held up her hand, adding, "No, forget it. I just want to go home. I don't want to be around him anymore."

"Och, the battle of heart and mind, aye?" He tossed in more herbs.

She blushed, fully comprehending Cathal's words. How could he see right through her? Was it so obvious? "It's complicated."

"The road to the truth is never a smooth one."

She blanched. "*Truth*? And whose truth are we talking about?"

Nodding, he stopped stirring and came over to where she stood.

Cathal loomed over her, placing both his hands on her shoulders as he spoke. "Brigid O'Neill, your people are also descended from the fae and were the original keepers of the relics. They were, nae, still *are* a mighty clan. It makes sense that the Guardian has entrusted the sword to a descendant of the first. I will share a truth with ye. Ye must ken Duncan did not intend to kill his sister. Blind fury and evil helped to wield the energy that night."

"What do you mean blind fury and evil?" Brigid demanded.

Speaking more gently, he added, "It does not absolve any of them from what happened that night, nae, yet it was not entirely their fault. There was..." Cathal touched a finger to his mouth in thought. "...an evil present for some time and it weaved its spell over the brothers. The Guardian understands, so this is why they must *all* take this journey—*this quest*. It is not only a fight to restore honor and the order, but a fight for their very souls."

"How did it happen, Cathal?" Her question but a whisper.

"Ye must ask Duncan. I do not have the answer. I only ken all is not lost."

Tears streamed down Brigid's cheeks and spilled onto her shirt. She could no longer contain them. Her armor of fear had slipped. Cathal had given her the greatest gift, one of *hope*. There was hope for Duncan and his brothers, and her, too. The Guardian had entrusted the sword into her care, as she was part of his quest. He could retain his honor, and she could return home.

Yet, her heart sank. Did she truly *want* to return home?

"I'm so confused. I'm drawn to a man I don't know. How do I *help* him?"

"Och, Brigid. Trust your heart. The answers ye seek are within."

Reaching up with shaking hands, she fell into Cathal's arms, crying against his shoulder.

Cathal's heart sank, for he almost wished he could shed tears with her.

Chapter 24

"To turn your back on a dragon, 'tis very foolish. However, to face the dragon even more foolish and brave."

Duncan spent a fitful night tossing and turning before the hearth. His thoughts and dreams were of a green-eyed lass, with a splash of sunspots across her nose and cheeks. Her dark red curls tickling his thighs as she placed kisses on his manhood. The dream so vivid that upon waking, he found himself cock sore from the hardness and on the verge of spilling right there on his wrap. Groaning, he threw his arm across his face, fearing the day would be far worse with them traveling together.

When he had returned to the cottage last evening after tending to Brandubh, he had noticed tears in her eyes. She then gave him a full smile, which showed a wee dimple on her cheek. It had nearly undone him, since he did not feel deserving of such warmth. It took all of his strength not to gather her back in his arms and devour the smile into his mouth.

The lass stirred a strange mix of emotions in him. His world had been dark too long. Now it was tossed on its arse, and he along with it. She had touched his soul, placing a warm thread of light within it. In just their brief encounter, the blackness he had cloaked around himself managed to thaw just a little.

Why he had this strong need to protect and claim her, he could not fathom.

Slowly, he eased himself up and went over to where she lay. She looked flushed, and her lips were in a pout begging to be tasted. He should walk straight out the door and soak his aching body in the icy waters of the nearby stream, yet, for reasons he could not fathom, his legs carried him toward her sleeping form. Kneeling, he brushed a stray curl from her forehead, bending to place a kiss upon her brow.

Instantly, her eyes fluttered open.

The trained warrior was frozen, unable to move. His mind screamed he needed to walk away, but her emerald eyes met his and reaching for his head, she pulled him down to her lips. He was the one to moan, drinking in her taste, and thrusting his tongue deep within her mouth as if he truly wanted to devour her. He tried to be gentle, but she demanded more with her tongue. Where one would tease, the other would take, and the sensual dance of the kiss became more intense.

Duncan moved to nip along her chin and slowly moved his palm over her breast. He was shocked to find some article of clothing under her shirt, hindering his touch. He raised his head in question.

"Don't stop, *please*," Brigid pleaded, and then did something so brazen by taking his hand and placing it back on her breast.

His mouth came crashing down on hers. Taking his hand, he slid it under her shirt, stroking the strange garment and caressing the tight nipple. He loved the sensual feel of the fabric. Tossing aside the furs, he yanked her shirt up and over her head so fast, she gasped. Placing both hands over her lush full breasts, he kneaded them gently, causing her to moan. His thumbs traced over the heart-shaped top of the fabric, and then he lowered his mouth over her taut nipples, biting through the fabric.

"Duncan," she gasped and watched as he brought his head up, a wicked smile curving his lush mouth. His eyes reminded her of the ocean, and she lost herself in them.

"Does this please ye?" he rasped, as he bent his head to continue teasing her nipples with his mouth.

Duncan heard the whistling first, and his head snapped up. Brigid went completely still under him.

"By the gods," he muttered. Placing his forehead on hers, he breathed in the smell of her desire and placed one last kiss upon her brow. Standing, he adjusted his plaid and stormed over to the door, nearly taking it off its hinges as he swung it wide, sending it crashing against the wall.

Brigid heard him yell something in Gaelic to Cathal. Grabbing her shirt, she hastily put it back on. Placing a trembling hand against her swollen lips, she could still taste Duncan—wool, peat, ale, *and man*. What a heady combination.

Cathal came striding in, still whistling a tune as he went over to his working table. "A blessed morn, Brigid," he nodded without looking at her.

She was so embarrassed. If it had been a few minutes more, both their bodies would have been stripped of their clothing. Standing, she attempted to straighten the furs, until Cathal brought over a mug and shoved it into her hands.

"Come, ye do not need to fuss. Break your fast."

Brigid sipped the ale and moved past Cathal to the table where bread, cheese, and berries were set out. She ate in silence, content to watch the flames in the hearth. Try as she might, she could not get the feel and taste of Duncan Mackay out of her mouth. Now, she was forced to make this journey with him, and the attraction she felt was making her life a swirling mix of emotions.

"I will leave ye to your thoughts, Brigid, and take this food to Duncan." Cathal had placed a gentle hand on her shoulder, but she could only nod.

****

Duncan had stripped off all of his clothing and plunged headfirst into the stream. The frigid water shocking his body, but not his senses. His soul was still on fire...still burning from her touch. He tried not to think as he kept on swimming.

Finally emerging from the stream, he flung water everywhere. Placing his hands on his hips, he glanced out from where he had come. He never lost control over a woman, *ever*. What possessed him to lose control with this one?

Raking his hands through his damp hair, Duncan blew out a sharp breath. He picked up a small stone and hurled it into the water. She had touched the cold darkness of his soul and soothed it, which was *not* what he wanted. He did not have time for such, with this lass, or with any other. In truth, each time he tried to banish her from his mind her face came back, haunting him.

Bedding her was now definitely out of the question.

Duncan heard the footsteps and cursed himself for not bringing his sword. Grabbing his dirk, he swung to face Cathal.

"Hmmmm...expecting the enemy, Duncan?"

"Humph!" Dropping his dirk, Duncan reached for his plaid, drying himself. Cathal handed him his tunic, and he hastily threw it on.

"I have brought food to break your fast and more for the journey. Here, let me take your wrap, and I will warm it by the fire. Ye will be wanting to leave soon."

Duncan nodded and took the food and drink, sitting down against a nearby tree, seeking solace in its strength.

"Who is she?" he asked between bites of the food.

With a sigh, Cathal stroked his beard and sat down on a boulder across from Duncan. "Brigid is part of the O'Neill clan, but not from the O'Neills we ken."

A frown skittered across Duncan's features. "And what clan would that be?"

Taking another deep breath, Cathal looked directly out across the water when he spoke. "The O'Neill clan...from the future."

Duncan sputtered on some ale. "Ye ken this *how*?"

"Brigid is under the protection of the fae and she had a Fenian warrior as her protector. She told this to me." Cathal turned his gaze back to Duncan.

"By the hounds of Cuchulainn!" Duncan roared. Standing quickly, his food spilled everywhere as thunder rumbled in the distance.

"Ye have a chance to make amends," said Cathal.

Duncan started to speak, his eyes turning to crystal shards, but Cathal stayed his voice with his hand. "The fae have entrusted *ye* with Brigid, and they have entrusted *her* with the sword. Your quest is interwoven, and one cannot be completed without the other."

Fists clenched, he backed away from Cathal.

Watching the flow of stream weave along the banks, he knew the words Cathal spoke were true. As much as he did not want to believe, in his heart...spoke truth.

Again, Duncan did not hear Cathal's approach. He never did with the old druid, but there he was standing next to him.

"Trust in the lass, Duncan. She has great power, chosen from her people to take this journey. The sword is hers until it is cleansed, and only then can she rightfully return it to ye."

Duncan's eyes narrowed. "What do ye mean, return it? It is mine."

"Nae, Duncan. It is Brigid's until the day she presents it back to ye. Trust me when I say, she will ken when the time is right. For the moment, she is scared and unsure. She will need your strength and help. Talk to her, Duncan. Let her tell ye where she is from."

"*Talk*?" Duncan uttered incredulously.

Duncan snorted and proceeded to walk away from Cathal.

"I warn ye, Duncan, she is under the protection of the fae."

Duncan swung back around. "Tell me this"— pointing a finger at Cathal—"who is her Fenian warrior?"

Cathal's jaw clenched as he just shrugged his shoulders.

"Humph!"

Cathal watched as Duncan stomped furiously away from him. When he was out of sight, Cathal exhaled deeply. There would be a reckoning when Duncan found out that he had withheld certain information.

He whistled softly, and watched as Sorcha flew

down from the tree branches, landing on the boulder next to him. "Watch over them, my lady. Be mine eyes and ears, for I can do no more."

Blinking once, she flew off through the trees, shrieking.

Chapter 25

"If you listen carefully, the wind will sing you a melody of colors."

After several hours on a horse, Brigid was feeling it well within her thighs. The sound of leaves and twigs snapping under Roan as they made their way along the path of pines, birch, and oak, and the occasional squawk of a bird, were the only sounds, giving her some time to think.

She had been grateful when Cathal had suggested she borrow his horse. The idea of being tucked so close against Duncan while riding on Brandubh frightened and excited her at the same time. Her feelings became a jumbled mess, and she could not think straight when she was in his arms.

Watching his muscular back sent shivers down her spine. His corded muscles moved with each movement as rider and animal moved through the glen. He had a ruggedness and vital power that drew her to him. Of course, he was also devastatingly handsome. Her body still burned from his kisses, and she placed her hand on her lips.

Shaking her head, she cast her vision to their surroundings. She caught glimpses of the loch down below as light filtered through a thick clump of trees. Brigid had never seen anything more beautiful. The loch was bluer than she remembered, and of course the trees were more prominent here than in her own time. Duncan had kept to the trail hugging the trees. She wished they could descend and travel along the water's edge.

Grasping a pine bough and pushing it aside, she saw a stag up on the ridge to her right. He stood majestic in his stance, and nodded once as if in greeting before turning away through the trees.

She loved Scotland in her time, but here, it captivated her senses.

Brigid saw movement in the trees ahead, but noticed it was only Sorcha. Moving Roan closer to Duncan, she called out, "Hey, why is Sorcha following us?"

Duncan slowed Brandubh and twisted to face her, "It's the way of Cathal. She will carry news back to him."

How could she not remember all the tales her grandparents told her of the druids? "He must be very powerful," she said half aloud, while rubbing a hand across her temple.

"Powerful? Aye, ye could say." Duncan came closer, a slight frown on his face.

She just waved a hand in the air, "Sorry, Duncan. I'm just new to all this magical stuff. I am still *adjusting*." Her eyes pierced him with her best showdown stare.

Duncan proceeded to dismount from Brandubh so effortlessly, walking over to her and Roan. Reaching up, he lifted her as if she was a feather. Slowly, he eased her down against him.

Placing her palms against his chest, she lifted her

head to look up at him.

"I thought ye could use some time to rest." Duncan reached behind her and pulled a sack off Roan, thrusting it into her arms.

"Rest? Food? Right," she whispered. *I really want to kiss that dimple in the middle of your chin.* Finally realizing she had been holding her breath, she let out a gush.

Suddenly, she frowned. "How do you know I need to rest? We can keep going."

Duncan kept walking away from her, stirring her ire just a bit more. "Wait a minute. Where are we *going*?"

Without pausing to look back at her, he clipped, "I can hear ye moaning and grumbling about your legs."

She looked mildly affronted, and then the anger took over. "Hey, mister! I'm sorry, I am not used to being on a horse for an extended period of time. You see in *my* time we have modes of transportation that travel quickly, and don't require being on the back of a horse for hours or *days* at a time." She stood watching as he kept walking away. "Damn it, Duncan Mackay!" He had now disappeared from her sight within the trees.

Half running and limping to catch up to him, she heard him give a low whistle and then saw Sorcha swoop down, landing on a small branch. He tossed out raw meat, which she instantly dove down and collected, disappearing back into the tree.

"Keep watch, Sorcha. Let me know of any riders," he said.

Brigid tried not to laugh, but she had to admit it was ridiculous a falcon would be their watchful guard. "Putting faith in a bird to alert you of intruders? Can you tell me where we'll be heading?"

Again, he ignored her questions and walked further within the trees.

"Bloody, dominating, medieval man," she hissed, rubbing her thighs to ease the soreness.

He halted and raked a hand through his hair. "God's teeth! Are ye ever quiet?"

Placing her hands on her hips, she narrowed her eyes at him. "Excuse me? Are you always so rude and obnoxious?"

Watching as he clenched his jaw, she actually jumped at the sound of thunder rolling nearby and yet, not a cloud in the sky. When he turned his back on her, she wanted to pitch something at him. Why did he stir such emotions in her? One moment, she wanted to kiss him, the other, she wanted to bash him over the head.

This time, she watched until he was completely out of sight. Leaning against a tree, she took in deep gulps of air and counted to ten. Taking one last deep breath, she pushed away from the tree and hoped he hadn't left her too far behind. "Where in the blazes are you taking me, Duncan Mackay?"

****

Brigid entered a small glade nestled in among the trees. It was small, but the sun's light filled the center. Wildflowers clumped in various sizes and colors carpeted the ground like a rainbow. The air was warm here considering it was late October, yet it held the scent of autumn with the golden hues of the leaves, which lent a presence of magic and serenity to the place. It reminded her of a faery glen, and against one of the trees, stood the most dangerous looking faery of all.

Letting out a deep breath, she noticed Duncan had placed a blanket and some food on the ground. The tension she felt earlier melted away and reaching her arms over her head, she arched her back, stretching out toward the sky. Perhaps, she did need some rest and food.

She glanced back at him. He stood with his back against a tree, arms across his chest, his form shadowed from the shade of the trees. He reminded her of one of those gods of nature, the silver of his torc glinting from the rays of the sun. There was a restless energy about him, and she felt his power touch her when a brush of wind swept past her. She had so many questions. It would be difficult not to probe or push, as was her nature. But what was she going to do?

Strength and courage she told herself. In her talks with Cathal, he told her she was chosen by the fae to right a wrong, but *how*? No one could answer *that* burning question.

Walking over to the blanket, she sat down with a sigh. Proceeding to tear off a piece of the bread, she took a swallow of ale to soften the hardness. What she would give for some water, she thought. It might be the thirteenth century, but surely, she could get a cup of water somewhere.

"Are you going to stand there and watch, or do you want some of this?"

The tall dark figure stepped from the shadows. "What are ye offering?"

Nearly sputtering on the ale, she watched as he stalked over to her. Clearly by the look in his eyes, he didn't think she meant food. Before she realized it, he was next to her, cupping her chin. Ever so slowly, he took his tongue and lapped up the drop of ale on her mouth, his shadow of a beard grazing her lips.

Brigid inhaled sharply at the contact. Instantly, desire flared in places she wanted so badly for him to touch and taste.

Raising his mouth from hers, she gazed into his eyes. Confusion marred his features and his hands fisted to his knees. Seeing the fight within, she quickly made the decision for both of them. She was tired, so very tired of fighting against him. She would give herself freely to this man, this *stranger* from another time, her tarnished knight.

With her decision made, there was no turning back.

Gradually, she stood, looking at him. Goodness, he was so big even as he knelt before her. Taking her braid, she unbound the mass of curls, freeing them and letting them flow around her. Next, she removed her shirt, and after slipping out of her boots, she unbuttoned her jeans, trying to control the shaking in her hands. She watched in fascination at how his eyes traveled her every movement, now noticing his hands were clenched at his sides.

Stepping back to give him a better view, she unsnapped her bra in the front and slowly let her full breasts spill out. Hearing his sharp intake of breath, she glanced at her nipples, which were taut from the air and desire. A growl rumbled forth from Duncan, and she smiled.

"Take me, Duncan…you have haunted my dreams far too long."

A long silence ensued, and she thought maybe he did not want her.

Snatching her hand, he grabbed her forward, his

face right above her lace panties. She placed a shaky hand across the stubble of his cheek, causing a shudder to ripple through his body. "I have never known such beauty." The burr of his voice sending shivers across her body.

Whispering low, she angled her head at him. "Do you not want me to remove these?" Her hand came to the edge of her panties to start pulling, but he stayed her hand with the touch of his lips, his breath hot and moist against her skin, and her legs trembled.

"Nae," he growled. "Let me."

His mouth nipped along her hip, and then he placed it on her soft center where her curls were nestled. Throwing her head back, she gasped in ecstasy, as his mouth kept sucking at her center. Finding her sensitive nub, he bit ever so slightly through the lace. Brigid let out a whimper and took hold of his head, running her fingers through his dark locks.

He slid his fingers inside the lace, delving into her folds. As he stroked and teased, his cock strained from her soft moans. With his teeth, Duncan ripped down the wet fabric, her musky scent filling his senses.

"*Pleeease*," she pleaded, almost a cry.

Growling, he plunged his tongue into her wet core and suckled, teasing her with his mouth. Duncan moved his hands on her thighs to cup her bottom, laving her core fully.

The rasp of his beard and tongue was a powerful combination, and Brigid felt her world tilt, the pleasure building. His tongue stroked once, twice, and she shattered into a million glowing stars, feeling reborn from his touch.

Duncan stood and clasped his hands on either side

of her face. "Bonny, bonny Brigid." His last words were smothered as his lips covered hers hungrily. She opened to the feel of them, giving him all. His tongue demanding hers and the air she breathed. He tasted of her and his scent, a heady combination of lust. Brigid could feel his hardness on her stomach and yearning flared again within her. His rough hands were on her breasts, teasing and pinching her nipples.

Breaking from her lips he looked deep within her eyes, "I cannae hold back, *leannan*. I need ye, *now*."

The look of raw passion in his eyes mirrored Brigid's. She needed him hard and fast, too. Taking a hold of his hand, she brought him down with her onto the ground, opening up for him. His hand cupped her core, and she arched in sweet pleasure. Using his fingers, he stroked between her womanly folds and then took his cock and rubbed it against her.

"Duncan, take me now," she growled.

A wicked smile curved his lips as he plunged deep into her, causing her to arch back to take all of him. It was flesh against flesh, man against woman. His lips brushed her nipples, and he took her harder and faster, sending Brigid racing with the storm. He grabbed one leg and pulled it up against him, pounding harder and she felt as if the wind was carrying them beyond time and space.

Duncan couldn't hold back, her body was so soft and lush. Watching her heavy breasts bounce with each movement of his cock, he wanted to consume her. His body was on fire, and she was the water to quench its thirst.

Feeling her pleasure about to release, Duncan could no longer stay in control. He was so very tired of being in control, and he wanted nothing more than to release it all.

Her screams echoed in his mind first, and he fell over the cliff with her, smothering her mouth with his cry of release.

****

What was he thinking by bringing her to this magical place? Protection, aye, but it also called out to his primal animal self, wanting to strip her clothes and mark her as his own there on the ground. She had become his pagan sacrifice. His hand moved magically over her soft breast, slowly circling the taut nipple as she lay on her back in the crook of his arm. Just the slight touch with her leg wrapped around him made him hard again.

Feeling her shift around, he kept his eyes closed and grunted. Finally, she snuggled back against his body.

Her fingers moved across his chest. "I find your dark curls, oh so sexy," and buried her face in them.

Opening his eyes, he had to fight the urge to slip her back under him. He wanted to hear the words from her lips. "Tell me what ye want, lass?"

"You, *again*," she whispered.

Duncan stretched, displaying a fully erect cock, and placed his hands under his head. "I am all yours, Brigid." His eyes held a playful gleam.

Arching her head and giving him her saucy smile, she straddled herself over him. Catching him off guard, she took him into herself in one swift movement.

He moaned. "Sweet Brigid." Clasping her hips, he thrust up into her.

Duncan watched in pure pleasure as Brigid took

control of his body, riding him up and down ever so slowly. She reminded him of some ethereal goddess with her mass of auburn curls streaming down her back, the sun casting a glow of copper throughout.

She was bewitching him.

Beads of sweat broke out on his brow as he tried to control his own seed from spilling too soon. He dipped his thumb to her center, taking her over the edge. The look of raw emotion on her face sent him into the abyss of pleasure, as he emptied himself to the last shudder.

The cool air swirled around them, as they lay wrapped in each other's arms still trembling from their joining. Duncan placed a kiss on her temple, turning her onto her back.

"As much as I would love to taste more of ye, we must get to shelter before darkness."

A small smile played at the corner of his mouth, and Brigid's heart slammed into her chest. God, he was so handsome. If only he would truly smile for her.

Instantly, she realized how much she was needed here. "To right a wrong," she whispered, brushing a lock of his hair away from his brow.

His hands stilled, and coldness flashed through his eyes. "What did ye say?"

"Duncan, I *know* of the curse." Brigid went to grab for his hand, but in one swift move he was up and throwing his tunic over his head. Suddenly, the air cooled, and she grabbed the plaid to wrap around her. She stood, looking at him. His fists clenched as he swung around to face her, and she realized the cold Duncan was back.

"What of the curse do ye ken?" he asked sharply.

"All of it...including the part where you took that"

—she pointed to the sword strapped across Brandubh— "and killed your *sister*." Brigid thought she should trend carefully, but she was tired of walking on eggshells around this man. If there was any sense to make out of this, she needed to know *all* of the details. The fae had sent her through time with the sword to help, and by God, that is what she would do.

With eyes blazing with fury and thunder rumbling in the distance, he kept silent.

Stepping closer to him, she looked right into the storm of his eyes. "Tell me what happened that night."

Thunder shook the ground around them as dark clouds blocked out the warmth and light of the sun, the wind whipping a mighty fury. Brigid knew of his powers, but she was not going to fear this man.

"Damn it, Duncan! Are you doing this?" she demanded, waiving her hand in the air.

"Aye," he growled.

"Then we are at an impasse, Duncan. I will *not* go any further with you, *and* I will not relinquish the sword until you tell me about the night." Poking her finger into his chest, she spat out, "I didn't come eight hundred years from the future with that sword for nothing! Which, by the way, I haven't figured out how in the hell I'm going to get back to my own time. That was one thing your Conn MacRoich forgot to mention in his brief parting instructions."

The storm stopped as suddenly as it started, and a look of shock crossed over Duncan's face. "Brigid, how do ye ken Conn MacRoich?" His voice was but a whisper.

"As I told Cathal, Conn was my guide in Scotland. It's all very confusing, but apparently, according to

Cathal, Conn is my Fenian warrior, the one who told me to bring the sword to you." Reaching up, she placed her palm on his cheek. "My protector there, until I came here and found *you*."

Suddenly, he grasped her hand, and she saw pain in his eyes.

Brigid was confused. "What is it, Duncan?"

"Conn MacRoich is a traveler between the realms. When ye finally do relinquish the sword to me, Brigid, he will come for ye, to take ye back to your time."

Placing a soft kiss in her palm, he turned and walked away from her, leaving a stunned and speechless Brigid wondering how she could have felt so much joy and pain all in one afternoon.

Chapter 26

"Mix one part shining star, one part dew, one part flower essence, one part sunlight, and one part hope. Then stir slowly and breathe into the mixture of wishes."

Journeying farther north in the great glen, Duncan shook his head. *The gods can be cruel.*

He should have *never* touched her.

His feelings went beyond simply bedding the lass, and there's where the thorn lay. She opened a door inside him, and he willingly stepped through. It was as if his soul possessed a mind of its own.

Now, he had to close it firmly tight.

He would do all he could to protect her, and when their quest was over he would make sure Conn returned her to her own time, a time he could not fathom. Of all the Fenian warriors, Conn was their elite. He guarded and made sure any human traveling the veils of time returned to their own.

He also was not on the best of terms with the warrior.

He lifted the breeze with a thought, a whiff of her scent brushed gently against his face, and he inhaled. Clutching Brandubh's reins more tightly, he swore under his breath. "What am I doing?" He needed distance and others around her to keep himself in order.

There was only one place safe enough, he thought. After the sword was cleansed, he would take Brigid to Castle Creag. There, she could get some proper clothing that would hide those curves and keep him at a distance from her.

Aye, it is what he would do.

If only he knew how long this quest would take. Cathal was of no help. Only telling him, they would both know the moment. The druid was a sly one, even his denial of the Fenian warrior, which did not sit well with Duncan.

Raking a hand across his face, he felt the growth of a beard, one that sorely needed shaving. "Humph! Very cruel indeed."

****

Brigid was numb, letting Roan set the pace. The past few days she had been on this magical journey. In the beginning, she was afraid, fearful she would never return home.

Yet, what *was* waiting for her in the twenty-first century? She had always felt out of sync in her own time. Always longing for the far off past, collecting old and sometimes rare antiques, reminding her of places that spoke to her spirit. All of her family was gone, except if you count Lisa, but even she was not enough of a pull to go back.

Her life tipped over the edge when she met Duncan. Watching him, she was fascinated how he held himself on Brandubh. Rider and horse as one, the warrior always alert. His ebony locks glistened in the sun, and she noticed his muscular legs, as if she hadn't seen enough of them earlier.

She'd never forget how magnificent he was

standing in the glade with nothing but his boots and torc on. It had been an afternoon that had ended too soon with a startling revelation—one where it would take her away from this place and *him*. Her heart told her that this was her home in Scotland of the past. It was her *feelings*, not only for the land, but also for the warrior with the dark and twisted soul.

There was more to his story, and she intended to get to the bottom of it.

The warmth of the sun brushed past her cheeks, and Brigid noticed they had emerged from the trees and were moving down toward the water. The loch shimmered with sunlight giving an effect of fractured jewels dancing on its surface. She could feel its energy ease away her worries as it hummed through her veins. The water called to her, beckoning her to touch and play, and the mountains loomed high as if they were guarding mystical waters.

She smiled. "Faery magic."

Roan snorted, and Brigid giggled, patting his mane with her hand. Looking up, she saw Duncan had stopped. "Let's not keep *him* waiting."

When they approached, Brigid noticed Duncan kept his focus out toward the water, and she let her gaze travel out there, too.

"We are at the northern end of the great glen. Here is where the last dragon slumbers beneath the loch. I will take ye down to the water's edge and call forth the dragon. Ye will then present the sword to her."

Feeling spellbound by the beauty of the loch, she almost didn't hear what Duncan was saying until she heard the word *dragon*. Snapping her head back out of her trance, her mouth dropped open in shock.

"Ummmm, did I hear you say *dragon*?"

"Aye." Duncan dismounted from Brandubh, leading him away from the water's edge.

"Oh no, no, no!" She shook her head, eyes wide with fear. "I thought you were teasing earlier."

"Do not come out from the trees, Brandubh." With a pat on his rump, Duncan sent the horse trotting away from the water.

In two strides, he was at her side and proceeded to whisk Brigid off Roan.

"I can't do this, Duncan," she protested. "I've only heard the stories. Now you want me to come face to face with a dragon? I just can't!" She started shaking again. "I know the sword is in my possession, but *you* do it."

"Brigid, lass, hear me, please," his tone laced with agony. "Ye must have courage. Only *ye* can do this."

Slowly, she stopped shaking her head and cast her gaze up into his eyes. His expression was one of hurt, and she noted his hands were fisted at his sides. He had become this stranger in just a few hours with his pain wound tightly around himself. She thought she had broken through with their lovemaking and yes, perhaps a bit more on her part, but she would never tell him that. No, she would not tell him she had feelings, *feelings* she still did not understand in just a short time.

Could he be upset that she had to leave when all was said and done?

Closing her eyes and clasping her hands in a silent prayer, she nodded her head in agreement. Hearing a sigh escape from Duncan, she softly asked, "Tell me what to do."

He hesitated slightly, but removed the sword from

its pouch on Roan. Then doing the same with Roan as he had with Brandubh, he watched as the two horses were nestled safely among the trees.

The thought of Nessie as an actual dragon was one Brigid had heard in stories...stories she would have preferred to read or hear about. Now, she had to come face to face with it. She watched as Duncan took the sword near the water. For a brief moment, she thought of taking off and standing with the horses.

Duncan turned toward Brigid, a look of sadness passing over his face. "I will call for the great dragon, and when I am done, ye will come forth and touch the stone on the sword's hilt. She will recognize ye as the guardian of the relic. Ye may speak to her outright or with the words in your head." Duncan glanced back toward the water. "If I am correct, she will ken why ye are here. Her words will tell ye what to do."

"I am ready." Wrapping her arms around herself, Brigid watched as Duncan lifted the sword up toward the sky, and she felt his energy start to pulsate, a tingling sensation under her skin. The wind spun, sending leaves fluttering past, and she lifted her head to the loch beyond him.

His voice was low and melodic as if he was singing a song. Brigid crept closer to hear.

"*Hail the north. I call upon thee from the mother that will set us free.*"

"*Hail the east. There are those I seek who will help with the peace.*"

"*Hail the south. The fire that will forge the bond.*"

"*Hail the west. Where all will journey to the next realm.*"

"*From the four quarters, I, Duncan Alexander*

Mackay, call upon the one who came from the stars with the Tuatha De Danann."

He lifted the sword high on the last word and with one swift movement, pierced the ground. The hilt bobbed gently as one with the lapping of the waves.

Brigid stood transfixed after listening to his words. As he walked passed her, she grasped for his hand. "Where are you going?"

Duncan cast his eyes to where she had placed her hand against his. Refusing to meet her eyes he spoke low. "I cannot be in the dragon's presence, for I am not worthy, nor a knight. Dinnae fear the dragon, Brigid. Ye are safer with her than with *me*." Squeezing her hand slightly, he let her go, slowly making his way to the horses and trees.

The music of the loch chimed in Brigid's ears causing her to turn away from Duncan. Her heart ached at his words. She wanted nothing more than to pull the sword from the ground and run after him, telling him the sword was his.

However, she couldn't. He wasn't ready to hold and possess it.

A sense of peace wrapped around her as she continued to watch the mists form around and within the loch.

Could the cleansing of the sword bring a sense of peace to him, she wondered? There were so many questions and simply no answers. The more she thought, the more that were added to the list.

A wisp of the mist brushed past her and Brigid felt...*warmth*. Remembering Duncan's words that she was safer with the dragon, she gave pause for a weak smile. "I will do it for you, Duncan. This time my actions will be for you." Lifting her head high, she stepped near the water's edge.

Grasping the hilt of the sword, Brigid ran her palm against the cool stone in the hilt. She swallowed the fear, needing her voice strong. "I am here, great dragon."

The air cooled slightly, but Brigid remained calm. There was no room for fear. On the contrary, it was as if she was floating on the mists, light and carefree. Light splintered through, casting a hue of multi-colored lights, and she gasped at their beauty. The water continued its rhythmic tune, reminding her of a harp.

Then the mists parted.

Brigid stared in awe as the dragon emerged from the depths of the loch, crystals of water streaming from her head. It was *incredible*. There was no other word to describe it. Her head was as big as a house, and it swayed with the movement of the water causing the color of her skin to change in iridescent shades of green and blue. Eyes the color of quartz sparkled and blinked, as if studying her.

How could she ever fear this creature? She felt as if she had known her all her life, only to be reunited after a very long time apart. "The last dragon," she murmured.

A thread of song filled her thoughts until she could hear the words clearly and understood it to be from the dragon.

"Greetings, Brigid Moira O'Neill, from the Clan O'Neill, descended from the order, who protected our kind a millennium ago. It has been eons since I have come upon your people. How do they fare?"

Brigid smiled. "Greetings to you, great dragon.

Well, how do they fare? Honestly, I don't know much about my people, which I am sorry to admit. Perhaps it is one I can rectify when I return home." A wave of sadness passed through her at the thought of returning to her own time.

The melodic voice of the dragon filled her mind again.

"You have the sword of the Order of the Dragon Knights. It is tainted with the blood of an innocent."

"How do you know?"

"I have read your thoughts and know why and how you came to me. You have traveled far within the realm, Brigid. You do your clan great honor."

"That's right. He told me you could hear my mind," her voice soft.

Clasping her hands behind her back to keep them from trembling, Brigid tilted her head up further to look into the eyes of the dragon. "Then you know what I am asking of you?"

There was a pause, and the flow of the water had a soothing effect on Brigid.

"Yes, Brigid, I do know what you ask, and I will purify the sword and purge it of its evil. However, the knight must also cleanse himself before the sword becomes one with him.

"Thank you." She let out a long held sigh.

If the dragon could read her thoughts, there was no harm in asking her next question. "Then you know what *I* seek, too?"

A tinkling of laughter echoed throughout Brigid's mind.

"Why do you think you were chosen, great warrior lady? I believe you have already found the key to unlock the darkness within his soul."

Brigid clutched a fist to her chest as she spoke. "I'm afraid."

"I have never understood why humans fear more from love than when they face an enemy. So, nothing has changed much in the last millennium. My spirit is sad."

"Perhaps, it is because love is the most powerful weapon of all. It is known to rip apart a body and soul. You might have underestimated the power of love, great one." She cringed, realizing she should not have chastised.

As the minutes passed, Brigid feared she offended the dragon. After what seemed to be an eternity, she thought she heard the dragon sigh.

"You have spoken truth, Brigid, but remember this, love is the greatest instrument of healing, and before your journey's end you will truly understand its power."

Biting her bottom lip, she nodded in agreement.

"Blessings of light and love, Brigid Moira O'Neill."

With the dragon's final words, the light and mist exploded in one shattering blast. The ground shook beneath Brigid, causing her to collapse. She fought to regain her breathing, noticing the sword was no longer next to her, but hovering above the water as if it was its protector. A bright flash of light seared across it, and she closed her eyes from the intensity. Her head was pounding, and she fought to stand.

Suddenly, all went still.

Breathing deeply, she dug her fingers into her thighs and tried to find her heartbeat. With great effort, she looked up to find the loch void of the dragon, and the shimmering lights only a memory. A bird's caw brought her back to her senses. Not only was Sorcha perched on a rock, but the sword was also lying majestically against it.

"You know, Sorcha, my grandmother told me when I can't hear my heart, it's because the cogs in my head have taken over."

Laughter burst forth from Brigid as she rocked back and forth upon the ground.

Chapter 27

"A knight's code of honor will be his shield until the day his heart is hardened into steel."

Duncan's heart pounded against his chest when the blast of energy shattered earth and sky, shaking him to his soul. The force of the blast had slammed him against the tree, causing his legs to buckle and collapse beneath him. He heard Brandubh and Roan snorting and stomping, but knew the great one would never harm any animal. He had been unable to see the great dragon speaking with Brigid. She was shrouded in the mist, and he was not permitted to witness their meeting.

There was no time for sorrow, nor envy, realizing it was the price he was paying.

Wiping a hand across his face, he slowly cast his gaze to Brigid, and his protective instincts screamed within. Lunging forward, he took off running toward her. His strong arms engulfed her against him. As her sobs lessoned, he could feel her heart beating wildly against his chest.

"Shhhh, lass, I am here." Duncan spoke softly, his touch gentle on her head.

Cupping her head in his hands, he peered into her eyes. "Are ye hurt, Brigid?"

Too overcome by emotion to speak, Brigid placed her hands over his and shook her head no.

Duncan wrapped her in his arms again. "Och, *leannan*, ye are verra brave."

Her teeth started to chatter. "I don…don't fe…feel brave," snuggling more into his embrace.

Casting his sight out onto the loch, Duncan held her close as her tremors subsided. His feisty Brigid had faced the dragon. She did not scream or flee in terror. And when did he start to think of her as *his*?

He lifted her to her feet and brushed a kiss along her brow. "I need to find us shelter, since darkness is falling."

Stepping away, he whistled for the horses. Gently, he lifted the sword and placed in the pouch on Roan. When he glanced over his shoulder, he saw her peering out at the loch, mumbling.

"What are ye doing?" he asked quietly noticing how the wind caught wisps of her curls. She stood transfixed.

Placing a hand on her shoulder, she angled her head up at him. "Saying good-bye," she replied softly.

His chest swelled at the respect she had shown for the great one. Holding out his hand, he gave her a small smile. "Come, lass."

****

Hours later, Duncan let out a sigh of relief. It had been many years since he had been in this part of the glen. Therefore, it had taken longer than expected to find the cave beneath the waterfall. When he spotted the old oak with the markings he and his brothers had carved into it that spring day, he realized he was near.

So many memories came rushing back, unleashing emotions he had held in check for over a year. Memories of when they made a pact to always stand united against any enemy, and to protect their baby sister from harm.

They had been young lads when Margaret came into their world. She was a beacon of light and hope in their family. A girl had not been born in over a millennium, and all thought it a blessing from the fae. Therefore, on an early spring morn, Angus gathered Stephen, Alastair, and himself, to go on a quest to thank the fae and swear their allegiance. They had been staying at Castle Creag and with their father's blessing, promising they would return by the last ray of light, they set out.

It was sheer luck when they found the waterfall after marking their path only on the oak trees, each with their own name in ogham. If any others should pass, they would understand its meaning as one of a passing druid and give it the respect due.

Angus had chosen the spot and started the fire, since this was his power. Stephen would call upon the fae, using his power of visions and water. Alastair being so very young, then tried to bring forth foxgloves from the ground, and succeeded only in thickening the grass under their feet. Duncan smiled at the memory and remembered how he brought the wind to circle around them instead of through them. He had mastered the wind and storms early in his life and took great pride in it.

As they had chanted their vows, each withdrew their dirks, and sliced it across their palm. Still chanting, they came together in a ritual only they would understand. Linking hands as one, they continued chanting until a white light cascaded over them and all went silent within the forest grove.

It was the first time they met the Guardian. She came forth in blazing colors, thanking each of them and marking on their foreheads her blessing as she passed. They returned many times after that first day to play and swim near the waterfall.

Yet, they never saw the Guardian again until that fateful night.

Duncan inhaled deeply, pressing the memories of long ago back within. Why he thought of this place now after all that had happened, he could not fathom. Perhaps there was still hope for his brothers. Brigid would be safe here amid the magic, a magic created by his brothers and himself that spring morning.

****

Brigid shivered. The last rays of the sun were descending fast, and she was cold, hungry, and tired. Her entire body ached. She certainly was not accustomed to riding horses, and her recent activity with Duncan made it more difficult to stay upright on Roan. What she wouldn't give for a warm bath and a soft mattress.

She arched her back more to stretch out the kinks when she heard the rush of water. They had entered another grove, but this one had its own waterfall, tucked against the mountain. The water had its own rhythm, slowly cascading over the rocks at the bottom. Green moss draped majestically over the stones on either sides, giving it an ethereal feel.

"Breathtaking, wouldn't you say, Roan?" Brigid gave a small rub to the top of his head, and he nodded as if he understood. She was captivated as the spray from the water danced along the rocks gliding into the stream, letting the hypnotic trance of the water soothe

the weariness within her.

Duncan dismounted, walking over to her. "There's a cave nestled to one side of the water where we will stay the night." Reaching up, he grasped her waist and brought her gently to the ground as if her five foot nine inch frame was nothing more than feathers. Tucking a stray curl behind her ear, he spoke so softly she almost could not hear him. "So very soft."

She trembled from the touch of his hand. Brigid didn't realize she had been holding her breath, until he stepped back away from her and started reaching for items off Roan. The great dragon had spoken of love. Yet, how could she possibly love this man so soon? It was probably only a one-sided love affair. He certainly didn't *love* her. Did he?

"Here, let me help." Brigid turned her gaze from him.

Duncan handed her the bag which held their food, and her stomach growled. She tossed it over her shoulder, the effort causing her to wince. Thank God, he didn't see, or he would think her to be some weak girl. Come to think of it, he never once asked about her time. Was he not curious? His life was ruled and dictated by magic, though, surely, wouldn't he have questions? She had questions—*questions* about his powers, the sword and of course, the great dragon, the one she called Nessie.

"Is he not curious about *me*?" she spoke softly. Hearing a snicker, she realized the only one listening to her conversation was Roan.

"Thanks for the support, Roan." Pursing her lips, she came to the conclusion it didn't matter. She would gather all the courage she possessed and see this quest through. It would be her gift to Duncan. He would never know her feelings for him, keeping the treasure under lock and key inside her heart, and taking it back home.

Strolling along, she saw the path they were taking was strewn among faery mounds. Wild mushrooms clumped together in a circle with foxgloves on one side, and wildflowers on another. Noticing Duncan was taking great care not to trespass inside them, she followed in his step. Her grandmother had taught her to respect these sacred places dear to the faery. Jumping over one, she landed smack against Duncan's backside, which seemed to be made of marble, he didn't even budge from the impact.

"Sorry," mumbled Brigid.

"Humph!" He shook his head.

Dropping their sacks and kneeling before the stream, Duncan cupped his hands in the water, taking a drink. Wiping his mouth with the back of his hand, he stood. "I'll gather some branches and tend to the horses. This will give ye some time for privacy."

She arched an eyebrow in question.

"We are safe here. I see no movement." Taking the reins of Brandubh and Roan, he added, "Ye can tend to your personal affairs."

Brigid gaped in disbelief as he led the horses away from the stream. "You're just going to leave me here to do what? In a very cold stream?"

She heard him chuckle as he continue to walk away from her.

Continuing to grumble, she sat on the rock watching the water gurgling in the stream and took a deep breath. "What I really *need* is heated water."

Dipping a hand slowly into the stream, Brigid withdrew it quickly. "Damn it!" Quickly splashing the icy water on her face, the sting bringing back life to her weary senses, she cupped her hands back in and drew forth some water to drink. Shivering as the water went down, she stood to shake off the last droplets, wiping her hands on her jeans. "This will have to do."

Darkness was now descending, and glancing up, she watched Sorcha take cover in a nearby tree. The wind shifted, and she felt warmth spread across her neck. She turned sensing Duncan was returning.

He *was* the wind, and she blushed.

"Are ye ready?" Duncan asked quietly.

Brigid nodded and followed Duncan until they approached a hilly mound, which went over a narrow part of the stream acting as a bridge. Moving closer to the waterfall and passing between two giant pine trees, she came to the entrance to the cave. Light spilled forth from a fire Duncan had built and the effect was inviting. Her stomach rumbled, *again*.

The entrance low as she ducked to step inside, gasping immediately. The walls weren't lined with dirt, but of stones that glowed with various colors. The firelight created an illuminating effect. Reaching out, she felt the smooth contours, marveling at their contrast. In the far corner, Brigid saw branches on the ground covered by Duncan's plaid.

"Come and sit. I ken ye are hungry. I can hear your belly speaking." A smiled played at the corner of his mouth.

Brigid snapped her eyes away from the bed and narrowed them at him, until she glimpsed the banquet Duncan had spread out on the other plaid. It was all they had, but she didn't care. It was food.

Duncan handed her the ale, which she gladly took a swig, plopping down to eat her feast of hard cheese and an oatcake. Spying something black she asked, "Blackberries, Duncan?"

"Aye."

"Here?"

"Aye. I cannot take from the animals here in this part of the grove, but fruit is plentiful."

"Why not?"

Brigid popped a few into her mouth, savoring the smell and taste as she closed her eyes. "Hmmmm, so good." Drops of the juice lingered on her lips, and she used her tongue to lap them up.

Duncan froze ale in hand. "Does food always bring ye such pleasure?"

She slowly opened her eyes and met his. "Of course."

"Ale?" he croaked out.

"Yes, thank you," she smiled. "Blackberry?"

"Nae. Ye enjoy them."

"Duncan what do you mean you can't take from the animals here?" Brigid started to gnaw on the oatcake, wishing she had coffee, tea, *anything*, to dunk it into. She almost thought of splashing some ale over the stale thing.

He wiped a hand across his face and stared across at the fire. "It is sacred in the grove. No animal can come to harm here."

"Oh. I did see the faery mounds. How did you find this place?" she asked taking another swig of ale.

"Angus found it."

Brigid's heart stood still for one beat. It was the

first time he had mentioned any of his family, and she took this as a sign of an opening. "Angus is the oldest, right?"

A deep sigh escaped Duncan, and he turned back to her, a frown furrowing his brow. "Aye, as ye already ken."

She leaned across and placed her hand gently on his forearm, keeping her eyes level with his. "Duncan, I've told you, where I come from I know the legend. It is written down and told in bardic tales, still."

He pushed away from her grip so fast she swayed back. Standing against the wall, Duncan placed one shoulder against it for support.

"Duncan?"

"Legends!" He snorted

Brigid heard thunder rumbling in the distance, from Duncan no doubt. She had to take his mind off that night until he was ready.

"Tell me about your brothers and their powers. Why did Angus choose this place?"

His face was taut, and the muscles tensed along his jaw, but she was determined to get him to talk.

"Blackberries then?"

He snapped his gaze back to her, and his lips quivered in a half smile. Shoving off from the wall, he walked over and placing one hand on the wall above the entrance, looked out on the night sky.

"We are descended from the fae, part man, part fae, each with our own power. Angus is the oldest, his is fire, and he carries the shield. Stephen carries the Stone of Ages, and can work magic with water. He also has the sight. Then there is Alastair. His power is of the great mother—the land, and he carries the axe."

Stepping back inside, Duncan brought the wind inside the cave. "I think ye ken what *my* powers are."

The air swirled around her and Brigid felt its warmth. A question marked her face, "You can control the temperature with the wind?"

Duncan frowned. "I do not ken the word."

"It means you can control its heat and coolness."

Understanding marked his features as he nodded. "Aye."

"The storms, too?"

He glanced upwards. "Aye, storms."

"What about the relics? Do they hold power, too?"

"Oh aye. Their magic blended with ours is mighty powerful."

"And this place?" Brigid waved her hands indicating the cave.

"Aye...this place. Angus led Stephen, Alastair, and me to the grove, marking it with the way of the druid. He claimed a fire burned within him and with each step, the heat of the flame led him to this place." Speaking more softly, he continued, "We had set out on our journey to thank the fae for the blessing of our wee sister, Margaret."

"Blessing? Why?" asked Brigid. She had risen, standing against the opposite wall.

"The legends speak of only males descending from the Mackays? Your legends do not tell of her birth, of a female, the first in over a thousand years?" His words laced with anger as he stepped closer to her.

"No, Duncan. They only tell of the knights, but I'm sorry to say Margaret was only mentioned briefly and she..." Brigid hesitated.

"Only of her death?" Duncan spat out.

"Yes."

Lightning flashed in the night sky, and thunder rumbled far too close, Brigid thought, causing her to shiver. Afraid, but determined to find out, she asked her next question.

"What happened that night, Duncan?"

The wind started howling through the trees, and the look on Duncan's face was one of anger and pain. He grasped her shoulders, his eyes shifting from sky blue to shards of white crystal, and his fingers bit into her shoulders. She did not flinch, or back away.

Brigid stood tall and looked into his face of fury.

"*Ye have no right*!"

Her voice, when she spoke, held a sense of calm, and Brigid fought to keep it from quivering. "Yes, Duncan, I do. If I am to help you, I need to know what happened that night. *All of it*."

"Do not ask me what I cannot speak of," he snapped.

Brigid slowly brought her hand up and placed it on his chest, feeling his heart hammering against her palm.

Her small, simple touch was his undoing.

His lips came crashing down on hers as he thrust his tongue deep within. He tried to control the kiss, but his beast would not relent. He sucked the air from her and gave it back. The kiss was one fused with anger and hunger. Anger for the one question he was not ready to answer, and hunger for her. He pulled at her bottom lip and sucked greedily, causing her to moan.

Picking her up in one swift movement, he strode over to the bed, collapsing on top of it. She pulled at his hair and twined her fingers in it. Taking her tongue, he let her caress his rough chin. Now it was his turn to moan, and he ravished her mouth again, taking her passion, and fueling his. The heat of her breath came out in small gasps. He wanted to suck all the air from her, as if it was not enough. His kiss was urgent and exploratory, and she responded back with her own passion.

Taking her hands, he held them above her head. Burying his face along the side of her neck, he raked his teeth along her skin, searing a path down to her shoulder. She tasted of flowers, berries, and her womanly scent. He wanted to bury himself in her.

Without thought, he ripped her tee shirt up over her head. With one flick of his thumb and finger, he unsnapped her bra. Cupping her breasts, he lavished each, smothering his face between her soft mounds. Bringing his hand up to one breast, he pinched her rosy nipples, watching as she screamed in pleasure, arching under him.

"Sweet mother Danu!" he choked out. Grasping her shoulder, he stared at the strange mark glaring back at him. He gently rubbed his thumb over her right shoulder.

"Duncan? What?" She tried to move, but he held her away from him.

"Ye bear the mark of the dragon, Brigid. Ye have been touched." Quickly gathering his senses, he released her. Grabbing his plaid, he draped it over her shoulders and stood.

Hands fisted at his sides, he turned and walked to the entrance of the cave. "Rest, Brigid. We leave at dawn." Giving her one last look over his shoulder, he shoved a hand through his hair and stepped out.

Brigid stared after him in disbelief. What just

happened?

Taking her hand, she touched her lips, lips that were still on fire from his touch. Closing her eyes, she inhaled deeply of his scent. Then remembering his words, she peered down at her shoulder and saw the mark. It was no bigger than a nickel, reminding her of Celtic knotwork patterns she had seen and greatly admired.

"*Great*. Now I've been tattooed by a dragon."

Chapter 28

"I skip and play through the meadows of time, but when I awake will I know who I am?"

Brigid awoke to birdsong. Sitting up slowly, she worked out the kinks in her neck and shoulders, watching as a small bird chirped at her from the entrance.

Tossing off the plaid and reaching for her leather jacket, she put it on and zipped it up. Glancing down at her partially torn tee shirt, memories of the night before engulfed her in sadness. "Damn you, Duncan, for making me feel this way." Bunching up the shirt, she rolled it within one of the plaids and folded the other as best she could. She swept her gaze one last time and walked to the entrance. There was no trace of Duncan having slept inside. She could only guess he probably spent the night outdoors.

Stepping outside, the sun was barely up over the hills when she heard...*chanting*?

She spotted Brandubh and Roan tethered to a nearby tree and walked over to them, putting her items into Roan's pack. Walking slowly, she followed the sound of the chanting, pushing past green branches of pine and stepping upwards away from the path and the waterfall.

Then Brigid saw him.

Duncan was up on a crest, facing the sunrise. Sword in hand and chanting in Gaelic, he would lunge forward, sweeping the sword up and over in an arc.

Brigid's mouth fell open.

Duncan had not one stitch of clothing on, except for his boots and the torc around his neck. Her heart started beating faster as she stood transfixed by the scene. Every move of his body accentuated his muscles, and her thoughts returned to her earlier images of him as a Celtic god. He moved with the air, and his words became a repetitive chant. Repeatedly, he would move with fluid movements—sword and man as one entity.

Brigid leaned against a tree for support, watching in awe and a growing respect for her Highlander. When did she start thinking of him as *her* Highlander?

Yet, that was precisely how she felt.

She let her eyes travel the length of his brawny torso, where the black hair curled in abundance across his chest and narrowed down the flat plane of his abdomen to his manhood.

The sunrise made its journey up into the sky and she watched it come up over the hill, touching its rays of light on Duncan as if in welcome. The light shimmered across his ebony locks. He threw both his arms up in greeting and spoke in words of Gaelic. Dropping down on one knee, he bent his head in silence.

To Brigid, he was the most powerful, erotic man she had ever met. And regardless of the outcome of her journey, she knew to the very core of her soul there never could nor would there ever be another. Her heart had sealed that fate the moment she met Duncan Mackay in her dreams.

"Oh, great mother," she whispered. "Help me to help him, and heal my heart when I am no longer here. I can't do this alone." Brigid swallowed, and moved silently away from the tree making her way back to the horses.

****

Duncan's breathing was labored. He remained kneeling until he heard her footsteps move away. He knew the moment Brigid stepped into view, and it took all of his concentration not to turn and look her way. Doing so would only disturb his ritual, and once his eyes met hers he would want to take her, *again*.

He cursed his body for betraying him when she was near as he continued to fight his lust—a lust that was stripping away his sanity. Yet, there was more than just the red haze of his cravings. She touched his soul and spread warmth throughout, reaching inside the darkness and vanquishing the demons.

Seeing the mark of the great dragon yesterday, reminded him of her purpose. She was not his.

Looking up toward the sun, he shook his head and uttered one word. "*Why?*"

Grunting at the mocking silence, Duncan grabbed a fistful of dirt and brought it to his lips. Kissing it gently, he tossed it back to the ground. Reaching for his tunic, he slung it over his shoulders and made his way back to the horses. If they rode hard, they would reach Castle Creag by late night. The sooner the better, he thought.

When he approached, Brigid was speaking to the horses in soothing tones, and he glanced to the right. She had spread what was left of their food and drink on a rock slab.

She approached him and her smile wavered. "I

200

hope you don't mind, but I filled one of the skins with water. It's cool and refreshing."

Wrapping his plaid around him, he strode over to Brandubh and procured a Celtic pin from his pouch, fastening it in place.

"I thought we should eat, though meager it is, before we leave," she stated taking a seat on an old log.

"Nae, later." He waved his hand nonchalantly.

Her shoulders slumped. "Duncan, you haven't eaten much since our journey. You need to eat, please?"

The look of worry on her face was too much for Duncan. Without uttering a word, he sat down and ate a piece of hard cheese and dry bread. He was thankful for the cool water, though a swig of ale would have tasted far better. It was going to be a very long day, considering his brat had her scent mingled in it.

"How long will it take to reach Castle Creag?" she asked softly, her eyes more on the hard food than on him.

"If we ride hard, by nightfall."

Brigid took a drink of water and asked, "I'm curious, Duncan, why Castle Creag?"

Rubbing a hand across the back of his neck, he gave her the only reason he could think of. "It is the safest place. With riders spotted in this part of the glen, we travel to a place where I can keep ye safe, and Cormac may have answers as well."

"Who's Cormac?"

Glancing slightly at Brigid, he answered, "He is laird of Castle Creag, and the only man I can trust."

Sorcha's caw brought both of them up short.

Duncan jumped up, reaching for his sword. He stood in front of her as her protector. Sorcha continued circling above them. Duncan nodded, and she flew off in a northern direction.

Moving around to face her, he placed his fingers across her lips in a plea for silence. Moments passed before he released his fingers from her lips. Her indrawn breath told him she had not even allowed herself to breathe. His eyes peered over her head as if awaiting the danger to come forth.

"We cannot stay. Sorcha has spotted riders in the distance." Cupping her chin with his hand, his gaze bore into hers with concern. "We have to ride hard and fast, Brigid. There will be no stopping. Can ye do this?"

Placing her hand against the growth of his rough beard, she gave him a smile of encouragement and strength, "Yes, Duncan."

Duncan's mind screamed not to do it, but his body betrayed him. Bending his head, he brushed a light kiss along her rosy lips. Taking his tongue, he licked up the last of the crumbs along the edges of her mouth. "Good lass. I do not want to leave ye behind." He released her with a wicked gleam of a smile as he gathered up the last of their meal.

Chapter 29

"Beware the cloak of doom, for thine enemies are close at hand. Shrewd and cunning, and they will rip one's soul out."

The guttural sound coming forth from his mouth was one of disgust and contempt.

Why could no one seem to find them? They slipped through the hills sight unseen, as if the very fae were assisting them. It was impossible, since they were cursed and their souls damned. However, days ago the veil of time shifted and someone had passed through. That was a possibility he had not counted on, and he contemplated its outcome in his plans. Taking a hand to his chin, he mulled over new plans, one of which he had to consider.

"Deep in thought again, Lachlan?"

Alex and a group of his men had come upon him, and that did not bode well. Now, he was faced with riding along with them. He thought to question them as to why they were in these parts, but then decided to keep silent.

Lachlan glared at him. "Your greeting is always with such reverence, Alex. One would think I was one of your men."

"My pardon, great one." Alex smirked.

Lachlan nodded, making a mental note he would

have to tread carefully around him. He knew of Patrick's disapproval of him, now Alex? They would know the might of his power when this was over. Then the whole lot of MacFhearguises would feel his wrath and give him their due respect.

"Have ye any news of Adam?" Lachlan asked.

Sighing, Alex sat forward looking down at the loch. "Nae. Not a word." He waved his gloved hand in the air. "It is as if he vanished into the mists."

Lachlan next words would anger the man and he counted on it. "Duncan Mackay is now on his quest to find the sword, and restore his clan's honor." He watched with shrewdness as Alex's face contorted with anger, his fist clenching.

"By Lugh's honor, is it true?" Anger and shock infused Alex's words. "By the gods, how can this be?"

Lachlan held up his hand to quiet him, reveling internally in the reactionary response he got from Alex. "A vision came to me, and I have sensed the shift in power."

Shaking his head Alex turned his full fury on Lachlan. "Vision? Ye base this on a *vision*? The Mackays were cursed and banished! Twelve moons have passed without a word from the blasted Mackays. They were disbanded. We have spies everywhere who would have spoken of this quest!" Pointing a finger at Lachlan, he continued his rant, "Might I remind ye, druid, that ye were the one to tell us that the relics no longer belonged to their clan and their names stricken from the hallow halls of the fae!"

Lachlan cleared his throat. "Might I remind ye, Alex, I am a *druid*, and visions are gifts from the gods and goddesses. Your skepticism I find—*disturbing*."

Alex's jaw clenched.

"Also, I have reported this to your brother, the laird, and he concurs." Lachlan did not want to divulge he sensed an undercurrent of discontent from Patrick.

Alex tore his gaze away from the druid.

Rubbing a gloved hand over a moon's growth of a beard, he yelled back to his men. "Sean, come forth!"

"Damnation! Where are ye, Adam?" Alex grumbled.

Sean rode to his side, giving a silent greeting of welcome to Lachlan. "Aye, Alex?"

"Lachlan tells me Duncan Mackay has taken up a *quest* to find his sword and restore the clan's honor and wipe the stain clean."

"Judas's balls! I did not think it possible?" Sean's steed snorted and stomped his hoof several times.

Nodding his head toward Lachlan, Alex continued, "It is true I fear."

"By the hounds of Cuchulainn! Do ye ken where the Mackay is?" Sean asked.

If Michael knew where the Mackay was, Lachlan would have shared the information, and the force of the gods would not be able to hold any MacFhearguis back from their revenge. But Alex still had to ask.

"Lachlan, can ye see him in your…vision?" Cocking his head to the side, Alex waited.

"Nae," he answered, shaking his head slowly.

Alex turned his gaze back to Sean. Reaching out, he clamped a hand on his shoulder. "I need ye to go on a quest." Sean raised an eyebrow in response as Alex continued, "Ride forth to Castle Creag. Ye have a spy within, and I need to find where this Mackay has ventured."

"So the Mackay has been at Castle Creag?" asked Lachlan glancing away to keep his fury from showing.

"Aye," responded Alex.

Sean slowly nodded in assent, a slow smile curving his ruggedly handsome face. "Aye, it will give me some long overdue nights with Morag."

Alex barked out a roar of laughter, giving Sean's shoulder a shake, "Oh, that I could take the journey with ye. Give her my regards."

"Nae, she might be looking over my shoulder for ye," he responded, a smile creasing his face.

Lachlan snarled inwardly wanting to spit. So, Alex knew where the Mackay had been all along. Now, he was sending his right hand man to search for information. He tried hard not to clench his fists at the thought of anyone finding him before himself. Alex was playing a game, which he would surely lose. Struggling with thoughts that would visibly be his undoing, he turned them inward toward another path.

Tapping his finger to his mouth while shaking his head, he said, "Hmmmm, a keen plan, Alex. One I should commend ye on." Grabbing the reins of his horse in preparation to leave, he added, "I go now to give this news to your brother. He will be anxious to hear of your plans."

Alex nodded his assent. "Give my brother my regards and tell him I will return by the first snows, though in truth I think the gods and goddesses have misplaced the seasons. It is too warm this close to Samhain."

"I will, though who are we to argue with what the gods and goddesses have given us?" Turning aside, he slowly made his way down and toward the path away from them, his mind reveling in his new plans. A cruel smile splayed across his features as he spoke quietly, "Aye, Alex, I will use your plans indeed, and if your man stumbles across my path, who's to say it was my dirk or that of the Mackays?"

A shadow of a rider emerged from the trees, blocking Lachlan's path. Lachlan nodded his head in acknowledgement. No words were exchanged as the rider followed in his wake.

"Do ye ken who he rides with?" asked Sean.

Alex rubbed the back of his neck. "Nae. Not my concern at the moment. Nonetheless, the druid is lying. Why would he be out in the Highlands near Mackay land? Lachlan has never ventured past our lands."

"He is a slippery one, Alex. Not to be trusted."

"Patrick warned me about him, and I would not listen. Besides, the news of the Mackay will overshadow any concerns regarding Lachlan."

Sean's hands rested on the horn of his saddle as he glanced at the northern end of the glen. "I'll pass through An Druim Buidhe and through the witch's teat to make Castle Creag before the night falls."

"An Druim Buidhe—yellow ridge?" A frown marred his features.

"Aye. It is quicker and few if any will pass along that road."

"Good, good." Shifting his gaze from the path Lachlan took, he turned toward Sean. "Do not be seen within the castle. Let the woman gather the information we seek. I cannot start a feud with the Murray, *yet*. I will return to the grove in four days.

With a quick nod, Sean rode off toward the northern part of the glen leaving Alex alone with a sense of unease. He watched him until he was no longer in his sight. His eyes caught movement and watched a hawk in the distance, soaring and diving. A smile curved his mouth, thinking it to be hunting its prey. Then his smile became a scowl, noticing the hawk was not hunting prey, it was following Sean.

"Bloody bastard, druid magic!" He spat out on to the ground. "Ye will rue the day ye crossed paths with this MacFhearguis." Until the day either Patrick or himself could present facts as to why they should no longer welcome Lachlan as their counsel, he would have to patient.

And his patience with Lachlan was ebbing away.

Chapter 30

"In the Book of the Beginning, there was a voice, and her melody sang a song of awakening."

Duncan slowed his pace when he came into view of Castle Creag, allowing Brigid a moment before they would descend. He could just imagine the questions they would likely have for her.

To say Duncan was proud of the lass riding with him would be madness, but that was indeed how he felt. Smiling slightly, he watched her approach, curls escaping from her braid and fanning her heart-shaped face. Her lips were pursed in a thin line, and he took it as a sign of torment, either mentally or physically. He had literally pushed them hard, allocating only one stop. Not a word had passed from those lips, and he silently praised her spirit and strength. She was not a good rider, but she kept up with his relentless pace.

Now that they were at Castle Creag, he would see she received some much needed rest and proper clothing. "Aye, clothing indeed," he murmured.

Closing the distance to her, he pointed to the massive stone structure. "That there is Castle Creag, home of Cormac Murray."

Tucking her curls behind her ears, she squinted. "Castle Creag? *Creag*, meaning rock in Gaelic?"

Duncan's eyes lit up at her knowledge of his

language, and his smile broadened. "Aye, lass. Ye understand."

Hells bells, thought Brigid. She had to hold tight to the reins to keep from swooning, but when this man smiled fully, her heart did a flip-flop. God, he was gorgeous, his teeth gleaming white against his slightly bearded face and the light from his eyes sparkled. All she could think of was that he definitely was part fae. No one could be so handsome without some magic thrown into their DNA. Brigid could only smile back and nod, like some daft lass she turned into every so often, *particularly* around him.

"Shall we?" He waved his hand toward the entrance.

Taking her gaze from the Highlander in front of her, Brigid's mouth opened at the sight before her. She kept Roan at a slow pace to absorb the feeling of seeing her very first castle. Who would have believed she, Brigid O'Neill, would be transported back in time and entering a real medieval castle in Scotland. It may not be Eilean Donan on the Isle of Skye *or* the great Edinburgh Castle, but it was stunning in all its glory. There were two towers, one facing east, the other west, wondering what it would be like to stand within one of those towers when the mists descended.

A parapet went around the entire keep and a stream flowed in the front and under a bridge. From her vantage point, she could discern not one, but two entrances. Sheep were grazing at the western end. The scene was one she wished to imprint in her memory forever.

As they crossed the stone bridge leading upwards, she peeked over the side to see some boys playing.

They were skipping stones across the water, their laughter filling the air. One of the boys pointed at her and Duncan, all play coming to a halt, their mouths opened in shock.

She just smiled back.

Duncan had seen the guard standing at the forward tower and raised a hand in acknowledgment. Making their way through the tunnel entrance, they passed under the portcullis. He was amazed at how many were now drawn to their attention, especially the men. They were gaping not at him, but at Brigid. The lass riding behind him in the strange clothing.

"God's blood!" He smacked his hand against his forehead. What had he been thinking? He glanced back at Brigid and saw her smiling at them. Did she not realize what she looked like—in her strange clothing, molding every inch of her body? Before he was forced to draw his sword, he needed to get her quickly inside.

A squeal and the pitter-patter of light footsteps came barreling out from the stables. There was only one person who would be so brave as to greet him thus. Finn.

Dismounting from Brandubh, he watched as Finn came running to a halt right in front of him. "Good evening, Sir Duncan. May I take Brandubh?"

"What is this? I did not recall such manners before I took my leave, and now look at ye?" A smile tugged at the corners of Duncan's mouth.

"Why, Sir Duncan, I ken manners verra well." Finn was standing still awaiting a nod of approval, but his hands were twisting behind his back, giving away his excitement. In truth, he believed Finn was happier to see his horse.

Taking a hand to Finn's hair, he rumpled it saying, "Aye, and tell Tiernan we have another horse as well." Turning to help Brigid dismount, his heart all but stopped when he saw Cormac had already taken a hold of her, placing his arms around her waist. He watched in horror as Cormac gently placed her down, only to keep one arm locked firmly around her.

Growling, Duncan lunged forward.

Cormac placed his other hand out, grasping Duncan's shoulder, arching an eyebrow in question. "I was just helping the bonny lass down, Duncan." Releasing his grip on Brigid first, he kept his hand firmly on Duncan's shoulder.

Keeping his gaze locked on Brigid, he asked, "Will ye make the introductions, Duncan?"

"Cormac Murray, this is Brigid O'Neill, and she is under *my* protection." Stepping away from his grasp, Duncan took her arm, placing it securely within the crook of his. He knew better than to look at Brigid, realizing her eyes were probably throwing him daggers. She tried to pull free from his grasp, but he was much stronger and held firm.

Palms held up in surrender, Cormac took a step back. Glancing back at Brigid, he bowed his head briefly. "Welcome to Castle Creag. I ken ye must be tired and hungry." Coughing into his hand he also sputtered out the last, "And in need of clothing, too, aye?"

Duncan's eyes narrowed, "Aye, and quickly, lest one of your men meets with the end of my sword."

Brigid tried to elbow him. "Oh, for pity's sake, Duncan, stop being an ass!"

It was as if her words had silenced the entire

country. Even the horses had gone completely still.

Releasing her, he placed his fists on his hips and lowered his face mere inches from hers, his eyes blazing as he spoke. "In case ye did not notice, Brigid, ye are a meal for these men in your outlandish clothing, and I will *not* be made a laughingstock with your words in front of them," he hissed out.

"Really?" Brigid snorted. "You seem to be doing just that all on your own."

Cormac proceeded to cough loudly into his fist. "Nell," he sputtered out. "Nell!"

A young lass came running out. She had flour on her nose, and her braids looked like they had been pulled as they had started to unravel. "Aye, Master Cormac?"

Taking a finger and wiping the flour off her nose, Cormac just shook his head. "Helping in the kitchens again?"

"Oh *nae*, Master Cormac. I ken better." Nell started fussing with her apron, twisting the ends as if deciding how to tell the story.

"Ye ken what Moira will do to ye if she finds ye swiping cakes again?" Cormac stood with his arms crossed over his chest.

"'Tis only one," she corrected.

Cormac snorted. "Then there was the mince pies, green pea pottage, and a basket filled with apples, which Moira found the other morning."

She lifted her chin. "They were for the stray dogs."

"The strays can forage for themselves." Holding up the finger with flour on it, he asked, "And what do ye suppose this is?"

"Dust?"

"Ye had better pray Moira does not find ye in the kitchen, since ye are banned from the place."

"I would *never* disobey an order." Her eyes wide.

"Good to hear. Take Mistress Brigid to the guest room on the east tower, and fetch Sienna to care for her."

"Aye, Master Cormac." Her eyes alight as she glanced Brigid's way.

Smiling, Brigid extended her hand out to Nell. "Lead the way."

Nell grasped Brigid's hand, tugging her along.

Brigid glanced back over her shoulder mouthing a thank you to Cormac before being whisked away.

Slowly, Cormac turned toward Duncan. With his arms folded across his chest, he asked, "Sweet Danu! Who *is* this Brigid O'Neill?"

Duncan continued following Brigid with his eyes until she stepped inside the castle. Letting out a long held breath, he turned aside and removed the pouch containing the sword from Roan. Holding the pouch under his arm, he gazed back to where Brigid had parted from them. How much could he reveal to Cormac?

Waiting a few more moments he spoke softly. "Brigid O'Neill was sent by the Guardian to bring back my sword and relinquish it to me at a time of her choosing."

Cormac slowly released his arms, the look of shock registering across his features. "The lass has brought ye your sword?" His eyes leveled at the pouch in disbelief. "What do ye mean, a time of her *choosing*?"

"When the time comes, she will give me back my sword. It is hers…temporarily."

Rubbing the back of his neck, Cormac grimaced. "Strange that a *lass* has brought ye back your sword, but who is she? Is she part of your quest?"

Glancing around, Duncan grabbed Cormac's arm, turning him away from the ears of his men. Hugging the sword more tightly, he quietly said, "The lass has come from another land and has been touched by the fae. I do not ken when the time will happen." Duncan could see the uncertainty in the face of his friend. "*Nor* do I believe she kens."

"A twist if ever I heard of, Duncan. Nevertheless, I do not feel sorry for ye."

Duncan frowned. "And why is that?"

Slowly smiling and with a twinkle in his eyes, he answered, "She is a very bonny lass and easy on the eyes. What with her style of clothing, I would very much like to visit her land."

Cormac never saw the punch coming, for Duncan hit him quick, knocking him flat on the ground. "Bloody hell, Duncan!" He rubbed his chin, and checked for loose teeth with his tongue.

"I told ye, Brigid is under my protection and ye should do well to remember it," his voice one of steel. Leaving a stunned Cormac sitting on the ground, Duncan stormed off toward the lists.

"Oh aye, Duncan Mackay, I'll remember." Standing, Cormac stomped his boots, shaking off the dirt and leaves. "So the big brawny knight has found himself a woman."

Could it be conceivable she would be his salvation? "By the gods, I pray it so."

Chapter 31

"Love is like a warrior's battle—easy to begin, yet hard to stop."

"More hot water, my lady?" Sienna stood with another pail of steaming water, and Brigid nodded in affirmation.

"I shall get the rose scented soap to help ye with your tresses, too."

"Hmmmm, so wonderful." Brigid thought she'd died and gone to heaven. Never in her life would she take something so simple as a bath for granted again. She didn't even mind that they had to haul those buckets of hot water up here for her.

When Sienna took one look at her and her clothing, she had pointed a finger at Nell to get Micah and the others to bring up the tub. She started tsking at her clothing, saying it was not proper for a woman to wear such material. Brigid just chuckled to herself.

Sitting in the chair by the fireplace, she waited for them to haul and fill the beautiful tub, not caring that she had to undress and give her clothing to Sienna. However, Brigid did let her know that she would be keeping those items and would tend to their cleaning, which only prompted more tsking from Sienna.

Brigid sighed, sinking more into the tub.

"My lady, if ye would dunk your head, I can lather

the soap in." Sienna pulled up a stool near the tub.

"Please, Sienna, just call me Brigid, and thank you for helping me with my hair. I can just imagine what it looks like." Giving Sienna a smile, she slowly submerged herself under the water, bobbing back up. Sienna started massaging the soap in, and the smell of roses and other scents soothed her weary body. After the past few days, she would have lathered with lye just to feel clean again.

"My lady—" Brigid held up her hand in warning to the reference, and Sienna giggled. "*Brigid*, where did ye meet Sir Duncan?"

So, thought Brigid, how could she explain their meeting? From what she discerned, Duncan was addressed as Sir Duncan and the people here still gave him the honor—one of a Dragon Knight. They continued to worship the pagan ways here in this time. However, would they comprehend time travel? Brigid smirked. "No, they would not," she whispered.

"Did ye say something, Brigid?" Sienna was leaning around giving her a queer look.

"No, nothing. Sorry, it just feels so good to bathe. To answer your question, Duncan and I just met a few days ago. I was traveling with family, and we became separated. Duncan is assisting me to search for them." *Holy crap! Where did that come from?* She just made up the biggest lie, and now she had to find Duncan fast to give him the details.

Plunging herself back under, she splashed water everywhere, causing a squeak to emerge from Sienna.

"Oh, so sorry, Sienna," gasped Brigid. "The water's getting cold, and I think I'm clean enough." Good one Brigid, another lie to add to the list. If you're not careful, you're going to be tripping over them before the day is over with.

****

Duncan had thought to work off some of his restlessness by training in the lists. However, after an hour, his emotions were more twisted than ever. What was he thinking in throwing a fist at Cormac? He rammed his sword into the ground and ran a hand through his hair. "God's teeth!"

Casting his gaze up toward the sky, he saw Sorcha circling. Going over to the bench, he grabbed one of his gloves and whistled. She circled once more and dove straight at his arm, landing as gentle as a feather. Sorcha was special, not only to Cathal, but Duncan, too.

"Good eventide, little lady." Stroking her gently, he spoke comforting words in the old language. Sorcha tilted her head to one side as if she understood.

"It is good to see ye and Sorcha have bonded."

Duncan whipped his head to the side, surprised to see the druid within Castle Creag. "Cathal? What brings ye inside these walls?" Looking back at Sorcha, he smirked, "Missing your feathered friend?" She blinked once at him.

"Nae Duncan. I believe ye needed her. I am here on another matter." He stood with his arms behind his back, a frown marring his features. "I need to speak with ye and Cormac."

Taking Sorcha to the edge of the lists, Duncan released her. Tossing off his glove and reaching for his sword, he asked, "Why is my gut telling me I will not like what ye have to say?"

"Go and wash. We will talk after the meal. I have made my greetings to Cormac and requested his presence with ye."

Grabbing his plaid, Duncan tossed it over his bare shoulder, walking away from Cathal. Coming to a halt at the entrance, he paused and turned around. "Tell me this, does it entail Brigid?"

Cathal stroked his beard before answering, walking over to where Duncan stood. "The sword, your quest, all of it *entails* Brigid. She is bonded to ye until the day of reckoning. Ye cannot keep fighting this. Trust in the fae." Placing a hand on his shoulder he gave it a firm shake. "Do ye understand my words, Duncan?"

"Oh, aye, I ken your words, until the day the Fenian warrior comes to take her!" he spat out. The wind whipped past, followed by a thundering boom.

"It seems ye still need to work on taming that angry beast of yours. I shall see ye at the evening meal." Shaking his head slowly, Cathal walked away from Duncan.

Leaning against the archway, Duncan closed his eyes. He had secured the walls around his heart with anger to block out the pain. And if he could not have Brigid…"Then I will *never* tame the beast," he growled, slamming his fist against the stone.

Chapter 32

"They wove a golden thread of time around their hearts, fearing they would separate from one another."

Laughter spilled out from the great hall, and the smell of food lured Duncan in like a woman. He did not know how hungry he was until the scents assaulted him, and his stomach responded in a fierce growl. Walking in, he saw the tables laden high as if it were a feast day. Then he remembered Cathal was here, and Cormac would indeed prepare a feast for the druid. It was not every day they had the great and mighty Cathal feasting at their table.

Music filtered from the corner and he smiled. It reminded Duncan of happier times when they celebrated the feast days together as one clan. "Feast days?" he muttered to himself. How could he be so blind? They were fast approaching the feast of Samhain. Strong magic always occurred on days such as these. Cathal had mentioned the day of reckoning. Would it happen then, and what would they have to encounter? Could it be possible?

Duncan's stomach growled again, and loudly. His steps quickened as he passed others in the great hall, and then he froze at the vision he saw before him. Sitting near the head of the table next to Cormac was the most bewitching woman he had ever laid eyes on.

"*Brigid?*" He croaked out.

Her dark amber hair framed her heart-shaped face and fell in a wild mass down her back. He had thought her beauty glorious in her strange clothing, but nothing could compare with her gown of dark emerald edged in gold trim, hugging her voluptuous form. No jewelry adorned her, and he thought none would do her justice, for she carried them in her eyes. Sitting next to her was Finn and Nell, and she laughed at something Nell said. He had never seen her laugh, and his breath caught in his chest. Her entire face lit up. Her laughter so infectious it spilled over to the young ones.

"By the Gods!" he whispered. "It is more than my heart that is bonded, Cathal."

"Sir Duncan, what are ye gaping at?" One of Cormac's men had come up behind him and shook him free from his thoughts.

The man cast his sight toward Brigid. "Oh aye, she is a bonny, bonny lass. Where did ye come upon her?"

Duncan flashed him a lethal look, one that let the man know his place when it came to Brigid. "I would hold your tongue when it comes to *my woman*," he snarled.

Holding up his palms, he stepped back. "Sorry, Sir Duncan. I did not ken she is your woman." Bowing slightly, he proceeded to walk away, taking his place at the far end of the table.

"Duncan, are ye going to stand there all night, or do ye plan on running a blade through one of my men?" Cormac arched a brow and waved him on over.

Duncan strode over to where Finn was sitting on Brigid's left and nodded for him to move down. Finn sighed, reluctantly moving out of the way. Duncan placed a hand on his shoulder. "Thank ye, Finn."

The glow in the young boy's face broke into a huge smile. "Gladly, Sir Duncan. I was keeping your place so no other would sit next to Lady Brigid." His chest puffed out proudly as he spoke.

Duncan cocked his head to the side in question. "*Lady* Brigid?"

"Oh, aye, Sir Duncan," Nell interrupted. "Lady Brigid has come from a faraway land with odd clothing and language. She *must* be a lady!" she exclaimed, causing Finn to nod in agreement.

A chuckle emerged from Duncan, and he turned to Brigid, "*Lady* Brigid, may I sit next to ye?"

"Yes, Duncan." Brigid waited until he was seated then leaned close whispering, "And please don't call me lady. I'm not royalty."

Her curls had touched his face, and he had to fight the urge to grab a fistful and bury his face within. Giving her a full smile, he asked, "Are ye sure? Ye *have* been touched by the great dragon, my lady."

Her eyes went round, and she placed her hand gently on one of his. "No, Duncan," she said softly," I'm just Brigid O'Neill from a land your people have yet to encounter."

The shock of her hand on his sent sensual waves throughout his body, and the blush creeping into her face told him she was feeling the same. Taking his other hand and covering hers, his eyes glowing blue silver as he spoke low. "It is of no importance from what land ye came from, Brigid. Ye are descended from the fae and ye are *my* lady."

When Duncan heard a loud cough coming from Cormac, he scowled at him. Must the man watch his every move?

Standing, Cormac took his mug of ale and held it aloft saying, "A toast, and welcome to the great druid Cathal, who honors us this evening with his presence here at our table."

All had agreed with a raucous cry of aye, pounding the wooden table with cheers.

Cathal stood, bowing his head slightly to Cormac. "It is I who welcomes your hospitality and gives thanks for this feast." Raising his hands out toward everyone, he continued, "Blessings of light and love my friends."

"Let us feast!" proclaimed Cormac.

Brigid's senses were on overload at the food before her. She had never seen so much food all at once. The scene was something out of one of her history books or a movie, down to the lavender scented rushes on the floor.

Slouched down, next to Cormac's chair was a Scottish deerhound. Every now and then, it would raise its large brown eyes, pleading for some scraps. Bending low, Brigid whispered, "If you're good, perhaps one small treat when I'm finished."

"Do not start to fatten up old Fergus. He has a way with the ladies when he gives them those looks." Cormac winked at her, as he took a knife and stabbed into a platter of onions and cucumbers in some kind of sauce.

The food made her mouth water, but it was the man next to her, who made her blood boil. The moment her eyes saw him, she had to stifle a gasp. Of course, he had marched into the hall with his ever-present scowl, making Finn move from his place by her side. However, in afterthought, he did say kind words to him.

No, it was a freshly shaved Duncan who had her staring in awe. How could he be any more handsome? Looking at the cleft in his chin only added more to his striking features. That he had bathed was evident in the smell of herbal soap mixed with his scent. His dark glossy locks shimmered in the candlelight as they fell in waves to his shoulder. There was the one lock that was forever slipping over one eye, tempting her to touch and play.

He had an intoxicating effect on her senses.

The tunic he wore was deep blue, threaded with gold and red and belted with leather. The belt had the gold clasp of a dragon, similar to his torc, which gleamed brightly from his neck. Duncan had chosen not to lace up his tunic, keeping it open. Whereas, not only could she see the torc, but his dark curling chest hairs. The only other item he wore were his boots, not the colored hose that some of the men wore. There were those who wore their plaids, and others wore chain mail.

For her, there was only one man who stood apart—*Duncan.*

"Are ye going to eat or stare at my face all evening?" Duncan asked, holding some kind of meat in front of her face.

Her tongue was stuck to the roof of her mouth and all she could do was nod her head. She always went to mush at the sound of his husky burr.

"Open then." A lusty look shone in his eyes.

Brigid complied. As he placed the piece of meat past her lips into her mouth, her tongue touched against his fingers, and she heard him groan. Closing her eyes at the pleasurable sensation of the meat, she sighed with satisfaction. Upon opening her eyes, she watched as Duncan placed the two fingers he used for her meat into his mouth, licking them clean.

"Tasty indeed." He smiled devilishly. "What shall ye try next?"

Brigid grabbed her mug of ale and drank fully. Setting it back down she didn't know where to begin. As her eyes roamed the table she asked, "What *is* all of this?"

"Well, ye have tasted quail, roasted with apples. Over there on the larger trencher is roasted lamb. Cabbage is in the bowls on either side of the salmon with dill sauce." Duncan leaned close and his mouth gently brushed against her ear as he spoke. "The salmon dish is a favorite of Cathal's, so no one will touch it, until they know he has."

Brigid closed her eyes at the sensation of his breath across her skin. "And the breads," she whispered.

"Och, lass, ye have a fondness for the breads, too? The one nearest ye is an oat and almond bread with honey for dipping, and yonder by Finn is rosemary bread." Duncan reached for the oat and almond bread, tearing off a large portion. Dunking it into the honey, he popped the piece into his mouth and finished by licking the drops of honey from his fingers.

"Moira kens I have a weakness for the bread and honey," he said, giving her a wink.

"Well, that makes two of us Duncan. I love honey, too."

"Do ye lass?" Ripping off another chunk, he dipped it into the bowl of honey. Brigid opened her mouth to receive the delectable piece along with the taste of his fingers. Again, she watched as he licked his fingers clean, and her cheeks flamed, feeling the blush extending down her neck.

"Here, let me fill your cup with some of Cormac's elderberry wine. He calls himself an expert with this batch." Duncan proceeded to fill her cup and then placed more food on her plate.

Brigid glanced around at the great hall rife with food, drink, music, and much merrymaking, that she almost forgot she was not a part of this time and place and pain stabbed at her heart.

"Bloody balls, Nell!" yelled Finn, as he removed the knife from the sleeve of his tunic. Laughter spilled out from the others, and Duncan placed a firm hand on the lad's shoulder.

"Dinnae cry, ye baby. I was just after some apple pieces from the inside of the bird," scoffed Nell, as she made to collect her knife from Finn.

"Whoa, Nell, I think you'd better let Finn help you," said Brigid, shocked not only by Finn's language, but also of the feisty young girl. "Come, Nell." She leaned back away from Duncan and stretched out her hand. "Sit by me. Then we'll ask Sir Duncan to pass us the food we want." Brigid gave Duncan a wink.

"Humph!" Nell muttered, as she took Brigid's outstretched hand and placed herself between Duncan and Brigid. Wiggling herself in, she bent across the table and stuck out her tongue at Finn, causing Finn to roll his eyes in disgust.

Duncan started heaping food on to her plate and Brigid asked, "How old are you, Nell?"

"Ooooh, thank ye, Sir Duncan," cooed Nell as she speared the apples with her recovered knife. Munching on some apples, she swallowed and gave Brigid a wide smile, saying, "I am seven summers."

"You are very brave, Nell, not to be scared of Finn. How old is he?" Brigid asked, taking another bite of the quail and apples.

Puffing her chest out, she exclaimed, "Och, Lady Brigid, I'm not afraid of anything." Then giving another glare at Finn stated, "He is only nine winters."

Glancing over the top of Nell's head, Brigid mouthed to Duncan, "Are their parents here at the table?"

Duncan's mouth went grim, and he shook his head in a negative response. "I will tell ye later."

Brigid watched their bantering, as the two youngsters kept giving one another smirks and wondered what could have happened to their parents. Was it possible they were orphans or part of the household staff? She did not think they were the staff, since they wouldn't be allowed to sit here. Yet, she did see a few of the help earlier eating and speaking with Cathal at another table.

The feasting continued with song and bardic stories bringing the meal to an end. However, merriment continued as many told their own stories in song, each one getting louder than the next. Nell had fallen asleep, curled up in Brigid's lap. As she stroked Nell's mass of golden curls, it reminded Brigid of her own ringlets. Glancing up, she saw Finn and Duncan playing a game of dice, and Cathal had moved to the corner of the hall in a battle of chess with Cormac.

Brigid smiled. All was well with her world, and for the moment, she would pretend she belonged in this place and time.

Chapter 33

"Harsh words are like a stone skipping across the surface of water. You'll never know how far their reach will extend."

One of the women had come and taken Nell from Brigid's lap. When she stood, she swayed a bit. Grabbing a hold of the table, Brigid realized that too much ale mixed with elderberry wine was not a good combination.

Duncan grasped her elbow to steady her as his other arm came around her waist. "Bonny Brigid, too much merry making?" He chuckled low into her ear.

"*I think*...I just need to lie down." Brigid looked up into his eyes.

"Och, Duncan, have ye given the lass too much to drink already?" Matilda stood on the other side of the table giving him a suspicious look. Walking around it, she placed her arm within Brigid's. "The poor lass has had too much excitement. Here, let me take her to her room. Cathal is waiting for ye in Cormac's chambers."

A look of disappointment creased his brow, but he knew Matilda was right. Brigid was beyond exhausted, and Duncan felt guilty from plying her with drink and lusty looks. What he ought to do was gather her in his arms and tuck her into her bed. Instead, he took her hand brushing his lips gently across, saying, "Go with

Matilda. She will help ye to your chambers." Glancing back at Matilda, he gave her a mock salute over his heart, as he turned to leave.

"Cormac told me to tell you to fetch the *uisge beatha*, too."

Grabbing the ewer as he passed by the end of the table, he waved to her over his head.

"Whisky?" asked Brigid, clutching at her head again.

"Tsk,tsk. Come lass, we shall make the slow steps together. This way you can tell me about yourself and how ye found the big bad wolf known as Duncan Mackay."

Brigid giggled. "Big bad wolf? I believe under his tough skin is a lap dog."

Matilda threw back her head and laughed fully. "Brigid, lass, how is it ye have known him only a few days, and yet it seems ye have grasped his soul?"

Both women smiled as they made their way slowly to Brigid's chambers. The room was warm from the fire and the bed of furs beckoned, but she fought the sleep that was claiming her eyelids.

"Tell me, Matilda, how long you have known Duncan?" she asked, sighing the moment she sat in one of the large chairs by the fire.

"Hmmm, I've known the lad since his birth. A strong loud wailing did he give when entering this world." Gathering a blanket around Brigid, Matilda went over to a small table where there was a pitcher and poured some liquid into it. Taking a packet from the pouch around her belt, she took a couple of pinches and placed them in the mug.

"Here lass, drink this. 'Tis some water mixed with

herbs. It will make your head feel better."

Brigid sniffed the contents. "Ummmm, peppermint?"

"Aye. It will help ye."

"Thank you, Matilda, water is definitely what I need. The elderberry wine is potent, sorta sneaks up on you." She sipped the cool water feeling refreshed within moments.

Taking a seat across from Brigid, Matilda asked, "Lass, ye have a strange mix of words, verra much like English. Where do ye hail from?"

Brigid snorted, "From a land far, far away."

"Not of this time and space." Matilda's eyes bored into her.

Her eyes went wide at Matilda's words. "How do you know?"

Chuckling Matilda took her hand, leaning forward. "I ken ye have the mark of the great dragon on your shoulder, *and* your coming was foretold. We did not understand the stories until now."

Placing her hand on her shoulder, Brigid understood there were only two people that saw the mark; one was Duncan, the other Sienna. "Right." Realization dawning. "So-o-o how *many* people know that I'm not from...this time?

"It is only myself. Sienna believes ye have been touched by the fae." Matilda gave her hand a squeeze and sat back in her chair. "A great storm is coming, Brigid, and I fear for ye and Duncan."

"But why, Matilda? We don't even understand what is to happen." Casting a glance over to another table, she saw the sword. Duncan had brought it up to her room, awaiting the time when she would turn it over to him. "I don't have one clue what I'm supposed to do with it." Pointing a finger in the direction of the sword, her words were one of frustration. "Do I hand it over to him now? Or am I to wait until he is healed? Actually, if you think about it, will he *ever* be healed? Tell me, Matilda, what *do* the stories say?"

Matilda hesitated briefly. "A love will come through time and space..."

Brigid finished the sentence. "To right a wrong within this place."

"Then ye understand the words. Ye must follow your heart," she stated, gently tapping her fist against her chest.

Brigid placed her fingers on either side of her temple to massage the ache. "My heart was lost the moment I stepped through the stones, and to follow it would do no good. When this is over, I will have to return." With a sigh, Brigid tilted her head back and gazed upwards.

"Brigid, ye followed your heart for a purpose. In truth, the Duncan who set out on his quest is not the same man I saw this night."

A blush crept up Brigid's face, and she feared that Matilda knew that she had slept with him. Is that what she meant? Only one way to find out, she thought. "How so?"

A warm chuckle came forth before Matilda answered, "Lass, Duncan Mackay left without so much as a farewell to any. The man has not uttered more than a few words in over twelve moons—more like grunts and nods." Brigid's eyes went wide, but Matilda kept speaking. "There is a change in Duncan, and *all* have noticed."

Then realization dawned, and she asked, "Matilda, what did happen that night, and *where* are his brothers?"

"Och, Brigid, I dinnae ken what happened, only that his sword was the one that killed his sister, Margaret. Duncan has not spoken about the darkness of that night." She pointed a finger adding, "I ken that is a question ye must ask him."

Brigid's smile was sad. "Oh, I've asked, and it was followed by thunder and wind. All I needed was rain and lightning."

Matilda nodded. "Aye, his temper is the worst of all the brothers. Ye dinnae want to be around when he fully unleashes it." Shuddering, she took her shawl and hugged it tighter around her arms. "Ye ken his power is the elements of sky, and it is powerful. He mastered it verra young and was a bit of a show-off. Angus would threaten to squelch the rain with his power of fire, or worse tell their father." She gazed off, remembering the days as if they were yesterday.

"Hmmm, and Stephen's gift is visions and water, Alastair is the earth, or you call it the great mother, but what about Margaret? Did she have any special gifts?" asked Brigid.

Nodding her head, smiling, Matilda replied, "Margaret was a special child. There had not been a female born in over a thousand years. Her birth so special it was foretold by the druids. Margaret's gift was that of a healer linked directly to the fae. She also possessed the Book of the Beginning." Tears glistened in Matilda's eyes as she continued, "Her death was a great loss to the clan *and* the fae." Spreading her hands across her knees, she smoothed her dress, then bowed her head in silence.

It was Brigid's turn to give comfort. Reaching out, she placed her hand on one of Matilda's. "I take it her gift was very unique, but what is the Book of the Beginning?"

Raising her head slowly, Matilda angled her head with a look of questioning on her face. "Ye do not ken the *Book of the Beginning*?"

"No, I don't. Why would I?"

She let out a soft sigh. "The Book of the Beginning, or as some call the *Awakening*, tells the story of the fae and how they came to us. Only two have been chosen to hold the book; one was Margaret, the other was from an ancient clan from Eirinn. Her name was Deidra Ui Neill."

Gasping, Brigid drew her hand back from Matilda's.

"Ye ken who she was?" A slow smile spread across Matilda's face.

"Yes, I do," whispered Brigid. Swallowing she continued, her voice gaining more strength. "The *Ui Neill* is the descendant of Niall of the Nine Hostages who lived around 400 AD and from where the O'Neill, *my family* is descended from."

"Aye. Now ye realize why they call ye *Lady* Brigid. They believe ye were sent from the fae, and ye are their hope, not only for Sir Duncan, but for themselves, too. Ye will understand what to do when the door opens."

Brigid grimaced not understanding her words. "Yet, Margaret is dead," she said softly.

"Aye, she is. Was this foretold? Nae, but perhaps from this, another thread of life takes the place of hers."

Matilda stood, rubbing the small of her back. Walking over to Brigid, she placed a kiss on her forehead. "Rest, lass."

"Thank you, Matilda."

Brigid watched as Matilda left her chambers. Standing, she went over and curled up on the stone seat by the window. Tucking her feet underneath her to keep warm, she gazed out at the night sky amazed at how many stars she could see. They lit the night with such brilliance, like diamonds of light glittering against black velvet. The moon was waxing and in a few weeks, it would be full. It illuminated the landscape below casting a dance of shadows.

She wanted—no needed to see Duncan. Visions of his honeyed fingers in her mouth sent chills of desire coursing through her. As much as her desire set her soul afire, she truly wanted to know what happened the night Margaret died. Remembering the words of Cathal, how he mentioned an evil was present that night, filled her mind with more questions.

Resting her chin on her knees, she had hoped to heal Duncan with her love. She prayed that was happening, but he turned away from her in the cave when he saw the mark on her shoulder. She lightly touched the mark with her left hand and then her head shot straight up.

"*Love*?" She gasped. Did she honestly love this man? He was a warrior, a Dragon Knight, scarred and tainted with the blood of his sister. She had *feelings*, but love? Was this part of his journey, and she, the instrument? Why would the Guardian show him love, only to rip them apart?

"Oh Goddess, please if you can hear me, I will

need your help when I go back to my own time, since I believe I have lost my heart to Duncan Mackay. I ask you to heal it, because I surely know it will shatter to pieces when I leave him." Brigid lowered her head back onto her knees, keeping a watch on the night stars.

****

Duncan watched the sleeping beauty curled peacefully by the window and marveled at how his body reacted every time he saw her. He did not intend to come to her chambers, but his feet carried them to her door of their own will. Just standing against the oak door, his body responded with a force to take and bury himself deep within her again.

He feared it was more than just a simple possession, and it grew deeper each day they spent in each other's company. She wove a thread around his soul, healing the ache with that thread.

Rubbing his hand against his face, he sighed deeply.

In his meeting, Cathal had revealed to them about his vision of an evil growing stronger each day—one which brought death. His vision could not show him whose death, but it was someone here within the castle.

Then Duncan mentioned the riders he saw, thinking them MacFhearguis, though each voiced their concern over what clan was stomping through the glen. The talk of reivers was mentioned; however, Cormac did not think he had lost any cattle. After much discussion and *uisge beatha*, they decided to take a few men at dawn's first light and search the surrounding hills.

Stepping away from the door, Duncan strolled over to Brigid and gently touched her curls. "Och, lass, what ye do to me. If only circumstances were different. Aye, I would make ye mine, and mine alone," he muttered softly.

Duncan gently lifted her into his arms, her head rolling against his shoulder, as a soft moan escaped her lips. Laying her tenderly on the furs and fighting the urge to join her, he brushed a kiss on her brow.

"Bonny, bonny Brigid, what have ye done to me?"

Walking over to the window, he bent and retrieved a stray ribbon that had come loose from her hair. Bringing it to his face, he inhaled her scent and then cast his gaze out into the night sky, speaking softly, "Oh great Danu, give me the chance to right this wrong that I have done." Glancing back at her, he kissed the ribbon and tucked it inside the top of his boot, realizing now he should stay far, far away from her.

Chapter 34

"For time has many doors and to choose only one will cause one to stand alone and bound to none."

Brigid woke instantly from a deep slumber when she heard a resounding crash of a door. Sitting upright, she looked around in confusion at her surroundings, until she remembered she had tumbled through to the thirteenth century and was now residing in a medieval castle.

She couldn't recollect the last time she had slept so well. She frowned, recalling her last thoughts were sitting over by the window. How in the hell did she get into bed? Rubbing the sleepiness from her eyes, she peered at the small creature digging its claws into her gown.

"Damn. I fell asleep in my gown." Which was twisted around her legs. Gingerly plucking the wee kitten's claws from the material, she saw Nell was standing next to the bed tapping her foot.

"Yes, Nell?" Brigid mumbled wearily. Looking at the kitten, she noticed it only had one eye.

"The sun is full high in the sky, and ye are still abed. I brought Whiskers to wake ye."

"*What?*" Gathering from the sun streaming into the room and Nell's version of full high, Brigid took it as being noontime.

"Well, thank you Nell *and* Whiskers." Dropping the tabby carefully onto the floor, she gathered her dress and got out of bed.

"Matilda told us not to wake ye, but I did not want to wait."

"Well, you know, Nell, I'm grateful you did. I think I've slept enough." Looking around, Brigid saw a pitcher and bowl and prayed there was fresh water to wash the last remnants of sleep away. Seeing that there was, she splashed the cold water on her face, then noticed another dress was laid across the chair with a woolen plaid wrap. Saying a silent prayer to whoever had been so kind, she turned back to Nell.

"Do you think it's possible to get something to eat, Nell?"

Nell started biting the upper part of her lip. Brigid became concerned until she remembered Nell had been banned from the kitchens.

"Why don't you wait for me, and we'll both go to the kitchens. I'm sure Moira won't mind if you're with me."

Puffing out her chest in mock display, Nell exclaimed, "Aye, Lady Brigid!" Then scooping up Whiskers, she went over to the window seat with a pillow and waited.

****

It seemed unusually quiet, except for the constant chatter of Nell, as they made their way toward the kitchens. Brigid kept questioning the direction in which they were descending, but Nell told her this was indeed the way. "How can you possibly tell which corridor leads you in the right direction?"

Nell tugged at Brigid's hand. "This way, Lady

Brigid."

Pushing a large wooden door open, the smells of the kitchen assaulted Brigid. Smiling, they stepped into the warm place.

Moira cast her eyes at Nell, a frown creasing her brow, but kept her mouth shut when she saw she was with Brigid.

"I know it's late, but would it be possible to get something to eat, Moira? I apologize for oversleeping. If you just show me where everything is, I will prepare my own meal."

"Och, my Lady—nae!" A look of shock registered on Moira's face, and she waved her hands about, causing Brigid to blanch.

"But I just want something to break my fast Moira?" pleaded Brigid.

"Aye, Lady Brigid, and I will see to it. What would my laird think if he came in here and saw ye preparing your own meal? Tsk, tsk." Moira grabbed Brigid's elbow and placed her near the hearth. Mumbling under her breath about strange talking lasses, she ladled some soup into a bowl, bringing it over to Brigid.

"Let me get ye some bread and cheese, too." She bustled to the other side of the kitchen.

Brigid gave Nell a quick smile, patting her hand on the chair next to her, indicating for her to sit down.

Leaning close to Brigid, Nell said in hushed voice, "Do ye think ye could ask for extra cheese and bread, Lady Brigid?"

"Are you hungry, too?"

"Nae," whispered Nell. "I need to feed my family." She peeked around to make sure no one was listening.

"Your *family*? I'm confused, Nell." Brigid recalled

Duncan mentioning that Nell and Finn did not have parents. Did she have siblings?

Grabbing the girl's hand, she bent low and spoke softly. "Tell me, Nell, where is your family?"

Again, Nell cast a glance over her shoulder before answering, "I will take ye after your meal."

Moira came bustling back in with a trencher of cheese, bread, apples, and a bowl of something that looked oddly like modern-day potatoes. Setting them down, she reached for a jug, pouring some ale into a cup. "There ye are, Lady Brigid. If ye be needing more, just let me know."

"Thank you, Moira, but I truly wish you would let me help."

"Oh, but ye have."

"I have? How?"

Moira placed a gentle hand on Brigid's cheek and her eyes gleamed with kindness as she spoke. "Och, Lady Brigid, ye have brought our Sir Duncan back from the darkness. There is light back in his eyes." With a smile she added, "We all can see the way he looks at ye, too."

Brigid swallowed hard, as if a stone was lodged in her throat, making her unable to say anything in response to her kind words. Instead, she gave Moira a warm smile.

They spent the remaining time in the kitchen in hushed silence. Brigid shared some apples with Nell, but for the most part watched as the girl gathered most of the food, folding it within her own plaid. Brigid requested more before they left to visit Nell's family.

Making their way out of the Great Hall, Brigid wondered what the rest of the castle looked like, and she told herself an exploration was in order. How could one not want to explore a thirteenth century medieval castle? And she already had a guide...Nell.

Stepping outside, there was a chill in the air and the sky partially overcast. Breathing deeply, Brigid felt as if she was inhaling Scotland. She could see the mists threading around one of the towers. It was the most magical thing she truly loved about this place.

Hugging her shawl more tightly around her, she followed Nell, careful not to step in any horse droppings. Cormac's men would nod as she passed or give her a smile. She could hear the clang of steel nearby, the noise coming from the lists. That would be another sight to see. *Oh yes, seeing Duncan in the lists.* He didn't go there this morning, since he and Cormac went out early beyond the castle walls. Moira had been kind enough to share this information.

In her heart, she had wanted Duncan to come to her bed during the night. He had teased her relentlessly with his fingers at their meal last night. Her thoughts returned to the glade, and she blushed just remembering. Touching her lips with her fingers, she whispered his name.

Passing by the stables at the end of the bailey, Brigid saw Finn with one of the horses. She caught his eye and waved a greeting, as he did the same.

"We're almost there, Lady Brigid," she heard Nell saying as they continued out a hidden entrance beyond the stables. Their journey took them through a clump of small trees where a small structure stood. It reminded Brigid of a storage shed, but made of stone.

"What is this place, Nell?"

"It is where my family lives," her smile beaming.

"Stay here, until I announce ye." Pushing the door open, which squeaked loudly, Nell, disappeared inside.

Brigid was horrified.

How in the blazes could Cormac, *or* Duncan, let this child and her family stay in such a small place? It didn't even have a fireplace, only two narrow slits serving as windows. She thought them men of honor and kindness, well at *least* Cormac. "I'll give you a piece of my mind when you both return." Brigid squelched her fury when Nell popped her head out.

"It is ready, Lady Brigid. Ye may come inside."

Brigid stepped inside, waiting for her eyes to adjust to the half-darkness, with only a small torch lit against the wall. Glancing at Nell's family, her eyes went wide. Tucked in the corner on some hay was a rabbit without an ear. On a table in a sorely fashioned wooden cage missing its door, was an owl, its wing bandaged. On the opposite corner, a mother cat and her kittens were sleeping. Sitting with a regal air about him, was a sheep dog, missing one of his front legs.

"This is your *family*?" Brigid exclaimed.

"Oh, aye!" Her smile wide and beaming as if she had brought them into the world.

Then realization dawned on Brigid. Nell was banned from the kitchens for stealing cakes and other items because she was feeding them. This was her family—a family of strays who were all under the same roof, and a quiet bunch, too. Not a peep out of them when she entered. She was positively stunned.

She turned toward Nell. "Where did you find them?"

Nell shoulders slumped slightly. "I just came upon them. They are lost and have no kin." She moved to the owl. "His name is Feathers. I found him in the stables." Moving next to the rabbit, she gently lifted it into her arms, placing a small kiss on its head. "I do not ken the story of her lost ear, but I have named her Faith."

"Do you take care of them by yourself?" Brigid asked softly.

"Some days Finn helps me to get food, but aye, I tend to them myself."

"Who is your guard dog?" Brigid noticed he placed himself in front of Nell, as if protecting her. She thought it best to stay where she was.

Tucking the rabbit back down on the straw, she gave the dog a fierce hug, burying her face into his fur. "This is Cuchulainn. He saved my life."

She had to hold back her smile at the thought of Nell naming her dog after a Celtic hero. Nodding her head toward the mother cat, she asked, "What's wrong with the family in the corner?"

"Och, Midnight is blind, but she needed a place to have her kittens."

"And how did Cuchulainn save your life?" Brigid saw the far off look in Nell's eyes, thinking that perhaps she shouldn't have asked the question.

Nell sighed, "It was night, and was fierce raining. I was lost. The wind kept pushing me toward the edge of the mountain. I dinnae ken where I was, and I slipped, my legs hanging over the edge." Nell nuzzled Cuchulainn again. "I was screaming, and then I felt something pull me away from the edge." She looked into Cuchulainn's eyes as she scratched his ears. "I stayed with him all night, huddled against a tree until morning."

If Brigid was shocked before she entered the house,

she was beyond that now. How Nell managed to keep a mixture of bird and animal at peace with each other was incredible. She was tending to their wounds, as if she were a healer. Then a thought occurred to Brigid. Where were her parents? Duncan never did have the chance to explain, and she chewed on the thought. She didn't want to ask Nell, for fear it would cause her pain.

Brigid continued watching as Nell soothed and spoke to each one of her *family,* placing small portions of food nearby and checking to make sure each had water in their tiny bowls. Cuchulainn silently followed at her heels.

Returning to stand next to Brigid, she grasped her hand. With a look of pleading in her eyes, she said, "Promise me ye will not speak of this with *anyone*, Lady Brigid."

Brigid bent down to her level, immediately hearing a small growl from Cuchulainn. "I give you my word, Nell, I will hold your secret safe in my heart." Then she turned and spoke to Cuchulainn, "I, too, give my word to take care of your mistress, for however long I shall be at Castle Creag."

Nell released her grip on Brigid's hand and hugged her tightly, whispering in her ear, "Och, thank ye."

Cuchulainn gave two short barks, then proceeded to place kisses on their faces. Fits of laughter burst out from both of them.

"I think Cuchulainn likes ye, Lady Brigid."

"Good! I don't think I want to be his enemy." Brigid gave him a scratch behind his ear and he rewarded her with more kisses.

Chapter 35

"Echoes of the silence—a soothing tonic to the chaos and cries of battle."

"Hells bells!" Brigid muttered, as she pricked her finger for the tenth time in an hour.

Nell giggled in a corner tending to her own stitching. Brigid tossed aside the panel she was working on in sheer frustration. Raising her arms over her head and stretching, she peered out at the gray sky. The weather had changed from an unseasonably warm one, to colder, crisper days feeling more like autumn in the Highlands. The mists descended over the mountains and folded gently down around them, curling their way around the castle and making their way to the valley below.

It had been three long days and no word of Duncan and Cormac. She knew they would be gone for a few days, but she desperately missed him. It wasn't as if he was packing a cell phone and could call and let her know they were fine. No, she had to wait patiently for any news.

She passed the time without anything to do, which caused her to become restless. No one would let her help with anything. Sienna was forever fussing over her, and Moira kept preparing meals with the help of the other women. She kept insisting she could be of assistance, but Moira would always shoo her away. Seeking out Matilda, she was informed by one of the men that she had gone foraging in the surrounding forest for herbs and such.

Looking in on the library proved just as frustrating, since most of the texts were in Latin. When she was about to tear her hair out, or worse—go to the stables and fetch a horse, one of the ladies gave her a sampler. It was part of a larger tapestry and the woman happily showed her some simple stitches. Brigid thought this would occupy her, except it was not going well at all.

The small bright light in her world the last few days had been Nell. She had followed her everywhere, and Brigid could not figure out if it was because she feared she would tell someone about her family of animals, or if she just wanted to be around her. It didn't matter to Brigid which one it was, since she had grown very fond of Nell. As soon as Duncan returned, she would inquire into Nell's story.

Casting her gaze back at her stitching, she knew she could not endure another moment with the panel. Turning to Nell, she asked, "Do you think we could go find something to eat? I don't know about you, but I'm famished just doing all this work."

Nell placed her panel on a chair and walked over to Brigid. She picked up Brigid's panel studying the piece with an expert eye. "Och, Mistress Megan will not be happy with these stitches, Lady Brigid." Then with a shrug of her shoulders, she tossed it back down. "She can finish the rest. I'm hungry, too."

Brigid gathered up her mending, placing it on a large table. She went over and opened the door. "Saucy little girl," she mumbled.

Nell had become braver in the past few days and somehow Brigid thought it was because the girl had a partner in crime to her thievery. Brigid had been taking more than her normal portions at each mealtime and giving them secretly to either Nell, or to Finn. He would grumble and roll his eyes, until Brigid had given him a glare one morning. From that moment on, he had been on his best behavior.

Stepping out of the chambers, Brigid waited for Nell and then suddenly asked, "Do you think you could show me around the castle before we eat?" The thought of exploring this medieval castle had been in her thoughts the past few days.

"Lady Brigid, this is a big castle." Nell gestured with her arms outstretched.

Brigid bit the inside of her cheek to keep from laughing. "Yes, I know, but I would just like to take a look around."

Nell pursed her lips, a frown creasing her brow before replying, "I'll take ye to a special place."

Taking Brigid's hand, she led her down the corridor. Instead of descending the stairs, she twisted left, going down a hallway lit dimly with torches. They continued on their exploration and the pathway became narrow in places, finally opening out.

Nell released Brigid's hand. "It is the chambers where they keep some of the swords and other weapons."

"Swords?" a shocked Brigid asked. "Nell, what made you think I would be interested in this room?"

A look of exasperation shown on her face and rolling her eyes, she replied, "Lady Brigid, ye have a *sword* in your chambers. I ken ye like them, so this was

247

the first place ye would want to see."

Smiling, Brigid said, "You truly amaze me, Nell. Let's see what's inside, shall we?"

Pushing open the door, Brigid stepped into the most spectacular room of weapons she had ever seen.

She had marveled at the swords all the men were carrying, and now she was in a room full of broadswords of various sizes. Shields hung against one side of the wall, and turning slowly, she saw several pieces of full chain mail, including helmets. Brigid reached out and gingerly touched the links on the mail and shuddered. This room was living history, and she was smack in the middle of it. It was positively freezing and a sliver of light came through a narrow window, casting an eerie effect on the weapons.

"Outstanding," she whispered, moving from one item to the next, picking up a dirk along the way. The handle was made of wood depicting horses, its artistry breathtaking. This room spoke to her in a way that made her nerves sizzle.

"Are ye done touching the swords, Lady Brigid? I'm mighty hungry." Nell was propped on a stool watching her.

Brigid sighed, "Yes, Nell. I'm ready." Taking her hand, she squeezed it, saying, "Thank you for showing me this room. Perhaps one day we can come back."

"Nae, *ye* can come back. 'Tis always too cold in here."

"Yes, it is!" Blowing on her hands and rubbing them fast to warm them, she gathered Nell's and left the magnificent room of steel.

They made their way through the corridors to the kitchens, and came to a halt. Baskets and baskets of plums were on the working table and on the floor. Moira had her arms across her chest and her face was scarlet as if she had just finished yelling at someone. Nell started backing out, but Brigid clamped a hand on her back prodding her forward. Moira was still muttering in Gaelic when she saw them.

"Och, Lady Brigid, do not tell me ye want something to eat?" A look of horror swept across her features.

"Well, yes, we did."

Moira slumped down on a stool.

"Moira, what's the matter?" Brigid asked, placing a gentle hand on the woman's shoulder.

Her hands flew to the basket as she spoke. "He is not supposed to bring these here. 'Tis too early, and I have no help to start with the tarts." Taking a floured hand across her brow, she added, "I just heard the men are returning home." She then buried her head into her hands.

Brigid smiled, not fully understanding about the tarts, but happy Duncan was on his way back...safe.

"How soon, Moira?"

A groan escaped her lips. "By dawn."

"Well, then, Nell and I will lend a hand." Moira started to protest, but Brigid bent down and clasped both of her hands. "Please let me help, Moira. I would be honored to help you in your kitchens, and Nell will be by side at all times. She can lend a helping hand, too. Nothing would give me more joy at the moment, since you have been so very kind to me."

Moira took a few moments to consider Brigid's words. Nodding slowly, she lifted her head up. "There is much to do, and we might be here all night."

Brigid smiled. "I think I'm up for the challenge, since I'm much better in the kitchen than I am with stitching panels."

"Och, 'tis truth, Mistress Moira," lamented Nell.

Moira laughed and squeezed Brigid's hands in return. "Weel, let me get ye a smock, and we can start on these plums."

Chapter 36

"You can only fool your heart for so long before it drags you back home by the balls."

The silver gray light of dawn was waving its hand over the eastern sky as Duncan and Brandubh waited for the rest of the men to catch up with him. He had risen early, wanting to be alone with his thoughts. They had encountered not one person on their journey, but they had spied deserted camps and fires. He had cursed himself for not paying closer attention to the men he saw the same day he had come upon Brigid. All was lost to his vision once he saw her standing over that boulder.

He had hoped being apart from her would cool the fire burning in him, but nae. He could hardly wait to return, the anticipation evident in his loins. Again, he cursed himself for having touched her.

"By the hounds," he muttered. "Bad enough I've been cursed, now I'm cursing myself, too."

"Eager to return I see." Cormac was now at his side.

Both horses snorted as puffs of white smoke billowed out of them in the early morning chill. Duncan did not want to engage in conversation and kept his gaze on Castle Creag, his body taut.

Cormac's lips twisted and he shook his head.

"Duncan my friend, best ye take her quickly and frequently, since I'm tiring of your foul humor when…"

For the second time, Cormac never saw the fist coming as the blow knocked his head back. Shaking his head and rubbing a gloved hand over his face, he squinted as Duncan rode off.

"Duncan Mackay, if ye do that one more time, I will personally ask the fae myself if I can take your sword and slay ye."

The bloody bastard had to open up his mouth again, thought Duncan. If only he knew he had bedded her and not nearly enough. He rode Brandubh hard, whipping past pine branches as they smacked across his face, the sting adding to the vain attempt of controlling his raging emotions. The wind rushed past him, urging him to keep riding past Castle Creag, to go forth and never set eyes upon her again.

She was not his—*ever*! She would eventually return to her own time, and it would finally be over. It was only his lust confusing him.

Pulling hard on the reins, he brought Brandubh to a hard stop before they crossed over the bridge. "Argh," he growled, horse and man breathing hard.

There was only one thing to do. Stay completely away from Brigid O'Neill.

He would bunk with the men in the hall, and take his meals in the kitchens. During the day, he would seek out Cathal and scour the surrounding hills. Yes, this is what he would do.

Strangely, his new plan did nothing to ease his mind.

Giving Brandubh a nudge with his thighs, he urged

him slowly forward into the castle and to the bailey. He saw Finn and dismounted, giving the reins over to him. "Thank you, Finn. Tend him well."

"I will Sir Duncan."

His stomach growled as he sought out the kitchens, nodding to a passing guard. There was no need to clean up if he was not going into the great hall. The smell of baking tarts hit him as he rounded the long corridor to the kitchens. Closing his eyes, he inhaled the aroma. "Damson tarts."

The plum and currant tarts were a favorite of his and he smiled inwardly knowing Moira had not only prepared them for the feast of Samhain, but for him, too. Samhain was fast approaching, but still over ten days out.

His stomach rumbled, and he quickened his pace.

Duncan's heart slammed inside his chest at the vision before his eyes when he entered the kitchens. One of the tables was laden with many tarts, but it was the scene in the corner by the fire, which undid him. He leaned against the wall for support and gazed on the sight. Brigid was slumped in a chair, plum juice staining her hands and mouth. In her lap curled up against her was Nell, both of whom were sound asleep. A slight snore escaped from Brigid, causing Duncan to smile.

The scene of hearth and home pulled at every emotion in his being and an ache akin to a lodestone gripped his heart, reminding him of what he could not possess. He pounded the stone behind him with the back of his head as he gazed up. "Why do ye gods punish me so?"

Perhaps, they were showing him what he had taken

from Margaret.

A sob from Nell brought Duncan out of his current thoughts, and he cautiously moved to where she lay. Brushing a feather light kiss on Brigid's head, he lifted Nell ever so gently out from her lap. Positioning her against his chest, another sob came forth. Duncan whispered soothing words in Gaelic as he took her out of the kitchens to her room.

All thoughts of food had banished.

****

Brigid's dream was again of Duncan, and when she woke, the air was filled with his scent. A sudden fear gripped her when she noticed Nell was no longer on her lap. Thinking he probably took her to her chambers, she relaxed.

Her body ached from peeling, chopping, and rolling out so many tarts. She had tried sending Nell off to bed, but the girl wouldn't listen and Brigid just did not have the heart to scold and send her off. Moira's heart had softened toward her so much so, that she pulled out a plaid and placed it by the fire for Nell to lay when she observed the slump in her shoulders and the countless yawns.

Stretching and rubbing the small of her back, she got up slowly and folded the plaid, placing it on the chair. "What I need is some black coffee and a shower." She stifled a yawn, deciding a partial bath would have to be sufficient.

Looking at all the tarts, she smiled, "Not bad for an evening."

Strolling out of the kitchens, she almost collided with a woman holding a basket in her arms. "Oh, I'm sorry. I didn't see you coming." Brigid moved back into the kitchens to let her pass.

"Och, 'tis fine, miss." She moved as if to set her basket down on the table and saw all of the tarts.

"Here, let me help you." Brigid moved some to another smaller table. "I don't recall meeting you."

The woman placed her basket of peas on the table. "I dinnae stay in the castle. I have a cottage not far from here. If ye dinnae mind me saying, ye sound verra much like the English."

Brigid thought she was very pretty. Dark curls framed her face, falling down below her waist. She was petite, compared to her. She often thought of herself as a large horse stomping through and longed to be small like the woman in front of her. She tossed her head, wondering where those thoughts came from.

"Well, I'm not. I come from a land farther than England."

The girls' eyes widened. "Do ye? Does this land have a name?"

Brigid surmised there would be no harm in telling, since her land would not be discovered for many centuries, but maybe it would be best to say Ireland. No, can't say that. It's called Eire. Should I give her my last name? "Oh, do stop thinking so much." She muttered under her breath.

"Pardon, miss?"

Shaking her head, Brigid replied, "Nothing. I come from Eirinn. My name is Brigid."

"Oh." The woman pursed her lips and gave her a curious look. "It is only across the water." She glanced at all the tarts. "Tell Moira I'll return before Samhain with more, and mushrooms, too." A small tinkling of laughter spilled out from her before she added, "I see

Moira is making tarts not only for the feast day, but for Duncan, too. If ye see Duncan, tell him to bring me a tart. I'll be waiting."

The woman scooted past Brigid, but before she was out of the kitchens, Brigid stepped forward, hands clenched by her sides and asked, "And what's your name?"

Tilting her head to the side and glancing back around at Brigid, she replied, "'Tis Morag."

Brigid watched as she sauntered down the corridor and out of sight. At that precise moment, all she wanted to do was grab any sharp object and fling it at her back.

"It'll be a cold day in hell before I tell him to bring *you* a tart."

Chapter 37

"The way was marked, the land was cleared, but without the compass they would lose their hearts in the abyss."

Four days had passed since the men had returned, and still no sign of Duncan. Brigid had filled her days with Nell and helping Moira. She looked for him at the evening meals, but he never showed. And no one seemed concerned by his absence.

Finn had kept them company in the evening and the bantering between him and Nell had provided her with some comic relief. Yet, as always, her heart and mind would wander to thoughts of Duncan.

What had happened? Did she say or do something? One moment the man was hot, the next cold and indifferent. She shrugged them off as nonsense. When she questioned Cormac one evening, he would only shrug saying most of the time Duncan kept mainly to himself.

By the fifth day, she truly thought he was spending time with that woman, Morag. She did mention her name to Moira, and when she saw the look of concern in Brigid's eyes, Moira told her not to fret. Duncan could not stand the woman, considering she had been with most of the men. The look of shock that registered across Brigid's face was enough for Moira to reassure her that she knows when a man lusts after a woman, and Duncan had eyes for only Brigid.

Still, it did nothing to quiet her nerves.

By the sixth day of not seeing him, Brigid decided she would rise early and check out the lists. Her nights were spent with little or no sleep, always awakening before dawn.

"If the man won't come to me, I'll go to him," she muttered, shivering when her feet hit the floor. Dressing warmly, she gathered her plaid tightly around her.

She crept quietly and slowly around the dark corridors. Nell had given her the tour of the castle with the approval of Cormac, and she had shown her several pathways out of the castle. Brigid was amazed at some of the corridors, which were illuminated with torches and tapestries. There even was one depicting the great dragon. Brigid smiled when she passed the tapestry, placing her hand gently over her mark. She was still stunned how much they worshiped the old ways here and questioned if there were any who believed in the new religion.

Passing the great hall, she noticed all was quiet. The men were absent, which meant they were either at the lists or out performing their duties. Heaving one of the great oak doors open, a blast of cold air greeted her, reminding her that autumn was definitely settling here in the Highlands.

Brigid took in a deep breath. "Ahhh, brisk Highland air, better than coffee."

Making her way slowly, fearing she would step in some slop or trip and fall, a noise caught her attention. Realizing it was only an owl, she let her eyes become accustomed to the darkness, and didn't see the man until she was practically in his arms.

"Ouch!" The man had firmly clasped both of her arms. "Hey, I'm sorry, but will you please release me!" she hissed.

"Nae."

The sound of his voice low and growling in that one word told Brigid all she needed to know.

"Duncan?"

"Aye?"

Again, the burr of his voice sent shivers down her body. "Where the blazes have you been?" She did not mean for the words to tumble out, but she was tired and frustrated.

The silence permeated the air around them and Brigid no longer felt cold, only warmth. She moved into his chest, which was bare and noticed he was wearing leather trews. How she had longed to see them on him. He was breathing hard, smelling of earth and all things primal that called out to her.

"Why do ye care?" He still kept his hands on her arms, his voice low, and threatening.

Brigid swallowed. What was wrong with him? Then taking her mouth, she brushed a soft kiss on his chest, causing a guttural moan to escape from his mouth, his grip intensifying. She tilted her head back up toward him. "I care, Duncan, perhaps I shouldn't, but I do. You'll have to deal with it."

His lips came crushing down on hers, the beast no longer holding back. Hands that were holding her at bay were all over her, kneading and fondling. She drew him in and caressed the tendons in his neck, twining her hands through his locks. His tongue was hot and probing. It was a kiss for her tired soul to melt into, leaving her mouth burning with fire.

With dawn approaching, the shimmer of the morning light danced over the hills and touched them. Duncan pulled back from ravishing her mouth and saying a low curse, scooped her up in his arms, and headed for the entrance. Crashing through the door, he kept walking toward the stairway.

Brigid's breathing was labored, and laying her head against him, she let him carry her. She didn't think her legs could remain steady even if he had put her down. They were headed straight to her chambers, and all she could think of was this aching need for another one of his soul searing kisses.

He placed her down when they came to her door. Shoving it open, he gently pushed her forward. Brigid turned around, but she saw he had moved over by the window. His hands were braced on the stone wall, and she could tell something was wrong.

Warning alarms went off within her. "What's wrong, Duncan?"

"I cannot be with ye," his tone one of steel.

Brigid reeled as if she had been slapped.

"Tell me why, Duncan?" she asked, trying hard to keep her voice steady.

Pushing away from the wall, he swung around to face her with eyes as cold as ice. Waving his hands in the air, he lashed out, "This cannae be! Ye are not mine, nor am I yours. I should have never touched ye." Taking his fist, he pounded the wall behind him. "Do not seek me out, Brigid." His face twisted with anger and thunder shook outside.

"What do you want from me?"

"Nothing," he answered.

"And your quest, Duncan?" she demanded, her heart pounding.

"Not yours to concern yourself with."

"Then what am I to do? Stay here for...*what*?"

He shrugged, cold emotion rolling off him.

Brigid's last thread of sanity snapped. "You bastard! This is *unbelievable*. Did you see me as a quick lay, easy for the taking? And now you regret it, because it might mean more?"

His silence was her answer.

Her fury boiling, she could not contain her next words. "Well, Duncan Mackay, I do care for you. More than you deserve and more than you will ever know. I *never* asked for any of this. But for some unfathomable reason, it did happen. Now you want to pretend that nothing happened between us, and you no longer need my assistance?"

He continued to glare at her.

"I see. My mistake," her voice laced with sarcasm. Pointing a finger at him, she threw the last out like a stone. "I am through with this crap!! You can work out your demons on your own."

Brigid stormed over to the table where the sword was laying. Shaking her head in frustration, she picked up the sword. Tears pricked her eyes, but she refused to let them fall.

He did not deserve her tears, only her wrath.

Walking back over to him, she held out the sword. "This is not my battle anymore, Duncan. You have made it very clear my services are no longer required." Shoving the sword into his chest, she glared right back at him. "Take it. It's yours. I'm done!"

Duncan stood like a statue, his eyes changing color

right before her. He refused to grasp the sword, so Brigid stepped back, letting it drop with a resounding thud on the wooden floor.

She shook her head and walked to the door. Before leaving, she spared a fleeting look over her shoulder, "The sword is now yours, Duncan. I am leaving to find a way back to my own time. If I have to seek out the great dragon, so be it. She can summon Conn to take me back..."

Brigid couldn't finish the sentence. Slamming the door open with such force, it crashed against the wall as she ran down the hall. She let the hot tears sting her cheeks, running hard and with deliberate intention of the entrance that she became lost within the corridors for the first time.

"Damn it!" Instead of finding the pathway descending the stairs, she came upon one with stairs leading upwards. The castle was a maze of too many halls and confusion overtook her senses.

What a fool she was. She had lost her heart and soul to this man.

"Which way do I go?" Leaning against the cool stone wall for support, she glanced up. She was drained emotionally and physically. All the previous days came crashing over her causing her to tremble.

Grabbing her dress, Brigid slowly made her way up the curved stairway. The path was narrow and dimly lit, but she stopped abruptly before an alcove. She hesitated briefly at the door, but her instincts told her to keep moving upwards.

"There must be at least fifty steps." Stopping to catch her breath, she looked back down. The thought occurred to her to go back the way she came, but the possibility of running into Duncan caused her stomach to flip. A stone lodged in her chest, and yelling loudly she uttered, "I'm not going to cry over you, Duncan Mackay!" Then with her burning rage and tears, she took to the stairs, wishing with all her might she could just click her heals and return to her own time.

Finally reaching the top, the biting cold whispered through the cracks in the door. She was at the parapet. Saying a silent prayer there was a way out on the other side of the door, Brigid thrust it open.

****

Duncan could not move. Her last words of seeking out Conn hit him like a punch to the gut. Is that not what he wanted? To stay away until such a time she would hand over the sword, and then send her back to her own time? Why then did he feel an aching loss? Looking at the sword near his feet, he bent slowly down to retrieve it. Somehow, it still did not feel like his, and he speculated if perhaps it ever would.

"Are ye going to stand there staring at that thing, or are ye going to go after her?" Matilda stood at the door, her hands clasped together.

"Do not get involved, Matilda." Duncan moved to leave Brigid's chambers, but Matilda put her hand out to stop him from passing.

"It is only an observation."

Sighing, he glanced up at the ceiling then back down at her. "What is it?"

"Why do ye war with your emotions, Duncan?"

"*Emotions*!" he barked.

Striding away and over to the window, he kept his gaze locked on the sky, trying to bring his *emotions* into check. "They have been the bane of my existence. It *is* who I am. A gift *and* a curse."

"Whist!" Matilda shouted, as she stomped her foot on the floor.

Duncan twisted around, arching an eyebrow in question.

Shaking her head, she crossed her arms across her chest. "Ye ken exactly what I mean, Duncan Mackay. We *all* can see how ye feel for the lass."

Pounding his fist against the wall he shouted, "Nae! Not for me! I am not worthy. The gods have sent her here for a purpose and then she must leave!"

"Tsk, tsk. Ye are truly blind, Duncan. Did it ever occur to ye they sent her, so your heart may open to love again?"

"I do not deserve love," his voice a low murmur.

Moving closer, she spoke softly. "Perhaps it is not about the sword, Duncan, but the healing of your heart."

Duncan slowly turned and with a look of anguish said, "Then the gods are cruel, Matilda. For in the end when all is done, Conn MacRoich will come for Brigid and return her to her own time. I do not believe they would punish me thus. I would rather take my sword and cut out my own heart."

A smile flickered across her face. "If they are not punishing ye, then why would they send the lass through time to get *her* heart broken? And, since when did ye listen to anything Conn ever told ye?"

"Humph!"

"Duncan, take hold of the time ye have with Brigid. Samhain is approaching, and the walls are already thinning. If the Guardian thought all was lost, then why did she send Brigid? If ye were cursed forever, she would not have placed this quest at your door. The Guardian is part of the fae, and at their core is *love*."

Matlida placed her hand on his arm, "Go to her, Duncan...*talk* to her. Ye have nothing left to lose." Letting out a sigh, Matilda slipped her hand away and left the room.

Keeping his gaze out beyond the hills Duncan whispered, "Ye are wrong, Matilda, for I do have one thing left to lose...*Brigid*."

Chapter 38

"The darkness overtook them and their path was empty, until the dragon blew her breath of light and the stars illuminated their steps."

The chilly bite of the wind caused Brigid to shiver, and she hugged her arms tighter around her. She regretted not having her wrap. Considering how she left her room rather quickly, it didn't give her time to think of grabbing one. Her hair was unraveling from her braid and she kept tucking the stray curls behind her ears.

Initially, she had intended to move quickly to locate another exit out of the castle. What stopped her on the parapet was not the cold blast which greeted her, but the sheer beauty of the landscape below. The mountains rolled beneath blankets of pine and others of oak and birch trees. Their leaves were ablaze with autumn colors of scarlet, orange, and copper. The sun filtered through puffs of white clouds and the scene reminded her of a painting, so rich in colors.

Walking slowly, she tipped her head up, letting the warmth of the sun touch her face. Breathing in deeply of the clean mountain air, Brigid closed her eyes and felt the wind shift. It whispered against her cheeks, soothing her.

"They say if ye can brave the North wall and her winds, then she will talk to ye."

Brigid eyes snapped open to find Duncan standing before her. Her anger at him was her shield and she used it to pull away, walking toward the other end.

He was at her side in two strides. Grabbing her waist, he tugged her close against her chest and whispered in her ear, "Do not run away, Brigid."

Her true feelings betrayed her just being in his arms, and tears pooled at the corner of her eyes. "*Why*?" her voice thick with emotion.

He held her close. "I do not want ye to go."

"But, *why*?" she demanded. She would yank every answer out of him.

"Is it not enough?" his breath hot and moist against her ear.

Pulling free from his embrace, she spun around to face him and saw the look of torment in his eyes. "No, Duncan. *What* has changed your mind?"

He cupped her face and placed his forehead onto hers. "Nothing...and *illumination*."

Brigid again pulled back from his embrace, shoving against his chest. "You make absolutely no sense." She had to get away. Her emotions teetered on collapsing right into his massive arms, and she was not about to do that.

She twisted to move, yet Duncan quickly moved in front of her. "Nothing, meaning nothing has changed. The facts are still as they are, Brigid. Illumination..." Duncan reached for her hand placing it over his heart saying, "Ye have opened the light within my heart, and I am a fool for not telling ye sooner. Ye cannot go...just yet, *leannan*."

"Duncan Mackay, I swear to you that I have never cried so much in my entire life!"

He lifted her chin with his fingers, gazing into her eyes as he kissed the tears that threatened to spill from the corner of them. "Do not cry for me, lass, not now." Taking her face in his hands, he bent and covered her lips with his in a slow drawn out kiss. When he broke free, he took his tongue and gently stroked her bottom lip, bringing forth a tingling sensation that shook her core. This kiss was different. It was one that was tender, seeking, not his usual demanding ones.

She opened her eyes to find him smiling down at her, his eyes ablaze with as much desire as hers. *God, how she loved him.* "Oh, Duncan, what *are* we going to do?"

"Well, I would like to show ye my chambers"— brushing a light kiss below her ear—"and I am verra hungry."

Taken aback, she asked, "Hungry?"

"Indeed." With one arm, he reached and pulled her close to his chest. With his other, he pulled at a stray curl, twisting it around his finger. He bent close to her ear. "I will make ye my feast, Brigid. I want to taste all of ye, from the top of your head to the tips of your toes. Then I will take my tongue and taste of your sweet honey that ye keep hidden." He started tracing slow kisses below her ear and down her neck. "I will fill myself of your scent and make ye mine." His hand had made its way to one of her breast, and she ached for his touch on her skin.

He spun her around and placed her against his chest, so she could look out toward the mountains. Brigid could feel his hardness against her bottom and she pushed into it as an invitation.

"Och lass," he growled. "Careful. If ye keep

wiggling your lovely bottom against me, I'll take my dirk and plunge it into your sheath."

Brigid squirmed. "You have a mighty big dirk, too."

In one shift movement, Duncan had lifted her skirts, the cool air blasting her legs until she felt his hand kneading her thigh, his fingers slowly finding their way into her folds. He took one finger, rubbing a slow circle around her nub. A sob escaped from her as she leaned her head back onto his chest.

"How big would ye say it is?" His breath hot on her neck as he continued his exploration, causing her to whimper. It wouldn't take much to grab his cock and thrust deep into her, but this was not what he had intended. He wanted to explore, give her as much as he could and take his sweet time in doing it. His finger kept stroking her swollen nub as she continued to grind into him. He muttered a soft curse and removed his hand, causing her to utter a cry of anguish.

Duncan wrapped both of his arms around her waist, the scent of her desire a potent drug that swamped his senses. "Before I take ye to my chambers and continue my feasting of your body, I want ye to look out yonder."

Keeping her head against his chest, Brigid tried to focus on the landscape, the ache between her legs demanding a release.

"Tell me, Brigid. Does Scotland still look like this in your time?"

She smiled. "Yes, for the most part. Here in the Highlands, its beauty is still one to be treasured." Brigid realized this was the first question Duncan asked regarding her time. She placed her arms over his and just stood still, gazing out at the land.

"When I first came to Castle Creag after that dark night, I slept out here for many moons, sleeping on the cold stones. I did not want comfort, just the longing of death. Each morn, I would awake cursing the gods I still existed. I would descend to the lists, or hunt, then return each night. Yet with each dawn I would gaze upon the beauty of the land and on some of those days I would let it calm the beast within." He took a deep shuttering breath.

"This was your haven, Duncan, your refuge."

"Aye still is...until ye came."

Brigid squeezed his arms more tightly, reveling in his strength and warmth. There were no words to express how she felt at this precise moment. All she wanted was to hold onto this tiny fraction of time, which held a promise of healing.

"Let me show ye my chambers." Duncan broke the contact, and she felt bereft, the wind snapping at her. He tugged at her hand gently, the warmth from it coursing through her veins. He walked her back the way she came. Descending the pathway she had previously taken, he led her toward the alcove.

Pushing open the massive oak door, he pulled her in and swiftly closed it shut. Marveling at the room, she let her gaze travel over it. She stole a look behind her and noticed he was standing with arms behind him against the door. She didn't know why, but Brigid was nervous, like this was their first time. Her palms tingled, and she brushed them across the material of her gown.

His room had a large arched window with a stone seating area with pillows scattered on top. To the left of the door, a hearth was blazing, and the warmth drew her like a beacon. A huge chair faced the hearth, but what caught her eye were the carvings on the armrests. They were shaped in the form of giant claws. She saw a small table and chest, but the only other piece of furniture was a very large bed covered in furs. Her face flushed just thinking of what Duncan was going to do her on those furs.

"Do ye like the bed, lass?" his voice a husky burr behind her.

She swung around and saw the heat of desire in not only his eyes, but also where something was protruding very prominently against his plaid. She could not take her gaze from it, and watched as he took a hold of himself and squeezed.

"Or do ye like this better?"

Brigid placed her hands behind her to keep them from trembling. "Don't tease," she softly whispered.

A rumble of laughter came forth, dark with lust as Duncan moved away from the wall. He approached her slowly. As their gazes locked on each other, he took her face in his hands and captured her lips with his. Hot and demanding, his tongue sought hers, until she melted into his embrace.

His hands moved down to her bottom, pulling her toward his erection and rubbing it against her, his kiss deepening with more urgency. Brigid took her hand and squeezed his arousal through his plaid. He responded with a growl, resonating deep into her as she continued to stroke his hardness.

A guttural sound tore from his throat as he stilled her hand. "Nae, I will spill myself before I have a chance to tease ye properly."

Taking a step back, he slowly removed his plaid, tunic, and dirk. Giving her a wicked smile, Duncan moved toward the chair with nothing on but his boots and the torc around his neck.

Brigid watched with pure lust at the most gorgeous ass she had ever seen. She bit her lower lip as he turned, crooking a finger at her to come forward.

Did that groan just escape from her throat?

She didn't think her legs could move. Her body was heavy with raw need. Standing before him, he started slowly removing her clothing, placing slow sensuous kisses starting at the hollow of her neck.

When she stood before him in only her shift, he gently slipped it down over her aching breasts. Then taking his calloused hands, he rubbed them over her taut nipples. Brigid closed her eyes on the powerful sensation.

"Open your eyes, Brigid." Tipping her head up, she opened them to shards of crystal blue. "I want to watch your desire peak until I thrust into ye."

With open eyes, she watched as he bent and flicked a tongue over one nipple and then the other before placing languid kisses around the sides and under her breasts, returning to her nipples. Brigid thought her knees were going to buckle and in one swift move, he grabbed her around the waist and gathered them both into the chair. Her bottom was on his large erection, and he hissed when she started to move.

He continued to lavish and savor each breast. Taking his tongue, he slowly trailed kisses down the middle, kneading them together. Her gaze never wavered, the storm of ecstasy so very close.

"Do ye like watching?" his voice a husky burr.

"Yes," she gasped.

Twirling a curl around his finger, he twisted and pulled. "Your hair is verra soft, lass, but not as soft as these curls near your sweet mound." Keeping his eyes on hers, his fingers played in her nest of curls.

"Is this what ye want, lass?" Duncan's burr was so thick Brigid could barely understand him. Lowering her gaze, she became captivated by his touch. His fingers stroked her folds until she felt one enter her.

"*Ohhh*, Duncan." Brigid clasped his shoulders, fearing she would swoon right off his lap. His finger kept moving in slow movements in and out and then up over her pleasure spot. Her eyes closed, until she heard him say, "Look at me, Brigid."

Opening her eyes, she was lost in his that shared her passion. Brigid whimpered when he removed his fingers and she tried to pull them back into her. Still keeping her eyes locked on his, she watched as he placed those fingers into his mouth.

His smile held a promise of more to come. "I must get a proper taste of your honey."

Brigid didn't have time to blink as she was whisked up and into his arms. Carrying her over to the bed, he placed her gently on the furs, the softness against her bare skin sending more sensations of pleasure throughout her body.

Her eyes were only for him as he sat and removed his boots and stood in front of her. Her mouth became dry at the vision of him—pure unabashed male. Massive would never describe Duncan. Oh no, he was beyond that. He fisted his hands on his hips, seeming to gain more pleasure as she continued to feast her eyes on him. His cock surged forward in invitation. Brigid rolled to her knees, reaching for him with her hand.

Her hand stroked him. "So hard...*and soft*."

Groaning, he took her other hand and placed it on his balls.

She could hear his labored breathing and saw the head of his cock now glistened with moisture. It beckoned to her to taste. Brigid lowered her head, and taking her tongue, she traced it along the top before taking it all into her mouth.

Duncan clenched his jaw as he fought to maintain control, jerking slightly. Her mouth was bliss. Never had he felt anything so searing in all his life. He was so close to spilling that he gave her only one more taste before yanking her head free. Toppling her back onto the furs, he crushed her beneath him, claiming her mouth with savage intensity.

Duncan rose up and taking her head in his hands, he barely rasped out, "Now I taste *ye*."

Brigid did not have time to protest as he pushed her thighs apart. She watched in a sensual haze as he descended down between them. He placed a kiss at the top of her curls and blew on them. Then he took his tongue and dove inside of her.

She clutched at the furs, arching up as he took his fill of her. The waves of pleasure were building quickly again. "Don't stop," she pleaded, wanting to yield to the burning sweetness that was captive within her.

His only sound was a growl and then he took his tongue over her center, teasing and biting, sending shockwaves of pleasure so intense she arched wildly up off the furs. A scream tore from her throat, as her world shattered in pure ecstasy, stars dancing behind her eyes.

Duncan shook with the raw need of release.

Sliding up over her, he took his cock and thrust deep inside her wet dampness. His need was one of possession; he could not be gentle any longer. With each thrust, he went deeper within her. She was *his*, and he wanted to mark her for eternity.

Sensing his need, Brigid arched more into him. Raising her arms above her head, she took him more into herself. He took her hands in his above her head and kissed her, savagely.

The tremors of release slammed into him, the shattering so strong. He shook violently, emptying body and soul into the woman he loved.

Chapter 39

"The art of the Celts and their spirals are pathways to one's journey in life. No beginning and no ending."

Duncan's gaze was on Brigid, who was lying across his body with one leg wrapped around his and her hand on his chest. She was his goddess, with her hair a riot of wild curls falling about her luscious skin, flushed from their lovemaking. Her hair reminded him of the leaves when they changed their hue.

He took his hand and caressed her backside causing a small moan to escape. She had fallen asleep, and the light from the window had cast shadows along the floor, letting him know evening was approaching.

Drawing her more closely to him, he wondered when he had lost his heart to this bewitching woman. How was he ever going to let her go back to her own time? Would she even consider staying here with him— a broken man without a home?

A soft sob came forth from her and Duncan spoke softly, "Shhhhh."

"Duncan?" she murmured, still half asleep.

"Yes, *leannan?*"

"Where do we go next?" she asked.

Duncan threw his arm over his forehead, not knowing the answer himself. "I ken only the moment."

Brigid turned from his arms, placing her chin on his chest. She took her hand and splayed it into his chest hairs.

"I'm hungry, Duncan," she stated now fully awake.

He opened one eye, saw the wanton look in her eyes, and smiled. Cupping her bottom, he nudged her over his swollen cock. "Hungry for more of this?"

"How did you know?" she asked huskily.

"Show me," he rasped.

Ever so slowly, Brigid made her way down his chest to his enlarged member, taking as much as she could into her mouth. She savored the saltiness, hearing him release a growl. She was going to tease him the same as he did to her. Sliding her tongue over and around the top, she cupped his balls, and took him back into her mouth.

Never in her life had Brigid been so bold.

When she looked up, she saw beads of sweat on his brow, his eyes watching her every moment. Taking it as a good sign, she continued with her ministrations. His hips moved more rapidly, until suddenly he moved to clasp her arm, but Brigid stopped him with a nip.

"Mine," she growled.

He groaned. "I cannae hold back much longer."

"Then don't," she uttered, taking him fully into her mouth again.

Her mouth on his cock was pure bliss. He never had any woman take him thus, and the sensation rolled over him in giant waves.

Brigid lapped up the last few drops of his release.

Thinking she was still in control, Duncan caught her off guard when he quickly tossed her onto her back, thrusting deep into her. "Duncan," she moaned, as he continued to rock slowly in and out of her.

She felt the laughter rumble in his chest before he spoke, "Aye, my wench."

He cupped her breasts, fondling the taut nipples. His hips grinding slow and methodical, wanting to take her over the crest of pleasure before he found his, *again.*

He stilled himself partially out of her, and taking his thumb, he found her sensitive nub. With a few strokes, she came in a rush, screaming his name. Duncan thrust deep into her, following in his own wave of bliss.

Rolling her on top of him, he held her close wanting to stay like this forever.

"I can hear your stomach *growling*," he muttered.

Brigid giggled and rolled off him. The two tapestries on either side of the fireplace captured her sight. Sitting up, she marveled at their colors and pondered if there was a story woven through. Ignoring her stomach for the moment, she asked, "Who is the man depicted in the tapestries?"

Duncan placed a soft kiss on her mouth before leaving their bed. He grabbed his plaid and wrapped it across his waist. Striding over to the fire, he put more peat into the dwindling blaze. Glancing up at the tapestries, he stood looking at them, hands fisted on his sides.

"Cinaed mac Ailpin, the Conqueror. He was the very first king of Scotland. *Chan eil carraig air nach caochail sruth.*"

"What does it mean?"

"There is no rock that the stream won't change." Titling his head to one side, he continued, "He was a great man, also descended from the fae."

"*The* Kenneth MacAlpin?"

"Aye."

The other tapestry was one of the king on a horse before a circle of standing stones. Brigid grabbed one of the furs around her and moved off the bed, her feet encountering the cold floor. Flinching, she walked quickly over to where Duncan was standing. A wave of shock swept over her as she recognized the stone circle.

"Duncan, this is where I came through." Her hand shook as she reached out to touch the fabric.

Instantly, Duncan grasped her wrist before she could touch it and brought her against his chest. He held her close for a few moments, and then tipped her head back gently. Looking into her eyes, he said, "It is the same place Meggie took her last breath."

"What happened, Duncan?" her voice barely a whisper, and she could feel his body tense.

Releasing Brigid, Duncan walked over to the window. He glanced back over his shoulder at the tapestry.

It was as if time stood still, and Brigid was afraid to breathe. There was no rumbling of thunder in the distance, only the sound of the crackling fire.

Brigid sat with shaky limbs on the fur rug before the fire, waiting for details of a night so horrific, she feared she was not brave enough to listen and hear the truth. All this time, asking and probing, now the moment came, and she was scared that it would change her. She took a deep calming breath and watched as he ran a hand through his hair in exasperation, leaning against the wall.

"The day was gray and a storm was brewing." He

cast a look at her and shook his head as if reading her thoughts. "Nae, not of my doing." Turning back toward the window, he let his mind drift back to that night.

"Meggie knew how we felt about the MacFhearguis. She argued many times with Angus, even calling him a pig-headed arse. I tended to side with her on the latter. No one suspected she had been secretly meeting the MacFhearguis for many moons. Alastair was the one who came upon them one morning and went immediately to Angus. I ken Meggie never forgave Alastair, for she barely spoke to him afterwards. She was very close to Alastair and this was akin to a dirk in her back. She wanted to explain, but he never gave her the chance.

"As the months passed, we thought Meggie had broken off with the MacFhearguis, but nae, she met him in secret. It was during that time, we all had taken to arguing over all matters. Angus had forbidden us to seek out the MacFhearguis, so we took it out on each other. We all itched to start a fight and fists and swords were drawn many a day. I was the worst. Stephen and Alastair feared to fight me in the lists; therefore, I would seek them out."

Propping a leg up on the stone bench, Duncan crossed his arms over his chest and continued speaking. "The storm was fierce that night and most of us were deep in our cups, when Hamish came running into the Hall stammering and frightened of what he was about to tell. Meggie had run off with the MacFhearguis to be handfasted. It was all I needed to hear to let loose the fury which had been building for months. I did not heed Angus's words; I just grabbed my sword and left for the stones. When I reached them, I had one purpose, and it was to slay Adam MacFhearguis. Meggie was holding him and would not let him go. He tried to pull away, but she held fast."

Duncan's voice became bitter as he continued, "I let the wind whip them both, not a care for my sister's safety, only the death of one. The blood rage had me in its thrall, and I used my powers to intensify it. I believe that is why Angus wanted me to stay behind. He knew that I had become unstable and perilous."

Duncan swallowed. "My brothers had arrived, and I gave no care for their existence. Angus shouted at me to stop, his shield pounding into my backside. Of course, I turned on him, lancing a blow on his arm. I could not hear Angus's words, for the blood was pounding in my ears. I saw movement to my right. It was Alastair moving toward Meggie and the MacFhearguis, and shoving with all my might, I clipped Angus, crashing into Stephen. Then I went for them, taking a swing at Alastair first, which caused a cry to tear forth from Meggie."

Duncan tore his gaze from the window, a look of excruciating pain etched on his face. "She feared I had solely injured Alastair. She broke free from Adam and ran toward me. Adam followed her. My focus was on killing this man, but somehow my sister stepped in front of him. My sword impaled them both. Meggie was mortally wounded, but Adam survived his injuries."

Duncan collapsed on the window bench and held his bent head in his hands. "She died in Angus's arms. All my fault," he choked out. "I damned them with my actions."

Brigid's heart ached. It ached for Meggie and

Adam, but mostly it ached for the broken man in front of her. She had questions, questions she was not going to ask Duncan. He needed her, and she would do whatever it took to right the wrong. Yes, her mind whispered, if all was truly lost, then why did the Guardian see fit to redeem them? At least for now, she finally had a big piece of the puzzle.

Slowly standing, she walked over to her distraught knight. Putting her arms around him, she cradled him, feeling him shake from the release of his emotions.

Several moments passed, and Duncan unwrapped himself from her arms. He placed tender kisses along her face. "Food, my lady?"

"Mmmmm," she smiled, keeping her eyes closed.

They both stood and dressed quietly. When Brigid went for the door, Duncan's hand stilled on it, holding it closed. Cupping her chin, he brushed a kiss softly on her swollen lips. "No matter what, Brigid O'Neill, do not forget ye are now mine. I will protect ye, *always*." Brushing his thumb across her bottom lip, he continued, "Ye have my heart, *leannan*. What ye do with it is up to ye."

Brigid placed her hand over his chest, her gaze never leaving his face. "Then I give you *my* heart to hold and protect."

Clasping her to his chest, he could find no other words, letting the silence wash over them in peace.

Chapter 40

"A year and a day, that is all I ask of my true love to give me."

The great hall was crowded with mostly Cormac and his men. When they entered together, Cormac arched a brow in mock display at Duncan, and then smiled broadly. Brigid had longed for a hot bath, but her stomach had grumbled in protest, again, which Duncan had heard. She had gone all day without eating, and the smell of food assaulted her as she entered.

"Here, Duncan." Cormac waved them both over to sit near him.

Duncan poured them both some ale, and he drank with gusto. Leaning forward, he took her plate and piled it high with food. He was being so attentive. Every so often, he would take her hand and squeeze it under the table. Her face felt on fire with the way he was constantly looking at her. There was something else, but she couldn't quite figure it out.

"Tell me, Cormac, where are Nell and Finn?" asked Brigid between bites of meat.

"Those two rascals are probably fetching some food for the menagerie of animals they keep." Cormac snorted.

Brigid choked on her food, causing Duncan to leap up and start pounding her back. *"St-o-o-pp*, Duncan."

She coughed some more. "I'm fine, please sit down."

She was sorry the minute she saw the look of concern in his eyes. "Really, I'm fine, thank you." Taking her hand, she brushed it against his thigh, getting the effect she intended when she saw passion flare instantly within his eyes.

Tilting her head back to Cormac, she asked, "How long have ye known?"

Cormac chuckled deep before answering, "Och, Brigid, we realized the moment she started taking from the kitchens. Finn keeps a watch over her and her brood, making sure they are safe."

Brigid's mouth dropped open in shock, and considered telling Nell. The poor little girl was so afraid someone would snatch her family away. Yet, it was just the opposite. They all shared her secret and were taking care of her.

"Why don't you tell her that you know?"

"Then she would become laird, giving orders to everyone." Duncan interjected between mouthfuls of food.

A bark of laughter came forth from Cormac, and he ventured to look around as if fearing someone would hear. "I tell ye, Brigid, Duncan is correct. The lass has a way of wrapping us all around her wee fingers," he stated, holding up his pinky. Then with a more solemn voice added, "She's already a mighty warrior for one so young."

Pointing a knife at Brigid, Cormac's eyes narrowed. "Do not say a word of this to anyone."

Palms held out in mock surrender, Brigid responded, "Not a word will pass these lips." Smiling, she reached out and laid a hand on his arm. "You are a good man, Cormac."

"Humph! I did not take them in. Look to your man. He rescued them."

Slowly, her gaze went from Cormac to Duncan who was entrenched in his meal, eyes downcast. "You rescued them? *How*?"

"It is nothing. They lost their families in a storm, and I happen to find them lost and shaken. They are under my charge."

"How kind."

Duncan's body tensed, "Nae not kindness, what had to be done."

"Yet you rescued them. How bad was this storm?" She looked to Cormac and saw his eyes were wide and he was shaking his head, pleading with her not to ask.

Then it dawned on her.

Duncan's voice was low when he spoke. "It was a storm that took more than my sister's life."

Holy crap! How bad was this storm—a storm that was a combination of elements and Duncan's powers? Her mind reeled. She could not comprehend how a man could be so lost after he kills his sister, and yet, he rescues two small children on the same night.

Brigid placed her hand gently on his.

The warmth of her touch shook him free from his thoughts of that night. She gave him one of those beautiful smiles that shook his soul, and he pondered what she truly saw in him. Many times, he thought himself a monster.

Duncan reached for her hand and placed a kiss in her palm. "Thank ye," he whispered.

At that moment, Nell came running into the hall with Finn following behind her.

"There ye are. Where *have* ye been?" Nell practically ran into Brigid's outstretched arms.

"Whoa, missy," laughed Brigid.

Sienna was not far behind, clucking and wiping her brow. "Nell Murray! What have ye been up to?"

Nell cocked her head to the side with a look of distain before answering, "Washing up."

Sienna just rolled her eyes. "Come, leave Sir Duncan and Lady Brigid be."

"Leave her. She can stay with us." Brigid gave her a reassuring smile.

"Thank ye," mouthed Sienna.

Finn had already taken a seat beside Duncan and Nell wedged herself between them. Duncan then rolled his eyes, and Brigid burst out laughing.

"Lady Brigid?"

"Yes, Nell?"

"When are ye and Sir Duncan going to handfast?"

Duncan had been drinking from his mug, when he choked on its contents sputtering ale everywhere.

Brigid swallowed. "Handfast?"

"Aye. 'Tis only right, especially the way he looks at ye and ye at him."

"Oh my. Well, ummmm..." Brigid's face burned, and daring a glance at Duncan, noticed he was fast approaching gluttony with the amount of food he was shoveling into his mouth.

Cathal came to their rescue. He stood directly across from them, hands clasped together in front. "Ah, Nell, I am sure when Sir Duncan and Lady Brigid decide to be handfasted, ye will be the first they tell."

"Humph!" Then looking at Brigid she asked, "Truth? Ye will tell me first?"

Duncan spoke before Brigid had a chance to compose her thoughts. "Aye, Nell. I shall come find ye myself."

The look he gave Brigid over Nell's head was one that spoke truth. He truly thought there might be a chance for her to stay, and he wanted to make it legal by handfasting with her. Could she hope, too? In her heart, she loved Duncan. But could he open his heart fully to love her?

The smile on Nell's face beamed for all to see. "Good. Now please someone pass me those neeps. I'm famished!"

The table erupted into fits of laughter and snorts, the latter coming from Finn.

"Don't you want some of the meat, too?" Brigid started to reach past for the trencher of meat, but Nell's eyes went round and her mouth started to quiver.

"Nae, Lady Brigid. I will not eat the animals. They are my *friends,*" her voice barely a whisper.

She patted Nell's hand. "I understand."

Well, there was one for the history books Brigid mused, a vegetarian in medieval Scotland.

****

Hours later, Duncan and Brigid stood on the parapet, watching as the moon made its way up over the hills, sending beams of light over the valley below, almost blotting out the night stars. Standing against his chest, she was wrapped in his arms, a cocoon of warmth and strength. His chin rested on the top of her head, as they basked in the glow of the rising moon.

The sound of bagpipes floated on the wind, creating a magic that whispered of old. Brigid sighed as her heart sang along with the tune.

"Calum is playing for the dead," Duncan drawled.

"What? I think it's beautiful."

"Nae. The song is one for the ancestors."

"What do you call it?"

" 'Journey to Tir na Og.' "

She sighed. "It's still beautiful, in a haunting way."

Duncan snorted and turned Brigid quickly to face him. "Enough of the pipes. Let me take ye to my bed and warm ye properly." Before she could answer, his mouth took hers in a searing kiss, and all thoughts of the pipes vanished from her mind.

Chapter 41

"The darkness of Samhain speaks to us as wisdom of light, ushering in the new beginning."

Duncan had made love to almost every inch of her body, and Brigid felt so sated that sleep beckoned, luring her to a far off slumber. That is until she heard Duncan ask her a question.

"Why were ye with Nell in the weapons room? Do ye like them?"

Sighing, she tried twisting to look into his face, but he held her fast against his chest. "Duncan, how do you know I was in there? Are you having us followed?"

"Nae, not me—Cormac. I find it interesting a woman would want to look at swords, shields, spears, and such."

Brigid could feel his chest rumble from laughter. "Spears, really? I didn't see any." Trying more to wiggle free, she finally gave up, snuggling back into his embrace. "In my time women are men's equals, well in most of the countries, and I just happen to love medieval weaponry. I did have a small shop with antiques from Scotland, Ireland, and England. I've always been fascinated by the craftsmanship of sword making."

"Hmmmmm. That's what I told Cormac." He placed soft kisses on her shoulder. "And the cursing?

289

Do women curse too?"

"Um, *well*," she gasped when he placed a kiss behind her ear. "As a matter of fact, Duncan, they do...oh, that *feels good*. She closed her eyes. "I don't curse that much."

Duncan chuckled and bit down on the side of her neck. "Nae, your language is strange, but the cursing I recognize."

Her eyes popped opened. "Duncan, stop! You're teasing me, right?"

His laughter rumbled against her and she finally got an elbow out to take a jab, when he grasped it, turning her to face him.

"It is a problem. One that I'll have to punish ye for." Taking his mouth, he kissed the side of her eyes, top of her nose, and pressed one on the corners of her mouth before he took his tongue and traced the soft fullness of her lips.

"You are *such* a tease, Duncan Mackay."

"Aye."

Leaving her mouth yearning for more, he rolled off the bed and strolled over to the table, where Brigid spied the sword. So, he had taken the sword from her room. Good, she concluded.

"I have a gift for ye. Since ye have a fondness for the weapons, I considered ye should have one." He held out the dirk, the very one she had admired that day with Nell.

"Duncan, it's beautiful," she whispered. "How did you know?" Taking the dirk, she still marveled at its beauty, tracing the carving of the horses with her fingers. It was small and fit snug in her hand.

"Nell. She told me if I wanted to win your heart,

then perhaps I should give ye a weapon. She suspected ye had a fondness for them."

"Oh, Nell, you are a wise soul, indeed."

"Aye, she is, lass. I take it ye like my gift."

"Yes, Duncan, I do." Brigid reached up and grasped his hand, placing it against her cheek.

Still holding his hand, Brigid glanced at the table. "What is the green stone in the hilt of your sword?" She felt him stiffen slightly, as he released his hand from hers.

Duncan walked slowly over to the sword, partially unsheathing it. "The stone is from Eirinn, blest by the fae when they came to this land. Legend says that the color so reminded them of their home, they anointed it with dragon's fire." Duncan ran his finger over the surface of the stone and then placed it back inside the pouch.

"Duncan, we call this stone Connemara marble and it still exists in what we call Ireland."

A look of shock marred his features as he turned quickly at her words. "How can this be?"

"It seems the faery, or fae, left a huge amount in the mountains on the west of Ireland, or as you call it— *Eirinn.*"

Rubbing a hand over the shadow of his beard, he shook his head in disbelief. "Brigid, what *is* the year ye are from?"

"Duncan, perhaps you should come and sit before I tell you." She held out her hand and motioned him to come to the bed.

He narrowed his eyes, and fisted his hands on his hips. "Nae! What *is* the year?"

Brigid tried hard not to smile. He looked so

scrumptious *and* stubborn at the same time, giving her his best glare while he stood stark naked in front of her.

"Okay, fine. I don't know if you remember that I did mention eight hundred years?"

He shook his head no, slowly.

"Can you handle the year 2013?"

Duncan's eyes did not even blink, nor did he move any muscles. He just stood very still. Brigid feared the shock was too much until she saw him swallow. Instantly, he was at her side in two strides.

Taking her head in his hands, he stared into her eyes, whispering, "Ye must be mighty special to the fae, for them to take ye from your time and whisk ye back here, *leannan*." His breath was warm, and she melted into his embrace as he smothered her against his chest and the furs.

****

Brigid woke later in the night, still in Duncan's arms. Moving slightly, she saw he was awake and gazing out toward the window, a frown creasing his forehead. "A penny for your thoughts?" she uttered softly.

"Huh?" asked Duncan.

"Sorry, just a saying we use when we notice someone is deep in thought." Brigid gave him a smile and brushed her fingers across the frown on his face.

Duncan continued to stare out at the window. "Do ye wish to return to your own time?" He asked softly.

Brigid sat up and looked at Duncan. "Do *you* want me to stay?"

Her heart started to beat wildly. What if he didn't want her? She cursed too much, could probably not keep a house, much less a castle. Wait a minute...this was Cormac's home. Where did Duncan live? Urquhart Castle?

He turned his head to look at her, keeping his emotions to himself. What if's...that's all she had. She went over what would happen to her heart *if* she left him. He might as well take his sword and stab her now, because returning to her own time would do the same.

"No," she whispered.

His mask of steel stripped by that one word, and he uttered a deep sigh, and her heart soared. "Aye, *leannan* I *do* want ye to stay." He reached out, touched her riot of curls, and spun them between his fingers. "Ye do not mind spending the rest of your life with a monster?"

"Are you asking me to marry you?"

"Aye. I am of the old religion. Does it bother ye?" His eyes held hers and waited.

"No, I will mar...handfast with you on one condition, Duncan."

His hand froze. "What is it?"

"Quit saying you're a monster, because I don't believe for one second you are one. Yes, you made a horrible mistake in judgment, but something else was going on that night. I think it's long overdue on finding out the truth."

"I killed my sister. That is *not* a mistake in judgment," he snapped.

Brigid pounded her chest with her fist. "Duncan, I sense there was an evil present on that night, and I don't suspect it was you and your brothers."

She watched as he clenched his jaw, but he kept silent.

"Will you accept my condition?" Brigid watched as his steady gaze bore into her, causing her to believe he wasn't going to accept. A simple one she reflected, realizing she was asking a great deal of him.

Brigid waited patiently as he battled with the decision.

"Brigid O'Neill, I accept your condition."

With those words, she saw the heart-rending tenderness in his eyes. Grasping his face, she brought her lips down to his, unlocking his soul and heart with her kiss.

"Duncan?" His hands started their pleasurable descent over her body.

"Where do ye want me to pleasure ye?" His eyes shifted to her naked breasts.

"I think we need to talk to someone about that night." Brigid let out a moan as Duncan placed another kiss along her collarbone with his hand gently kneading her breast.

"Aye, I've already thought of it, too," his breath hot against her skin.

"Then you know who I mean?"

Lifting his head from his pursuit of her body, he answered, "I shall seek out Cathal in the morning. He will give us council on this, and the other, too."

"What other?" she asked, leaning more into him.

"The one of handfasting, lass. I *have* accepted your condition."

Brigid's eyes went wide. "Oh Duncan, do you truly think Cathal can help?"

"He is a great and powerful druid, so aye, I believe he can."

The idea that Cathal could help sent her heart soaring, but before she could ask any further questions, Duncan started kissing her shoulder, and she moved toward him, impelled by her own passion. Her hands caressed his broad shoulders.

"Where do ye want me to explore next?" Duncan was kissing the spot below her ear, which he deduced to be one of her favorite pleasure spots. Then taking his fingers, he teased the curls at the center of another pleasurable area.

"Everywhere," she gasped. Her body melted against his and her world filled with him.

Chapter 42

"If on a clear starry night, when you tilt your head a certain way you can see the doors to Tir na Og."

"Judas's balls! How long has he been in there?" Alex paced back and forth in front of Michael's chambers, his hands clenched behind his back.

Patrick leaned against the wall, arms crossed over his chest, his expression a mask of stone. "Lachlan's been with him most of the morning. It seems the news he brings is one for his ears only."

Alex's face twisted with cold fury. He glanced back at the door and walked over to Patrick, clamping his hand on his shoulder. "Brother, we need to talk and best we do it not here in the corridor. Agreed?"

Patrick's smile was without humor. "I pondered when ye would want to talk about the druid."

"Come, I have some wine in my chambers," motioned Alex.

"Stealing from the cellar again?" Patrick gave a low chuckle.

"Nae, not from ours." His mouth curved into a mischievous smile. "From Cormac Murray's."

Patrick's eyebrows rose in amazement. "Ye jest?"

Alex's laughter was low as he shook his brother before glancing back at the door. "Let us drink and I shall tell ye what I have learned."

They descended through the long corridor. Alex caught up with one of his men, giving him orders to send for him when Lachlan finished speaking with their laird.

Upon entering his chambers, Alex went over and retrieved the bottle of wine he had in his pack. "I would rather share this with our brother, but as ye can see I am not sure where his loyalties are."

Patrick was quiet for a moment, more interested in how Alex got the wine from the Murray. He watched as Alex poured some into two mugs, handing him one. He proceeded to sniff the contents and a frown wrinkled his brows. "It is elderberry wine, Alex. Did ye realize that?"

"Nae, never asked when Sean gave it to me." He took a swig, letting it settle in his mouth. "Not bad, brother. The Murray knows his stuff."

"My preference is whisky, as ye well ken." Taking a swallow, he nodded as he glanced up. "Ye are right, not bad."

Patrick took another swig, then arched a brow in question. "Tell me, Alex, how did Sean happen to steal the Murray's wine?" Holding his palm up to stop the negative response forthcoming from Alex, he added, "Do not take me for a fool, brother." Placing the mug on the table, he faced his brother, hands fisted on his hips. "Does this have anything to do with Adam?"

Alex took one last draw from his mug and placed it down alongside Patrick's. Striding over to the window arch that overlooked the stables, he rubbed his hand over his rough beard. "Sean is keeping watch over Castle Creag, since Duncan Mackay has been on a guest there this past year." He let out a sigh before continuing, "Also, Duncan now has a woman with him as guest of the Murray. Her name is Lady Brigid O'Neill."

He heard a choking sound behind him and spun to find Patrick had braced his hands on the table to hold himself. "*Why* would an O'Neill have anything to do with a Mackay? And how do ye ken he's been there these past twelve moons? Sean?"

"Sean has eyes in the castle, verra beautiful eyes as a matter of fact." He gave Patrick a wink. "Do I ken why she is with the Mackay? Nae. Only that she is *his* woman and"—Alex pointed a finger at Patrick—"I do not think he knows the whereabouts of Adam."

"Michael will use the woman in his quest for vengeance, ye ken this?" Patrick stated, finally pushing off from the table.

"What makes ye say that, brother?"

"Lachlan also knows about the woman. I overheard him mention this in passing when he was not aware of my presence. He spoke of an O'Neill and that is when he thought it best to speak in private."

Alex slammed a fist against the wall, glaring back at Patrick. "We waste time with the Mackay, instead of searching for Adam! I tell ye Lachlan has other plans, and I do not trust him. What say ye?"

Slowly, Patrick poured some more wine into their mugs, his decision made the moment he stepped into Alex's chambers, one that would divide them against not only their brother, but also their laird. In truth, he had been unsure of Alex's loyalties and uneasiness quelled inside of him. Walking over to Alex, he handed him his mug.

Patrick sighed heavily. "I have never trusted

Lachlan, ever since the verra day he came back telling us of our father's death. He is as slippery as an eel and he reeks of evil. I have suspected that all he wants is the relics of the Dragon Order in order to gain the power for himself. I was unsure of your loyalty to the druid for many years. Then, there is Michael. He has always heeded his counsel, more so, after the death of our father."

Alex lifted a brow. "Brother, I have held my tongue far too long. It seems as if the corridors have eyes everywhere. We have a problem if Michael continues to listen to his council, since the druid bends Michael's will to his." Slugging back the wine, he added, "I believe he's using *us* to get to the Mackay. When did Lachlan return?"

"Late last night."

"By the hounds!" Alex rubbed a hand on the back of his neck in frustration. "Then we have a problem, Patrick. I met up with Lachlan over seven days ago."

"And?" Patrick gave a noncommittal shrug. "Do ye not think he had other plans before he returned?"

Slashing out a hand in a negative response, he replied, "Nae, he was determined to give Michael the news immediately. I tell ye, the druid is up to something." There was a bitter edge of cynicism in his voice.

Silence descended in the room, as the fire hissed and snapped. Patrick felt cold dread clutch his chest. Perhaps he had been wrong in confronting Alex with his concerns. He despised the druid. But would Alex turn against the Lachlan and their brother, *the laird*? He had years ago. Yet would Alex be willing to turn against their clan in order to save them?

Patrick's cold impersonal tone broke the silence. "Then we must gather only our most trusted men and confront the Mackay at Castle Creag."

"Christ, Patrick! Did ye not hear me? We should be searching for Adam, *not* the bastard Mackay!" he exclaimed in a harsh, raw voice.

"Alex." He leaned forward clamping both hands on his brother's shoulders, meeting his angry scowl. "I grow weary of this feud and no news of Adam. Hell! I do not want the relics! They have never been ours, and to continue a feud over them and the land is costing us dearly." Patrick pushed away and went over to the fire. Placing both his hands on the stone mantel, he stared into the flames.

"Then we are of like mind, my brother, but why seek out the Mackay?" Alex had lost some of the fury in his tone.

Patrick glanced back over his shoulder with a mischievous grin. "I say we go straight to the devil, asking *him* the whereabouts of Adam."

****

"So, the bloody bastard has been at Castle Creag all these months." Michael took the mug from Lachlan and watched as he poured some for himself.

"It would seem so." Lachlan strolled over to a massive chair, facing Michael and sat. He was weary, and that made for mistakes.

Michael hesitated, and then took a sip. He approached Lachlan. "Tell me again, what of this woman."

"She is an O'Neill, yet how she came here is uncertain. She has no kinfolk with her, and for the moment, she plans to stay there. They say Duncan is protective of her and calls her his. There is talk he even took a fist to the Murray over her."

Michael only smirked on the last remark. "What of the sword?"

Lachlan betrayed no emotions when he answered, "None."

Michael cocked an eyebrow in question. "I find it hard to fathom that Duncan Mackay is so besotted by a woman's charms, he has abandoned his quest for the sword." He walked over to the table and placed his mug down.

Lachlan was hesitant to say more, but he needed to convince Michael that the key to the sword was through this woman. He silently placed his mug on the ground and steepled his fingers. "Perhaps this woman is the key to finding the sword and Adam."

He watched as Michael turned and leaned against the table, his arms crossed over his chest. "Go on."

"We need to speak with this woman. Perhaps, gain her trust."

Michael let out a bark of laughter. "Lachlan, ye surprise me. *Talk* to a woman? Gain her *trust*? Nae, that is why ye are the druid and I am the laird." His look turned sinister when he added, "I say we just take her. With her in our possession, it won't take long for the Mackay to be at our door."

"Ah, yes. Your plan would be wiser." Lachlan steeled himself from gloating at how he manipulated Michael. Standing, he went over to Michael, a frown forming on his face.

Holding his hands together in front of him, he said, "I fear we may have another problem."

"What would that be?"

"Alex and Patrick. They may not be willing to kidnap the woman."

Michael's eyes narrowed. "I am their laird, and they *will* obey me. Do not worry about them." Turning, he strode out from his chambers issuing orders to the man outside.

A slow smiled curved ever so slightly on Lachlan's mouth, his thoughts plotting out the next step.

Chapter 43

"Tell me the flowers of the faery, and I'll whisper to you their meaning."

"Ouch! *Blast* that hurts." Brigid brought her pricked finger to her mouth, tasting blood and spitting out the small prickly thorn. She heard giggling to her side and saw Nell hunched over, a hand clamped over her mouth. Her eyes narrowed on the small girl.

"Hey, it's not like I do this every day. I think I'll take back my dirk I gave you to make it easier."

"If ye think it will make it easier for ye, here." Nell handed her the dirk hilt facing Brigid with a broad smile on her face.

Bridgid reconsidered. "Thanks, but I think I'll move on to something say—*softer*."

"Ye are funny, Lady Brigid," snickered Nell.

"Yeah, I'm a regular comedian." Brigid stood straightening her dress. It was days like these when she longed to be wearing her jeans and boots. Nell suggested they pick some wildflowers for the Samhain feast tomorrow, so trying to pick wildflowers in a gown was one aspect of medieval life she was still adjusting too.

Stretching her arms over her head to work out the kinks in her shoulders, she stood taking in the beauty of her surroundings. They had ventured out early this morning with Finn and one of the guards, since Duncan and Cormac had insisted they not leave the castle without protection. They never did find out whom, or if one of the MacFhearguises was traveling on their lands. Duncan had been fierce in his protection of her, another issue she was still coming to terms with.

Brigid clasped her arms around her waist reliving the past few days with Duncan. During the daytime they were apart; however, on occasion, they would run into each other along the dark silent corridors, filling them with passionate kisses—a promise of what they would have come nightfall.

She may have been weary from lack of sleep, but she would not trade it for anything. He filled her body and soul. Every time she saw him, it was as if she fell more in love with him. The only thorn, which was not the one in her finger, was the one when Conn would return for her.

Then there was the situation with the sword. It struck her that there had to be more than just handing it over to Duncan. Hell, even Duncan mirrored her thoughts and they spent many an hour discussing the same, with no solution. It was after one of their heated discussions regarding Conn and the sword that Duncan decided to seek out advice from Cathal. One of these days, she would have to ask Duncan how he knew the Fenian warrior.

Cathal had left yesterday morning to prepare for the feast of Samhain, and Duncan had ridden out soon thereafter. The druid required solitary meditation and would return the day of Samhain to celebrate with them.

The wind brushed against her face and for a

moment, she expected it to be Duncan, but he wouldn't be back until Samhain. She placed a hand against her cheek. "Hurry back," she whispered.

Her head snapped around when she heard the anguished cry of an animal in the trees ahead. Glancing back at Nell, she saw the girl heard it, too. Before she could utter a word of warning to her, Nell was up and running toward the sound.

"No, Nell!" Reaching out to grab her, Brigid tripped and fell slamming to the cold ground with such force she had to catch her breath. Quickly hauling herself up, she twisted to see Nell already dodging into the thick grove of trees.

"Finn? Dougal?" Brigid yelled. "Blast! You were shadowing our every move and *now* when we need you..." Brigid couldn't wait and took off after Nell.

Another cry from the animal echoed out from among the trees. Brigid ran as fast as her feet could carry, the dress hampering her efforts to move quickly.

"Nell!" Brigid screamed praying Dougal or Finn had heard her. She was trying hard not to panic, since she heard nothing from Nell. Slowing her pace, she entered the grove of thick pine trees. Brushing past them, she stepped over several logs coming to a halt. Scanning the dense thicket, she let her eyes adjust to the semi-darkness. "Nell, where are you?" she snapped.

Creeping along gradually, she froze when she heard a low growl coming from her right. Turning, she peered down and noticed Nell sitting down beside what looked like a wooden cage. Moving forward cautiously, the animal's growl intensified, bringing her to a halt. She also saw that Nell held up her hand in warning to stay her footsteps.

"What are you doing?" hissed Brigid. "Come here this instant!"

Nell shook her head no, and spoke quietly. "Och, gray wolf, I'm sorry we have scared ye, but I can help ye out of that ugly cage. I ken there are awful persons who would do such cruel things. If ye would be so kind, I would like to move a bit closer to take a look at the latch."

Brigid's heart pounded and she refused to let a small girl tell her, the adult, what to do. It occurred to her they wouldn't have much time before the wolf lunged and broke free from his bondage, only to feast on the girl in front of him. Taking small steps forward, she inched slowly toward Nell.

The wolf snarled and snapped at Brigid.

"*Please*, Lady Brigid," pleaded Nell. "I ken what I am doing. Gray wolf is frightened and if I can soothe him, he will trust me. Ye are not helping."

"Bloody hell." Irritation lacing her voice. "What are you planning to do?"

"To set him free." Nell continued speaking in hushed tones to the wolf.

Brigid watched, and then realized if only she had her dirk. Why did she not take it back when Nell offered? *Where in God's green earth are you, Finn and Dougal? This is insanity*. Quickly scanning her surroundings, she looked for anything that could be used for a weapon. Perhaps, a large heavy branch or rock? However, that would require her to move, and the animal kept eyeing her every few minutes then back again to Nell.

Enough she thought. Her only hope was to run, gather Nell, and hurry as fast as she could out of the trees, praying Dougal was nearby. Just when she was about to lunge at Nell, the wolf silently made a whooshing sound as if sighing and lay down. She gaped and watched in horror as Nell lifted the wooden latch from the cage and sat back down.

As if sensing her fear, Nell said softly, "Dinnae fetch me Lady Brigid. I will come to ye."

Brigid swallowed, and the lump that was in her heart now lodged inside her throat. If need be, she would run and place herself in front of Nell. Time stood still as she waited what seemed like eternity, fear rooting her to the ground. Brigid had no doubt her bravery would take over if the wolf decided to make Nell his next meal.

Nell gradually stood up. Muttering something in Gaelic, she blew the wolf a kiss. Then Nell did something that Brigid concluded was utterly foolish, she turned her back on the wolf and made her way toward Brigid. She kept her eyes steady on the wolf until she felt Nell grasp her hand. Pushing her toward her side, she stepped back ever so slowly.

The wolf raised its head and sniffed the air causing Brigid to halt her steps. She watched in horror as the wolf casually stood and stepped through the cage. Giving them one last look over, it sauntered away through the thicket of trees.

Brigid's shoulders slumped, and her breath came out in a rush. "Sweet Mother." Her eyes narrowed as she pivoted around to look at Nell, who was seemingly unaware of the danger they had just faced.

Trying to keep her anger at bay she asked, "What could have possibly possessed you to go over and open the door for that wild animal?"

Nell gave her an insolent look. "It needed my help."

"That wolf"—Brigid pointed to where the wolf had been—"could have eaten you alive!"

Innocent eyes of a child gazed into hers saying, "Och, nae, it just wanted to be set free."

There was no convincing Nell she was right in this matter. So Brigid bit her tongue and counted to ten, fearing she would lash out and be more of a threat than the wolf. Nell's hand squeezed hers ever so gently, which brought her focus back down to the smile on the little girl's face, melting her anger. Brigid dropped down on her knees to her level.

"Lady Brigid, dinnae be angry. The wolf is gone."

All Brigid could do was hug her tightly. Then standing, she took her hand again saying, "Let's go find Dougal and Finn, okay?" Nell shook her head in agreement.

A brisk breeze brushed passed them, its cold tendrils touching Brigid's face, and she shivered.

Standing at the edge of the grove was a man dressed in a long robe, similar to the one Cathal wore. His hair was black with steaks of silver, and he had it tied back. The look he gave her was sinister. He stood still, hands clasped in front with his head tilted to one side as if studying her. Behind him was a large giant. She thought Duncan to be tall, but this one was much taller. He reminded her of some wild caveman. His hair was long and dirty and he had a deep scar that ran from his brow to chin, and he carried an axe.

Her instincts told her to run. *But where*? And where in the blazes was Dougal?

Her heart started to pound and she gripped Nell's

hand more firmly, pulling her close to her side. She nodded in greeting and made a move to walk away until the giant took several steps forward, blocking her path.

Then the other man spoke. "Greetings, *Lady* Brigid. It would please me immensely, if ye and the young lass would accompany us."

Swallowing the fear creeping back into her throat, she narrowed her eyes. "I believe we are expected back at Castle Creag, and I am with several armed men."

His smirk was more of a snarl. "If it is your one man, I am afraid to tell ye that he is dead." Nodding to the giant in front of her, he continued, "He did fight bravely with my man, Thadeus." Then the snarl became one filled with anger. "Ye and the lass *will* accompany us, now!"

Nell whispered, "Lady Brigid, what..."

"Shush, Nell. It's going to be okay." Brigid realized what Nell was about to say, and considered it best to keep silent about Finn. Nell's eyes went round, but she nodded in agreement, and Brigid thanked the gods that for once, Nell kept quiet.

"Why did you kill Dougal?" Fear and anger knotted inside her.

"He was of no use. However, the young lad, Finn, is that his name?"

Nell gasped, and Brigid nodded in agreement.

"Good. Finn will deliver my message, a bit bloodied, but they will ken my meaning."

"What do you mean, a bit bloodied? What did you *do* to Finn?" Her voice rising.

"*I* did nothing, Lady Brigid. Thadeus was the one who removed a finger from the boy."

Brigid held her ground, bile forming in her mouth

as she felt Nell quake with silent sobs. "We are not going anywhere with you—*you monster*!" Releasing Nell's hand, she pushed her behind her.

"Enough!" His hand whipped the air, and Brigid reeled as if she'd been slapped.

Gasping, she half turned and yelled, "Run, Nell!"

Thadeus was too quick for either of them. He grabbed Nell, tucking her under his arm, as her screams tore through the grove.

"Stop! Please let her go!" Brigid stood motionless, hands clenched at her sides.

Pointing a gnarled finger at her, he rasped out, "Ye will come, and to insure that ye do, we will bring the lass."

"Who the bloody hell are you, and what do you want?" demanded Brigid.

Without warning, he slapped her hard across the face, his sardonic laughter filling her ears. "I am the druid Lachlan, and what I *want,* is the heart of your Duncan Mackay and his Dragon Knight sword."

Brigid stood unmoving, icy fear gripped her heart as the warm blood from her cut lip trickled down her chin.

Chapter 44

"When all is lost and the path is filled with darkness, call upon the dragon for her to light the way."

Duncan's gaze scanned the horizon. The wind snapped past him, whipping his plaid, and dusting him with leaves ripped from their limbs. It spoke to him of the coming storm, which he could see the dark ominous clouds gathering in the distance. He could hear the rumble of the beast.

Brandubh gave a loud snort and shook his ebony mane. Duncan patted the side of his great warhorse, soothing him with his touch.

"Aye, ye smell the fury of this one, my friend. It is a storm to herald in Samhain." Brandubh bobbed his head as if in agreement. Duncan's gut twisted, such was a storm like this on Samhain that Margaret had died. Could this be an omen? What if this was the battle Cathal had spoken of? He could not shake the fear that snaked within him as he envisioned Brigid caught in the conflict.

"Let us search out Cathal." Nudging Brandubh onwards, he made his way across a small burn and through a thicket of pines. He spotted wisps of smoke and the light from a small fire. Slowing the pace of Brandubh, he brought him to halt a few paces from the small clearing. In the middle, resting against a tall praying stone, he spotted the druid roasting neeps over a small fire. Duncan had entered a sacred place.

"Ye may enter, Duncan." Cathal spoke without looking up to greet him.

Duncan dismounted, tying Brandubh to one of the trees. Then pulling a carefully wrapped leather bottle out of the pack tied to the horse, he strolled over to Cathal.

"Thank ye." He handed the bottle to Cathal.

The fire snapped, sending hot sparks up into the night sky. Cathal pulled out the long branch with the roasting neeps from the heat and laid it across his legs, gesturing for Duncan to join him on the ground.

Removing the cork, Cathal sniffed its contents. "Ahhhh, ye bring *uisge beatha*?"

Duncan smiled and nodded.

Closing his eyes, he took a sip. When he opened them, he cocked a brow. "The water of life, how kind of ye."

He then handed the bottle back to Duncan and he took a drink, savoring the flavor of the fiery liquid. Wiping his mouth with the back of his hand, he placed the whiskey on the ground between them. Silence ensued, as Duncan waited for Cathal to speak.

Cathal uttered a deep sigh. Reaching for the dirk lying next to him, he sliced a portion of the neep, handing it to Duncan. He bowed his head. "Blessings to the great Mother, who has given us our food this day."

The two men ate in communal silence, sharing the whiskey every so often. No words were spoken, nor needed.

Some time had lapsed and Cathal tossed a few

more branches, including the one used to roast their meal, into the fire. Duncan once again passed the bottle back to Cathal, but he held out his hand indicating no more.

"The battle is coming, Duncan."

His words caught Duncan off guard and frowning he asked, "Do ye mean the storm?"

"Why are ye here, Duncan?"

Duncan blinked and shook his head in confusion at the change in conversation. "I need to know if there is a way to keep Conn from entering this realm and taking Brigid back. And before ye ask, aye...this is what she wants, too. She has agreed to handfast with me."

Cathal's eyebrows shot up in surprise. "Truly?"

He gave Cathal a broad smile. "Aye."

Duncan watched as the druid made to stand, grasping his staff. The druid's smile held a glint of sadness, and he waited patiently to hear his words.

Leaning against the prayer stone, he shook his head. "Ye cannot bend the will of the fae to yours, Duncan. Ye ken who Conn is and *what* he is."

"*That* I understand," growled Duncan. He stood abruptly, striding over to the edge of the trees, his hands fisted on his hips. Shaking his head in frustration, he looked back over his shoulder at Cathal. "I love her," his voice but a whisper.

The pain etched across Duncan's face was one Cathal had feared. He had found his heart and now he must let her go. Cathal's own heart was sad, since he had no answers for the Dragon Knight.

Then the light of knowledge illuminated his thoughts. This was not only about love, but also Duncan's honor—honor that had to be fought for. Hope surged within Cathal, and he nodded with the realization not all was lost.

Stepping toward him, Cathal clasped a firm hand on his arm. "The battle is coming, Duncan. Ye must fight the evil and restore the balance."

"So the storm that is coming *is* the battle I must fight?"

Cathal only nodded in affirmative.

Duncan rubbed the back of his neck to ease the tension, recognizing exactly what he would do if Conn should come for Brigid.

"I will see this to the end, but hear me on this, druid, when Conn steps through the mists, he will have to come through *me* to get to Brigid."

A wry smile formed on Cathal's mouth. "Aye, it is something I would like to see. Come, ye shall stay the night, Duncan, and we will finish off that liquid amber."

Chapter 45

"Is reality truth or myth? Are dreams meant to harm or save? Do you believe in dragons?"

Duncan awoke from a deep slumber with a pounding headache and the rumble of snores emanating from Cathal. The drink they had consumed the previous night was not the cause of his pain, but of the coming storm that kept itself at bay, slowly weaving its tail across the Highlands.

Standing slowly, he breathed deeply of the icy brittle air. Snow was accompanying the storm, he suspected, and it might even dust them on Samhain. Saying a quick blessing of thanks for this morning and the ancestors, including Margaret, he flexed his shoulders easing the tension. Something other than the storm was niggling at him, and his thoughts turned toward Brigid.

"Snow is coming, Duncan," yawned Cathal.

Duncan grunted, glancing out toward the dark cloudy sky.

"Where's Sorcha?"

Cathal was now standing. When he bent to retrieve his staff, he paused, a frown forming on his already wrinkled forehead. He gave a sharp whistle and waited.

"She's been gone since last morn," he answered.

Cathal closed his eyes and leaned on his staff.

"She's out of my vision, and it causes me to worry."

Duncan's eyes roamed the broad expanse of the pine trees. "I believe it is time we return."

They had ridden swiftly after quickly breaking their fast. Duncan would have pushed off immediately, but deduced it was important for Cathal to break his fast for the hard ride back to the castle.

It was midday when they saw the stone fortress in the distance. A light drizzle had started, and the wind but a whisper of portent of what was to follow. The ride had cleared Duncan's head, but casting a sideways glance at Cathal gave him pause to worry. He mulled over that he was possibly still worried about Sorcha. The druid had a long day and night ahead with the feast of Samhain without any rest. When the last rays of light drifted away, the darkness would herald in a new beginning. Then he would disappear until winter solstice.

Pulling up gently on Brandubh's reins, he slowed their pace to a mere gallop. He spotted extra men stationed near the portcullis and ramparts, and an uneasiness settled over him.

"Something's amiss, Duncan."

"Aye, I sense it, too."

Upon entering through the portcullis and through the second gate, Duncan dismounted. He immediately unsheathed his sword and took note that Finn had not come forth to tend to Brandubh. The niggling had turned to a prickling sensation of unease and when Cormac greeted them in the bailey, he had the look of a warrior ready to do battle.

Instantly, Duncan understood.

"Brigid?"

Cormac did not hesitate. "Taken with Nell, Dougal killed."

The blow of his words struck him with such force that Duncan stumbled, taking a few steps backwards, his sword scraping the muddy ground. His vision blurred. The combination of the storm's building power and his, was too much to contain. A guttural cry tore from his throat and thunder boomed so loud over them, the ground where they stood shook, causing panic in the men and animals. Even Duncan's great warhorse whinnied, throwing his head back.

He kept his hands fisted at his sides glaring at Cormac.

"When?" he rasped out.

"Yesterday."

Before Duncan had a chance to unleash his rage onto him, Cormac held up a cautionary hand, sword extended in the other. "I suspect your next question, and the answer lies with Finn. He is resting in one of the rooms off of my chambers."

"*Resting*? Lugh's balls! He will get himself down here, now!"

Duncan took a step forward, just as Cormac stepped in front of him blocking his path. A dangerous move, thought Duncan. He would not let him interfere. Dark fury flared in his eyes, but still Cormac refused to stand down.

"Nae, Duncan! Finn is injured. The bastards cut off one of his fingers."

Duncan flinched.

Cormac's voice softened. "He's a brave, strong lad—walked back holding his bloody hand last evening, looking for ye. The lad would not rest, nor has he taken any sleeping draught for the pain. He says he has a message for ye from those who took Brigid and Nell."

Duncan's expression was tight with strain. "We must make ready, Cormac."

Cormac nodded. "Yet ye must hear out the lad before we can move against this evil." He spat on the ground. "The only thing Finn would say is that ye must come alone."

Duncan arched an eyebrow in question, since he knew damn well Cormac would never sit back and let some vile creature dictate to him. And he was grateful. Thunder crashed again around them, and the sky opened up with a torrential downpour.

"Do not think to not include me in this." Raising his sword up in an arc, Cormac plunged it into the ground. Then holding out his arm, he waited for Duncan to acknowledge him.

Duncan grasped his outheld arm. "I would want no other, though hear me on this"—his lips curling in disdain—"I will be the one to thrust my sword into their heart, until it beats no more."

"Aye, that I will give ye. Now go see to Finn. Matilda is tending him."

****

Duncan entered the chamber seeing Matilda sitting in a chair by the lad's side. She was telling him a tale about the great Cuchulainn and his hound. The boy was listening with rapt attention holding his bandaged hand and nodding, taking in her every word. Duncan gave a small smile remembering it was one of his favorites as a young lad, too. Leaning against the door, he listened to Matilda's calm voice, trying to answer the many questions the lad kept tossing out at her.

"Are ye sure he only had one hound? Some say he had two."

"Now, Finn, the tale that was told by the great druid Cathbad, was he only had one."

"Humph! Do ye think his chariot was big enough for more than one hound?"

"I dinnae ken."

"Humph!"

Duncan pushed off from the wall and walked over to Finn, hearing a small sigh escape from Matlida.

"It is good to see ye, Duncan."

He reached out as she gave him her hand, gently squeezing it.

"I hear ye have been having the same problem with the telling of Cuchulainn and his hound."

"Ye both seem to think he had *two* hounds." The worry shone bright in Matilda's eyes.

Duncan bent and placed a kiss on her brow. "Why don't ye get something to eat? I will tend to Finn. I hear he has a message for me." Casting a glance over to the lad, he noticed fear when he saw it. The lad would now have to tell him what he witnessed.

"Thank ye, Duncan."

Standing slowly, she stepped close to Duncan's side speaking softly. "When he is finished, I have prepared a draught. He has not slept since returning." Patting his arm, she turned to leave.

They both watched as Matilda left the room, gently closing the oak door behind her.

Duncan saw Finn swallow, understanding it was fear lodged in his throat like a lodestone. He did not want to push the lad, but time was their greatest enemy. Each hour that passed was another hour the bastard held

Brigid and Nell captive.

"Are ye ready to tell me the message?" his voice low, but firm. Duncan sat forward in the chair, his arms resting on his knees. He gazed into the lad's somber eyes.

Finn swallowed again and nodded affirmative.

"Good."

"We did not see them coming. The taller man came at Dougal with his axe. He went down hard and never got back up." Finn's eyes went wide in the telling. "I could not move and when I did, I ran into the other man." Finn twisted the edges of his wrap with his good hand.

"So there were only two?"

"Aye, just the two...the big man and the druid."

"Druid? Are ye sure, Finn?"

A shadow of alarm passed over Finn's face. "Och, aye, Sir Duncan. He told me so, and he carries a staff like Cathal's."

Duncan reached out and squeezed the lad's leg in reassurance. "Go on, Finn."

"The druid told me ye are to bring the Dragon Sword to the stones where your lady came through. Ye must come alone, too."

"This is all he wants, Finn?"

"Aye."

Finn's shoulders started to sag, and Duncan realized the lad was fading quickly.

"Can ye tell me why they cut your finger off, Finn?"

He glanced down at his bandaged hand, and a small tear threaten to spill forth as his voice took on a more angry tone. "The druid said this was a message meant for ye, and they would harm more than a finger on the lass." Finn's gaze returned to Duncan's, and the searing look he gave him was one of steel. "He then said that for your lady he would remove her heart and give it to ye as a gift."

Duncan sat up slowly and fisted his hands on his knees, his face flashed in anger.

Finn leaned forward. His voice was quiet, yet held an undertone of cold contempt. "He may be a druid, but I think ye need to take his heart out."

Duncan gave the lad a sardonic smile, his mind already getting ready for the battle ahead. He stood and placed his hand on Finn's shoulder. "Ye were very brave, lad. Ye have shown great courage and strength. Understand this, Finn—I am proud of ye."

Finn's jaw started to tremble, and he quickly cast his gaze away from Duncan. "Och, Sir Duncan..."

"Nae, Finn." Duncan sat down on the bed and leaned close. "From this day forward, there will be no more *Sir* before my name. I give ye permission to call me Duncan. Do ye hear me, *son*?"

Finn's head snapped up, a look of shock registering over his features and his mouth agape at Duncan's words.

"Do ye mean Sir—I mean Du...Duncan that I'm under your protection *forever*?"

One corner of Duncan's mouth twisted upwards. "Forever, son."

"I thank ye, Duncan," his voice but a whisper.

Then in a voice hardened with steel, Finn added, "Now go, and bring our women back from those bastards."

"I will indeed, Finn. Now rest."

It struck Duncan that the young lad would make a great warrior one day. One he would want by his side. Rising from his chair, he walked quickly toward the door.

"Duncan?"

"Yes, Finn?"

"I forgot to tell ye the druid's name."

Duncan paused at the door half turning. So, the bastard had a name. "What is it?"

"He told me his name is Lachlan." Finn spat as if the very word was foul tasting.

A feeling of cold dread washed over Duncan as he braced his hand against the door. Never did he think to hear that name again.

"Thank ye, Finn."

Matilda came through the corridor, and he nodded to her in passing.

He hastily climbed the stairs to his chambers, striding over to the table where his sword lay. His hand froze but for a brief moment over the sheath, before removing the sword. Walking over to the window, he opened the shutters.

Honor. Family. Love. Three powerful words, which had been absent from his life these past twelve moons. He considered himself unworthy of them, until *she* walked into his life. She gave herself freely to him, understanding all that he had done. Brigid had given her love to his wretched soul, ripping apart the blackness that almost destroyed him. Did he feel worthy of her love? Nae, but perhaps one day.

Duncan glanced down at the sword in his hand, realizing he had one more task to complete.

Leaving his chambers, he ascended to the parapet

and walked along the wall to the northern end. Here there would be no one to witness his actions. The wind howled at his back and the rain pelted his face with an icy sting.

Raising the sword slowly out in front of him, he called out to the ancients. "By the elements of sky, I claim ye as my own. By the blood of my fae family, I claim ye as my own. By the code of the Dragon Knights, I claim ye as my own!"

Holding the sword face down, he kissed the green dragon stone in the hilt. His blue eyes scanned the ominous dark sky as if in search of someone or something. Bending down on one knee, he placed the sword down on the ground in front of him.

"Forgive me, Guardian, I ask of ye. Let me regain my honor to redeem those ye have sent. If I must die, then so be it."

Lightning tore across the sky in a dazzling brilliance of light and energy. Its intensity pulsed within his body and flooded him with renewed strength.

The stone in the hilt of his sword shimmered and with a steady hand, he grasped hold of it. Standing and angling it high over his head, the heat of stone seared up the length of his arm, quickly spreading throughout the rest of his body. The effect knocking him back against the wall. He was breathing in short bursts as he brought his sword arm down.

Duncan appeared...different. *Changed.*

Gently, he brought the hilt up to his lips and kissed the dragon stone again, content that the Guardian heard his words. Stepping away from the wall, Duncan made his way to his chambers to prepare for a battle that would save one life and take another.

Chapter 46

"When all hope is lost, put your ear to the ground, and listen. If in your heart you believe, then you will hear the heartbeat of the great dragon, and you may call upon her for help."

Brigid heard the wailing in the distance, and she rubbed her tired sore eyes against her drawn up knees. Curled up against her was Nell, her eyes round with fright. Brigid could not tell if it was from the wailing, or the monsters that were holding them captive. Their hands and feet were bound, and Thadeus was sitting on a boulder several feet away, his back to them.

They had traveled most of the night, stopping only when Nell had started to whimper. In an attempt to silence her, Lachlan had threatened to remove her tongue. Brigid had tried unsuccessfully to reason with the druid, and he slapped her hard again.

They trudged on until the first glistening rays of dawn descended over the hill. It was a dark and gloomy day, one filled with rain, which made it more difficult to travel.

They were permitted to relieve themselves, but Thadeus stood guard a foot away. When it came time for Brigid, he held a knife to the girl's throat and she had to hold back a vile retort.

The wailing continued, and Brigid heard Nell

whisper something.

"What is it, Nell?" her voice low as she watched the back of Thadeus.

Nell looked up into Brigid's eyes, so deep and piercing. "Banshee."

"No, sweetheart. There's no such th..." Brigid stopped in midsentence, realizing it seemed ridiculous to tell Nell that banshees did not exist. Especially, when she had traveled over eight hundred years into the past, encountered a dragon, and watched a man manipulate the wind, and the elements of the sky.

She recalled from her history that banshees only meant one thing. Their cry was a foretelling of a death, and it sent shivers down her spine. Yet, the only death she longed to see was the giant in front of them and the druid.

Brigid stretched out her legs, easing the cramps in her calves.

"Nell, lay down across my lap. You need to get some rest."

Silently, she did as Brigid told her to do, keeping her gaze on the back of the giant.

She sensed the moment Nell had drifted off to sleep, by the deep sigh the girl let out. At least they tied Nell's hands in front, instead of behind her back as they did with hers.

If only I had my dirk, she reflected. Taking a deep breath, she tried to relax her shoulders. She closed her eyes, but realized the early morning birdsong was quiet within the forest right before she drifted off.

Dreams of monsters filtered through her sleep. Brigid awoke with a pounding against her leg, and the glare of Lachlan looming over her. He had been kicking her for several moments and neither her, or Nell had awoken fast enough.

"Get up!" Spittle from his mouth flew into her face, and she swallowed the acid rising in her throat. Nell's head snapped up, and Brigid thanked the gods she remained quiet.

The rain was now a steady downpour causing her to slip twice. She observed Nell trying to keep up, wincing every now and then. However, she gave the girl credit for being strong and brave. Ducking under a low hanging pine bough, they emerged into a circular group of oak trees, which she recognized. "Damn," she muttered under her breath.

Brigid knew precisely what was waiting beyond those trees. The stone circle she came through, and the place where Duncan's sister died.

Was blood to be spilled again?

They kept their pace along the trees, never venturing within. The trees had lost most of their leaves and the stones stood starkly through the thick branches. A strange tingling sensation sent a tremor through her and at the same time, she saw a familiar face. Hope soared when she spotted Sorcha perched in one of trees.

Brigid sent out a mental prayer of thanks to whoever was watching over them. Could it be possible the dragon was watching, too? She smiled slowly and bumped gently into Nell.

Nell gazed up frowning at her.

Brigid nodded her head discreetly in the direction of Sorcha. She wanted to share a bit of hope with the girl.

Tears glistened in Nell's eyes, and she bit her lower lip to keep them from spilling forth. A smile flitted briefly, fear still keeping Nell petrified of her captors.

They walked with more spirit than they had in the past twenty-four hours and even the rain and mud could not dispel their new spirit of faith.

Chapter 47

"Sometimes the broken heart of a warrior cannot be healed by love, but must be completely reborn."

Duncan stood next to Brandubh, strapping his sword on the great warhorse. He had chosen to wear only his leather trews and plaid. When the moment presented itself, he would strip off his plaid and fight like the warrior he was trained to be, since the moment of his birth. He would fight with his fae blood and gain honor back for his family.

The wind and rain descended in freezing pellets, and he relished its fury. For the first time, Duncan had somehow mastered and tamed his own beast. After saying a prayer to the Guardian, he honed his own power as one of a shield and surrounded himself with it. He would not unleash it, unless it was necessary.

Cormac was giving last minute instructions to those of his men who would stay behind and guard the castle. There was a quiet strength in his friend, one that helped him many times in the past year.

He owed him his life and more.

Duncan understood Cormac considered it a weakness for anyone to take women hostage, especially ones so young. He confessed to Duncan that he had a soft spot for the wee lass. They all had formed a bond with her and with Brigid. Cormac had one hell of time keeping him and his men at bay until Duncan arrived. They wanted blood for this action.

Duncan reminded Cormac of Nell's family and gave instructions for food to be taken out to the animals. Strangely, the one to volunteer was Moira. She was grief stricken when she heard Brigid and Nell had been taken. Cormac was insistent a guard accompany her, since they had no idea how the animals would respond.

There was only one last message to deliver before they left, and he saw the one person he had to speak with come slowly through the yard toward him.

"Greetings, Cathal." Duncan watched as the druid made his way cautiously to his side.

Cathal leaned forward on his staff. "Fine weather for this Samhain."

A wry smile formed on Duncan's mouth, "Aye, indeed. I believe I may have found the source of evil in all of this."

Cathal's white bushy brows arched upwards in surprise, "*Truth?*"

"Lachlan."

"He's dead," Cathal uttered in a strained whisper.

Duncan shook his head. "Nae, he gave his name to Finn. He travels with a giant who carries an axe, and he wants me to bring the Dragon Sword in exchange for the women."

"Sweet Danu, *nae!*"

Duncan's voice was as cold as steel when he spoke. "Ye ken what I must do."

"How can this be? Why would the gods and goddesses not show me Lachlan? There can only be one answer. Lachlan has chosen the path of evil, and my visions, clouded." His shoulders slumped. "I will come with ye."

Duncan placed a hand on Cathal's shoulder in compassion. "Nae, ye are not the one to do this, nor should ye be. I believe he has had a part in this from the beginning, and I must be the one to end it."

He only nodded and Duncan squeezed gently before leaving.

"Duncan. I ask one favor."

Half turning, Duncan asked, "What is it?"

"Bring me the heart of my brother, so I can burn the evil that is within. *Is buan gach olc*. Evil lives long," Cathal lamented.

Duncan gave a quick nod of approval and mounted Brandubh. The wind howling at his back, he motioned for Cormac to follow.

No sooner did they leave the castle, than the MacFhearguis brothers, Alex, Patrick, and a few of their men greeted them. At once, all men unsheathed their swords, the sound of steel piercing the air. Horses snorted, their hoofs stomping the cold muddy ground.

Brandubh already sensing the battle was ready to charge onward. "Hold." Duncan pulled hard, his sword held high.

Alex raised his hand in greeting and nudged his horse slowly forward. He was the only one not to unsheathe his sword.

The wind whipped past him, and he was uncertain if this storm was of Duncan's making. The man looked feral and then he noticed the sword.

"By the gods! The Mackay has the sword back in his possession," said Patrick, keeping a slow pace next to his brother.

Alex cast him a quick glance. "*Aye*. So be it then. It never was intended for our family. My only concern is to do whatever it will take to call a truce and find Adam."

Patrick nodded in agreement and halted his horse a few paces back.

Bringing his horse to a stop, Alex held the reins tightly. "Hail, Duncan."

The air hummed with energy around Duncan. "Ye take great risk in coming here, MacFhearguis!" he said with a snarl.

"Aye, as ye can see my sword is sheathed. I come to speak with ye."

Duncan sliced the air with his sword, and Alex quickly raised his hand. "Hold men!"

"Ye *dare* to have an archer poised at me? Words laced with lies!" Duncan spat out. He knew Alex well; having spotted the man perched in the tree. "I have no time to deal with ye, MacFhearguis. Step aside *now*!" he growled. Duncan detected his control slipping, and if the man did not move, he would have to take him down. Time was something he did not have, chiefly for Alex.

Alex refused to move saying, "I've come to ask ye for help in searching for Adam. He has been missing these past six moons."

"I will ask ye only one more time, MacFhearguis, then, *if* blood is spilled, it will not be mine," his voice turning deadly.

Keeping his features closed, Alex gave a sharp nod. Giving way to Duncan and his men, he gave the signal to let them pass. He waited until they were out of sight to speak with Patrick, who had ridden over to him.

"That went well, brother."

"God's teeth, Patrick!" The rain pelted them harder.

Sean came thundering through the trees with a look Alex understood well. He brought news, and Alex prayed it was news of Adam.

"What news, Sean?"

"Bloody hell, Alex! Ye are damn lucky the Mackay did not take your head! What were ye thinking?"

Alex blanched, since he had never known Sean to question his motives.

"Sean, ye overstep."

"Nae, Alex. Ye have not heard the news. Someone has taken the Mackay's woman and a wee lass."

"God's blood, nae!" Alex rubbed a hand over his face in frustration.

"There is only one person I can think of at the moment who would dare to take her, especially on Samhain." Patrick had spoken with dead calm.

"Michael, of course," said Alex.

Patrick shook his head negative, a cold expression settled on his features. "Nae."

His gut twisted as realization dawned on Alex. "It's happening again."

"What?" asked Sean.

"Do ye think it was *him* last Samhain?"

The grim look Patrick gave was his answer.

Sean was growing impatient. "*Who* took them and *what* is happening again?"

Alex rubbed his chin. "I ken of only one man who would gain from this, and I believe he has been using us to get what he wants."

Sean threw his hands up in frustration.

"*Lachlan*." Alex spat out.

Chapter 48

"When a wounded knight has found his strength, will he relinquish all that he has been taught?"

The storm was at full strength, and Duncan relished its fury, and they sped as if the wind carried them. Cormac and the select few who accompanied them rode along at a distance. This was Duncan's final quest, but he was smart in realizing he might need his friend. They were not dealing with any ordinary man, but a powerful druid.

Again, his mind drifted back to the night with Margaret. Could it be possible Lachlan was involved, weaving evil magic? It was a thought to ponder later. This was now, and he needed to save Brigid and Nell. Bile rose just thinking they were in the grips of this black-hearted monster. Pushing Brandubh faster through the hills, pine boughs smacked his face, their biting sting giving him more strength and focus. They rode as one and spittle from his horse flew out into the air.

He rode today like a warrior.

Duncan heard a bird screech and spotted Sorcha circling in the distance. Night was descending; its blackness combined with the storm would mean that it would be difficult to see. He urged his horse faster, knowing the path to the stones well. Sending out a thought of thanks to her, he sent her on her way, realizing she knew where they were.

****

Brigid could not quell the fits of shaking from Nell. She had noticed the blue of her lips and worried she had taken a chill. They sat huddled together under a large oak tree away from the stones. Their ever-present guard was perched low on one knee on the ground, his back to them. Every now and then, he would half turn to gaze at them, causing Nell to shiver more.

The storm had abated, and Brigid could see the full moon peeking out of the dark clouds. The moonlight dusted the branches with its pale luminosity and cast a shining radiance off the stones. She took solace in the light, giving her hope.

She suspected Duncan would come for them, but what would be the price? The words of her note and those of the curse blazed forth in her mind.

"So this is where it ends," she whispered.

Brigid's arms were numb from being tied behind her back for so long, but it was her heart that now ached. What she wouldn't give to have her dirk. Shaking her head in frustration, she gazed up again at the moon, saying a silent plea of protection, not only for herself and Nell, but for Duncan, too.

"*Fear not my daughter*," a gentle voice pierced her thoughts. Her mind recognized at once whom the voice belonged to, and her head snapped around in anticipation of seeing the great dragon.

Then she felt a warm breeze touch her cheeks and sensed Duncan nearby. Hope surged anew, and she bent over to whisper into Nell's ear.

"Help is close by, Nell."

Nell only nodded and huddled more against Brigid's chest.

The air hummed with energy, and Brigid kept her focus on Thadeus. She had no idea where the evil coward Lachlan was hiding; therefore, she kept her gaze out toward the stones. The first chance she had, she would see Nell to safety, even if it meant blocking the path of the giant.

The warm breeze swept over again, and this time she smiled. "If you can hear me, Duncan, hurry, my love." Her words infused with love were sent back on the breeze.

It was in that moment she saw Lachlan step out from across the stones. He stood directly in the middle as Duncan rode in, dismounting from Brandubh in one swift movement. He had thrown off his plaid and stood as a mighty warrior. He kept his sword across his forearms, waiting.

Brigid started to let out a cry, but held back. He knew she was alive and to distract him, but for an instant, could mean his death.

"Will it be a battle of power we shall fight?" Duncan's tone edged with steel.

Lachlan cocked his head to the side as if studying some lower kind of prey. He then proceeded to punch the ground with his staff and lightning split the sky.

"Do not play games with me, druid." Duncan held his sword out and with his other hand slapped the air, causing Lachlan to lose his balance as if he was the one slapped. His nostrils flared with fury.

"Enough!" snarled Lachlan. "Ye understand what I want!"

Keeping his gaze fixed on Duncan, he yelled out,

"Thadeus bring out the woman, and ye ken what to do with the other. I would be careful on what ye do next, Duncan. If ye want the woman to live, ye will give me the sword."

Duncan froze. His face a mask of fury, arms clenched with the need to seize and snap the druid's neck. Cormac was still some distance away and he needed more time. Tapping down his rage and power, he took in deep gulps of cold air, letting them out slowly.

Thadeus went over and tossed Nell aside as if she was a rag doll, her head bumping on a nearby log.

"No!" yelled Brigid as she tried to kick the giant in vain. He held her down with one arm, slicing through the bonds at her ankles, and yanking her to her feet.

"Damn," Duncan hissed quietly. Where *are* ye Cormac?

He turned his gaze back toward Lachlan. "Was it ye, druid, last Samhain?" his voice bitter, but controlled.

Lachlan's laugh was sinister in its tone. "Since ye are about to die, ye might as well know. Your clan does not deserve to hold so much power. It should have been placed within a druid." He spat out the last.

"Ye were all so easy to stir the beast in each of ye." His smile was one of pure evil. Pointing his staff at Duncan, he sneered. "I used *your* powers against ye, so very simple to have ye at each other's throats. I must say, it was easy to tap into your anger, Duncan, using it to control ye." Tapping his finger against his mouth in a cruel jest he continued, "The plan was to have ye kill the MacFhearguis, but I must say Duncan, I relish your ending more." Lachlan's eyes lit up almost gleefully.

"To kill your sister, *was brilliant*!"

The sky erupted in a thunderous clap and Duncan's eyes turned lethal, as his sword threatened to slice through the druid's throat. Never had he shook with so much rage to kill. It took everything he had within to hold himself back. "Ye mock the fae, druid." he growled.

"*Nae*, they are no more, hiding below when they could wield so much power out in the open." He flung out his arms on the last.

Duncan realized he was insane. No one would dare go against the fae.

"Ye will pay the price for this, druid." Duncan aimed the sword at his chest. They were many feet away, but he was sure he could slice it out in two strides.

"Thadeus?"

Duncan turned slowly to see Brigid standing by the outer edge of the trees. She was ragged, and her face bruised. The man had a dirk to her throat, and a trail of blood trickled down her neck. Blind rage tore at him, wanting to rip apart these men.

He felt helpless.

Brigid gave him a small smile and mouthed the words, "I love you."

It was all the power and strength he required.

His power was not in the relic he held. Nae, his power not only flowed through his blood, but also for the woman he loved. He loved Brigid more than life itself, and it was the most powerful weapon of all. Yes, he would give the sword to the druid, and then he would not only feel his rage, but that of the fae, as well.

Duncan lowered his sword, presenting the hilt out

toward the druid. Yet, before Lachlan had a chance to reach for it, they heard a loud howling.

Thadeus never saw the animal coming, the growl piercing the night in all directions. He gave a loud roar as the wolf jumped and clamped his teeth into his thigh. Letting go of Brigid to spear the wolf, she tumbled to the ground watching in horror as the wolf tore through an artery, blood gushing everywhere.

Brigid scrambled back away from Thadeus, who was trying in a strangled effort to reach her. She tried to stand, but her feet flicked mud and leaves causing her to slip. He caught her heel, and instantly the wolf went for the kill and lunged for his neck.

Brigid screamed, and watched in horror as the wolf snarled at the man after he had killed him. Then he sauntered several paces away, sat down, and proceeded to lick his paws.

Thadeus was dead.

"That was a verra bad man. Thank ye, gray wolf." Nell was sitting up besides the log, and her eyes held the look of one who thought justice had been served.

Stunned, Brigid tried to stand on shaky legs. "Oh, Nell."

Immediately, she saw Cormac come up behind Nell and whisper something behind her back. Brigid watched as he cut the bonds from her arms and feet. Tears streamed down her face as Nell lunged into his arms.

Another man Brigid didn't recognize came over and sliced through her bonds behind her back. Her shoulders sagged with the relief of freedom.

"Thank you." Brigid flexed her hands, and rubbed at her sore wrists.

The man merely nodded, stepping aside to go stand by another man.

"Traitors!" screamed Lachlan.

"I would hold your tongue, druid," spat Alex. "I believe our brother would be very interested to know what ye have been doing behind his back."

Duncan still had his sword leveled at Lachlan, and then he heard Cormac give a shout that Nell and Brigid were safe.

The druid was shaking with fury, his eyes blazing.

Duncan shifted slightly. "It would seem as if ye have made new enemies this night, Lachlan, and I might add that I am still alive. I am sure *my* brothers will be interested in learning what transpired with your *evil magic*."

The glare Lachlan gave him would have cut any other man to stone, but Duncan held firm, considering that the druid's days were numbered.

"Hear these words well, druid. Not only will ye die, but I will make sure your heart is delivered to your brother, Cathal. Blood will not be spilled on holy ground this night. Therefore, I will release ye. Take heed, for ye will never ken the moment I strike ye down."

Lachlan took his staff and pushed the sword away from his body, his face infused with rage. He turned and stomped away.

It was over.

"Duncan!" Brigid could no longer contain herself. Tears streaming down her face, she stumbled quickly toward her knight.

One moment Duncan's face held the look of one to embrace his love. The next, horror of what was about to happen, and he could not move fast enough.

Brigid's focus was on reaching the man she loved, and she never saw the dirk until the moment Lachlan plunged it into her.

Grabbing her braid with his other hand, he whispered into her ear, "How does it feel realizing I just killed the soul of the man ye love?" He flung her aside as if she were nothing.

A guttural roar of anguish tore from Duncan. Gathering his power, he hurled it out toward Lachlan, sending the druid flying where he landed against a large stone, his head hitting the ground.

Duncan was at Brigid's side in two strides. Dropping down next to her, he cradled her in his arms.

"Du…Duncan?" Brigid tried to raise her hand to his face. He took hold of it, placing it against his chest.

"Whist, *leannan*, I am here. Dinnae move." Duncan glanced down at her abdomen, where her wound was bleeding profusely.

Without realizing it, Cormac was beside him ripping apart his tunic with his sword. "Here, Duncan, place this against her wound." Duncan took the cloth and held it over the open wound, causing Brigid to moan, blood pooling out of the now drenched material.

"Nae, she's losing too much blood." Duncan blurted out, fear knotting within.

"She needs the healer, Duncan, the wound is grave." He turned to look at his men and shook his head.

"*Nae!*" Nell screamed, running toward them. Cormac caught her in midflight holding her against his chest as he stepped away from Duncan and Brigid.

Brigid's eyes fluttered back open. She had drifted

off and was fighting hard to stay conscious. The look on Duncan's face told her that the wound was severe. His hair hung down with the one wild lock hanging over his brow, tempting her to brush it aside. She smiled bravely into those crystal blue eyes she loved. "Have I told you how much I love you, Duncan Mackay?"

"*Leannan*...," his voice overcome with emotion.

"I'm not going to make it, am I?" She swallowed.

His lips trembled and he shook his head. He was helpless. How could this be happening? She was not sent here to die, was she? His mind reeled. There was only one thought, one last deed.

"Brigid O'Neill, I love ye as no other. My *soul* is yours forever. My *heart* is yours forever. I will never love another." Reaching down, he pulled out the ribbon he had stolen many weeks ago from her room. Her eyes went wide when she saw it, and he wrapped it around her wrist and his, letting it dangle over his arm.

His voice shook. "I take ye my heart, at the rising of the moon, and the setting of the stars, binding my heart and soul to ye—in this life and beyond." His lips grazed hers in a gentle kiss.

Her voice trembled. "Duncan Mackay, my one true love, my dream lover, my heart. I will love you forever and a day until the end of time." She reached up and placed her hand firmly against his chest willing herself to stay focused, feeling the life literally drain out of her. Staring into his eyes brimming with tears, she added, "I will wait for you, my love, in the land of forever, *Tir na Og*."

"We are married," he said smiling down at her.

"We are handfasted," she whispered.

Brigid's head rolled back unable to hold on any longer.

Duncan let go of his unshed tears, cradling her as he placed kisses gently over her face.

"Let me save her, Duncan."

Without looking up, Duncan recognized the voice. The air hummed with his energy, and it belonged to only one.

"Can ye truly, *Conn*?" Duncan choked out, tearing his gaze from Brigid to glare at the Fenian warrior standing beside him.

Conn knelt in front of Duncan and placed a hand across his shoulder. "Aye. In her time, there are great healers. I must hurry, though, her life force is draining."

Duncan nodded slowly. Carefully rising to his feet, he held Brigid firmly in his arms.

She wrenched out a cry of pain. "Shhh, *leannan si*," he whispered softly across her face. Conn followed silently behind him.

The mists had encased the stone circle like a blanket, and the moon bathed them in its luminous glow.

"*Beannachd leat*—goodbye, my faery lover. I will love ye always." Duncan kissed Brigid one last time, and then laid her in the arms of Conn.

"I will hold ye to your word, Conn."

Conn glanced down at Brigid before returning his gaze to Duncan.

"I give you my word—*Dragon Knight*."

The air shimmered. Duncan took a step back, and watched as Conn stepped through the veil until they both had disappeared from his sight. Instantly, the veil closed, leaving nothing but silence.

Duncan stared down at his hands covered in Brigid's blood, the only physical proof left that she had ever existed in his world. His steps faltered and he dropped to his knees. Brigid was gone—forever to some distant future, a future that would never include him. He felt lost as the waves of raw grief rocked within him.

"*Why?*" he roared out in pain, staring up at the night sky.

He heard a twig snap behind him. "Go away," he growled. He was in no mood to look upon another person.

A small gentle touch on his shoulder brought Duncan back to the surface of the living. "Did Lady Brigid go back home with the faery?" Nell asked softly.

Duncan found it difficult to speak, and just shook his head in agreement.

"Then we shall not be sad, Sir Duncan. Maybe they will let her come back for a visit."

Nae, Duncan reflected. Brigid would never be allowed to return, but he would never tell Nell. Letting out a long sigh, he uttered, "Perhaps."

The bump on Nell's forehead was visible and fury rose in him again. He slowly rose to his feet with strength he did not think he had. Glancing down at Nell, he said, "Ye were a verra brave lass." Taking her hand, he squeezed it lightly. "I promise ye, Lachlan *will* be punished."

Nell tilted her head up, squinting as if in thought. "Do not take too long."

"We have a problem, Duncan." Cormac had drifted over to where he was standing, sword extended.

Duncan dropped Nell's hand, peering over

Cormac's shoulder. Glancing to the spot where Lachlan *had* been.

"By the hounds!" he roared in frustration. Bending down to reach for his sword, Duncan let its energy hum throughout his body and wounded spirit. He stood transfixed letting it soothe him for the first time.

"What the *bloody hell* happened?" His question more for Cormac, keeping his gaze on the two men standing by his side.

"We were focused on ye and your lady that no one paid heed to him," interrupted Alex.

Patrick stepped forward. "Truth? I thought him dead."

"*Ye*, who would stoop to treachery. Why would I trust ye?" Shaking his head in irritation, Duncan paced the ground in thought. Suddenly, he sliced the air with his sword leveling it at Alex. "Why are ye here, *MacFhearguis*?"

Alex did not flinch, his steely gaze boring into Duncan's. "We have long considered the druid was not one to be trusted."

"And ye have known this for how long?" Duncan scoffed.

"Since the day he told me of our father's death," interjected Patrick as he glanced at Alex.

"What of Michael?" asked Duncan.

Alex let out a groan. "He follows the council of the druid." Pointing a finger back at Patrick, he scolded, "We have much to discuss later."

"Agreed." Patrick nodded solemnly.

"And now the source of this evil has vanished," sneered Cormac.

Duncan pointed his sword at the brothers. "Hear

me well. I will deal with the druid. He is *mine*."

Alex and Patrick both nodded in agreement.

"We will take this news of what happened here to Michael," replied Alex.

They both turned to leave until Duncan had one more thought. "Why do ye seek Adam?"

"Adam has been gone these past six moons. He left no word." Alex grimaced when he added the next. "We thought foul play with ye, or one of your brothers."

"We will help ye search for him," Cormac pledged, keeping his gaze on Duncan.

Alex gave a curt nod before taking his leave.

They watched as the MacFhearguis brothers left the stone circle.

Duncan's shoulders slumped. The weariness crept over his body, enveloping him in sadness. As he peered across the mossy grass, the moonlight cast a glow on the spot where he held Brigid in his arms. The loss of his love—*his life*, just a memory, reminding him of the mists; here one moment, gone the next.

He observed Nell gathering some flowers. She went and placed them on the spot where Brigid had fallen. "Cormac, I need ye to see Nell safely back to the castle."

"Aye."

They both watched as Nell gently arranged the flowers in a circle, humming a tune of mourning.

"She will be sorely missed, Duncan—by many." Cormac lamented.

Duncan tilted his head back toward the night sky unable to respond to his friend.

Cormac shifted and placed a hand on Duncan's shoulder. "Do not be away too long."

"I am heading back home to Urquhart. I need to find out what has happened there in my absence and search out my brothers." He angled his head to look at Cormac. "I fear I may need more than my powers alone to defeat the druid."

"Aye, true. Then, there is Cathal. Can he not call upon the druid council?"

"Nae." Duncan let out long sigh. "We must contain it here. I dread there may be others who believe as Lachlan does. Give the news to Cathal, and see what he thinks. I shall return by the winter solstice, or sooner, depending on the snows."

"Safe journey, Duncan."

"Thank ye, my friend."

Cormac watched as Duncan slowly made his way to Nell. He bent low speaking to her. At the last, she flung herself into his arms, pressing a kiss to his cheek.

Chapter 49

"Let me go back to my dream, for this reality is far too agonizing to bear."—Brigid O'Neill, as told to the Guardian

The sound of sweet music filled the air, and Brigid's eyes fluttered open to a shining brilliance that astounded her. The colors filled her vision were too bright, and she blinked several times trying to adjust to them and her surroundings.

She was lying in a cocoon of flowers—roses, lavender, foxgloves, tuberroses, evergreens, and gardenias. Their heady scent filled her being and soothed her soul. Her hand brushed over their petals, the colors dancing in front of her eyes. Brigid watched as a hummingbird, the color of emeralds, hovered in front of her before dashing away. Dragonflies flitted over her, gently gliding over to a small pond, the color of light blue crystals.

Then Brigid's heart froze.

"*Duncan*," she blurted out. A warm breeze ruffled her curls.

Instantly, all her memories came back in a sudden torment of pain. Sitting up on her elbows, she glanced down at herself and noticed she was wearing her dress still stained with blood. She found she could move without any pain. The wound was still there, but the bleeding had stopped.

Sitting up, she hugged herself rocking back and forth, great sobs racking her body.

Gone forever.

Her love, her Dragon Knight...her life.

"I did give my life for him, didn't I?" she sobbed out. "The dream was *real*." Brigid bent her head to her knees, letting her grief pour out.

"Yes, my child. You gave your life."

The melodic tone of her voice was like a silken caress over Brigid, and she lifted her tear-stained face to the most dazzling beauty she had ever seen. She moved toward Brigid as if she was floating on air, her radiance almost blinding.

The woman was a shimmering rainbow of colors and then she smiled at Brigid.

"Wh...*Who are you*?" Brigid whispered.

"Walk with me, Brigid."

Brigid looked down at herself. Could she really walk?

"Yes, Brigid. In this place *anything* is possible."

Her head snapped up, jaw gaped opened. "How did you know?"

The Guardian laughed the sound of tinkling bells.

Taking a deep breath, Brigid rose up slowly to find not only was there no pain, but also, she seemed— lighter. She cautiously stepped over to where the woman stood, gazing out to a valley below them. Brigid squinted, noticing that there were three paths leading downwards.

"Where am I?"

"I am the Guardian, Brigid, and you are in my realm of veils."

"Is this *Tir na Og*?"

"Yes...and no." She tilted her head to the side to gaze at Brigid.

"I am giving you a gift, Brigid, but it is up to *you* to choose."

Chapter 50

"To know love for only a brief time is worth more than any riches a man may acquire on his journey. I would endure the fire of the great dragon for one more touch."—Duncan Mackay, as told to the Guardian

Duncan took hold of Brandubh's reins, pulling back and bringing him to a stop. The smell of winter permeated the air, crisp, cold, and clean. Snow had dusted the ground during the night creating a magical effect, and he paused to stare at Castle Creag. He had been gone almost two moons and was grateful the weather held until he was able to pass through the glen.

He heard the crunch of something on the snow-covered ground. Peering over his left shoulder, he spied a reddish-brown stag foraging for food. Watching as it ambled off into the trees, Duncan brought his attention back to the castle.

His journey back home had been uneventful and frustrating. Urquhart was devoid of his brothers, and no one had seen, nor heard of them in over a year. The few that stayed at Urquhart were overjoyed to see him return, and he vowed to unite his brothers and bring them back. Making sure they had all they needed to survive the long winter, he set out to retrieve Finn and Nell. They were now part of his family—under his protection, a promise he had made to them both.

Brandubh tossed his head and snorted, puffs of air billowing in the icy air.

"Are ye anxious for a warm bed and food?" A sad smile spread across his face, and the ever-present ache lodged in his chest swelled just a bit more.

He reckoned it would be painful, returning to a place where memories of her would remind him of all he had lost. Rubbing his chest with his palm, he tried in vain to ease the ache. "It will be a verra long winter," he muttered, as he gave the signal for Brandubh to continue onward.

When entering the bailey, he saw the usual activity of men, and one of the guards saluted him in welcome. Dogs ran past barking, and some of the lads followed along, wooden swords in hand. Laughter spilled forth, and as one of the women spotted him in passing, she greeted him with a wave.

This is what he wanted for Urquhart—warmth of family and friends, children playing about, life rich with people. How did he forget this? The yearning so great, he made a silent vow to the gods and goddesses that he would return Urquhart Castle to one such as this.

He would do it for his brothers and for *her*.

"*Duncan!*" A shrill scream echoed from the entrance, and Nell came bounding out toward him, Cuchulainn following closely.

He dismounted from Brandubh just in time for her to fling herself into his arms. Wrapping her arms around him, she gave him a fierce hug, burying her head into his shoulder.

"It's good to see ye, too, Nell."

Duncan spotted Tiernan approaching, with Finn running past and skidding to a halt in front of him. He ruffled the top of Finn's head before taking one arm and embracing him in a hug.

"I'll take your horse, Sir Duncan," said Tiernan.

"Nae, I believe the task still belongs to the lad." He glanced down at Finn's hand, which was slightly bandaged. He would not treat him any differently.

Finn stepped back from Duncan his mouth gaped open. "Oh, thank ye, Duncan." A huge smile broke out on Finn's face as he proudly took the reins of Brandubh, leading him away.

"We still give him duties, but I believe ye have just given him the greatest one of all," Tiernan said quietly.

Duncan nodded in agreement. He noticed Cormac near the entrance, arms across his chest, watching with a knowing smile.

"Nell, I swear ye are growing bigger each time I see ye." He placed her down upon the ground where she eagerly put her hand into his. They ventured on over to where Cormac stood.

"Good to see ye, Duncan." Cormac clamped a hand across his shoulder in welcome.

"I could use some of your whisky to warm myself."

"Oh, and some plum tarts with honey, too," Nell squeaked.

Duncan wiped a smidgen of the evidence off her cheek with his thumb. "My favorite..." His thoughts returning to happier times.

"We knew ye were coming, and that is why Moira made them."

Duncan frowned slightly, looking back at Cormac. "Ye did?"

"Cathal," replied Cormac. "He sensed your energy

and suspected ye to be nearby."

"I have to go and help Moira." Nell gave him one more squeeze before she scampered off.

Duncan crossed his arms over his chest, giving Cormac a questioning look. "Nell is helping in the kitchens? Cathal is still here? Next, ye will be telling me Matilda has moved into the castle along with all of Nell's family."

"Well..." Cormac rubbed the back of his neck wincing at the stunned look Duncan was giving him.

"Ye have gone soft, Murray," grunted Duncan.

"I could knock ye one for that, Mackay," Cormac spat out before glancing around to make sure none of his men had heard Duncan's words. "I had reasons for bringing Nell's *family* into the castle, and as for Nell, Moira took her under her wing when we brought her back. She needed the woman's touch after ye left. I think it may be difficult to pry her loose from the woman when ye plan to leave here with her."

Duncan rubbed at the several days' growth of beard. "Aye, could be."

Walking along the corridor to the great hall, he glanced up the stairwell and stopped for a brief moment, remembering. Duncan angled his head back toward Cormac.

"And Matilda?"

"We needed the healer," Cormac said softly.

"Cathal?" Duncan glanced back up again.

"To assist Matilda."

"What are ye *not* telling me?" He shifted uneasily.

"Come, Duncan, take some food and drink. I will send someone to fetch Cathal."

Duncan snapped, "Nae, tell me Cormac." Then his

thoughts reeled. "Ye have found one of my brothers?" His fists clenched.

The look on Cormac's face told him all he needed. "Where?"

Cormac let out a long sigh, "If ye must know—in your chambers."

Duncan made rapid strides across the hall taking flight up the stairway. His heart was pounding as he weaved his way along the circular steps and through the corridors.

Which brother would he find?

When he got to the oak door, he found his hand was shaking when he placed it on the latch. Lifting it, he shoved it open.

At first, his eyes had to adjust to the light streaming in through the open window. Sunlight had broken through and it danced off the snow, flooding the room with a dazzling effect.

Sitting on the bed was Matilda. She was speaking softly to someone. Cathal was standing next to her, making it difficult for him to see who was lying in his bed.

Cathal twisted to one side, giving Duncan a huge smile. "Welcome back, Duncan."

Time stood still, and Duncan's heart froze.

Matilda slowly eased up from the bed, so that he could see.

His world spun, and tilted; the ground opened beneath him.

"Brigid?" he croaked.

"Yes, my love." Tears of joy streaked her face. She held out her hand beckoning him to join her on the bed.

Cathal strolled over to Duncan giving him a nudge.

"She's real, my son. Go to her."

He glanced incredulously at Cathal before snapping back to stare open-mouthed at Brigid.

"Damn it, Duncan!" she pleaded through choked sobs. "If I could, I would leap out of this bed and throw myself into your arms, but I can't. Don't make me wait another moment to touch you."

He staggered forward, reaching out to touch her outstretched hands, weaving his fingers with hers. "My *leannan si*—ye are truly one of the fae," he muttered, dropping down to the bed.

"Duncan..." Reaching up to touch his face, Brigid brushed at his lips with her fingers, and in one fell swoop, he gathered her in his arms crushing his mouth into hers for a soul-searing kiss, devouring her sobs with his own.

He finally broke free as they both gasped for air. Taking his hand, he cupped her cheek and held it gently, letting his gaze roam over her face. "I did not think to ever see ye again. How can this be, *leannan*?"

"The Guardian, Duncan. She gave me a choice on which path I wanted to call home." Brigid saw the stunned look on Duncan's face, and smiled. "It may be hard to believe, but she wanted to give this to me—to *us*."

Bending and pressing his forehead against hers, he inhaled her scent, marveling at the gift he was given. Suddenly, he realized Cormac had said that Matilda and Cathal were needed. Casting his gaze down her body, he placed a hand gently on her abdomen.

"Yet, she did not heal your wound?" he questioned. The jubilation Duncan was feeling became overshadowed by the thought Brigid was unwell, or hiding something else.

Seeing her bite her lower lip, he whispered, "Tell me."

"She was able to stop the bleeding, but since I chose to return to you and this time, I had to rely on healers in this century. I did not want to go back to my time, and I certainly did not want to stay in the land of *Tir na Og*!"

"Sweet Danu!" he groaned. "What have ye done?"

She grasped both of his hands, "I love you, Duncan. It was simple. I could not choose an existence in my time without you." Duncan started to speak, but she placed a finger on his lips to silence him. "My body may have been healed, but my heart would always know the pain of loss, and that my love, is something no doctor, or healer could ever cure. Life without you would not be a life."

Duncan heard the shuffling of feet, and remembered Cathal and Matilda were still in the room. Half twisting toward them, he saw that they both held grim looks. "I want the truth. Can she be healed?"

Matilda stepped forward, hands clasped together. "Aye, we can heal some of her wounds"—she took a deep sigh—"and some we cannot mend."

Duncan's head snapped back toward Brigid. His heart pounded within his chest, the blood rushing through his ears. This could not be happening again, he thought.

He heard the door to his chambers close softly, realizing they had left, leaving him alone with Brigid.

"What is she not telling me, Brigid?" His eyes bored into hers.

Brigid's shoulders slumped. Here was the decisive

moment, one where he would take her either as she was, or leave her. She had no idea how he would react. He was a medieval warrior, and the news she was about to give him, might just leave her entirely alone in this century. Could he love her as a damaged person? Was their love strong enough? Oh God, she thought, what have I done?

Looking up into his blue eyes, she gently brushed the ebony lock from his forehead, placing her palm on his cheek. "I cannot bear you any children, Duncan. The wound was too severe—the damage of my womb beyond the healing powers of Matilda." She kept her gaze locked with his adding, "Will you take me as I am, unable to give you any sons or daughters?" Anxiety twisted her gut as she waited for him to respond.

He stared at her baffled. "Ye will not die?"

"No." Hesitation filled her voice. "Not I pray, until I am very old and wrinkled."

"Then, *wife*, I will take ye, be it wrinkled and old, for I cannae be without ye for another day."

A cry of relief broke from her lips before he took them once more, leaving her mouth burning with the fire of his healing touch.

****

The hours passed as they lay in each other's arms, whispering, laughing, and sharing their fears, hopes, and dreams. Dusk of twilight was settling in, the fading light ebbing from the windows. Brigid had told him how Conn had returned her to Castle Creag with a message to Duncan that all debts had been paid.

His eyes narrowed, but he would say no more.

"One of these days, you are going to have to tell me what it is about him you don't like."

"This is not one of them," and he silenced her words with his mouth.

Moira had sent Nell and Sienna with supper for both of them, and Duncan made sure Brigid ate every last morsel.

"*Please*, no more, Duncan." Brigid waved off his attempt at one more spoonful of meat broth. "I feel like I'm going to burst."

"Humph! Ye must gain back your strength," he stated with a determined look.

She cocked her head to the side and pointed to the tray. "I *will* take another plum tart." She giggled as one sexy eyebrow rose in question. He reached for one, placing a portion into her mouth.

When he concluded she had enough, Duncan stretched out next to her. He played with a curl that had escaped from her braid, placing it against his lips. The lust for her blazed hot in his eyes, "I cannot wait until ye are healed, *leannan*. I want your silken tresses draped over my body."

Giving him a slow sexy smile, Brigid crooked her finger to come closer. When he bent his head close to hers, she placed her hands on his face and whispered into his ear, "I can hardly wait for that day, too." Then taking her teeth, she nipped at his ear sending shards of pleasure pulsating down his body.

Duncan sucked in a sharp breath, "Och, my lusty *leannan,* do not start something ye cannot finish."

She chuckled low. "Who says I can't finish?"

Uttering a growl, he took possession of her mouth, and sent their world colliding with the newly shone stars.

****

When Duncan felt the stirring of dawn's first light, he woke to find his love cradled asleep next to his chest, softly snoring. Smiling, he sent a silent prayer of thanks to the Guardian for all she had given him. There was still much to do, and once again, he made a vow to bring together his brothers and restore life back into Urquhart Castle.

He mulled over the knowledge where to search for one of his brothers. Cathal had shared some news with him recently, explaining his brother Stephen was at Arbroath Abbey. He could not fathom why he was at the Abbey. Cathal had mentioned that perhaps it was possible Stephen was considering joining their order and becoming a monk.

"I will not let ye, brother," he said quietly.

Then there was the matter with the children.

Brigid stirred in his arms. Her hand was on his chest playing with the dark curling hairs. "Good morning, my love," she whispered.

Grasping her hand, he placed a warm kiss in her palm. "Aye, it is."

She observed his slight frown and asked, "What is it?"

Duncan held her hand in his, fearing her reaction to his words. "I need to discuss the children with ye."

Brigid's heart slammed into her chest. *Oh God, he does want children.* She tried pushing away from him, but it was useless against his vast strength.

"Let. Me. Go," Brigid said through gritted teeth.

"Brigid?" Duncan's tone was wary.

"Children?" she hissed. Tears stung at her eyes. This could not be happening. Perhaps she had misunderstood, or did he?

She felt his hold loosen. Taking the opportunity to free herself, she pushed upright. Sitting on the edge of the bed, she kept her back to him. She couldn't look at him.

"I wish to speak with ye about Finn and Nell, Brigid. I have made a promise to both that they are now under my protection. They will be coming with me to Urquhart Castle. I cannot ask ye to take on this responsibility with me." He let out a sigh. "Yet, I was hoping ye had come to like them..."

She slowly turned back around, wincing at the movement. "*Like*? Oh, Duncan, I love them both! They will be our family—*our children*."

His heart soaring, Duncan lunged across the bed gathering her gently into his arms and onto his lap. Tenderly, he wiped away a tear that had escaped with his thumb. "I do not deserve ye, Brigid, but hear me well, no one will take ye from me—*ever*. Ye are *mine, leannan si.*"

The tenderness in his voice melted her senses, his grip tight.

"Always yours, forever mine," Duncan avowed, before his lips touched hers.

Chapter 51

Seattle, Washington—Present Day

"Listen and believe, for the story I am about to tell you is one of truth, and if you so choose to believe, then you are one of the rare and special ones."

Lisa fought the wave of sadness as she blindly watched the rain tapping at the window in Brigid's bedroom. How many days had she stood in this room as the day turned into night, and still no word from her friend, *or* from the professor? She had called the college, but they told her Professor McKibbon had left his teaching post, and returned home to Scotland.

Even the cottage where Brigid supposedly stayed told her she had left to return home.

Yet, there was no recorded flight information confirming she did return home. It was as if Brigid vanished from the face of the planet. Even Scotland Yard was of no help, claiming the caretakers of Rowan Cottage said she had a marvelous time, then left. The only other option she could formulate was to hop on plane to Scotland and search every place her friend had been.

Leaning her head against the cool windowpane, she murmured, "Where are you, Brigid? At least call me." Sighing, she hugged herself as a shiver of cold air brushed past her.

The bell on the downstairs door chimed, letting her know she had a customer.

"Darn! I thought I locked the door."

She had taken to closing the store early most days, and on some, she did not bother opening, instead putting her focus into finding Brigid.

"Well, I hope these customers don't stay too long," she snapped. Descending the stairs, she pasted on her best smile.

The moment her foot took the last step into the room, she froze at the sight standing in front of her. Mouth gaping open, she reeled at the most gorgeous man that ever walked the earth. He was beyond gorgeous with his tight black jeans, black tee, and black leather jacket. His blond hair was pulled back to reveal a set of pale blue eyes. However, it was his size, thinking he had to be over six foot five, maybe six, that stunned her. His presence loomed over her, reminding her of a Viking god.

Thunder shook her out of her trance, but not before hearing a low rumble of laughter—from *him.*

"Why do you lassies always think of me as a *Viking god?*" He cocked his head to the side, giving her the most dazzling smile.

Lisa swallowed. "How do you know that's what I was thinking?" she asked blushing.

The Viking god strolled over to her. "It's a...*gift.*"

Thunder boomed again, and Lisa took control of her senses. She had no idea who this man was, but uneasiness crept up her spine. Taking a few steps backwards, she decided some distance between them would be best. Stepping on the other side of the counter, she peered behind him, hoping someone else would come through the door.

"Is there something you're looking for?" she blurted out.

The Viking god scanned the store, his brow furrowing, taking everything in.

"Nae." He brought his blue gaze back to hers. "I bring ye a message."

Lisa swayed. "*Brigid*?"

The Viking god moved with such speed that it seemed to Lisa more like a blur, and the next moment, she was cradled in his arms.

"You all right?"

Shaking her head no, she inhaled deeply of male, leather, and something else.

Cupping her chin, he raised it to gaze directly into her eyes. "Brigid is well, lass, and verra happy."

Pushing away from him, she shot back, "Then where in the *hell* is she?"

"If you must know, she is with Duncan Mackay and they are"—he paused in thought—"most likely married now, or soon to be."

"Duncan Mackay?" Lisa started to tremble. "Not the Mackay of the thirteenth century?"

"The one and only." He stood smiling at her, arms crossed in front.

"You're *insane*!" she spat out.

His brow drew together in thought. "Aye, she told me you would say that."

Turning, he walked toward the door.

"Wait!" Lisa lunged for his arm. "Where is she, *really*? Please, whoever you are, don't do this! If this is some kind of joke, it's a sick and twisted one. I realize how much she loved living in the past, but you and I both know that it's impossible."

He leveled his gaze at her, and Lisa could have sworn the color of his eyes shifted.

"Brigid is indeed alive and living in the thirteenth century with Duncan. She was chosen to travel the veil of time to help Duncan restore his honor and to return the sword. She told me to tell you, all your answers will be found in the book of ancient clans—the leather bound one."

"I know of it. So?" Lisa threw up her hands in frustration.

He took her face in his hands, lightly brushing a kiss against her lips. "My name is Conn MacRoich, and I am a Fenian warrior for the fae." His kiss sent shivers down her body.

Conn's gaze bore into hers breathing the last, "*Believe...*"

Lisa closed her eyes expecting another kiss, when the next, she felt nothing but cold air. Snapping her eyes back open, she blinked in disbelief.

Her Viking god—Conn MacRoich—had vanished.

Her heart racing, she tore up the stairs halting before Brigid's open bedroom. Scanning the bedroom, she saw it. Taking slow, shaky steps, she stopped and stared at the book. How many times had she seen it lying there these past few weeks, and never once looked inside?

With trembling hands, she picked up the large tome. Holding it against her chest, she veered over to the bed. Opening it up, she took her finger over the names that were written down until her finger stopped on the one that held a hope of promise. "Mackay Clan of Urquhart," Lisa whispered. Flipping the yellow pages carefully, she searched for the Mackay clan. Her palms became sweaty, and finally when she could not stand it any longer there it was, the Mackay's and their clan's crest—*The Dragon Knights*.

Lisa scanned the page until she came to the one name she wanted to see—Duncan Mackay. "Duncan Mackay, born in the year 1175, married to..." Lisa gasped, peering closely at the writing. "...married to Brigid Moira O'Neill, (birth unknown) in the year 1205. They had two children, one son, Finn, the other a daughter, Nell. Deaths unknown, but legends tell of them living well into advanced age."

"You did it, Brigid." Lisa choked back a sob. "You *really* did it!"

Lisa spent the next hour clutching the ancient text to her chest rocking back and forth between fits of laughter and tears.

Epilogue

Winter Solstice—1205

"Forever and a day," said the knight to his lady. "For that is my pledge to thee."—Duncan's vow to Brigid

Laughter rang clear through the crisp snow-filled morning of Duncan and Brigid's wedding. They had chosen to celebrate their union on this feast day of light. Neither wanted it held indoors, so they chose a place outside Castle Creag. It was partially up the mountain where they could glimpse a portion of the great glen through the snow-covered pines, and one large enough to hold many people. The day was gray, but the beauty of the landscape and those of everyone shone brightly, creating an enchanting scene.

Cathal had officiated. At the end, he gave them a druidic blessing, giving them length of lives and light on their journey, which was interwoven into each of their souls.

Brigid smiled, hugging her fur cloak and hood more snugly around her. A loud ruckus of laughter ripped through the air from Duncan as he responded to something Cormac had said to him, then punching him in the shoulder. Cormac put up his hands in mock surrender.

There were so many clustered together, but her intent was focused on one man—*Duncan*. He looked magnificent in his cloak of dark blue, trimmed in silver, and fastened with a silver brooch. Sienna and Matilda had made it, and his face did not hide how he felt when they presented him with the gift.

She heard shouting from the children nearby, and she reflected on those she would never give Duncan. Yes, she had healed; however, her heart would always ache just a bit. Then there was Finn and Nell. Her love for them was fierce, and she found instant motherhood not only a challenge, but also one of great joy. They were strong children. The trauma they had endured left both with scars. Nell had nightmares on occasion, and Finn had become more reserved. With time and love, she prayed they would heal.

They never did find Lachlan, infuriating not only the wrath of Duncan and Cormac, but also Cathal. He had decided come spring, he would seek out the druid elders. His own brother bent on evil was still a bitter pill for him to swallow. There were still many unanswered questions, but for now, they would just have to wait until springtime.

"Spring," she murmured, when Duncan and the children would set out for Urquhart Castle. The snows were too heavy to travel, and he reasoned it would be best to stay through winter. The wind whipped gently at the folds of Duncan's cloak, and she caught a glimpse of his sword belted low on his waist, her proud Dragon Knight.

"Thank you, Guardian, I believe I chose wisely."

Their gazes locked, and heat flared within her, as his eyes roamed over her body from the distance.

Striding over, he pulled her into his arms, his breath a warm caress across her face.

"Happy, wife?"

"Very," she proclaimed, angling her head back to look into the eyes she loved so well.

His torc glinted from beneath his cloak, and Brigid reached out to trace her finger along the dragon's head. "I was thinking that perhaps after we are settled at Urquhart we should pay our respects to the great dragon."

He drew her closer against his body, placing his head on top of hers. "Aye—we should. Though, now I think it best to take ye back and warm ye." He brought her chin up and tweaked her nose with his finger.

"Stop that," she protested, batting his hand away.

"It is like ice."

Brigid tried to wiggle her nose. "Just a bit, yet I'm warm here in your arms." She placed her hands underneath his cloak to be closer to him.

A lustful gleam was in his eyes as he bent down to capture her lips with his, plunging his tongue deep into her mouth. His kiss was raw and needy, and Brigid responded with equal fervor. Instantly, they heard howls of laughter and bawdy remarks emanating from the men.

They broke off their kiss with Duncan turning to give them his fiercest scowl. What followed were more hoots and hollering. Turning his gaze once more to his beloved wife, he whispered into her ear.

Brigid reached out and placed a finger along his lower lip, watching as his smile turned sensual. "Take me to bed, Duncan."

"With pleasure, *leannan*."

Scooping her up into his arms, he whistled for Brandubh who promptly came forth from the trees. Placing her on top, he swung up behind her, grasping her close. Her hood had fallen back, and she leaned against his hard body.

"Always yours, Brigid."

"Forever yours, Duncan."

A word from the author...

I am a constant daydreamer and have been told to remove my head from the clouds. Yet this is where I find the magic to write my stories. Not only do I love to weave a good tale, but I have a voracious appetite for reading.

I have traveled to England, Scotland, Ireland, and France. There are those who know me well when I say, "My heart is in the Highlands." I believe I have left it there, or perhaps in Ireland.

When I'm not writing, I enjoy playing in my garden—another place where magic grows. Of course, there is time spent with my family. They are the ones who keep me grounded.

I enjoy hearing from readers and you can find me at:

http://www.marymorganromancewriter.com